In *The Book of Lost Light*, Ron Nyren tells the heartbreaking and fascinating story of a man who wants to stop time, and his son. These beautifully written pages follow father and son through several earthquakes—the large one that wrecks the city of San Francisco and the several smaller ones that wreck their tiny family. I love these wonderfully stubborn characters and I love how, despite everything, time carries them to a new place. A ravishing debut.

—MARGOT LIVESEY

As deep and luminous as a sequence of platinum prints, Ron Nyren's novel freezes time and sets it free, captures what was once, and what might be. A lovely and contemplative work of art.

—ANDREA BARRETT

This is a brilliant novel that shimmers with extraordinary beauty and power. It achieves one of the profoundest desires held by this band of memorable characters: to bring the soul to light in the surface of a work of art, to break through to something timeless, significant, transformative. A subtle, achingly gorgeous work of fiction that brings light and restoration to our human world.

—HARRIET SCOTT CHESSMAN

THE
BOOK
OF LOST
LIGHT

RON
NYREN

 Black
Lawrence
Press

www.blacklawrence.com

Executive Editor: Diane Goettel
Book and Cover Design: Zoe Norvell

Copyright © Ron Nyren
ISBN: 978-1-62557-829-7

Published 2020 by Black Lawrence Press.
Printed in the United States.

For Sarah,
for my mother, Lita Nyren,
and in memory of my father, Fred Nyren

CHAPTER ONE

From the time I was three months old until I was nearly fifteen, my father photographed me every afternoon at precisely three o'clock. When I was an infant, my cousin Karelia held me up for the camera. In later years, I walked on my own to my father's portrait studio, tossed my cap onto the hat rack, shook hands with customers, and waited for my father. In school, I was known as a strange fellow, daydreaming and bookish, terrible at throwing balls, overly theatrical. But in my father's studio, I was part of a grand scientific experiment. In one sense, standing at the eye of the Tetrascope was as commonplace for me as washing my face in the morning. In another sense, it was the most significant moment of each day—one more step in the staircase I believed my father would someday ascend to greatness.

When my father called me in, we might exchange a few words, but we would always fall silent as we waited for the clock to strike three. Karelia's voice drifted in from the reception area as she flirted with a customer to cajole him into buying extra prints or purchasing a more expensive frame. I felt the hour approach as distinctly as if the clock's hands brushed the nape of my neck.

A few minutes before three, I removed all my clothes and set them on a chair, taking care to avoid shifts of weight that could translate through the floorboards and misalign the mirrors in the Tetrascope's tubes. The noises of the street below faded—the shouts of paperboys touting news, the clop of horses' hooves, the infrequent bleat of an automobile horn. I savored my approach to the focal point, the point toward which the Tetrascope's four lenses bent their forces; it seemed to glow, like a dust fleck in sunlight. I cupped my heels in the white semicircles painted on the floor, and the golden point floated right behind my breastbone.

When I remember my father in those days, I think longingly of his half-smile when Karelia or I said something that bemused him, or of him murmuring to a camera's broken shutter as he repaired it. He would concentrate as he held up a comparison print to make sure that I kept the same stance as always. "Raise your chin a quarter inch," he would say, or, "Flatten the left hand a little and bring the thumb in." I stifled the urge to fidget or make faces.

He finished adjusting the Tetrascope, and I felt myself come fully into alignment, edges sharply defined. It was as if yesterday's session had only just ended, as if tomorrow's would immediately follow, a long chain of photographs leading back to before I could remember and forward into all the years of glory to come. Finally, he lifted a finger in the air, and I held my breath until the shutter clicked.

One afternoon not long before we lost everything, when I was fourteen, he wondered aloud why time moved in only one direction. "If it reversed, would we notice?" he asked. "Or would we forget, second by second, until it began going forward again?"

I don't remember if I said anything in response. By then, I had grown self-conscious before the lens, doubtful of the value of his project, uncertain whether he was a genius or a madman. My mind was wandering, and I was restless to be off.

*   *   *

Eadweard Muybridge had fired my father a dozen years before I was born, but my father bore him no ill will. In fact, a photograph of Muybridge hung behind the reception desk in my father's portrait studio. It had been taken at Governor Leland Stanford's farm in Palo Alto in the summer of 1879. Muybridge stood at one end of a long shed. A long row of assistants—photographers, jockeys, grooms—squatted along the shed's whitewashed wall, from which protruded the lenses of twenty-four cameras. At the opposite end stood my father. At first glance, it could be difficult to tell him apart from his employer. Both he and Muybridge had beards reaching to their breastbones, both had their arms folded, their right foot slightly forward—even their hats were alike, though my father's had a shorter crown, perhaps out of deference to his mentor, and his beard then was black, while Muybridge's was gray. Like nearly all of my father's photographs, this one was destroyed long ago.

More voluble in those days, my father told his customers about his work with Muybridge. "Photographing a pigeon in flight was one of our most difficult enterprises," he would say, or, "Before Muybridge designed his electromagnetic shutters, it wasn't possible to photograph a horse at a gallop." If my father had no appointment scheduled, I could easily convince him to tell me more. We would sit in the reception area chairs, which creaked alarmingly with age, and I would listen and try to piece together the events that had led to our great secret enterprise.

On July 12, 1878, thirteen years before my birth, my father met Muybridge in the chambers of the San Francisco Art Association. My father was in his thirties, working as a mechanical engineer, but already a skilled amateur photographer; a self-portrait from that time showed him with a long oval face, round cheekbones, thin light-colored hair combed from a side part, and a short beard trailing from his chin, his mouth a grave line. He read in the morning *Chronicle* that Eadweard Muybridge—well-known for the 360-degree panorama of San Francisco he'd taken from the turret of the Hopkins Mansion on Nob Hill—would lecture that evening on "The Stride of a Trotting Horse." Though my father had no particular interest in horses, the phrase "instantaneous photography" piqued his interest.

I imagine a warm evening, the men in the audience shrugging off their jackets, the women waving their fans, Muybridge's assistant opening windows to let out the stale air as he drew the shades to darken the room. Muybridge strode to the lectern, gazing out from beneath the fierce shelf of his brow. He cleared his throat, and the room fell silent.

Although artists were the first to attempt to depict the attitudes of animals in motion, he said, throughout the ages they all adopted the same conventions in rendering those attitudes. His aim was to show that their notions were inaccurate.

Muybridge's assistant dropped slides one by one into the projection lantern. A series of life-size photographs of a horse appeared, first standing straight, its rider erect; then both leaning forward as the horse began its run, only one foreleg on the ground; then trotting at full clip, legs folded beneath the body, none of them touching earth. Until these experiments were made, Muybridge said, it was a question among even very experienced horse drivers as to whether a horse was ever clear of the ground during a trot or always had at least one foot touching down. The slides advanced as Muybridge showed the audience what no human eye had ever detected. His photographs proved conclusively that at a moderate trot, the weight of the body is entirely unsupported.

Even eminent painters depicted horses striking the ground with a bent leg. "False!" he said. In other cases, they had the poor beast looking like a hobbyhorse. On the screen next to the projected photograph, a slide of a painting appeared: a horse with forelegs stretched out before and hind legs stretched out behind. I imagine a nervous laugh broke out among many of the audience members; what had looked so familiar all their lives now revealed itself as absurd.

My father seldom laughed; he would have leaned forward instead, pressing his tongue to his upper lip as he often did when concentrating. Muybridge's photograph was so precise, even the tip of the rider's whip was visible.

Muybridge explained how he had sent a horse trotting past a row of twelve cameras fitted with a double-acting slide frame shutter of his own devising, each camera attached to a thread stretched across the track. The horse broke each thread with his breast as he ran, triggering each shutter in succession.

When the lecture was over, Muybridge remained talking with a pair of well-dressed men while his assistant packed up the lantern slides and projectors. My father lingered nearby, eager to approach. Apparently mistaking my father for someone else, Muybridge said, "Here's a young man so interested he has attended two of my lectures in a row. Or are you one of my skeptics?"

"I believe you're a genius," my father answered.

Muybridge nodded, pleased, before turning back and resuming his conversation. One of the men asked Muybridge if he planned to extend his experiments to the locomotion of other animals. Muybridge answered that this was difficult—it was easy to send a horse running down a trackway strung with threads, but this would not work with goats or deer or hogs.

"Have you considered connecting the camera shutters to a clock-work mechanism instead?" my father said.

The two men, who had politely stood still during the first interruption, shifted on their feet. My father's clothes were likely shabby, and though I've heard that Muybridge too was careless in his dress, my father lacked the dignity of age or accomplishment to compensate for the fade of his shirt or the fray of his cuffs.

"Are you a clockmaker?" Muybridge asked.

"I was a mechanical engineer. Now I'm a photographer." In saying this, my father decided it was true: he would quit his job the next day and devote himself solely to the art of fixing images. "You could easily design a mechanism that would automatically take a rapid succession of exposures, rendering threads unnecessary."

Muybridge seemed amused. "Have you experience in the darkroom?"
"Yes."

Here came my favorite part of the story, Muybridge's three questions.

"In a collodion negative, transparent spots may be caused by undissolved particles of iodides in the ether and alcohol; what would you add to prevent this?"

"A drop or two of water, or bromide of ammonium, or diluted alcohol."

"An albumen print suffers from mealiness. What's the remedy?"

"Submerge it for about ten minutes in two ounces of water mixed with eighteen grains of acetate of soda."

"Can I see your hands?" Muybridge examined the silver nitrate stains on my father's fingers. "I don't have any use for you now. Write to me at this address." And he gave my father his business card, along the top of which were printed the words "HELIOS, the Flying Studio."

My father had bought his first camera years ago, intending only to disassemble it and discover how it functioned. He had taken a few photographs, but didn't pay it much attention until, the year before he met Muybridge, the steamship Pacific had sunk off the coast of San Francisco, drowning my father's parents.

He kept his father's medical bag as a memento on the dresser in his bedroom. The only medical instrument remaining was a stethoscope, which, once I grew old enough, my father sometimes allowed me to handle. The bag also held a few Finnish coins, *markka*, from my grandparents' homeland; a brooch of my grandmother's; a newspaper clipping describing the steamship accident; and an envelope with the sole photograph he had taken of them.

"After they died, it struck me how remarkable it was to have an image of them as they were when they were alive," he told me. My grandparents stand stiffly side by side, not touching but quite close, in front of the small white house in Sacramento where my father and his brother William grew up. Slight overexposure blurred their features in the sunlight. I suppose that when my father had gazed at the photograph in the wake of their deaths, their faces must have been still fresh enough in his mind that memory could fill in what was lost.

Some months after the lecture, my father wrote to Muybridge offering his assistance again. He received no reply. By now my father was working as a photographer for the South Pacific Coast Railroad, documenting construction work and supplying publicity photos of depots and trains. He wrote Muybridge again a month later, sending him his own experiments in capturing time: photographs of an apple decaying over the course of a week; a grove of trees viewed at morning, noon, and afternoon, slashed by three different slants of shadow.

In May 1879, nearly a year after the lecture, the newspaper reported that Muybridge was resuming his work with motion on a grander scale. The next day, my father rode the train to the peninsula and walked to the farm of the former governor and immensely wealthy railroad tycoon Leland Stanford, the project's sponsor, who had initiated the original experiments by hiring Muybridge to determine whether a horse was ever entirely clear of the ground during a trot.

At last my father reached a long white shed alongside Stanford's training track. On the opposite side of the track, a high wooden fence had been draped with white sheets marked with equally spaced, numbered vertical lines. A jockey cantered at the far side of the field while two men stretched fresh threads across the track.

Muybridge came out of the shed, calling back sharply to someone.

"My name is Arthur Kylander," my father said. "We met in San Francisco some time ago, and I offered you my services—I've fifteen years of experience as a mechanical engineer and nearly a year as a professional photographer. I wrote you letters, but I assumed you were too busy to reply, and so I thought I would visit the farm myself—"

"Yes, take up cameras nineteen and twenty," Muybridge said irritably, gesturing to the shed entrance, and stalked on to examine the readiness of the track.

As he learned later, Muybridge had fired one of his photographic assistants for botching a print that morning. He had recently doubled the number of cameras he used for his experiments, but had trouble rounding up enough capable men to operate them.

My father quit the railway company. He found the work at Palo Alto Farm exhilarating: inside the shed, he and the other assistants each coated a glass plate in viscous acid, then slid it into a camera. The horse ran past, the shutters clicked in sequence, and all along the length of the shed, each assistant snatched plates and developed them in the dark-room behind them before the plates dried and the image was lost.

Depending on the day's needs, my father would supervise the oper-ating of the cameras, or repair touchy shutters, or correct short circuits. Together, he and Muybridge perfected the clockwork mechanism that made possible the photography of dogs and goats in motion.

Governor Stanford himself visited during one of their first trials of the device, and afterward, Muybridge told Stanford that my father had been essential to the work, that he possessed "exceedingly fine skills with all things mechanical." Stanford shook my father's hand and said, "I expect great things from my you." My father felt honored, galvanized, even, not only by the compliment but also by the electricity of the governor's phys-ical presence. With the backing of someone as influential and wealthy as Leland Stanford, what great visions might they not all realize?

One September evening not long after, my father was returning from Palo Alto Farm to his boardinghouse on the California Avenue streetcar, standing in a crowd of men wearing the same kind of hat—members of some club, no doubt. I've always pictured the hat as a short-brimmed affair with a flat crown and red stripes, but likely this was my own invention—my father didn't tend to notice or remember clothes.

Preoccupied with his own thoughts, he almost missed his stop. As he rushed toward the door before it closed, he collided with one of the club members. The red-striped hat flew off and landed in a young woman's lap.

She picked it up with delight, as if it had landed from the sky, and put it on her head. "Thank you," she said. "I felt so left out until now." The club members laughed. She looked up at my father and, mistaking him for the hat's owner, stretched it out to him.

In confusion, he took it. "Thank you," he said, and their fingers touched. The man he had collided with beckoned impatiently. My father returned the hat, blushing at the thought that he might be perceived as a thief. The door closed, and the streetcar resumed its journey, so my father grasped a pole and stared straight ahead until the next stop, where he disembarked without a word. Yet he followed the streetcar with his eyes as it continued on. At the next stop the young woman disembarked and walked up a staircase into a house.

Later he would try to recall the color of her eyes, he told me: green, he thought, and her hair was black. He wished he had been able to study her face until he'd memorized it. From then on, whenever he returned from work, he hoped to glimpse her, to talk to her, though he didn't know what he would say. He calculated that she had gone into one of three houses. Once he saw a hand adjust a curtain on the second floor of one of the houses, and several times he saw children running to or from a house, but he never saw her.

I believe it was not long afterward that my father's relationship with Muybridge began to deteriorate. One evening, my father was alone in the shed repairing a camera. Muybridge came in carrying a heavy object, which he placed at one end of the long room. He began to assemble it—it consisted of a magic-lantern slide projector and an apparatus with a hand crank and two vertical disks. Muybridge extinguished the room's lamps, lit the device's lantern, and began turning the crank, rotating the disks. Against the opposite wall, the silhouette of a phantom horse began trotting in place.

Tonight, Stanford was holding a party, he said, hosting the wealthy of San Francisco—owners of banks and railroads and mining enterprises and shipping concerns. "I've decided it's time for the Zoogyroscope to make its debut."

Jerky and stiff, composed of a sequence of twelve images of a horse that repeated themselves, the gleaming square of light nevertheless gave a convincing illusion of motion.

"Astounding," my father said. Muybridge had made a few references to his latest invention, but this was the first my father had seen of it. "They'll talk of nothing else for days."

Muybridge must have heard reluctance in my father's voice. "I suppose you have a mechanical improvement to suggest?"

My father circled the device, examining it, but said nothing.

I imagine Muybridge letting go of the crank and the horse slowing, becoming twelve horses again, drifting to a halt between two slides, the front half of one regarding the tail of another.

"If you have a concern, you must tell me," Muybridge said.

"Your design is impeccable," my father said. "My only hesitation is that the value of the work we've been doing is that it shows what the eye cannot see on its own. To reconstitute these images into an apparently moving picture reproduces what we see in everyday life. Will it advance everything you've worked so hard to document, or overshadow it? Will people still be interested in the insights we gain from capturing and studying a sequence of moments, or will they only clamor for the illusion of motion?"

"One project doesn't preclude the other."

"Of course," my father said. He bent to look closely at the projected image.

"You're right, that is not a photograph," Muybridge admitted, though my father hadn't spoken. "I hired an artist to draw elongated versions of the horse based on each image in the sequence. I tried using photographs, but the images weren't distinct enough to make out from a distance, and they appeared compressed because of the swift rotation of the disc."

My father chose his next words carefully. Muybridge had murdered a man only five years earlier—his wife's lover—and been acquitted by the jury on grounds of justifiable homicide. Muybridge estimated him highly, but had a temper. "They're very skillfully drawn. My only fear is that this device might lead susceptible people away from a true understanding of time."

Muybridge extinguished the Zoogyroscope's lantern, plunging the room into darkness. He opened the door and stood, silhouetted in the fading light of evening, gazing across the field. At last he turned back to the Zoogyroscope. The discs he slid into cloth sleeves. The rest he lowered into a canvas bag, which he hoisted. Without a word, he left my father alone in the room and walked toward Stanford's mansion.

My father was correct in predicting the success of the Zoogyroscope—it was received with excitement at Stanford's party, and when Muybridge demonstrated it in subsequent lectures in San Francisco, the size of his audiences more than tripled. Muybridge suspended the photographic work at Palo Alto Farm whenever he traveled outside the area to give a lecture, often letting weeks elapse. For my father, these interruptions were a lost opportunity.

Hoping to reignite Muybridge's interest in their original work, my father suggested doubling the number of cameras from twenty-four to forty-eight and lengthening the shed so that more of the animals' transit could be recorded, thus permitting a comparison of changes in gait over time. Or else keep the shed the same length, but pack forty-eight cameras into the space of twenty-four, and in this way they could study every muscle movement an animal made. "Ideally, of course, we'd take both measures at once, but the challenge of operating ninety-six cameras simultaneously and developing the film would be significant," my father said.

Muybridge shook his head. My father changed tactics. "Another possible improvement, which Stanford might find of great interest, would be to photograph the same horse running the same pace on days of different weather conditions, to see if temperature affects the gait."

"I have plenty of ideas of my own," Muybridge said, and walked away.

From time to time, Stanford would visit the track to see how the project was going. One evening, when my father was walking back to the train to San Francisco, Stanford rode up on Mahomet, a horse they had photographed many times, and stopped to chat.

"You're Muybridge's mechanical engineer, aren't you?" Stanford asked, perched on his saddle, his new leather boots gleaming despite the dust covering them. "The operation has expanded considerably in recent years."

"He runs everything with great efficiency," my father said. Stanford continued to ask more questions, probing ones, which my father answered as best he could.

"Tell me," Stanford said abruptly, "how long until this enterprise has discovered all that it can discover?"

My father hesitated. He worried that Stanford had grown bored of the project and would shut down the operation. So he said that plenty of possibilities lay ahead and described with enthusiasm the ideas that he'd suggested to Muybridge. Then he stopped himself. "Of course, he has ideas of his own, and if you ask him, I'm sure he'll tell you."

Stanford turned his horse toward a figure riding in the distance from the farm—Mrs. Stanford. "He's more of a showman than I suspected," Stanford said. "Will we lose him to the lecture circuit?"

My father had the same concern, but he said only, "He may spend more time on the road, but he's shown every sign of devotion to the work you've hired him to carry out. And he has, in me and in his team, men fully capable of carrying on his vision if he is not present, should you deem it necessary."

"I appreciate your honesty." Stanford spurred his horse and rode off to join his wife.

Two mornings later, when my father's train pulled up at Mayfield Station, one of the other photographers met him on the platform. "Arthur," he said. "Muybridge sent me to say that you need not come anymore."

"Need not come?"

"He said that you were no longer welcome."

My father stood silently for a moment. "There must be a misunderstanding."

The man looked abashed. "He and Stanford got into one of their arguments again last night. Apparently you spoke ill of him to the governor?"

"Then the governor has misconstrued my words. I'll go to Muybridge and straighten this out."

"I was told to make sure you do not."

My father walked toward Palo Alto Farm anyway, leaving his colleague to follow behind fretfully. He rehearsed what he might say, trying to check his anger, knowing that Muybridge's temper was swift and prodigious. He would appeal with rational arguments, he decided.

Muybridge was at the track, giving directions to the owner of the pair of oxen they were scheduled to photograph that morning. Muybridge ignored his approach and finished the conversation. When the man walked back to his animals, Muybridge turned and glared at my father.

"Eadweard," my father said. "If Stanford believed I criticized you in any way, he's mistaken. Why would you send me away? I'm your most useful pair of hands, you've acknowledged this—I understand your work and your thinking completely, I can do any task as well as you can."

Muybridge spat in the dirt by my father's feet. "The world doesn't need a second Muybridge," he said. He stalked toward the camera shed, pausing only to turn and shout, "Nor do I!"

*   *   *

"It was a terrible blow to me, to be fired in front of so many of my colleagues, to be exiled from the great enterprise we had been working on so long," my father told me. "For a week, I could hardly do anything, I was so miserable and angry. But I came to see that Muybridge and I were too much alike, after all, to work together for long. And Stanford was really the one at fault, I believe. A great man, a visionary, yet he didn't trust Muybridge enough, and that made him a poor patron in the end. He would later go on to betray Muybridge."

When Muybridge was giving lectures in Europe, Stanford published a book about the horse in motion with drawings based on Muybridge's photographs; on the title page, Stanford credited a physiologist friend of his as the book's author, and mentioned Muybridge only once, in the preface, as a "very skilful photographer" he had employed. When this came to light, Muybridge was humiliated in front of the council of the London Royal Society for appearing to claim greater credit than he was due, and his remaining invitations to lecture overseas were revoked.

In exile from Palo Alto Farm, my father was out of a job. He knew two things: he didn't want to go back to photographing for a railway company, and he wanted to see again the woman he'd met on the streetcar. Even though her face remained elusive, he hadn't forgotten her, the graceful way she'd put the hat on her head and then extended it to him. Now that he didn't have work to consume him, he thought of her more and more often. Of course, he knew she might have been only visiting on the day he'd seen her—she might live somewhere else entirely.

He had business cards printed with the words "portrait photographer" below his name. He showed me one once—the a's stood slightly higher than the other letters, as if jumping into the air, a typographical error he hoped no one would notice. "I didn't want to wait for the printer to correct it," he told me.

He had never taken any portraits, so he persuaded the widow who owned his boardinghouse to let her two daughters sit for him. When he'd printed portraits to his satisfaction, he slung his portable darkroom over one shoulder and set out for California Avenue.

No one was home at the first house. He tried the second, where an elderly man gladly sat for his portrait. I picture him talking the whole time about his parakeet, who had died early in the year, and who, whenever the man was sad, would fly up and rest its head against his cheek—but I believe I'm importing this detail from one of the customers who buttonholed me at my father's studio once. By now, I've thought of this story so often, it's as if it's one of my own memories, and I no longer remember which parts my father told me and which I imagined.

As my father approached the third house, he could hear a piano playing, which stopped when he rang the bell. He waited. The house needed a good coat of paint. I imagine his nervously wobbling a loose brick in the step.

An older woman opened the door. "We had our portraits done at Symes not two months ago. Are you going up and down the street? I've told all of our neighbors to go to Symes. They do fine work and they don't mark up their prices like some others do."

My father was about to turn away when he heard someone coming down the staircase. A young woman's voice said, "Mother, I hate that portrait of me. I look like a statue of Dignity."

She had black hair and green eyes, and my father found her lovely, with high cheekbones, a small chin, and a birthmark he hadn't noticed before on the line of her jaw. She was taller than he recalled. She said, "I've been telling all our neighbors to go to anyone but Symes." Did she recognize him? She gave no sign. "Let me see your samples," she said. "Symes had samples, of course, but I let my mother delude me into believing that it was the people in them who were ill favored, rather than his style of photography."

She leafed through the samples he had brought. "These resemble real women," she told her mother. "I like them."

"Do you have references?" the mother asked.

"Your neighbor," my father said, "Mr. Vignola."

"I can't bear him. How much do you charge?"

He told her the fees he had worked out in advance, this much for this many portraits, that much for these kinds of prints, and an awkward silence fell—he suspected his rates were much lower than Symes's.

"Please, mother, you know I've been unhappy about that horrible image of me. I'll pay for this myself, out of the gift Aunt Helen gave me."

The mother shrugged, and the young woman clapped her hands. They agreed he would return the following afternoon for the sitting. "You have my card," my father said, "but I don't know your name."

"Emily," she said.

The next day, in the back parlor, my father unfolded the legs of his portable darkroom and started to work. Beneath its cloak, he coated a number of glass plates with collodion and silver nitrate solution while Emily's mother brushed her daughter's hair. He still had little experience with portraits, so he allowed Emily to sit as she pleased, her mother standing by the window watching. First Emily sat stiffly, looking directly at the camera. "Don't make my birthmark disappear," Emily said, touching it lightly with her fingertip. "I won't recognize myself."

"Of course not," he said. He pretended to adjust the camera; gradually she relaxed, and he photographed her unawares.

"Have you been a photographer long?" He began telling them about his work under Muybridge. She had read about Muybridge's work in the newspapers. "I've never ridden a horse," she said, "but now that I know that they barely touch the ground when they run, I want to."

"We've also photographed athletes," he said. "Fencing, boxing. An extraordinary series of a man turning a back somersault—each stage is astonishing. First he's standing straight, ordinary in every way. Then you see him slumped forward with his knees bent. Then he's tilted at an impossible diagonal, with his toes lifted right above the ground. The next plate shows him perfectly horizontal in the air, as if a magician has levitated him. Next his legs are drawn up as if he's sitting in a chair, with his hands beneath his knees, except that there is no chair and he's upside down. And in the final image, he stands safely on his feet again, as if he has never moved."

"I would love to see that," she said.

"Are you photographing a circus?" put in her mother. She still held the hairbrush, turning it around in her hands as if she were ready to rush in at any point and smooth straying locks.

"Athletes from the Olympic Club," my father answered.

"I plan to be an actress," Emily said. "Will you take me as Antigone?" she said, draping the end of a sheer white curtain about her head.

"Antigone's veil would be black," her mother said.

"If my art is good enough," she answered, adopting a grief-stricken expression, "then it will look black."

She insisted that he photograph her in motion "à la Muybridge," and when he said he lacked the equipment for that, she had him take three pictures of her, posed as if she were at different stages of her stride. When he developed the negatives and showed them to her, she said she had never liked her image better. "See," she told her mother, pointing at the Antigone negative, "my veil is black, and my hair is white with grief."

He promised to bring her prints by the end of the week. As the two women showed him to the door, Emily asked, "Do you photograph weddings?"

"Symes—" her mother began.

"Weddings?" asked my father.

"The date hasn't been set precisely yet, I'm afraid."

"Symes is—"

"Symes could be disinvited," Emily said.

My father took off his hat and held it tightly. He hadn't noticed an engagement ring on her finger—the possibility hadn't even occurred to him. He had spent the whole time concentrating on her face, which he could look at without stint through the viewfinder. He felt he couldn't look now. "I offer my congratulations, but I'm not a wedding photographer." He turned and walked down the street, lugging his camera on one shoulder and the darkroom on the other.

Although my father was deeply disappointed, he nevertheless developed the images and returned to her house with the prints later that week. She exclaimed over them and insisted that she would introduce him to her friend, that Symes must not be allowed to tarnish her friend's memories of her happiest day. The wedding Emily had mentioned was not her own, then.

And so my father was invited back to the house to meet the friend, and again to go over the arrangements once the day had been set. As he was departing after this last meeting, my father said that he planned to take his camera to Woodward's Garden soon, and he would be honored if Emily and her friend would be willing to come along and enliven his photographs. She said yes.

Emily told him she did have a suitor, a law school student, whom her mother favored as a prospect, but she found him wanting: listless at his studies, always complaining about the dryness of lectures. She loved to hear my father describe his work with Muybridge. She said my father was a genius.

My mother and father eloped in 1880. My father joined a large portrait photography studio on Market Street. For a long time, they lived in a tiny one-room apartment on Steiner Street in San Francisco, behind a German restaurant; my mother came to hate the smell of sausage.

In the first seven years of the marriage, my mother gave birth to two children, neither of whom survived past the first month. Her own mother died during this time, and my father preferred not to describe those sad years.

I was born August 1, 1891. When I made my entrance into the world, my mother said, "This one will live. I can tell from the expression on his face." My father was skeptical, as I was a scrawny thing.

Or perhaps it was Karelia who told me those were my mother's words.

What everyone agrees on is that toward nightfall my mother began hemorrhaging, and before dawn she died.

*   *   *

My father would never say much about what happened in the weeks following, except that he drew the curtains and spent nearly all of his time in bed. After a few days, he managed to write two letters. One he sent to the portrait studio where he worked, to notify the owners of his wife's death and to say that he would not be able to carry out his duties until further notice. The other he mailed to Paul Whitaker, who had been a friend of his and his brother's when they were young and living in Sacramento. He hadn't seen Whitaker or his brother since the two had traveled north together to settle in Canada not long after the sinking of the steamship Pacific. He wished he could have written to his brother, but William had died.

A Hungarian family in the flat above, the Hajdus, looked after him. Two of the Hajdu daughters had recently given birth, and they wet-nursed me. In the evenings, Mrs. Hajdu brought my father paprika chicken, potato soup, pork gulyas, and cabbage noodle dishes. He ate little.

One morning in early September, a knock came on the door, at first so hesitant he thought it was only footsteps on the stairs. Too heavy with grief to rise, he dozed off.

A loud pounding woke him. He climbed out of bed, opened the door, and was nearly hit by a shoe. A skinny girl in canvas overalls and a heavy coat stood in the hall, her pale hair blown about, in one hand the shoe with which she had been banging, in the other hand an envelope with his name on it.

He took it, mystified, and scanned the letter inside. *We offer our deepest condolences.... We are sending you your niece Karelia....She is very capable and knows how to look after infants. She is not happy at home, and we believe she will be of great help to you during this difficult time.*

Quickly she slipped inside and set down the sack she carried, as if to establish a claim. Her gaze quickly fixed on something behind him: the loaf of bread the Hajdus had left the night before.

"I'll cut you a slice if you wash your hands," he said. When she did not move, he clarified: "You'll have to wash your hands first." They looked filthy. Also, she stank. He led her to the sink and turned it on for her—he wondered if she'd seen running water before. She spent nearly five minutes scrubbing her fingers. He buttered a slice of bread and watched her devour it. He cut her another slice, gave her a drink of water, and reread the letter from Paul Whitaker.

"Did anyone travel with you?" he asked.

Having eaten the second slice of bread, she sat, unmoving, at the kitchen table.

"Can you speak?" said my father.

"Yes."

"How old are you?"

She gripped the table.

"Fifteen."

He judged her to be no more than twelve or thirteen.

"I'm sorry," he said. "I wasn't expecting anyone. He might at least have sent the letter beforehand." How this scrawny untalking girl could be of any use was beyond him. "Are you tired?"

She gave him a glazed, imploring look. He rose, stripped the sheets from his bed—which hadn't been washed in weeks—and remade it clumsily with fresh ones. She crawled on top of it fully clothed and fell asleep.

CHAPTER TWO

That was my father's version of the story of Karelia's arrival. Karelia told me she wouldn't have knocked with a shoe. "My knuckles were harder than shoes, from working on the farm," she told me. "He didn't offer me anything to eat or drink until I asked him. He looked half-dead—unwashed, with big circles under his eyes. If anything, he was less talkative than I was. The idea that I was mute when I arrived must be his invention."

My father and Karelia often remembered things differently, or perhaps it's more accurate to say that they told different stories. For example, Karelia had never met my mother, but sometimes, when I was very young, I found this difficult to understand, and I would ask her what my mother had been like. Karelia would say, "Your mother was a tall and elegant woman, who always wore pearls, even when she was cooking dinner," or, "She loved to play the violin so much she would stay up all night practicing." Once she told a long story about my mother trying to buy a violin that she recognized as a Stradivarius in a junk shop; unfortunately she could not conceal her excitement, and the proprietor, realizing that it must be very valuable, kept raising the price.

When I repeated Karelia's tales to my father, he would sigh. "None of that is true," he would say. "She never played the violin."

"You photographed her playing it," I said.

"The violin belonged to a friend of hers. I don't know why Karelia makes up these stories."

Karelia would have been eighteen or nineteen then, beautiful, restless, and increasingly given to wild inventions. I could never resist encouraging her—the photographs of my mother proved too tempting a source of inspiration. "Tell me about the time my mother scared off an outlaw with her sword," I would ask. And Karelia would oblige. My father hung photographs of my mother on the walls of every apartment we lived in. My mother concealing her mouth with a paper fan; my mother wielding a fireplace shovel in a fencer's stance; my mother striding, in three successive images, across a room; my mother gazing dolefully up from a book as if resigned to being photographed. She almost never gave my father a straight face. For that he had had to catch her unaware by tying Bloch's Detective Photo Scarf around his neck, the lens protruding through the fabric in cunning imitation of a stickpin. In the resulting images, grainy and dark, her features are not composed for effect or animated by her will. She is waiting for a streetcar, she is holding onto her hat in the wind, she is mortal.

The only portrait of my mother that has not been destroyed is the simplest—the one he took on his second visit to her house. Her dark hair curved gently as it fell, framing her high forehead, her slightly plump cheeks, her long neck. She smiled the way people often do when they hope to smooth their features into a pure face for posterity, unmarked by hopes and worries. The portrait's very ordinariness appealed to me. For the first fourteen years of my life, I kept it in a frame on my nightstand.

*　　*　　*

According to Karelia, her journey from Canada's Okanagan Valley to our flat in San Francisco began with the incident of the hayloft.

Every year at the end of summer, little salmons known as kokanees swarmed the rivers and creeks of the Okanagan Valley and trapped themselves in the irrigation ditches. That August, they had died in such numbers that the farmers had to plow them under or bury them to dispel the reek.

One afternoon, she watched her brothers through a knothole

as they buried kokanees. When the wind changed and sent the odor through the gaps in the barn walls, she dipped her nose into the sleeve of her cotton dress, then climbed down the ladder to press her face into the flank of the cow. She felt sorry for the fish and wondered why they couldn't be ushered out of the ditches and sluiced back to freedom.

The hayloft belonged to a neighbor; Karelia had already spent an afternoon and a night hiding there, her whereabouts known to no one but the cow, whom she had milked that morning in the dark. She'd drunk from the pail, rinsed it, and dried it with a handful of straw so that when the neighbor, an elderly widower, came to milk, he would suspect nothing.

The stay in the barn was not the first time she had run away, although it was the longest, and because of the fish, the hardest. She had no plan. From the hayloft, she studied her brothers as they flung dirt, eyeing them for clues that her absence grieved or worried them.

Karelia's mother had died four years earlier, when Karelia was eight, and her father had died when she was ten. Her father had left the family and the household to Karelia's sister, the eldest of the siblings, who most days found reason to whip Karelia's legs with the riding crop. Karelia tracked dirt into the house, swung her legs in church, hid among branches in the apple orchard to read, rode the family's pony into the woods without asking. She loved to let the pony take her where it would, making its own path until they came to a cool glade; she loved to lie on mossy ground and sketch the pony's head. Her most recent offense, the one that had driven her to run away, had been to draw a portrait of the cat on a scrap of paper using a charred twig from the fireplace; contemplating the angle of the ears, she had let her hand stray and smudged the sofa. Her ankles still stung.

"On the second morning, I overslept," she told me. "When I came down the ladder, our neighbor was beginning to milk the cow. I bolted toward the barn door and accidentally knocked over the oil lamp he'd set down. The straw caught fire. We had to rescue the animals. We got them all out, but the barn burned." By afternoon, she said, nothing remained but a mound of blackened wood that smoked for days.

A few days after her return to the family, Mr. Whitaker, the family's guardian, came to dinner. There were nine places at the table: Karelia's sister and her sister's husband, their two little children, and Karelia's three brothers. Mr. Whitaker had soft brown eyes and a small mouth whose lips moved little when he spoke, as if reluctant to disturb his face. Although he had been friends with her father, Karelia knew only that he worked at the bank in town.

"Mr. Whitaker received a letter from your uncle in San Francisco," Karelia's sister said.

"I didn't know we had an uncle," said Karelia's younger brother.

"We were at school together in Sacramento before your father and I moved here," Mr. Whitaker said. He had shaken salt heavily over all of his food but had eaten almost nothing yet. Perhaps sensing the eyes of everyone at the table on him, he dutifully forked corn into his mouth and chewed carefully before speaking again. "He writes that his wife has died, and he's left alone with his only child, an infant."

Karelia felt a brief envy at the phrase "only child."

Her sister leaned forward. "I've been telling Mr. Whitaker how unhappy you've been, Karelia, how nothing we've tried has worked. We hate to see you unhappy. And you know how to take care of little ones."

"You want to send me away?" Karelia cried, shoving back from the table.

Her sister covered her eyes with her hands. "Of course not," she said, and for a moment the table was silent while she wept. When she had dried her tears on her apron, she said, "We're only saying that if you were unhappy, you could go help your uncle—he has no family there.

And you've always said you wished you could take drawing lessons, but there's no one here who could do that. In San Francisco, there is an art school. You could find a student who would teach you."

"I want to go too," said Karelia's younger brother.

Mr. Whitaker said, "At it happens, Karelia, Mrs. Boklund is traveling through San Francisco in a few weeks on her way to Los Angeles to visit her son. If you decided to go, she would accompany you."

"I'll go," Karelia said.

"You don't have to give an answer tonight."

"I'll go," she repeated. She could see that the swiftness of her response hurt her sister. She didn't dare look at her other siblings. They never understood why she fell afoul of their oldest sister. "If you do what she says, she's easy to get along with," one of her older brothers had said once.

She called for someone to pass the greens. It seemed as if food had become too large for her throat, but she forced herself to swallow.

Mrs. Boklund was a tall Swede they knew from town. She knitted constantly on the long sea journey from Vancouver. When the wind rose and the water grew choppy, and Karelia became seasick, Mrs. Boklund came to check on her often, laying a hand on her forehead as if she had a fever. When the waters calmed, Karelia sat on the deck as far from the waves as possible, wrapped in a blanket and fighting panic: she wished she'd never left the safety of her home.

Her younger brother had given her the two-volume English translation of the *Kalevala*, the epic poem of Finland, their mother's copy, tales of ancient Finnish heroes and magic.

She opened it now and read the first story, which told how the world came to be created: one day, Ilmatar, the Daughter of the Ether, grows lonely in the empty expanse of heaven and descends to the ocean to relieve her boredom, only to be caught in a storm that tosses her among the waves and makes her pregnant and too heavy to return to the air. For seven hundred years, she swims back and forth, weeping with homesickness, her child refusing to be born. When at last she begs the creator to help her, a "beauteous duck" descends and lays eggs on Ilmatar's knee; when Ilmatar twitches her leg, the eggs fall and break, the fragments becoming the earth, the sky, the moon, the sun, the stars, and the clouds. Now Ilmatar passes the time shaping the land into hills and valleys, carving bays and lakes, molding reefs and islands, until finally her child—Wainamoinen, already ancient, already weary, fated to become the great hero of the Finnish people—climbs out of the womb himself and swims away.

A peculiar birth, Karelia thought; mother and son never exchange a word or even a glance, and he doesn't even need to suckle, as every newborn animal she'd watched had to do. She read on, but the poem seemed to forget about Ilmatar. Did she return to the air, having delivered her child? Did she mourn him and look for him? Karelia looked at the waves and no longer feared them. If I were Ilmatar, she thought, I would stay on earth and keep on sculpting the land, digging harbors with my heel and filigreeing the mountains with my fingers.

"The *Kalevala* wasn't like anything I'd ever read before," she told me many years later. "It made little sense, like a dream, or like life, and that's why it comforted me."

Mrs. Boklund warned Karelia to watch out, once they reached San Francisco, for men trying to lure her into a brothel. The city had blocks lined with saloons and houses of prostitution, sailors mad with loneliness. Even some of the finest restaurants had places of dalliance on the second floor. Karelia peppered Mrs. Boklund with questions: Was it true San Francisco had a whole city inside it where people from China lived stacked on shelves? Did miners still walk around with gold in their pockets?

Their steamer was delayed in landing as another vessel unloaded at the wharf, and when it was time to disembark, the passengers, weary of days at sea, crowded to reach dry land. In the crush of people, Karelia lost her grip on Mrs. Boklund's dress and was separated. When the passengers dispersed, she couldn't see Mrs. Boklund at all.

No doubt Mrs. Boklund had doubled back and was searching for her. But Karelia knew Mrs. Boklund regretted having given herself only one day to spend with her relatives in San Francisco before continuing on to Los Angeles, and so she assumed her guardian had hurried on without her. She dug out the letter Mr. Whitaker had sent with her and noted the address.

"I was terrified," Karelia told me, "but I suppose I was also half-pleased, to be alone with my chances, to finally be in charge of myself."

Karelia gave different accounts of what happened next. When I was very young, she said she followed a trio of stilt-walking street performers juggling wooden pins, assuming that wherever they were going it would be safe, and eventually she spotted the street my father lived on. Or she said a policeman led her to my father's door.

When I was eight or nine, she told me that two friendly young men volunteered to take her straight there and carry her suitcase for her. They kept getting lost, however, and she wandered the city for hours with them, until evening fell and she realized they had no intention of taking her to her uncle. One of the men tried to kiss her. "I'd never been so terrified," she told me. "I wished I'd never left home."

She grabbed her suitcase away from him and ran down the street. A Spanish washerwoman who spoke little English took her in and let her sleep on her floor. Early the next morning she asked someone the way and walked seventeen blocks to my father's flat.

*   *   *

My father found her a bewildering presence. Later Karelia discovered a journal he kept and read the entries he'd written about her:

> She prefers to sit in the chair by the window and look out at the street all afternoon.
> I could hardly persuade her to take a bath, and then she spent an hour at it.
> She regards Joseph as if he were a bundle of clothing.

When the Hajdus first crowded into my father's flat with a cabbage-noodle dish and her squalling infant cousin, Karelia retreated into the bathroom. My father communicated to them who she was and why she had come, and the matriarch of the family tried to coax her with crescent-shaped cookies.

When she glimpsed her uncle at the edge of her vision, he was her father's echo. Like her father, he rolled pieces of bread into beads before eating it; he tapped his fingertips to his thumbs when thinking or agitated; he spoke little. Unlike her father, however, he read the newspaper each day. From time to time he would lean over and point out to her a particularly egregious example of fakery: Winchester's Hypophosphite of Lime and Soda, which claimed to cure pulmonary diseases, or Tutt's Tiny Pills, which promised pep. Reading about psychic mediums inflamed him.

Once, when he fell asleep on the sofa, she sketched his head. He had the same high Finnish cheekbones as her father's, the same deep-set eyes, the same gray-flecked beard. His face was longer, she supposed. She wished her hand could obey her eye and make smooth, sweeping marks on the paper that conjured what she saw instead of something wobbly and misshapen. She crumpled the drawing.

One day when the Hajdus arrived, they brought a cat, a striped tabby missing an ear. Karelia sat in the middle of the floor and took the cat in her arms. When the Hajdus left an hour later, she hadn't moved, and the cat had fallen asleep. On later visits, the family enlisted her aid. Mrs. Hajdu convinced Karelia to help make dumplings for a stew on my father's stove, which hadn't been used for cooking since my mother's death; one of the Hajdu daughters handed me to Karelia to hold while she swept the flat. My father noted in his journal when Karelia laughed for the first time while sewing with the oldest Hajdu daughter. She would change me and feed me and walk me around the room when I cried. Gradually she took on the running of the household, the cooking and the cleaning, preparing the recipes the Hajdus had taught her. He wrote nothing of his own grief, and only one line about the tabby: I *rue the cat*.

Though she'd never enjoyed church, she was surprised that her uncle didn't attend or insist that she go. He told her, "We must treat religion as a form of superstition, unless someone proves by scientific methods that a god exists." It had never occurred to her that she could live without church, any more than she could forgo washing her face in the morning no matter how cold the water. On the first few Sunday mornings, she gazed a little wistfully out the window at the women walking in their dresses and bonnets.

Two weeks after her arrival, he began to take an afternoon walk. On his return he would often lie fully clothed on the bed, hands over his eyes, until dinner. This is what Karelia recalls. He stopped writing in his journal. I believe, however, that chronicling the daily changes in Karelia may have helped inspire the project that was to consume his life.

One morning in late September, less than two months after I entered the world, my father got up early and began shaving. Karelia had never seen him with a razor in his hand before. When he emerged from the bathroom, she nearly did not recognize him; he had shaven his beard off entirely, and his skin glowed, the lines of his jaw sharp and pink. His drying hair stood out in damp ringlets.

"As soon as possible, we must go to the studio," he said.

She wasn't accustomed to hearing him speak in such energetic tones, and it made her uneasy. And she had no idea where he was proposing they go. He had told her that he was on leave from his job as a portrait photographer, but she didn't connect the word "studio" to that profession, which remained as mysterious to her as when she had arrived. She changed and bottle-fed me and ate her own breakfast. He held her coat for her.

My father was tall, and she was hard pressed to keep pace with him, especially with me in her arms. They walked down Montgomery Avenue, past the barber's, past the bakery where she gazed longingly at the pastries placed in the window. The streets were full of horses, with and without carriages; newsboys proclaimed the urgency of the day's headlines. A cold wind undid my father's collar on one side and made it stick up like a wing, which embarrassed her.

On Market Street they entered a five-story building and began climbing the stairs. At the third landing, my father stopped to catch his breath.

"I've been doing a great deal of thinking," my father said. He swabbed his face with a handkerchief and took the next flight two steps at a time. She hastened after him, trying not to jostle me, because although my eyes were still closed, I was beginning to move restlessly. I was prone to cry and, according to Karelia, had lungs of unusual capacity.

We burst into the photographic studio of Devereaux & Grant. The receptionist, Mrs. Ruthinger, was showing a young couple a selection of frames and didn't look up until my father had already hurried past her desk. She called in her deep froglike voice, "Who is your appointment with, sir?" When he turned, she seemed amazed to recognize my father.

"Mr. Kylander, I beg your pardon. We weren't expecting you. Your room is in use—Mr. Billings is at work."

"Who is Mr. Billings?"

"A freelance photographer," she said. "Mr. Devereaux brought him in to handle your clients."

"I need my room as soon as he is done," he said.

Mrs. Ruthinger extended her open hand in the direction of the couple who had been looking at frames, and who were now watching the interchange with much curiosity. She said, "They are scheduled for a four o'clock appointment with Mr. Billings."

The young woman, who had been smiling fondly at me, said, "We don't mind waiting a bit. How old is he?"

Karelia wondered if they thought that I was her child and that she was my father's wife. "Five years old," she said, to flummox them. The couple stared at the tiny bootie on my foot kicking up and down. "He's very small for his age," she added. They asked no more questions.

The door to my father's studio opened, and out came a husky man with wire rim spectacles that seemed too small for his face. "Mrs. Ruthinger will show you the sizes of prints we offer," he was saying to the elderly woman following him. "I'm sure you'll find something satisfactory."

"I'm Arthur Kylander," my father said, "and I need my studio for half an hour." He shook Mr. Billings's hand and beckoned to Karelia. She hurried after him. But no sooner had she reached the door than she ran into him, because he had stopped still.

"What's all this clutter?" he said. A large backdrop of a meadow rested on a carpet of artificial grass. In the corner of the room stood Greek columns, two papier-mâché boulders, and a rustic-looking fence. Several other painted landscapes leaned against the wall.

"I find that customers appreciate a variety of backdrops," Mr. Billings said.

"I know what their purpose is," said my father. "And they have nothing to do with portraits. For God's sake, the woman you just photographed likely hasn't set foot in a meadow in years. If people insist on being photographed with a meadow behind them, take them to a real one. Remove these items!"

Mr. Devereaux emerged from his office. "Arthur, what are you doing here? My deepest condolences about your wife." He paused. "You are well, I trust? Are you evicting Mr. Billings?"

"I'm evicting his paraphernalia," my father said.

"It's all right," said Mr. Billings. "I'm happy to remove it for the moment, Mr. Devereaux, happy to be accommodating."

Mr. Devereaux possessed the most neatly trimmed beard Karelia had ever seen, silvery and coming to a point so sharp it might cut glass. He regarded my father in astonishment. "But Arthur, are you sure you are well enough yet?"

"Quite well," my father said.

Behind him, Mr. Billings carried out a backdrop of the Alps.

Mr. Devereaux's eye twitched, but he said nothing. Soon Mr. Billings had removed all his props and with a bow and a flourish directed my father and Karelia into the studio.

By this time, Karelia felt self-conscious. She had never been inside a portrait studio. And although she had been living in our flat for a month, she hadn't had time to get used to my father—she had only seen him in his melancholic state.

My father placed a chair for her in front of the plain backdrop that he always used and motioned for her to sit. Mr. Billings had left behind a papier-mâché boulder, which my father shoved into the corner. By this time, I was awake, but although I jerked my head around solemnly at the unfamiliar surroundings, I hadn't yet decided to cry.

"Why did you bring us here?" Karelia asked my father.

"To take a portrait." He removed the lens of the camera and began to focus on her.

She hadn't been expecting to have her own photograph taken. No one had ever photographed her. She looked down at her dress, a patched, worn thing the Hajdus had given her. She hadn't even had the chance to brush her hair, yet she feared that if she asked for a brush, my father would think her vain. Surely he would offer her one.

As he focused the camera and adjusted the shades that let light into the room, he spoke to her. "I wish photographers wouldn't turn their studios into a theater stage. It's bad enough that people want us to retouch the negatives."

Now Karelia knew he wouldn't think of offering her a brush.

"The camera is an instrument of science," he said. "Muybridge showed us that."

She watched my father cross the room and remove from a cabinet what looked like a long flat box. After inserting this into the camera, he once again disappeared beneath the cloth. She had to stifle an urge to leap off the stool and run out of the room with me. "Hold him in the air in front of you so his legs hang down," he said. He gave her various instructions—higher, lower, turn the right side closer to me. "Is it warm enough in here to undress the child?"

When I was naked, he said, "Now hold him before you again, as straight on as possible." He studied them through the lens of his camera. "A half-inch lower."

She did not like holding me this way, as if I were a prize fish being recorded for posterity, and I did not like it either. I kicked and squalled. Her arms were tired. She heard a click. Was it as simple as that? She'd imagined a professional photographer's equipment to be much more complicated, involving rods and levers.

My father directed Karelia to turn me forty-five degrees so that he might photograph my right profile, then my back, then my left profile. "You may put him down now," he said, and she did so gratefully, her arms aching as she dressed me again.

A knock came, and Mr. Devereaux walked in. "Arthur, you've had your half-hour and some extra. May I ask your intentions for the rest of the afternoon?"

"I'm done for today," my father said. "And you can count on my return to work tomorrow morning. I'm invigorated by this project, which may well bring renown to the studio. I've an idea to extend Muybridge's work, to create the first scientific record of the development of the human body over time. I'd like Mrs. Ruthinger to clear a half hour in my schedule so that I may repeat this session with my son and my niece each afternoon."

"Each afternoon?" Karelia cried.

Mr. Devereaux went over to the windows and pulled up a shade, flooding the room with light. "Arthur, you know I grieve with you at the loss of your wife. At the same time, Mr. Billings is doing an excellent job with us. It is true that his approach is different from your own—I side with your aesthetic preferences here—but the customers are pleased with his work, and I feel I'm bound to allow him room to develop in his abilities. You have an excitable nature, Arthur, it wouldn't do for you to rush back into work. I believe the best course for you now is to consider yourself free from studio responsibilities at Devereaux & Grant. Perhaps at some future point, after some months or even a year has passed, we may come to a new understanding."

"I see," said my father. Karelia, who had succeeded in calming me, watched him warily, wondering if he was about to start a row. Mr. Devereaux had called him excitable, and since he had lain in bed much of the time she had known him, she had no experience of her own to go on except for the events of the afternoon. My father stood in the middle of the room, frowning, as if mulling over Mr. Devereaux's words. "Please let me have two weeks," he said. "Too much time has been lost already, and I can't afford any gaps in the sequence. And I ask for a half-hour each afternoon at three o'clock to continue my project. I'll gladly shorten my lunch hour to make it up. I've worked for you for more than four years, Mr. Devereaux. Two more weeks, that would only be fair, wouldn't it?"

Mr. Devereaux agreed with a sigh.

My father shook Mr. Devereaux's hand absently and motioned for Karelia to follow him out of the studio. Mr. Billings lurked by the door. He sprang back hastily, as if fearing my father might strike him. But my father seemed preoccupied with his own thoughts. Karelia felt the eyes of everyone in the waiting room. As I began to cry again, she tried to slow her step so as not to appear to be hurrying obediently after my father.

By the time my father and Karelia returned from the studio, I had fallen asleep, my head burrowed under her chin. My father shut himself into a closet she had never seen opened since her arrival—his dark-room. When he emerged, he put before her what he called the best series of prints, one of each quadrant of my infant body. "The left profile suffers from blur," he said. "The dorsal view is slightly overexposed. Still, a fair start."

Karelia was glad to see that my father had cropped the photographs tightly. Only her hands were visible, holding me up.

"But do I have to hold Joseph for the camera again?" Karelia asked.

"Bring him to the studio at three o'clock each afternoon. Do you remember the way?"

"For how many days?"

"For as long as it takes for him to learn to stand on his own."

She considered a moment. "I want something in return. I want to have drawing lessons."

He looked at her in surprise.

She expected him to say that drawing was a childish waste of time.

But instead he said, "Of course. Drawing is a useful way to train the eye."

*   *   *

In mid-November, my father opened Aethon Photographic Studio on Market Street. "In Greek mythology," he explained to me once, "Aethon was the name of one of the horses that pulled the chariot of the sun for the god Helios." In this he showed that he no longer harbored hard feelings toward Muybridge. However, within a year, my father would change the name to Kylander Photographic Studio. He grew tired, he said, of customers asking for Mr. Aethon.

After opening the studio, he moved us to a less expensive apartment in the Italian quarter and diverted some of our furniture to the studio; now at home one chair remained, which Karelia and my father transferred from room to room as needed; at meals my father sat on an orange crate. He posted flyers, advertised in the newspaper, and wrote to his former Devereaux & Grant customers. Karelia cooked bean and cabbage soup, bought scrap meat and salted codfish to save money, spread butter as thinly as possible on the slices of bread she baked. She darned his pockets, which the keys to the studio kept wearing through.

"I was homesick for the orchards," Karelia told me years later. "So many people and so few trees. And I had to beg your father for new clothes—I wore cast-offs neighbors gave me, which never fit. I hated the way other women looked at me on the streets, the way the merchants smiled at me. Girls my age were in school."

After my Sunday afternoon portrait session, my father walked Karelia to the flat where Miss Pettit, a student at the California School of Design, lived with her mother. Karelia drew still lifes of potatoes and bowls and urns; she drew a bust of Molière; she drew Miss Pettit's head. These were Karelia's happiest days yet. She drew a self-portrait and mailed it with some of her other drawings to her younger brother. She once showed me a rough sketch she'd kept: her face, framed in a round mirror, her sharp cheekbones shaded to exaggeration, her ash-colored hair bound in a scarf, her eyes wide as if she were startled or skeptical to find herself there.

For Christmas, Karelia baked star-shaped pastries filled with prune jam, which her mother had made. "What are these?" my father asked. *Joulutortut,* she told him, and at his blank expression, added that they were a traditional Christmas recipe in Finland. "My father preferred not to remember anything of their old life there," he told her. "He and my mother never spoke the language in front of us, and he had her serve us only American dishes." When Karelia teased my father and said of course he wouldn't want to eat her cookies, he reached for one and said he had no objection, because he'd never known Finland and therefore couldn't be reminded of it.

Karelia was named after the place where her mother had been a child, a territory extending from the Gulf of Finland to the White Sea. Though she'd never seen it herself, she drew it for me, the region of Karelia, which she rendered with vast spruce forests and lakes, boulders taller than men. Her most valued possession was her two-volume translation of the *Kalevala,* which she read to me at nights, her head on the pillow next to mine. The ancient singer Wainamoinen, swallowed by a dead giant, sets up a forge inside the stomach and forces the creature to cough him up. The reckless wizard Lemminkainen, arriving uninvited to a wedding, is served a mug of writhing serpents and lizards to provoke him into a duel of magic. The master blacksmith Ilmarinen, grieving over his wife's death, fashions a bride of gold and silver, but she lies lifeless in bed, chilling his skin. The three of them join forces to fight Louhi, the queen of Northland, to gain back the magic Sampo, a mysterious object that grinds flour on one side, produces salt from its second side, and mints coins with its third. How these tales fascinated me. I would make up my own stories about the characters after Karelia kissed me goodnight, and they so stirred my mind that sleep would be long in coming.

Each afternoon she brought me to the studio around three o'clock and held me for my portrait. At first, she believed that my father, mourning his wife, had found a way to preoccupy himself for a while. Her own father had taken to splitting wood for hours after her mother died—the mountain of logs he produced over the course of several months nearly reached the height of the house, until one day he stopped.

"Keep his chin still," my father said from behind the camera. "Straighten his left leg and his right arm."

"I only have two hands," Karelia said.

One evening after supper, about a month after the project began, my father asked her to let the washing wait and to sit back down at the table with him. She thought that he was angry at her; she had been ten minutes late to the studio that afternoon, and he had been even more quiet than usual ever since. He drew out a large, leather-bound book of prints entitled *Animal Locomotion: An Electro-Photographic Investigation of Consecutive Phases of Animal Movements* by Eadweard Muybridge and gave her a pair of white gloves to put on. The leather gave off the odor of birch bark.

This book contained a hundred plates that Muybridge had created under the University of Pennsylvania's auspices in the 1880s, after he'd left California. "Muybridge was a great man," my father said. "He revolutionized our understanding of the physiology of animals, including humans."

Karelia looked in wonder at the pageantry of wildlife that moved through its pages: horses, tigers, oxen, cats, buffalos, pigeons, ostriches, cranes. It struck her as odd that they all moved through the same blank environment—peering more closely, she made out what looked like an ordinary wrinkled bed sheet stretched as a backdrop behind the buffalos. In other images, the actions were performed before a grid of white lines on a black surface.

Most of the humans wore no clothing—this was to reveal their musculature, my father explained. Men jumped, wrestled, swung a scythe, hammered an anvil. An amputee walked with crutches; a legless boy climbed in and out of a chair. Women picked up clothes, threw a kiss, climbed stairs. One naked woman poured a bucket of water over another, a cloud of droplets shattering in the sequence's final three frames.

At this one, Karelia laughed.

My father smiled. "Muybridge sometimes diverged from the purely scientific, it's true. Still, you will find all of the images of value to study as you practice the art of drawing."

When she had finished looking through the plates, he said, "What Muybridge has achieved in chronicling motion, I intend to achieve in chronicling time."

"You're going to photograph Joseph for the rest of his life?"

"It's my hope, yes." A look of sadness crossed his face, perhaps remembering that his other children hadn't lived long, or thinking that he himself would not see his project completed. "Now do you understand why it is so important that you arrive on time each day?"

He might be a great man, she thought, like Bell or Edison or Muybridge. She looked at me, a four-month-old infant, and tried to imagine me as an old man, white haired and stooped, with my father, even older, training his camera on me.

CHAPTER THREE

My father began building the Tetrascope a few months after I learned to stand. He accumulated a number of cameras, some broken, which he now began to disassemble and tinker with in a spare room at the studio. He ordered small mirrors from a European manufacturer, ground to exacting standards. From plumbing supply stores he purchased lengths of pipe, and from junk shops he accumulated clocks that he disemboweled for gears.

He and Karelia warred over the flat surfaces of the house. She needed them for cooking and baking, he for spreading out the plans he was drawing up, which he worked on late at night after a day at the studio. When he built another table in the corner of the room by the window, it left hardly enough space for Karelia to squeeze out of her bedroom in the morning, and the amount of papers only increased, leaving the battlefield larger but no less contested.

One morning Karelia returned from the grocer's to find that my father had, before leaving for work, spread out a sheaf of drawings over the pie tins and rolling board she had laid out on the table. She threw the papers out the window. On his way back to the flat for lunch, my father saw a boy run past wearing a paper hat that bore familiar sketches of a gear assembly. Another sheet he found in the gutter, marked with hoof prints.

On his return Karelia did not meet his eyes. He said nothing. He washed his hands, sat on the orange crate, put his napkin on his lap, and waited for Karelia to serve. As soon as she had placed a hot chicken pie in the center of the table, he picked it up barehanded and flung it out the window.

"What are we going to eat now?" Karelia cried. She was very hungry. Chicken pie was one of her favorites. The scent of it still hung in the air.

My father looked at the reddening marks the hot pie plate had left on his fingertips.

Karelia stared at him. Then she began snatching things up from the table and hurling them out the window; the forks and knives clanged tinnily on the pavement below, the porcelain saltshaker gave off a muffled report. Passersby shouted up from below. I began to cry. My father grabbed Karelia's arms. For a moment she struggled to break free, then went limp. "Go ahead," she said. "Throw me out the window too. I didn't ask to be here."

He let go, and she picked me up and ran into her room. She rocked me and petted me, but I didn't quiet down. After a while she heard him rummaging in the kitchen area. Evidently he found some bread and butter; she heard a knife scraping the cutting board. She stared out the sole window in her room, which for some reason the builders had placed in the closet, requiring her to leave the closet door always open; it looked out into a gray light shaft. I grew calmer. Karelia heard the front door close and my father's footsteps retreat toward the stairs.

One afternoon a week later, when she arrived at the studio, he motioned her in to the studio's spare operating room. Beneath the skylights were four cameras on short tripods facing each other, forming the points of a square approximately ten feet wide. Pipes rose from the tops of three of the cameras, angled, then bent again to converge inside the fourth camera. It looked to her like a mechanical spider; she found it unnerving.

"I call it the Tetrascope," he said. "It has the ability to photograph its subject from four sides at once." When I ran to one of the cameras, Karelia followed to pull me away, but my father said, "Let him touch the cameras. I've screwed them to the floor and braced them to hold the weight of the tubes overhead. These pipes contain mirrors that reflect the images from each of the three satellite cameras, directing the dorsal and two lateral views of the subject into the master camera, where they take their positions next to the ventral view. In this way I can place all four views in a row on the same negative simultaneously. The mirrors are the most challenging aspect. The slightest movement of the building can throw them out of alignment. I still haven't completely solved the problem. But I expect it to be ready in a few more days."

The next week, my father asked Karelia to bring me into the room with the Tetrascope. He placed a block of firewood in the center as a dummy and began focusing and adjusting the mirrors. Then he removed the wood. Karelia undressed me and placed me at the center of the lenses. "Let him stand by himself," he said, waving her to the side of the room. I stood blinking, and my father took my picture.

For my father's plan to work, it was essential that I stand completely still, in more or less the same posture, each day while he took my photograph. I had only recently learned to stand and walk unaided, however, and stillness was not a skill I had any interest in. First he devised a sort of restraining pen out of smooth rods of wood, but Karelia protested that this was inhumane. And this method proved unsatisfactory anyway, because I could still twist about, and the bars of wood obstructed portions of my anatomy.

So he began to train me to stand still. As a youth in Sacramento, he had raised dogs; he decided to praise me and feed me candy when I remained still for any length of time.

These proceedings he concealed from Karelia by asking her to stay in the waiting area, reminding her that any movement could jar the mirrors. One day, however, she crept in to watch. After several weeks of training, I had become quite good at stillness; it frightened her. "What are you doing?" she asked when she saw him give me a chocolate after the image had been taken. When my father explained, she snatched me up, dressed me, and hurried out in a fury.

All the following day, Karelia was agitated. At two thirty, she took me down the street to the confectioner's and fed me as many sweets as I wanted. When we reached my father's studio, I had great difficulty settling down. "Be still," my father said, and I darted about, climbing the low table where he kept frames. He caught me and smelled my breath, redolent of chocolate and caramel.

"Karelia," he shouted. He strode into the waiting room, where she was leaning on the front desk talking to our receptionist, Mrs. Salamanco. A customer had come early for his next appointment, so my father did not shout anything further to Karelia. He returned to the Tetrascope and tried for another fifteen minutes to take my portrait, then gave up and handed me back to Karelia in disgust. This was the first gap in the sequence.

Not for the first time Karelia contemplated stealing me away, taking me with her back to Canada. And yet she pictured her oldest sister watching her approach the house after her year's absence, the attempt to put on a welcoming smile. Or she might be arrested for kidnapping. And where else could she go, with or without me? She was mindful of Mrs. Boklund's warnings. Miss Pettit had told her about a house in the city where runaway girls as young as eleven were forced to serve the pleasures of men. Karelia, thirteen at the time, didn't know what that meant, but she knew she couldn't bear such a life.

Karelia began to arrive at the studio late or early, either of which infuriated my father—if she arrived early, and I were fussy, we would disturb waiting customers; if she arrived late, my father had to rush or delay his next appointment. She always had a story—she had forgotten to wind the clock, she had lost her keys, she had been held up by a crowd surrounding a man who promoted a cure for baldness.

Early one afternoon, two weeks after the chocolate incident, Karelia packed a picnic basket and her sketching-pad and carried me to the studio, where she passed a note to my father's receptionist. It read, "At three o'clock, please tell Mr. Kylander that Joseph and I have gone to spend the afternoon at the beach." She put her fingers to her lips, and Mrs. Salamanco gave a fearful glance at the operating room. But Karelia was already backing out.

We took the streetcar to the ocean. The afternoon was unusually warm for San Francisco. She didn't understand how the horizon could be such a perfect straight line, when everywhere else the glittering waves were constantly roiling and shape-shifting. She scanned the shore for the elements of a still life: broken sand dollars, crab skeletons, delicate fanned shells of the scallops, pearly slices of oyster shell. She knew enough to keep me away from the occasional congealed mound of a dead jellyfish.

For hours she sketched and watched me run about on the sand. I grew weary, and she made a shady nest for me with her shawl and some driftwood. While I slept, she sat on the beach at the edge of the wet zone of the sand, her eyes opened as wide as possible. I can picture her, though surely I was too young to remember any of this. In later years, I often asked her to tell how I received the scar on my temple, and she would tell me about this day.

The beach had nearly emptied of other people. As a thick gray wall of fog advanced across the waves toward her, she had a mystical experience. Here, at the borderland between the civilized world of the land and the raw unruliness of the water, she saw that what truly mattered was the elemental wildness of nature. She felt the sea and the fog calling to her. She would build fires out of driftwood. She would learn how to catch fish herself, rather than haggle with fishmongers over the corpses of fish with already dulling eyes. She didn't have any idea of how to live off the sea, but after all, neither had the first people to walk the earth.

They had had to learn everything themselves. They didn't have ovens and water closets, spoons and hammers, stairways and streetcars. They had only their own fingers and what tools they could make from the things that nature had strewn around them.

She turned her head to better hear the waves and what they were saying to her. It was then she noticed that the tent of her shawl had collapsed, and I had disappeared. Wildly she looked up and down the beach through the whitening air. There I was, several hundred yards away, watching her. I ran off again, to get her to chase after me, I suppose. She jumped to her feet as I fell.

When she reached me, she found me wailing—I had cut my forehead on a piece of driftwood or shell. The wound was more bloody than deep, a line three-quarters of an inch long in the center of my forehead. Karelia washed the injury in sea water and tore a strip of cloth from the bottom of her skirt to bind my head. Thus disheveled, she carried me back across the beach toward the streetcar that would take us home, forgetting entirely about her shawl and the picnic basket.

"I was angry at you," she would tell me in later years. "You had interrupted something important. I wished I had left you with a neighbor and come out to the sea alone. And then as we left the beach, you stopped crying and put your arms around my neck, and suddenly my anger disappeared and all I felt was love." And here she would run her hand through my hair, stroke the faint white indentation on my forehead, and I would relax and lean into her. The scar was what had bound us together, when she had rescued me and I had rescued her; I felt it was a sign we would always be together.

When we returned to the flat, my father was standing near the door. Apparently I pulled a crab claw from my pocket to wave at him. My bloodied bandage was sliding off my temple, my eyes half closed. "What happened?" he cried. I turned in Karelia's grasp and held my arms out

to him sleepily; he took me; I turned again and held my arms out for
Karelia. When he did not give me back, I let out a cry.

"He's all right," Karelia said. "I took him for a day at the beach, and he
had a wonderful time. He just fell, that's all, but you can see he's happy."

My father carried me to the sink and bathed my forehead,
examining the injury with the thoroughness of a surgeon before apply-
ing a bandage. "He could have been seriously hurt."

Karelia said nothing.

"If you're not able to look after him, you should return to your
sister's household."

"How would you live without me?" she asked.

"I would hire someone to clean and cook."

"With what money? And who would put up with you but me?"

My father put me to bed himself. Karelia stayed awake for a long
time alone in her room. He didn't understand her, and he never would.
She tried to remember the afternoon at the beach, the sound of the
waves, the cry of the seagulls. Instead she heard the laughter of drunken
men passing by on the street. The walls around her were nothing but
brittle paper, the bedspread a flimsy tissue. Now she knew that the
city was nothing to be frightened of; man had paved over the soil with
asphalt and erected buildings like toys, but they would not endure like
the sea, the land. If she had to stay here, she would raise me to know
what was elemental and what was false; she would not let my father
alone shape my soul.

For breakfast, she made biscuits; he ate three and said they were
delicious.

"I was thinking in the night," he said. "It isn't necessary to photograph Joseph seven days a week—the three of us could take Sundays off
and go on expeditions to the beaches and forests. We can start by taking
the ferry to Larkspur this Sunday for a picnic."

She looked at him in astonishment. She couldn't imagine him sitting on a beach, holding a sandwich in wax paper under the trees, let alone wading into waves or hiking up a hillside. His obsession with photographing every day would prove too strong: she predicted his offer would last at most two weeks.

But my father kept his promise for many years. On Sundays, we visited shores and streams, climbed Mount Tamalpais and Mount Diablo, picnicked under redwoods and bay trees. Karelia pointed out beauty in spider webs, sunsets, anemones, and ladies in their hiking dresses, while my father taught me the chromatic properties of rainbows, the biology of earthworms, and the concepts of depth of field and shutter speed. Those days are a lost paradise: a cabinet of curiosities. I most like to remember my father as he was then, as willing to admire the speckles of a fallen blue robin's egg with me and Karelia as he was to explain the mechanics of a falcon's wing spread against the sky above us.

My father helped me construct my own pinhole camera, and on our excursions, I tried to capture the world, while Karelia went on ahead without the intermediary of a lens, sometimes stopping to show me a leaf or an insect and insisting I simply look, fix the moment in memory rather than on film.

Once, we came across a fallen tree layered with striped orange fungi like sea creatures. I took their picture, and my father remarked, "If we come this way next Sunday, you can photograph them again and we will be able to show how they have developed or diminished."

Karelia said, "Not everything needs to be scientifically useful."

"Everything *is*—" my father began, then stopped himself. He gave a small, rueful smile. Softly, he said, "But if it isn't, how am I to make any sense of it?"

I wish I'd captured my father at that moment, his look of dismayed, amused wonder. I wish I'd photographed him more often in general.

Instead, I focused on dragonflies and branch shadows, hikers resting against a tree, my bare feet reflected in a pool, any number of useless arrangements of light. I should have put on Bloch's Detective Photo Scarf and followed him around with it. But even if I had, those photographs would have been destroyed with all the others. Despite all the sophisticated devices and chemicals we had—the electric shutters and the extending lenses, the stop baths and the fixers—time has its own blunt instruments.

We moved to a different part of the city every few years, my father always seeking lower rents or quieter lodging. I found each school I attended a foreign country of sorts, with sub rosa allegiances and unspoken laws. Once, called upon in history class to answer some question about Caesar, I panicked and instead recited lines from Shakespeare's play, which I'd been reading with Karelia, dazzled by Caesar's calm solidity moments before being stabbed:

> *I could be well moved, if I were as you;*
> *If I could pray to move, prayers would move me;*
> *But I am constant as the northern star,*
> *Of whose true-fix'd and resting quality*
> *There is no fellow in the firmament.*
> *The skies are painted with unnumber'd sparks—*

The teacher cut me off. My schoolmates laughed and from then on referred to me as "Unnumber'd Sparks," when they did not ignore me entirely.

None of them had a genius for a father. I would sometimes gaze at them, hunched over their desks writing, and think I was fortunate not to lead an unrecorded life like them. I felt sad, not only because they had little documentation of the trace they had made in their brief existence, but also because I was my father's only subject; we had no data for comparison of the differences in development among individuals. And if some afternoons I looked longingly out the studio's window at a group of them kicking a can down the street together and laughing, I told myself that it didn't matter.

*   *   *

At the beginning of 1905, when I was halfway through the eighth grade, a rival photographer opened a studio in the building next door to my father's. The man put up an ostentatious display case at street level, twice the size of ours, to show his portraits. We heard he had a Vandyke beard, a parrot, and a store of anecdotes of his travels through the west photographing Indians. Muybridge had left California years ago to return to England, where he'd died, and my father's stories no longer had the same cachet they'd once had. Our customers dwindled.

Karelia asked the milkman to bring only one pint each day, and she baked savory pies only when the butcher discounted meat scraps. The grocer's man delivered a gigantic sack of white beans, which slouched on the kitchen floor like a reproachful animal.

That was when my father decided it was time to begin revealing his project to the world. First he would need a backer. He scanned the newspaper for the names of wealthy San Franciscans and wrote them letters mentioning that he'd been the protégé of the famous photographer Eadweard Muybridge. He hinted that he was at work on a secret project that exceeded his mentor's work. He reminded them of the renown that Governor Stanford had gained from supporting Muybridge, the first photographer to capture the horse in motion. If they came by the studio, he would show them an enterprise in scope beyond anything photographers had attempted before.

Most of the wealthy men didn't respond. One wanted to know if my father had any of Muybridge's photographs of horses to sell. Another sent a letter that my father crumpled and tossed in the trash. Karelia rescued it: the person desired "photographs in the manner of Muybridge, with women in certain poses I'll describe further when we meet." This made her laugh, though she wouldn't tell me why.

In a few cases, secretaries sent polite replies that so-and-so was very busy and could not consider all the ventures that came his way, or they sent less polite replies that so-and-so was not interested in the least. Sometimes my father came home from the studio with a letter like this in hand and lay down on the floor of his bedroom or, once, in the hallway. He would get up only for dinner, eat a boiled egg or piece of cheese, and go to bed. For days he would move sluggishly.

Karelia would tell him, "Your ideas are too advanced for everyone to grasp." Or, "They read your letter when they were suffering from eating too much beef at lunch." I would ask him to tell me again how he met Muybridge, how he won his way into a job with the man at the height of his fame in California. Soon we would wake to find him at his desk again, rapidly writing away with new enthusiasm, the ink flying from his pen.

We moved to a small third-floor apartment in the Hayes Valley neighborhood because my father's payments to the landlord of our previous place had fallen behind. The possibility of having to dismantle the Tetrascope and find a new studio for it as well hung over us all. To save costs, my father began storing the negatives without printing them first. He went through the old prints and destroyed nearly all those from 1898, declaring they'd been printed on inferior paper and would have to be redone someday.

One afternoon, I arrived at the Tetrascope room to find it empty, and when I went to look for my father in his operating room, he seemed surprised to see me.

"It's time," I said.

"It doesn't matter. No one has expressed interest in our project. We shouldn't be wasting film on it."

Of course it mattered, I told him. No one had ever attempted a project as ambitious as this. I reminded him that before Muybridge was hailed as a genius, he'd been derided: cartoonists had mocked the poses of the horses he'd photographed. I said that if Muybridge had had an easier time funding his project, it was because his backer had hired him in the first place—it wasn't even Muybridge's idea to photograph the horse in motion, after all, it was Stanford's. My father was the true visionary, and we must not give up hope.

I don't remember what else I said, but at last he rose to his feet and we went into the Tetrascope room. Our whole life revolved around our great endeavor. I couldn't imagine what would happen if we were to stop. If the Tetrascope gathered dust, if the long trail of photographs petered out, it would be as if I'd stopped existing.

Finally, one Friday in September 1905, a stagnant, hazy heat took hold of San Francisco and gave the light in my father's photography studio the muted tone of a sepia print. I had just turned fourteen. In the breezeless air of late afternoon, Karelia and I played gin rummy in the waiting area and fanned ourselves with large mailing envelopes. Our sole client scheduled for that afternoon had canceled because of the heat. I brought a glass of water to my father in the back room and found him asleep with his head on the desk, his silvering hair bunched up against the retouching frame. I left the glass on a low table and tucked the negatives he'd been working on into a box, so that if he stirred in his sleep he wouldn't knock them to the floor.

At five o'clock, Karelia put up the CLOSED sign while I locked the frame display cases. Mrs. Salamanco now left early three days a week to care for her ailing mother, and so Karelia had taken to covering for her on these afternoons. She was not as patient with the customers as Mrs. Salamanco, but they liked her better, especially the men, and sometimes they brought her bouquets. I believe she was happier in those days, that although she sometimes complained about having to be "your father's handmaiden both at work and at home," she appreciated the chance to be out in the world and to help people.

That afternoon, however, the heat had made her irritable, and so I grabbed the broom without being asked and began sweeping the carpet.

It was seven minutes after five when someone knocked. I always knew precisely what time it was without needing to consult a clock—a skill I had learned to conceal from my schoolmates, since none of them seemed to possess it.

Karelia called out, "We're closed for the day," but the knocking continued until I answered it.

The man on the other side of the door stood well over six feet tall. He was perhaps in his early forties, with a large oval head topped by fine, fair hair, and his stout frame fit snugly in a suit of gray cloth, which gave off the sweet odor of pipe tobacco. He said his name was Thomas Hallgarten.

"Did you come to pick up prints?" I asked.

"No," he said, gazing at the studio with eyes crinkled and curious. His hat dangled from his fingertips, a curious style I'd never seen before, soft felt with a narrow brim that angled down in the front and turned up at the back.

"Did you come to schedule a sitting? We're usually booked a week in advance, but there may be a cancellation." In fact, an alarming swath of my father's schedule was free these days. "I'll check the calendar for you."

"I didn't come for a portrait," he said.

Karelia came up behind me. "You don't look like a creditor."

He laughed. "That's one thing I can be grateful for, then," he said.

"Tell me, what do I look like?"

She observed the mother-of-pearl cufflinks at his wrists, the gleaming black shoes. He wore four rings, one ornate and scrolled and set with tiny gems, the second bearing an amber-colored stone, the third thick and dark with the image of a dolphin stamped in the metal. The fourth was a simple gold band.

"A gypsy violinist," she said.

He grew solemn. "You have put your finger on it. I have the soul of a gypsy violinist, and yet I occupy the body of a businessman."

"How sad for you," she said.

"Better that than the soul of a businessman in the body of a gypsy violinist. I'm here to see Arthur Kylander. He wrote me about a project of his."

I liked his solidity. I tried to catch Karelia's eye, but she was regarding him with a half-smile. "Mr. Kylander is in the operating room and will be out soon," she said. She gestured toward the chairs by the entrance. "Please sit down."

Instead, Mr. Hallgarten walked about, revolving his hat in his hands and examining the room.

"That's my father with Muybridge at Palo Alto Farm," I said, pointing out the photograph behind the reception desk.

"I know a few artists who still remember their great chagrin when Muybridge proved them wrong about horses," he said.

This gave me hope. I hurried into the back room to get my father. It was empty. He wasn't in the operating room, the Tetrascope room, or the office. I knocked on the darkroom door. "Father, there's a man here to see you—one of the people you wrote a letter to." He didn't reply. I knocked more loudly, in case he had gone to sleep on the floor.

"Yes, Joseph," he called. "I'll come in a moment."

The week had been especially difficult. The unseasonably warm weather made his subjects' faces shiny with sweat. On Wednesday, two customers had arrived believing themselves scheduled for two o'clock and had nearly come to blows.

When I returned to the waiting area, Mr. Hallgarten was still wandering, peering avidly at the framed photographs on the walls. Karelia pointed in his direction and rolled her eyes at me. I glared at her. Had she even offered him a glass of water? It irritated me, too, that my father hadn't rushed out to greet him.

The carpet in the studio's waiting room was threadbare, the chairs' leather upholstery had split, the flowers on the reception desk had wilted in the heat. I feared that these things would put Mr. Hallgarten off.

"He'll be out soon," I told Mr. Hallgarten. "I'm Joseph—Dr. Kylander's son." The title I'd bestowed seemed to amuse Karelia, but it had a scientific ring that struck me as truthful in essence. "And this is Karelia, his niece." It seemed important to call attention to our visitor that we were a family, of sorts, to imply that we were all deeply invested in the project he'd come to learn about. I hoped that Karelia would conceal her doubts.

Our visitor drew near to the little table next to the frame display cases. On it lay a pile of proofs of photographs Karelia had taken on a recent beach excursion. To distract him, I said, "Why don't you look at these?"

"Those aren't the work of my uncle," Karelia called out. "They're mine. I'm not expert." But Mr. Hallgarten had already begun to spread them out, creating a landscape of seaweed sprawls and driftwood. He slid a stray sheet of paper beneath one to scoop it closer. It was a view taken from a position of about twenty feet back from a cliff top, with the ocean in the distance; in the foreground curled silhouettes of densely packed cypresses, bent from a lifetime under the wind's hand. At the print's right-hand edge, what looked at first like a stumpy branch resolved into the head of a woman, also in silhouette, peering out from behind a trunk as if testing the air. The silhouetted head was Karelia's.

"This one is like an image from a dream," he said.

"My uncle says I have a good eye, but my exposures are uneven and my printing technique is rotten."

"It's beautiful." Mr. Hallgarten lowered the print to the table. "What put you in mind of a gypsy?"

"Those rings of yours."

He held his hands out before him. "A gypsy likely wouldn't be so ostentatious," he said ruefully.

The operating room door opened.

"Father, this is Mr. Thomas Hallgarten," I said.

Mr. Hallgarten shook my father's hand. "I own Hallgarten Paper Company. You wrote to me some weeks ago at my office. You said you were extending Muybridge's work from the spatial dimension to the temporal?"

"Yes, the temporal dimension," my father said, blinking. The solitude of the darkroom sometimes left him deep within himself.

I moved away from Karelia's hand. "My father has photographed me every day since I was born. Would you like to see the preliminary photographic record?" Without waiting for an answer, I ran to retrieve the album of contact prints from my father's office.

As I returned to the reception room, my father was saying, "We think of ourselves as traveling in time, from point A to point B, in the same way that we move through space. But I've come to believe it may be more useful to think of ourselves as vessels."

I moved Karelia's photographs to the side and put the album down, pausing a moment before opening it with a flourish. "This has a small sampling of days from different years," I said. "Our goal is to print every day since I was born."

It occurs to me now that Mr. Hallgarten might have thought it odd, a child proudly showing a stranger a series of photographs in which he appeared unclothed from head to toe. Yet I felt no embarrassment. I'd been accustomed to my father's project all my life, and I'd grown up studying the plates in Muybridge's *Animal Locomotion*. If none of the nude models in Muybridge's photographs had been embarrassed, there was no reason for me to be. In my father's images—so exact in regularity, showing the ventral, the dorsal, and the left and right profile views for each day—I wore the cloak of science. If I had any reluctance in showing the photos, it was only that I found my younger self a little stupid-looking. The dreamy, slightly pudgy face, the flat chestnut hair that floated thinly around my skull, the almost comically large ears.

"Uncanny," Mr. Hallgarten said. "Month after month, he has the same expression on his face. He holds himself in exactly the same way. One could almost imagine each photograph taken in the same afternoon. And yet he's clearly getting older as they go along."

My father stood straighter now, and the vigor had returned to his eyes. "I have a theory," he said, "that we never entirely leave our youth behind."

"Yes?" Mr. Hallgarten said.

My father picked up the album and began turning the pages, advancing from my infant days. "Think of Russian nesting dolls, how each contains a smaller doll, identical except in size. Suppose instead of losing our childhood selves, we enclose them, each day adding another layer of self."

"That explains a good deal," Mr. Hallgarten said, patting his broad frame. I laughed to show I appreciated his joke, then stopped when I caught Karelia's wry gaze upon me.

"For instance," my father went on, "if a child breaks his arm at age five, he may very well have forgotten the experience by age twenty. But the fracture in the tibia could still be detected with an x-ray. The body contains all the events that it has undergone, it has been marked by them, even if we currently lack skills to detect those marks."

"An entertaining theory," said Mr. Hallgarten. "But what difference does it make one way or the other?"

"If we are containers of all our past days, then we are not lost," said my father, snapping the album shut excitedly. I turned my back on Karelia so I couldn't see her. How happy I felt to see him come back to himself.

"A traveler must leave one country behind to travel to another—he lives in perpetual exile. Even if he returns to the first country, he has lost the second. If we are vessels, however, we contain within us all our past days. If we knew how to, we could read the self and see each day spread out, we could look through a kind of microscope and see down through the layers. Just as fossils are buried in the strata of the earth, so every day of our lives is buried within us."

My father opened the album again. "This is May 23, 1897, Joseph. Do you recall what happened on the day? Look closely."

I glanced at my four-year-old face. "I don't remember," I said.

My father looked disappointed. I hastened to add, "But it's hard to tell. Because it's not only a record of the particular day, but of all the previous days as well."

"That's true," said my father.

"Maybe if you printed the sequence of the day before, and Joseph studied them both together, he could subtract one from the other," Mr. Hallgarten suggested.

"Or you could bring him to a hypnotist who could put him in a trance," Karelia said. "Then Joseph could reveal what he had for breakfast, lunch, and dinner each day—it would be an invaluable scientific record."

I elbowed her into silence.

Next Mr. Hallgarten asked to see the device that produced such images, and so my father invited him into the Tetrascope chamber.

As we followed them, Karelia took my arm.

"Don't raise your hopes," she whispered.

My father demonstrated how he could focus all four of the Tetrascope's lenses from the master camera. "Ingenious," Mr. Hallgarten said. "Could I pose? With my clothing on, of course."

"It's currently set for Joseph's height," my father said, "and although I designed it to be adjusted as he grows, I never took into account someone as tall as you. I'm afraid the images would not encompass your head, unless you kneel."

Mr. Hallgarten said he'd be willing to kneel, and so my father sent him to the dressing room to clean his face. My father raised all the window shades to make the most of the late afternoon light. When Mr. Hallgarten returned, he lowered his bulk carefully to the floor, his knees resting on the semicircles where my heels went. "I've always insisted that my left profile is much better than my right. But I've never had documentary evidence before."

I felt a pulling sensation in my chest as my father adjusted the mirrors and loaded the film; I had watched many clients pose before my father's portrait camera, but Mr. Hallgarten was the first to be the subject of the Tetrascope. As much as I was glad to see a potential patron excited by the project, I must have frowned. Mr. Hallgarten said to me, "Don't worry, I'll reimburse your father for this portrait." He turned to my father. "Your son has a good business sense. Tell me, Mr. Kylander, when should I attempt to look civilized for the lenses?"

"The photograph has been taken," my father said.

"Already? I hoped for a puff of smoke, or something dramatic." He rose to his feet and checked his pocket watch. "I must catch the ferry home to Berkeley. My family will be wondering where I am, as no doubt your wife will be too."

"My wife is deceased," my father said.

"I'm so sorry." There was a moment of silence.

As we walked to the door, my father promised that the prints would be ready the next day. "But please don't show them to anyone or speak of the nature of my project," he said. "I'm not ready yet to share my findings with the world."

Mr. Hallgarten said he could be counted on to keep it utterly secret, and that he would stop by next week. "I'd also like to learn about your work with Muybridge, which you alluded to in the letter," he said. "And I want to see more of your work, too, Miss Kylander."

When he had gone, Karelia swiped her hands together as if dusting them off. "Well, that's the last we'll see of him."

This seemed to startle my father. "What makes you think that?"

"His shoes," she said. "They cost more than all of your cameras put together."

"Why would that matter?" My father tucked the album of photographs under his arm and patted it. "Too much wealth makes a man yearn to engage it in a meaningful enterprise. We intrigued him, didn't we, Joseph? Won't we see him again?"

"Of course we will," I said, and I ran to prepare the darkroom.

CHAPTER FOUR

I had never expected Karelia to become a photographer. She started in 1903, after she had been courted for half a year by Fulvio, a thin Florentine studying at the Mark Hopkins Institute of Art. She would have been twenty-four then. She'd had several suitors over the years, but I believe the only one she'd lost her heart to was Fulvio.

I went with her once to his attic studio, full of his nocturnal land-scapes: a shadowy row of cypresses on a cliff top, a solitary fisherman's shack with one lit window, a lighthouse outshone by the full moon's glitter on the sea. One night at the end of August, Fulvio said that when he graduated, he would move back to Florence, and would she come with him as his wife? She said she couldn't leave me. He implored her to change her mind. "Joseph has his father," he said. "We'll have our own children, you and I. Your uncle and cousin can visit us whenever they like." Years later she confessed that she nearly said yes.

After her refusal, they saw each other less. He wouldn't tell her the date of his departure; she learned he had gone from a postcard. How she cried that day, how listlessly she moved in the weeks afterward, except when she went up onto the roof with her friend Violet Wellingham to share a cigarette. Crouching by the window in my bedroom, which gave out onto the light well, I could just make out their conversation. "Why would you want to marry, anyway?" Violet said. She belonged to a suffrage association and had taken Karelia to hear Susan B. Anthony and the Rev. Anna H. Shaw speak at the Alhambra a month earlier; eighty-five years old, Anthony had never married, and Violet believed, as Anthony had once predicted, in a future era of single women; for her, the institution of marriage promised only subjugation.

Though I didn't mind Fulvio's going, I thought him a fool for choosing Italy over Karelia. She was smart, and she was lovely. Her eyes were large and mobile and questioning, and when she turned them to look at you, you felt she had focused her attention completely on you. She said she had learned flattery late, only once she started working at the studio, and perhaps because of this, she deployed it with a gusto that made it more pleasing to men than a long-practiced coquetry might have. More than once, I spotted a customer, standing next to her while she set out frames for consideration, gaze at the nape of her neck and half-consciously lift a hand as if in a desire to undo the pins that held her hair up. As she darted to lift a catalog down from on top of the filing cabinets, she gave the impression of a wild creature, some relative of the caribou or gazelle, under a temporary, slipping enchantment.

My father seemed to notice Karelia's sadness, and even though the housekeeping suffered and our meals were frequently late or burned, he didn't complain. She had let her art lessons lapse the year before, frustrated by the wobble of her line, and now she even stopped sketching in the evenings.

One evening, he returned from the studio with a brand-new Brownie and offered it tentatively to her. "I know you said you didn't ever want to learn photography, but that was a long time ago, and if it seems interesting to you, I'm happy to develop the images myself, or show you how."

"Thank you," she said dully, and put it in her room as if he'd gotten her a necklace she'd never wear. I thought it strangely hopeful of him, to think she would take up the camera now.

But one June afternoon, I came home from the studio to find all my shirts draped in piles on the kitchen table, my trousers on the chairs, my books stacked in a corner. All the flat's curtains lay in a heap in the hallway. Every bedroom's mattress, shorn of its coverings, stood on end. The windows were all open, and the breeze stirred papers like leaves. I picked my way over a jumble of coats and skidded on a thimble. Karelia was an indifferent housekeeper, but once each year she pulled everything out into the open to clean, organize, and make decisions. Usually her energy flagged after three days, and so whatever she hadn't sorted was thrust back into the closet and the drawers and the dressers, not necessarily the ones they had once occupied. Only my father's room went untouched, at his insistence, during these cleaning periods.

Karelia was nowhere to be seen. In chagrin, I began restoring my glass bottle collection to my bedroom's window shelf, which had been half-dusted. Then she and her friend Violet appeared at the door, red-cheeked, their hair windblown, laughing. Karelia cradled the Brownie in her arms. "We've been on the roof," she said breathlessly. "Wait until you see the pictures we've made."

She took the Brownie to the beach on Sunday and had me clown for her lens, which I was glad to do. To my surprise, she asked my father for darkroom lessons. I expected this would end badly, but he taught her with unexpected tenderness, and she listened with unaccustomed patience. Sometimes he critiqued one of her works a little too sharply, and she challenged him or sulked, but later acknowledged he was right.

She had a much better eye than I did, a gift for framing landscapes, for catching people's expressions in moments when they revealed what usually remained hidden. I was prodigal with film and often silly, staging bizarre scenarios with spoons and shoes, or capturing moments on the street when a passerby's mouth formed a grotesque shape—these too were unheralded moments that only the camera could show us, I claimed, but deep down I knew my parodic take on my father's great enterprise derived from a sense that I didn't have a gift for this, whatever a gift might be, and however much my father insisted there was no such thing as a gift, only diligence and practice. Karelia had the gift, it was clear at once.

That Christmas, when she unwrapped my father's present, a 4x5 Buckeye, she kissed him on the cheek. It made me extraordinarily glad to see them aligned with each other.

*   *   *

On Monday evening, three days after Mr. Hallgarten's visit, we closed the shop at five o'clock as usual. Although none of us spoke of him, and although he hadn't promised to come on Monday, we all took unusual care that evening in our closing duties. Karelia changed the water in the reception desk vase, which she'd filled that morning with an exuberant bouquet of flowers. I had already polished the display cases on Sunday, but now, when I finished sweeping the floor, I took out my cloth again and made sure the glass gleamed. My father rearranged the photographic manuals in the office bookshelf according to some new system. Karelia unearthed the duster from beneath the reception desk and swabbed the top of the big clock on the wall, releasing several gray cloudlets that I had to chase with the broom.

That afternoon, only two customers had come, one so elderly that I had to help her down the staircase. "I will recommend your father to my friends," she said, but it was unclear to me if her friends would be sturdy enough to make the climb.

At twenty-four minutes after the hour, when we had begun to give up hope, Mr. Hallgarten knocked. "Sorry to arrive so late," he said, taking off his hat with a flourish. "My second in command is always eager with suggestions for improving the business, and I must hear him out, because he is the brains behind it all."

My father presented him with his Tetrascopic shots, which he had mounted and framed in a row. "Excellent," Mr. Hallgarten said. "I'll hang it in my study, where the mounds of paper frighten everyone away, and where the maid is forbidden to go, so no one but I will see it."

He wrote my father a check, which, from the degree to which my father's eyebrows lifted, must have been for a much larger sum than he expected. To Karelia, he said, "I hope to own one of your landscapes too someday."

"To hang where no one can see? You have a high estimation of my abilities."

"I'll give it a place of honor in my living room."

"Ah. You'll want something decorous and quiet, then."

"The opposite! Give me a landscape that is wild and tempestuous, where the trees reach greedily for the sky and even the grasses are in tumult."

The idea seemed to please her.

Reluctant to leave, he sat in one of the reception chairs, undeterred by the creak its old wood gave out, and the rest of us followed suit. His father had founded the paper company in the 1870s, he said, and after his death, Mr. Hallgarten's older brother had expanded it into a thriving business, only to die himself four years ago, "leaving the whole enterprise in my clumsy hands," as Mr. Hallgarten put it. "Before that, I had the title of vice president, but shirked my duties as much as possible to go to the opera and art exhibitions. Sometimes I've caught myself wishing I could return to those days."

"Time is a habit," my father said. "If we could break ourselves of it, we could move freely back and forth from past to future."

Mr. Hallgarten smiled. "People are always giving up habits, but then they fall back into them."

"Suppose you are in the habit of gambling," my father said. "If everyone you know is also a gambler, you're unlikely to stop. On the other hand, if you can put yourselves among people who do not share this habit, you can rely on them for assistance and encouragement. But in this matter of creeping forward in time at this same rate, we're all guilty of the same vice."

"Now you're calling time a vice," Mr. Hallgarten said.

"Sometimes I believe it is."

"I wouldn't like it if we were all moving back and forth in time," said Karelia. "How could you ever work it out to meet other people? Suppose you wanted to meet a friend in 1905, but he had gone back to the 1600s."

"Yes, that's true, Arthur, she has you there. Or suppose you were having a conversation with someone, but she was a minute ahead of you? She would be answering your questions before you asked them."

"You may be right," my father said. "Nevertheless, I wish I could travel back to the days when Muybridge and I worked together. Together, we could have done so much, if only I could have persuaded him to listen to me. And Emily was still alive."

I wished he wouldn't talk to Mr. Hallgarten about our private lives. And this made me wonder, not for the first time, if he blamed me for my mother's death. I didn't want to travel back in time, but I wished we could bring her forward with us, I wished I could have known her.

Mr. Hallgarten said, "If there's a habit to break, perhaps it's the habit of longing for the past."

After that, Mr. Hallgarten dropped by the studio at least twice a week around closing time, joking with customers if we had any, or with Karelia if she happened to be working that afternoon. When my father emerged from the operating room and turned the CLOSED sign around, we all sat down in the reception area and discussed the nature of time: whether we could ever describe it without resorting to the language of space; whether it was best considered as the fourth dimension or as something else entirely. Many times, I scarcely followed the conversation, but I always found it fascinating, and Karelia did too. When opinions differed, she seemed to delight in taking my father's side as much as Mr. Hallgarten's.

A new urgency possessed my father. He spent several evenings a week in the darkroom making prints from the project. He stood straighter, jumped up during meals to jot down notes, shook the hands of his customers with a firmer grip. Yet he also seemed more capable of relaxing. He bought a chess set and taught me to play, holding each piece in his palm as he explained how its form determined the type of movement it could make. In the beginning, whenever I made a foolish move, he would note the likely jeopardy I faced, speaking in such a bemused tone that it didn't occur to me to be ashamed. After a week of allowing me to undo my wrong moves, he suggested that we play in full accordance with the rules. I appreciated that he treated me as a serious opponent. Although I never won, his compliments whenever I happened to make a good move gave me so much pleasure that I felt this was good enough.

Mr. Hallgarten's only misstep was to give my father a copy of H.G. Wells's *The Time Machine*. My father—who as far as I knew had never touched a novel before—read it as if tasting something bitter. It had nothing interesting to say about time, he told Mr. Hallgarten the next week. First of all, travel into the future was impossible, like jumping up to the tenth flight of a staircase when only two flights had been constructed. Travel backwards in time was the only desirable movement, because the past gave meaning to the present. Mr. Hallgarten didn't seem offended—his eyes glittered with interest. "There's nothing halfway about you, Arthur," he said.

One afternoon, Mr. Hallgarten suggested that my father extend Muybridge's work in a way that would capture the public's attention, preparing the way for the introduction of his life's project—which, although brilliant, he said, was perhaps more subtle in its significance for the average person to grasp.

"After all, Muybridge made his name with an arresting image of a horse in mid-trot, and only later moved on to documenting a variety of animals and humans in more ordinary movements," Mr. Hallgarten said. "There must be some activities that Muybridge didn't think of chronicling. A woman giving her suitor a slap. Karelia, one of your suitors might be willing to help us out."

"I don't have any suitors at the moment. But we could advertise for one. 'Wanted, one suitor, must be willing to start with a slap. Potential to end with a kiss.'"

"You'll have them lining up at the door, if you'll only run a photograph of yourself with the advertisement." Mr. Hallgarten said this lightly, as he said almost everything, and he wasn't looking at her, but she blushed all the same.

The glow of Mr. Hallgarten's regard inspired us. That the owner of the city's largest paper company should visit us so regularly meant that we were indeed special. At the beach, Karelia photographed wind-gnarled cypress trees and had me act out scenes. Once, she and I devised a sequence of photographs that told a story. In the first image, a woman carrying a picnic basket along the beach passes a mound of seaweed. In the second, the seaweed rises up and she recoils. In the third, she smashes it with her picnic basket. In the fourth, she continues on her way, the seaweed scattered on the sand behind her. I remember how long it took her to stage the photograph while I shooed away flies under dank green ribbons.

Karelia presented Mr. Hallgarten with the sequence as a gift one afternoon in early October. He laughed uproariously. "You have beaten Muybridge at his own game," he said.

My father, coming in from the darkroom, overheard this and smiled, even as Karelia and Mr. Hallgarten fell silent and looked away from each other. "Thomas," my father said, "what if I were to use the techniques of rapid motion photography to document a man laughing, from beginning to end?"

"Brilliant," Mr. Hallgarten said, standing quickly. "But I hope you weren't thinking of me as your subject."

"Of course, it's one thing to ask a model to walk across the room or throw a discus," my father said. "It's another to ask him to laugh, especially if it requires a number of attempts to get it right. It might be artificial, and then it wouldn't be of any use. And I would need to build a chronographic camera that could take images in quick succession—a Marey wheel."

"Hang the results in your display case on the street, and you'll have customers coming in droves. I know just the man—he can break naturally into the most hilarious of laughs." Mr. Hallgarten pulled his checkbook out of his suit jacket. I ran to grab pen and ink from the reception desk and held the ink for him while he wrote my father a check.

It took my father two weeks to build his chronographic camera. Not long afterward, Mr. Hallgarten arrived at my father's studio with a young red-haired man. A manager at the paper company, he had a heart-shaped face and an impeccably tailored suit. While my father prepared his film, Mr. Hallgarten warmed up by telling some jokes. The jokes were not particularly good. But he delivered them with a wry amusement, as if to say, we know this is poor material, but it doesn't matter, a joke is nothing more than an agreement to have a pleasant laugh. Soon the subject was lost in broad paroxysms of laughter, my father smiling wryly as his shutter clicked in rapid-fire succession, at a rate of one image per second.

The next time he came, Mr. Hallgarten gave Karelia a magazine we hadn't seen before: *Camera Work*. I stood by her side as she paged through it. An elderly Franciscan monk, head bent with age, walked along a wharf in Venice. A small band of hikers picked their way through snow remnants on a high mountain ridge. Ghostly pedestrians on the Riva Schiavoni promenaded toward the dark statue of a martial figure on horseback, his sword aloft. Professor John Young of Glasgow University gazed with the regal bearing of a nobleman, dressed in a heavy robe with big cuffs, the furred collar swallowing his feathery white beard. Except for their sepia tones, all the images looked more like paintings than photographs. They seemed to have been photographed in a haze, and in several I couldn't make out the faces of the people; in others, the photographer had clearly altered the images, turning the people on the Riva Schiavoni into transparent shadows through which you could see the pavement.

"I didn't know this was possible with a camera," Karelia said.

I remember that a photogravure by Alvin Langdon Coburn fascinated her in particular: "Study—Miss R." A young woman's face framed by the smoke of her dark hair, the planes of her face deep in shadow except for a stripe of vertical light down one side of her nose. Her neck and shoulders were lost in darkness and blurred by brushwork, leaving only a barely perceptible sense of the mass that supported her head. Her long straight mouth was lax, and she stared with melancholy intensity. The image's granular texture suggested that the fabric of space was too old to bear much more existence.

"You can hardly see her," I said. "Why did he make the photograph so dark?"

She read to me from the essay at the back of the magazine: "the aim of a picture is not to demonstrate any theory or fact, but is to excite a certain sensory pleasure." At this heresy, we both glanced at the door of the operating room, where my father was photographing a customer. She kept the magazine in the top drawer of the reception desk, and at slow moments in the afternoon, she would study its pages with such absorption that she would fail to register the approach of customers until they cleared their throats or rang the little bell on the desk.

*   *   *

My father printed the series he called "Man Laughing" and hung it in his display case outside the building's entrance, where it attracted a good deal of attention. The *Call* ran an article about it; a political cartoonist for the *Chronicle* drew a parody of the image. We sold many prints of the series, and my father's portrait business picked up as well, allowing us to purchase new clothes and shoes. My father paid the landlord all of the back rent, replaced the cracked leather of the reception room chairs, and had the landlord repair the discolored portion of the ceiling.

One weekend, my father, Karelia, and I repainted the studio's reception room. He was in an unusually fine mood. On Sunday evening, we hung his portraits back on the walls, and after he had placed "Man Laughing" directly opposite the entry door and straightened it carefully, he stood back and admired it.

"You could make more like this," I suggested. "'Man Coughing,' or 'Man Yawning.'"

He looked at me in surprise, and I was afraid I'd offended him with my joke. But he said, "Yes, I suppose I could." He pondered a moment. "'Man Hiccupping.'"

"'Man Sneezing!'"

To celebrate my father's success, Mr. Hallgarten invited us all to a performance at the Tivoli Opera House in early December. He insisted Karelia's friend Violet come too. She brought her brother, a tall man with close-cropped hair and a little golden mustache flecked with silver, who was in the import business and had a habit of humming a certain note in the back of his throat from time to time, as if always trying to keep a pitch from vanishing out of memory. Violet greeted Mr. Hallgarten with much interest, and regarded him throughout the evening with a mixture of merriment and watchfulness. We saw *Il Trovatore*. I remember it disappointed me, because Karelia and I had seen it done much more grandly at the old Tivoli, which had been declared a fire hazard and torn down a few years earlier.

Late one night, about a week later, I woke and sensed that Karelia had come quietly into my room. She had been at the opera again. Now she stood in the thin moonlight, an unmoving shadow at the center of the room. She kneeled by the bed and touched her lips to my scalp, whispering, "Don't wake up." Her coat smelled of something I recognized but couldn't place—distinctively sweet and silky. I sat up.

"What opera did you see?"

She didn't respond at first, so I thought she hadn't heard me. Then she said, "Handel's *Semele.*"

"Tell me the story."

"You should be sleeping." But she after a moment, she said, "A princess named Semele fell in love with the god Jove. Disguised as an eagle, he bore her away to his sky fortress, where they lived together happily. But Jove's wife, Juno, tricked her into making him swear to show his true form, which was lightning, and Semele was destroyed."

"That's sad," I murmured, drifting off.

When I woke some time later, she was still there in the darkness, sitting on the foot of my bed. I turned over onto my right side and settled the blankets around me ostentatiously to show her I was awake. I brushed her hand as I did so and found it damp.

"Are you all right?" I asked.

"Yes, yes," she said. Then, after a pause, "I was wondering about Semele—what did she think she was doing? Did she recognize herself?"

Dozing, I came to realize—through that slow accumulation of sense memory with which one remembers details from a dream—that the familiar scent on her coat was Mr. Hallgarten's brand of pipe tobacco.

*   *   *

The next morning, Karelia hurried me off to school. When I reached the studio that afternoon, Karelia was showing a customer our selection of frames, and so I sat at the reception desk and looked through the listings in the newspaper.

I found no notice that an opera company was putting on *Semele* at the time. I remembered she'd gone to see it with Violet a couple of years ago. I assumed I was missing something. She'd run into Mr. Hallgarten at the opera, but she didn't want to tell me. I tried to recall the way they behaved together. I had only a dim idea of what falling in love would look like. Everything I knew came from the operas Karelia had taken me to: the singers would clutch their breasts and their voices would soar and quaver with pain and longing. If a married man or woman was involved, knives or poison would ensue. Once, Violet had gotten involved with a married man and had her heart broken. Karelia had told me about it and added that no good could come of an affair. I felt certain that Karelia and Mr. Hallgarten wouldn't do anything foolish. They were both interested in photography and could discuss it in a way she couldn't with my father, whose interests were so different from her own.

I leafed through *Camera Work* until I came to the page where Miss R. resided and stared at her as if somehow she could explain something to me. When I looked up, the customer had gone, and Karelia was watching me. Slowly she lifted an empty frame to her face and assumed the pensive, hollow gaze of Miss R. I had to look away—she was playing with me in a way that made me feel uncomfortable, because I sensed some truth under the joke, though it eluded me. As if seeing her error, she put the frame down, smiling in a way that was complicit and yet faraway.

I began watching her more closely. She had never been a model of punctuality, but she became more erratic. My father complained that she was arriving too late for her shift at the studio, and that it was impermissible for customers to arrive with no one to greet them; Mrs. Salamanco overstayed her shift on a few occasions until Karelia came, but she said this could not go on. Karelia's cooking had always been uneven, but now her pie crusts came out tough as shoes, and her stews were a mélange of burnt onions and half-raw carrots.

She began going to the opera one or two nights a week; she said Violet's brother had been so enamored by *Il Trovatore* that he'd become an enthusiast and begged them to accompany him. I tried to keep awake until she returned, and on the few times that I succeeded, I would creep out and sniff her coat after she'd gone to bed. I always smelled Mr. Hallgarten's smoke on it. But perhaps Violet's brother happened to like the same brand of tobacco, and puffed on his own pipe as he walked Karelia and Violet back to our apartment.

One morning, I teased her that she was in love with Violet's brother. "You like him because he's like your best friend, but he's a man," I said.

"He can't be like Violet, because he's a man," she answered.

"If you married him, you would be sisters."

She gave me a wary smile. "Do you like him so much? No, he courts a girl who teaches ballet at Miss Lydia's—he likes a girl to be tiny and dark-haired and to giggle with her hand over her mouth."

It didn't occur to me then how much raising another man's child might have dimmed her prospects of marriage. Fulvio had given up, but I thought that was because he insisted on moving back to Florence. Yet even though she wasn't my father's wife, she might as well have been, and it seems possible that her other suitors had been put off by her role in our household and her attachment to me. I wonder how much this was on her mind in those days.

*   *   *

Karelia and my father were getting on more harmoniously than they ever had. She asked him questions about the finer points of developing negatives and printmaking. My father was delighted. They had an argument one night over use of the darkroom; he was always in it, it seemed, when she wanted to develop her own images, and he couldn't bear to give up any time now that he finally had backing to print the project. "The darkroom is large enough for the two of us," he said at last. "We can both work at the same time."

For Christmas, my father presented Mr. Hallgarten with a black leather-bound album. The first page bore the words, "Book of Months: Joseph Kylander, September 1891–November 1905" written in my father's hand, along with a dedication to Mr. Hallgarten. On each page, my father had placed four rows of prints, each row depicting four profiles of me taken on the first Tuesday of each month. "It's only a précis of my work," my father said. "But I wanted you to have something tangible in return for your support, since it will be some time yet before a full daily record is complete. Please keep it secret."

"This will be worth a lot once you've earned your fame," said Mr. Hallgarten.

To my father, Mr. Hallgarten gave a copy of Darwin's *Expressions of the Emotions in Man and Animals;* to Karelia, the latest issue of *Camera Work*; to me, a watch. The spades at the tips of its hands curved elegantly, as if eager to point out the hour and the minute. At the six o'clock position, a smaller dial marked out the seconds. The watch seemed too expensive for a fourteen-year-old boy, and after I unwrapped it, he rocked back on his heels and gave a little hum, as he did when embarrassed. "Thank you," I breathed. My father looked stricken, as if on the verge of telling me to return it, but he did not. Karelia pressed my shoulder. "Thank you!" I said again, more loudly, fearing I had seemed insufficiently enthusiastic.

"You're more than welcome," he said. I didn't understand why he gave me such a gift. Perhaps a business associate had presented it to him, or he had bought it on a discount in some way. Certainly no one had less need of a watch than I—a fact that I now unwittingly underscored by setting the correct time without glancing at the clock on the wall behind me.

Karelia gave Mr. Hallgarten a photograph of a cliff at Ocean Beach, two cypresses at the top, both bending the same way. I studied him as he unwrapped it, the delight in his face, his elaborate bow of thanks. "I can't imagine finer gifts than these," he said, sweeping his hands to include the Book of Months and the bottle of cologne I had chosen as my gift to him, much to Karelia's bafflement. It had a strong sweet odor, which I thought might rub off on Karelia's coat if indeed they were together on her opera nights. He likely never tried it.

I wound his watch faithfully and kept it on my night stand in a box that had once housed wooden matches, behind the photograph of my mother. This was to conceal it from any potential burglars, though, despite the cotton balls I tucked it in, the ticking still gave it away. The sound helped me sleep, because it reminded me we had a patron to look after us now.

CHAPTER FIVE

Shortly before the new year, a letter arrived from Karelia's older sister to say their younger brother had fallen quite ill. The doctor believed he might not survive the winter.

Karelia hadn't ever gone back to Canada, but she and her younger brother had corresponded often. I had a dim memory of him visiting San Francisco when I was four years old. He was her favorite, she said. She wanted to see him before he died.

She worried that my father wouldn't remember to feed us while she was gone, so she made arrangements. She convinced the Wellinghams to promise to have us over for dinner on Wednesday nights. She charmed Mrs. Pulkkinen, the elderly Finnish woman who lived two floors below us, into agreeing to cook us meals on Mondays and Fridays. Mrs. Salamanco's neighbor's daughter Minnie would fill in for Karelia at the portrait studio when Mrs. Salamanco was unable to cover for her.

For the journey, Karelia borrowed a heavy brown coat from another neighbor, because she owned nothing appropriate for Canadian winter, and it gave off the odor of mothballs tinged with mildew. She pressed her cheek to mine. "I won't be long, Joseph," she said.

The letter from her sister had arrived on Thursday; she left on the following Tuesday morning.

"You'll be alone for weeks—how will you survive?" Mr. Hallgarten said when he visited. "Come spend a weekend with my family."

"Thank you," my father said, "but we wouldn't want to impose on them."

"What are two days out of thousands? My daughters and my wife would love company. We're still new to Berkeley, and our house is a bit isolated. The hill behind our house looks out onto a little canyon. In the morning you can see the quail running through our backyard and the deer nibbling the grass." Mr. Hallgarten held up his hand. "I have an idea. I'll commission you to photograph my house, Arthur. You'll find it fascinating. The geranium and the roses and the lavender are still young, but all the better, the architecture will be more apparent. And I would like you to photograph it several times over the course of the day, all from the same vantage point. For a house, like a person, exists over time."

My father considered. "It would be possible, with sufficient moon, to show the house at night as well. One could then chronicle the house over twenty-four hours."

"Splendid!" said Mr. Hallgarten.

"Of course, a house doesn't grow and change the way a human does, it has no thoughts or memory. We would only see the change of light and shadow over time."

Mr. Hallgarten said, "We could think of the inhabitants of a house, moving back and forth behind the windows and having their little domestic dramas, as the thoughts of a house."

My father tapped his fingers against his thumbs in quick succession. "It would make for an interesting technical challenge." He looked up the next full moon, which was January 21, 1906.

The weeks until then passed with agonizing slowness. At home and at the studio, with Karelia gone, I became aware of an immense silence, as pervasive and insinuating as fog. When Mrs. Pulkkinen made stuffed cabbage rolls and boiled potatoes for us the first Monday night, she had a large store of conversation ready to unreel while we ate: she told us about her poodle's escapades, her neighbor's insistence on playing records, the bursitis in her hip. But the silence remained, a constant steady background hum, and perhaps she heard it too and wanted to cover it up with her voice.

On Tuesday, we made ourselves peanut butter sandwiches. Wednesday night at the Wellinghams, we dined on chicken and mushrooms in an atmosphere of jokes and clamor. Thursday evening, we ate canned corn beef sandwiches. On Friday, Mrs. Pulkkinen returned, this time with what she called Finnish macaroni, a jiggling mass of noodles suspended in a pale sort of custard; I managed to consume a few forkfuls before declaring myself not very hungry. When Mrs. Pulkkinen brought pork blood pancakes on Monday, my father noticed I could not bring myself even to taste them, and instead of reprimanding me, he allowed me to eat bread and butter. As she was leaving, he told Mrs. Pulkkinen that he was grateful for her cooking, but would no longer need her to come, because we'd been invited to dine with the family of Karelia's friend—he omitted to mention that this invitation was for only one night each week. It was the closest I've ever seen my father come to telling a lie, and I was grateful to him.

The next Wednesday we arrived at the Wellinghams', but their house was dark. Apparently they had forgotten we were coming. Karelia, I imagined, was at this very moment sitting at the bedside of her brother, holding his hand, listening to his breath rasp—a taller version of her, with an elongated face and a stronger chin.

My father made the only meal he knew: patties of cornmeal mush, left over from breakfast, topped with fried eggs. Although slightly burnt, they were tasty enough the first night. After the third night of this, noting my waning enthusiasm, he said, "I'm sorry, Joseph. Tomorrow night we'll go out for dinner, and from then on we'll assemble our food from the delicatessen."

We ate huge bowls of spaghetti with thick wedges of garlic bread at a small restaurant in the Italian quarter. I watched the other diners and tried to eavesdrop on their conversation, distracting myself from a growing awareness that the silence emanated from somewhere within my father—even when he spoke, the silence nearly canceled out his words, though his voice was no more or less quiet than anyone else's. Had it always been there, and I hadn't noticed until now? Or did it spring from Karelia's absence?

At home, I took out the two dusty volumes of the *Kalevala* and decided I would read the whole thing, though it was more than 700 pages long. It had been years since Karelia read any of its tales to me, her voice pitched low, her head close to mine, the scent of her hair in my nostrils, the book above us like the sky of another land. I opened it and read the start of the first rune:

> *In primeval times, a maiden,*
> *Beauteous Daughter of the Ether,*
> *Passed for ages her existence*
> *In the great expanse of heaven,*
> *O'er the prairies yet enfolded.*

We received a postcard. Karelia's brother was so thin, she said, that he looked as if he might disappear, as if one morning they would wake and find his bedcovers smooth and flat.

One evening when we were closing the studio, my father sat at the reception desk, pulled out her *Camera Work,* and paged through it. "I don't understand what Karelia sees in this," he said. Yet he continued looking at the magazine for a long while.

A letter arrived from Karelia with the news that her brother had died. Snow was starting to fall as she wrote the letter, and there was some question as to whether a storm would delay the funeral.

* * *

On the Friday afternoon of our ferry crossing to the East Bay, hazy and cold, the setting sun laid a long gleam on the surface of the water behind us. I wished I had borrowed Karelia's long red woolen scarf, but she had taken it with her.

Mr. Hallgarten met us at the Oakland Ferry Terminal in his automobile. We almost didn't recognize him, because he wore a soft brown leather driving cap, with gloves to match, and a jacket of brown corduroy. With a sweep of his arms, he directed us to climb into his car. "How are you faring without Karelia? You must be at loose ends. Have you been eating? We'll get a good dinner into you. What news of her?"

My father told him her brother had died.

"I'm very sorry." Mr. Hallgarten bowed his head for a moment. Then, as if he'd been suppressing the question until a respectful time had passed, he asked, with a mixture of eagerness and irritation, "When will she return?"

Something about this embarrassed me, and I looked away.

My father handed me his camera to set between my feet in the back seat. "We don't know."

Mr. Hallgarten climbed behind the wheel and seemed to master himself. "Let's hope nostalgia for snow and freezing winds doesn't convince her to stay," he said.

He drove slowly. "It can reach speeds of up to forty miles per hour," he told my father, "but I won't demonstrate on this trip, so as not to jostle your equipment." I had never ridden in an automobile. The wind struck our faces, cold and damp. I didn't mind. The smooth black leather of the seat was so taut I could feel its gleam with my fingers. Stroking it, I came across walnut shells, presumably left by his daughters. As I dropped them over the side of the car—they seemed undignified for such a sleek machine—I wondered what the girls must be like. They had not been real to me before.

The sky was clear in Berkeley, and Mr. Hallgarten pointed out the rising full moon, which appeared to rest on the top of the hills above us. "My grandmother, in her later years, forbade us to look at the full moon.

Schauen Sie weg vom Mond! She seemed to think there was something obscene about it." He laughed. We rode up a street that sloped diagonally up the side of the hill, buckeye and laurel trees on either side.

Mr. Hallgarten's house stood near the top of the hill; its only neighbors were two houses several hundred feet away, both still under construction, timbers skeletal in the moonlight. The landscaping was still young, and save for a few cypress trees on the east and north sides of the house, the ground was bare around it. We climbed out of the car and carried our luggage toward the side door. An owl landed in the cypress and hooted; a window on the second floor swung outward and a small arm dumped the contents of what looked like a tea cup.

The Hallgartens' house was not like the ones I was familiar with, the delicate Victorians that lined our neighborhood. It had a wide rustic frame, dark unpainted redwood siding, a peaked roof, and a low-walled balcony with apple-shaped cutouts in the wood along the front. Four tall windows, grouped together, presented us with a discontinuous reflection of the starry night sky. Mr. Hallgarten told us it had been designed by Bernard Maybeck and said, "It looks like a Swiss chalet, doesn't it?" The words sounded magical. I repeated them under my breath: "Swiss chalet, Swiss chalet."

"I should begin shooting as early as possible," my father said. "Tomorrow night might not be as clear."

"Tomorrow will be fine for starting. Tonight, you are our guest."

We entered the foyer. A broad staircase before us led upwards. From above, a violin began playing the Marseillaise while a clarinet ran through scales, accompanied by random chords from a piano somewhere at the back of the house.

A small, auburn-haired woman came out. "I've been telling them all day to practice their music," she said, a French accent burnishing her voice. "Yet they choose this moment to begin!" She glided to the foot of the stairs and clapped her hands, "Thomasine! Sophie! Adele!" The music continued.

Mr. Hallgarten said, "This is my wife, Celeste."

For some reason, I had imagined her as tall as her husband, but she hardly stood higher than I, and although she was round-faced and much younger than her husband, not too many years older than Karelia, she gave off the air of a taller and older person who had been compressed into a smaller body, with a resulting excess of energy that had grown feverish in its confines. She had pulled her hair into a tight chignon, as if to rein herself back. "So you are the family of photographers," she said, taking our hands between her warm palms. She looked at us through exophthalmic, delighted eyes.

She led us into the living room, which was paneled with unpainted redwood from floor to ceiling, giving it a rich red glow. A fire burned in a large brick fireplace. Brass lanterns hung from the ceiling, which was supported by large, rough-cut redwood beams. The curtains were of soft tan leather, and two Oriental carpets covered the wood floor. Although the overall effect was rustic, the newness of the construction, the smoothness of the wood, and the elegance of the lamps made it luxurious. It seemed like an elaborate stage set that we had been invited to walk into. I noted with pride that on the walls, interspersed with still life paintings, hung "Man Laughing," a print of my father with Muybridge, and several of Karelia's photographs.

Two girls came down the staircase, and a third from the living room doorway opposite us. The two younger ones, perhaps seven and ten years of age, hung back by their mother and said hello quietly. They were blonde and had an irritating solemnity about them. The oldest, who was about my age, had her father's oval face and strong chin and her mother's brown hair, cut shorter than her sisters' and parted in the middle. Her eyes moved beneath her bangs with searching hazel intensity; from time to time, they fluttered up as if in some droll private assessment. She shook first my hand and then my father's, her grasp cool and strong. Next, she extended her hand to the empty air beside my father as if toward an invisible person. "Wasn't there supposed to be someone else?" she asked.

"I told you, Mr. Kylander's niece Karelia is in Canada now, her brother died." Mr. Hallgarten said. "I'm sure you'll meet her someday."

Did he really imagine introducing Karelia to his wife, his children? I thought of Juno, jealous of Semele, deceiving the poor girl into insisting that Jove show his true form. What would it be like to be married to someone whose true form was lightning?

"Thomasine is my oldest daughter," Mr. Hallgarten said. "She's the smart one. Adele is the youngest, she's the beauty of the three. And Sophie, she has the best manners, I suppose." I was a little startled that he would describe them this way. But they kept their faces impassive, except for Adele, who beamed with pleasure. "They were a bit put out this afternoon when I told them they had to give up their rooms for our guests and sleep with their mother and me." He laughed.

"*Papa,*" said Thomasine, "*Vous ne devriez pas leur dire cela.*"

Dinner consisted of steaks, baked potatoes, and greens cooked in butter, along with the fluffiest rolls I had ever eaten. Sometimes, Thomasine stared at me. Each time I caught her at it, she seemed unabashed, and only after a moment or two did she look away to study a spot on the wall above me.

While we ate, Mr. Hallgarten told us that although he'd been born in Stuttgart, he'd lived in San Francisco most of his life and was still getting used to Berkeley. "It was Celeste's idea. She grew up in the French countryside, and never felt at home in San Francisco. She fell in love with Berkeley's rolling hills, and now that we have moved here, she's part of a regiment to defend them."

"We want to encourage those building in the Berkeley hills to fit their houses into the contours of the landscape," she said passionately, rounding her hands through the air to show us how. "To preserve the trees and plant gardens, to use natural materials like stone and wood instead of painted plaster. American houses are generally shoddy. You gum up your buildings with wallpaper and stucco and paint and other shams to hide their poor construction. Good workmanship is its own ornament. A simple building, that lets wood be wood, that harmonizes with the landscape—this is the ideal."

"That's enough, Celeste," said Mr. Hallgarten, smiling in a way that made me uneasy. "Our visitors aren't planning to build in Berkeley just yet."

Mrs. Hallgarten stared straight ahead, as if absenting herself from the moment. Then she said, "Shall we have dessert in the living room?"

Not only was the cake slathered with white frosting, but the pieces Mrs. Hallgarten cut for us were twice the size we ate in our house, great lopsided wedges studded with raisins. Now Mr. Hallgarten had my father recount his time with Muybridge. Mrs. Hallgarten squinted as he talked, interrupting only to ask about the animals' personalities and how they affected the photographing. Something about the tilt of her head, the way she offered more tea and the way she concentrated on the pouring of it, expressed a judgment held in reserve. I hoped that my father would stop before he told the part in which Muybridge fired him, but he did not. Still, the moment in which Muybridge spat in the dirt at his feet briefly roused the younger girls, who had consumed their cake swiftly and dozed while he talked. Thomasine paid keen attention all the way through, and I liked her the better for it.

"Thomas tells me that you're going to photograph the outside of our house over the course of a day?" Mrs. Hallgarten said. Her voice was quiet, yet her tone seemed to call the whole idea into question, as if my father had announced he would photograph nothing but his shoelaces for a day.

"Yes," my father said. "We shall see how your house harmonizes with the landscape at all hours, from sunrise to midday to sunset and under the stars, won't we?" And it seemed he had scored a point, and she lifted her chin slightly as if in admiration for a good play.

Sophie and Adele had by now fallen asleep on the sofa, and Mr. Hallgarten said it was time for everyone to turn in.

I was to stay in Thomasine's room, he said, and my father would sleep in Sophie and Adele's; the master bedroom was large enough to accommodate all three of their children. "I generally sleep in my study these days," Mr. Hallgarten said, "so that my snoring does not plague Celeste." Thomasine asked to be allowed to sleep in the living room, but her mother said no, and told her to show me upstairs.

Thomasine led me to a small bedroom with a slanted ceiling on one side. "Wait here," she said. "And don't touch anything."

I was too tired to even look around. And I was uneasy, because I had wanted Mrs. Hallgarten to admire my father. But of course, I reminded myself, she knew nothing of my father's true project.

Thomasine returned with towels.

"Why were you staring at me all evening?" I asked.

"You looked familiar. Name one thing that dirt and mirrors have in common."

"I don't know."

"One point for me," she said. "Your turn. Name two things and I'll try to guess how they're similar. If I can't, you win one point. They can't be opposites, like black and white."

It took me a moment, because I was very sleepy. "Eggs and wire."

"Both smooth. I lead, two to nothing. Scissors and eternity."

"That's not fair, eternity is just an idea."

"Right. And scissors aren't."

"I give up."

"Three to nothing. Your turn."

"Don't you have to explain how scissors and eternity are similar?"

"No, that's not part of the game. They aren't similar, that's why I chose them."

My eyes kept closing of their own accord. "Fire," I said. I looked around the room again for help.

"And?"

"Bed."

She thought about that for a moment. "The maid makes both of them. A boot and the queen of England."

This one had me stumped for the longest time. At last I said, "They both have a sole."

She made a noise of exasperation. "Puns don't count."

"It isn't a pun," I said. "The queen has a sole on the bottom of her foot. And both have tongues. And eyes. And I bet she even has laces—in her drawer of fancy linens."

"Four to one, then. You didn't do too badly for your first time."

My eyes were closing again, and she showed me where to wash up before I went to sleep.

*   *   *

The next morning I woke to the sound of a squirrel pattering on the roof. Through the windows opposite the bed, sunlight shone in, finely filtered by the needles of a cypress. The room's redwood-paneled walls and ceiling made the room warm and cozy. The bed and the sheets were much softer than my own, and I felt as if I were floating on cream. The night's sleep had been deep. I remembered Mrs. Hallgarten's description of the ideal house, and I thought she was right, this was an ideal house:

magical, as if it had grown out of the ground. The houses of San Francisco, which I had once thought beautiful, now seemed nothing but a sham, with their Victorian gingerbread, their ornate cornices, their little spindles—decorative features that the builders had mail-ordered, my father had once said, and stuck onto row after row of identical houses.

I jumped out of bed and went to the window. In the yard below, a line of quail bobbed along, calling out in little pips. How I wished that I lived here, instead of in the noisy city, spending every afternoon working in the portrait studio, my shoes always tight because I'd outgrown them, my stomach rumbling because there hadn't been enough food. I wished that I was part of the Hallgarten family. The disloyalty of this thought gave me a pang, which I tried to appease by imagining that Karelia lived with us too, and of course my father somehow.

The quail disappeared in the grass further up the slope, and I began to sense a presence in the room. I turned. Across from the bed, near the door to the hall, stood a massive redwood armoire. With its unadorned lines and dark wood, it seemed of a piece with the house and with the Berkeley landscape. A row of carved wooden birds perched on top. I tugged the doors open, revealing Thomasine's dresses, which gave off a woodsy odor. I realized I looked forward to seeing her.

At breakfast, however, she had the look of a crumpled butterfly emerged too soon from its cocoon. "I had a wretched night," she said. "All they want to do is chatter, or make me tell them stories. And Sophie talks in her sleep. 'Get the hammer, get the hammer.' I did want to get a hammer." Her sister wrinkled her nose at her. Mrs. Hallgarten must have passed a sleepless night as well; pale circles underscored her eyes, making them seem even larger than usual, and she darted about the kitchen with an unsteady ferocity.

I was further distracted by the presence of a servant, a young woman named Lilly, who poured tea and coffee and ferried food from the kitchen and back. She was an undergraduate at the university, Mr. Hallgarten told us, and worked four days a week while studying anthropology. To have a servant waiting on us made me clumsy—I hastened to hold out my cup and bumped the teapot, slopping tea over the rug. "Stay calm," Lilly said, holding her hand out to prevent me from leaping in with my napkin. She whipped off her apron and used it to soak up the liquid. I had the impression that we were all not fully real to her, that with one part of her mind she performed her duties efficiently, and with another she was thinking about her textbooks.

After breakfast, my father surveyed the front yard and picked the spot to set up his camera. The first exposure was to take place at eight o'clock, and he had decided to take the photographs in intervals of one hour, culminating the next morning at seven. "When will you sleep?" Mr. Hallgarten asked, and my father insisted that sleep wasn't necessary. It was a fine morning, the air already growing warm.

Mr. Hallgarten brought out two chairs and set them up near the camera; he said he would chat a while with my father. Mrs. Hallgarten led the rest of us on a walk up to the rim of the small canyon above the house and down into its valley. She pointed out to us more quail, a flock of deer, and even a bobcat that sat as peacefully as a house cat not a hundred feet from us. Sophie missed her footing crossing the creek and soaked her left shoe and sock, but neither she nor her mother seemed perturbed. Thomasine and I were shy with each other at first, but soon we were exchanging stories—her family's summer in Paris the year before, my stories from the *Kalevala*.

Mrs. Hallgarten gave the names of the trees and grasses and other plants that we passed, and she asked her daughters to tell me how to distinguish them from each other by the shapes of their leaves, which they did proudly. "When I first came to this country, all the plants were unfamiliar to me," Mrs. Hallgarten said. "And so I pestered everyone around me to tell me their names so I would feel at home." She pointed to a low shrub with glossy red leaves. "Poison oak—do you know it? The only one I can't love." Her daughters laughed and teased her about some incident in which she had developed a violent rash, and she laughed, too. I felt envy. How splendid it seemed to have siblings and a mother and to live in such a beautiful landscape.

When we returned, we found Mr. Hallgarten and my father sitting by the camera. To my surprise, my father was stroking a large orange cat splayed in his lap. He greeted us. The cat yawningly turned over, exposing her white underbelly.

"Lilly should be finishing setting out lunch for you," Mrs. Hallgarten said. "I have a meeting with my Hillside Club committee."

"Stay one moment, Celeste," my father said. "I haven't had the chance to tell you about my work, which your husband has been so kind to invest in."

Mrs. Hallgarten folded her hands in front of her, as if to keep in check a leaping, loping energy that lay beneath the perfect motionlessness of her body.

"For the last dozen years, I've been working on a project of great magnitude and scope," my father said. "I've asked your husband not to speak of it, because I've wanted to ensure utter secrecy so no one had a chance of copying me."

As my father spoke, Sophie and Adele drifted away and pulled out a length of string to play cat's cradle. Thomasine followed my father with the same watchfulness as her mother, although she darted glances at me from time to time.

When my father finished, Mrs. Hallgarten laughed. It was a direct, startled laugh, like a dove taking flight. "Arthur Kylander, you may be a genius, or you may be a madman," she said, shaking her head. My father looked at her in perplexity.

Two women walked up the street, and Mrs. Hallgarten greeted them, said goodbye to us, and went off with them, presumably her fellow committee members.

Mr. Hallgarten rubbed his hands. "Lilly must be wondering what's keeping us," he said. "And you children must have worked up an appetite on your walk. Let's go inside." My father rose from his chair, dazed. "Arthur, don't be distressed by Celeste's reaction. She is fascinated by entomology and botany and zoology, but she takes little interest in the hard sciences—you would capture her attention if you were photographing the growth of a newt or a sunflower. If she sometimes seems blunt, I attribute that to her being French."

We walked inside to the dining room, where sandwiches had been cut on the diagonal and piled artfully on trays. I felt embarrassed. The word "madman" seemed excessive. I decided I no longer liked Mrs. Hallgarten. Adele and Sophie seemed not to have listened to my father at all, but I worried that Thomasine would ask me questions. Fortunately, she seemed so famished that she paid me no attention.

I wished Karelia had been among us to explain my father. Of course, Karelia had never believed in the project either. I experienced a strange sensation, as if I were only a projection of light upon a wall, as if I were flickering and about to go out.

After lunch, Mr. Hallgarten said the two older girls had to practice their instruments—Thomasine the violin, Sophie the clarinet—or their mother would be unhappy with him.

"Would you play Noah's ark with me?" Adele asked. I agreed readily, glad to be pulled into something simple. I had only a vague idea of the Noah story, something to do with a long sea journey in a boat full of pairs of wild beasts, which struck me as a dangerous endeavor. Adele brought down a large wooden ark, poured out painted animals from its hold, and began sorting them. My attention wandered. I could hear

Thomasine playing in her room upstairs, and although she halted whenever she made a mistake and played the offending passage over several times before continuing, I found it very beautiful and plaintive.

"Here—" Adele grabbed my hand, as if aware I was distracted by her sister's music, and handed me two wood animals. "You can play with them because you're the guest—they're my favorites." She looked up at me with her brown eyes as if to assess my gratitude. "The gazelles."

"The gazelles," I repeated. Thomasine found her way into a long passage where she made no mistakes, her bow striking and caressing the strings with a tone as rich as fur, so that I could almost feel the animal pelts under my fingers, and I closed my eyes.

As evening came on, fog flowed in from the bay and up the hill toward the house. "For some reason I imagined that the East Bay was free of the city's fog," my father said.

"Sometimes it passes before nightfall," Mr. Hallgarten said. "If it doesn't, however, I declare you completely free of your commission. It was, after all, only an excuse for me to invite you here."

My father didn't answer, regarding the fog as if contemplating how he might choose the right lens or exposure to compensate for its presence enveloping the house.

After dinner, Mr. Hallgarten suggested we play a game of Flinch. My father went out to his camera, although by now there seemed little likelihood that any image could be obtained. Mr. Hallgarten called out "Flinch!" with great relish. Then Mrs. Hallgarten took Sophie and Adele upstairs to tuck them in, and Mr. Hallgarten went out onto the balcony with his pipe, the smoke curling to join the fog, leaving Thomasine and me alone in the living room. She still sat at the card table, shuffling the deck in expert arcs. The fire gave off deep crackles and hisses, and I wondered where Karelia was, if she was on her way home.

An awful thought struck me.

"Thomasine."

"Yes?"

"Why did you say I looked familiar?"

"Did I?"

"Last night."

"I don't remember that. You must have been falling asleep."

She avoided my gaze. A cold heat swept through me.

"You've seen my father's photographs of me."

Now she looked at me full on. "Don't be embarrassed. I've seen photographs of people with no clothes on before."

"No one was supposed to know about the project. Where did you see them?"

She shrugged. "Now I know all about it." But she led me upstairs to her father's study, past the master bedroom, where Sophie was reading a book to Adele. Mrs. Hallgarten sat with her head turned to the black glass of the window, her hand resting on the sill almost as if she wished to push the casement wide and climb out of the window.

In the study at the end of the hall, photographs crowded the walls, few of them plumb. Most were landscapes, or portraits of ancestors. Some were nudes, women lying on elegant sofas or wrapped in flowing gauze. My father's Tetrascopic prints of Mr. Hallgarten hung above a photograph of a woman standing on tiptoe to pick a rose from a bush. On top of one bookcase leaned a print of Karelia's photograph of herself wound around a cypress, the one Mr. Hallgarten had said reminded him of a dream. An unmade bed crammed against the window, flanked by a desk on one side and stacks of papers and folders on the other. More piles covered the desk's surface and the bookcases. Thomasine picked her way through the mess until she found a black leather-bound album, which she pulled out and gave to me.

I flipped through the pages, my skin prickling, to make sure all the prints were there. She looked me over. "You're not as pudgy as you used to be, although your ears still stick out."

With as much calm and condescension as I could muster, I said, "Your father shouldn't have shown this to you."

"He didn't," Thomasine said. "I come here and look at things when I'm not supposed to."

"This is scientific work. Did you show anyone?"

"No. How could you stand the same way every month?"

I said nothing.

"We have to put it back," Thomasine whispered. "He won't like it if he knows we've been in here."

With a glare, I returned the album to her, indicating that she wrung this concession from me at great cost to our former friendship. She slid the album back into its pile. "If it's scientific, why are you embarrassed?" she asked.

"I'm not embarrassed," I said. But now I could see my younger self the way Thomasine must have: the flabby tummy and chest of the early years, the babyish nipples, the shrunken spout of the penis, the torso gradually shrinking and elongating until the ribs protruded, the dollar-coin-sized birth mark on my left hip, the shoulder that was always slightly higher than the other, the protruding ears, and most of all the foolish, unknowing, proud look in his eyes, standing there without any thought of who might gaze at him in the future. No doubt Thomasine had shown the album to Sophie and Adele too, and they had spent an afternoon giggling. "You're not able to see it the way a scientist would. We're keeping the project secret so no one can replicate it before we reveal the project to the world. He's almost ready."

"Oh, I see," she said drily. "You're afraid someone will see this and photograph their own child for fourteen years?"

I glared at her, walked into my room—her room—and closed the door.

Mr. Hallgarten had said he would stay up and keep my father company as long as he could. After everyone else had gone to bed and the lights had been put out, I headed back to the study. The darkness here, so much more complete than in the city, seemed to vibrate. The curtains hadn't been drawn, but only a faint illumination came from the large window. Terrified that I would knock the piles over and they would blend into each other, I inched toward the corner where I remembered seeing the portfolio. Lightly I brushed my fingers over the stacked papers until I touched its rough leather spine. I pulled it out.

As I left, the rasp of a door came from downstairs. Presumably this was Mr. Hallgarten retiring for the night. I hurried into Thomasine's room and shut the door as the top stair creaked under his foot. What if he'd seen my door closing, what if a pile had toppled, would he suspect me, would he light a lamp and look for what was missing? I listened for a long time; first, the splashing of water in the bathroom, then footsteps down the hall, then the study door closed. After ten silent minutes, I breathed more easily.

The fog hadn't lifted. Would my father really continue photographing the house all night? Could anything be visible on the film?

In the low light of Thomasine's lamp, I opened the Book of Months. Notes in my father's handwriting described more deviations than I recalled, days when I had been too ill with the flu, or the chicken pox, or a cold. He had redone the 1898 prints he'd destroyed, but October 1899 was not represented at all; a note read, "negatives currently missing."

I could slip the album into my suitcase, take it home and hide it under my mattress. It wouldn't be stealing—the photographs belonged to our family, and Mr. Hallgarten had no use for them. Surely I, of all people, had the right to decide their fate. The knowledge that Thomasine had looked at them knocked things off kilter.

What if Karelia found it in my room it during one of her annual housecleaning enthusiasms? I'd have to tell her. However, even then, I couldn't count on her not to absent-mindedly put the album in a pile where my father could see it someday, when she had forgotten my motives for concealing it. I could drop the album into the bay on our ferry ride home, but this seemed too final, and it gave me a chill to imagine dropping my younger self into the cold water.

At breakfast, I only half-listened to the conversation. My father ate briskly and seemed full of energy. The fog was lifting. "All may not be lost," he said. "We shall see what I can do in the darkroom."

When it was time to go, I gathered my things from Thomasine's room and weighed the portfolio in my hand, pacing the room. The baseboard, I noticed, kept the back of the armoire from lying flush with the wall behind it. With effort, I wedged the Book of Months into the gap, poking it deep into shadow with a walking stick I found under her bed. The armoire seemed so heavy I couldn't imagine anyone ever moving it. Perhaps someday, we would visit again, and I could retrieve it. This way, however, I had done nothing wrong—I hadn't stolen it, after all, merely changed its location slightly.

When my father and I had brought our luggage out into the front yard, Sophie said, "*Bonne journèe*," and Thomasine gave me a mocking glance. Adele surprised me by giving me a hard hug, apparently having forgiven me for my distracted ark-playing.

Mrs. Hallgarten, her hair now loose, kissed my father and me on the cheeks. "Come again with Karelia when you need a respite from the city," she said. "I'll show her the hills, too—there's such deep life here." As we walked to Mr. Hallgarten's car, the orange cat rose out of the bushes by the door and followed us. But when I turned around to pet her, she darted off, frightened no doubt by the suitcase in my hands.

*　*　*

Karelia returned on a Friday evening at the end of January, a week after the visit to the Hallgartens. My father and I were eating fish soup from the delicatessen. Karelia embraced me tightly, her coat giving off a marine tang. I made her sit next to me. She looked too thin, her frame birdlike and fragile. One of her gloves had fallen into the water as she disembarked, so her left hand was cool as porcelain.

"Tell me everything about Canada," I asked. "Go through each day and say what you did."

My father brought her a cup of soup. "Karelia's worn out, Joseph," he said. She ate rapidly, and he brought her another. I'd never seen him so solicitous. And she did seem more tired than I'd ever seen her. She had dark circles under her eyes and moved with unaccustomed slowness.

While she ate, I told her about our weekend at the Hallgartens, describing their place as if it were a cross between a tree house and a palace out of the Arabian Nights. I repeated Mrs. Hallgarten's words about the sham of most architecture, how it was better to let the joists show. "We should take down our ceilings," I said. "It would be more honest. And I want to see what the underside of the floor above us looks like."

"Why not do away with the whole floor, and the roof too?" she asked, smiling for the first time since her return.

"That would be too honest. And cold."

She sipped the tea my father brought her. "I'm glad to be here again, where it's warm—you don't think it's warm because you've never spent a winter in Canada, Joseph. Oh, but it's also beautiful there, I wish you could have come." She closed her eyes and fell asleep.

Karelia told us only a little of what happened in Canada. When she arrived in the Okanagan, her oldest brother's wife, Orie, picked her up at the train station in a cart. Karelia's older brothers were out cutting blocks of ice from the lake to haul back to the ice-house. Orie took Karelia to the house she'd grown up in, and they looked in at her younger brother sleeping. Then Karelia helped her with the wash. They hung the clothes on cords in the living room, because the laundry would freeze if left to dry outdoors. She and Orie moved the houseplants away from the windows to keep them warm for the night.

Since Karelia left, her family had rebuilt the barn, doubled the size of the orchard, planted pear trees in the field in front of the house, and constructed two other houses for each of Karelia's oldest brothers and their wives to live in. Her younger brother, never married, had lived in town until his illness became too severe. Her older brothers had grown tall and gone silent like their father. She felt more comfortable with Orie and her other sister-in-law; between them they had six children ranging in age from three to ten years old.

Her younger brother slept most of the time, so she was able to speak to him only a few times before he died. He smiled, clasped her hand, said her name. She told him that she had taken up photography, and that I had grown into a healthy boy. His fingers, hardly more than bone, pressed hers. "You haven't married either," he said softly. She admitted she hadn't. "And your uncle, did he remarry?" She said no. A frown creased his forehead. "We thought you would be gone only a year or two," he said. "We thought he would find a new wife and you would come back."

"Do you wish you'd gone back?" I asked her now.

"No, of course not!" she said. But I could tell the trip had dislodged her in some way, that we had become shadows while she was there, surrounded by her family and all their children and the desolate magic of winter.

CHAPTER SIX

Now, each time I undressed for the Tetrascope, Thomasine gazed wryly down at me, as if I were in a photograph she held in her hand. I didn't know how to present myself anymore, I tried to call to mind the face of whichever customer preceded me and reproduce the expression. When my father noticed, he told me to look natural. I didn't understand what he meant. After all, when a customer with wide-open eyes and pursed lips sat down before the camera, my father didn't tell him to look natural. "How do you know what's natural for me?" I asked my father. "I'm too young."

"You're too old already," he said. "Too old for your youth."

I took note whenever he failed to notice I was wearing someone else's face. Sometimes I would try to combine the looks of several customers, hoping my true face would arise from the blend. Sometimes, at the studio, I would pull out older photographs of me, hoping to recognize my true face. Perhaps when I was three years old I had been young enough to wear my proper expression without thinking about it. To my eyes, the younger versions of me looked rather blank.

* * *

On the Sunday afternoon following Karelia's return, the three of us walked to the studio, where she developed her negatives of the Okanagan Valley and my father and I reviewed our stocks and wrote a list of items for Mrs. Salamanco to order. Then Karelia emerged from the darkroom and asked him for assistance in making prints. Usually when they worked together, I was not permitted in, because there was little room, but this time, my father didn't object when I squeezed in too.

They worked in silence for a while, their faces illuminated only by soft ruby glow of the darkroom lamp. Karelia lifted a print of a landscape from the developing bath. It showed a few trees and white mounds—greasewood bushes covered with snow. Next, a print of her brother, his head cradled in a pillow like a hunk of bone. Pain shadowed his eyes, but some softness still remained about the mouth. Her hands trembled as she held up the print. She wept for a moment. Then she rinsed it and dropped it into the fixing bath.

"He was the only one I could talk to when we were children," she said. "You can't tell from this picture, but when he smiled, he could charm the wool off a lamb. He often talked himself out of chores, which fell on me instead."

"His face reminds me of my own brother's," my father remarked. "I'm sorry that we had so little communication, he and I, for so many years. Even as boys we didn't have much in common. From an early age he loved to plant seedlings and water and tend them. It made no sense to me—plants grew on their own, I pointed out."

When she finished developing her few prints—she hadn't thought about her camera much during her stay—my father beckoned us into the Tetrascope room.

"While you were gone, Karelia, I made some improvements to the Tetrascope—now it's possible to raise and lower all the cameras at the same time. It's simple. Here." He gestured, and she dutifully turned the crank. Slowly the cameras glided higher.

"I've marked numbers along the support," he said. "Bring it back down to thirty-three and three eighths of an inch. That centers the focus at the current level of Joseph's navel. As he becomes taller—and it won't be too long now before he is growing rapidly—small adjustments can allow the cameras to maintain their relation to his body." He motioned me to stand in the center and directed Karelia to look through the viewfinder.

Karelia gave me a questioning look. My father had rarely spoken to her about the Tetrascope since their clashes in the early days. Yet she stepped up and peered at me.

"You see all four sides of him in a row, yes?" my father said. "If the row isn't exact, you can adjust the mirrors to change the alignment, like this."

She turned the knobs as he indicated and straightened up for him to have a look.

"Excellent," he said. "It's not so complicated now as when I first constructed the device."

He took her hands. She regarded him with surprise.

"Unless the natural order of things is disrupted, Joseph will certainly long outlive me. My aim has always been to record the full span of Joseph's life. Promise me that, when my death comes, you'll continue my work, you'll take my place as the operator of the Tetrascope."

Karelia looked pleadingly at him.

"Joseph may outlive you, too," he said, "and so it may be necessary to find another successor many decades from now—I would leave that up to your judgment."

She pulled away from his grasp. "No," she said. "Please don't ask me to. How can you? You might as well require a cat to take the harness over from a horse."

She fled the room. My father stood, his head hanging, not stirring even when she reappeared.

"Why didn't you ever remarry?" she said. "Then you could have raised a whole brood of photographers to carry out your dreams."

She went out again. The coat rack must have tilted as she grabbed her coat, because we heard a rocking sound, and then the studio door closed and her feet faded down the steps.

The quiet settled over us like a blanket of snow. I wished I could have gone with Karelia to Canada and held my tongue out for snow-flakes. It seemed impossible that they could not be sweet, though Karelia had assured me they had only the flavor of water.

"It's nearly three o'clock," I said, hoping that by carrying on with our routine we could bring everything back to the way it was.

"Is it?" He shook his head slightly, as if he too felt the snow. His face seemed longer than usual. I undressed and cupped my heels in the lines on the floor. It would be strange if anyone but he were to operate the Tetrascope. It seemed that he was the one at the center of the project, not me. For someone else to take over his role would be as pointless as if another boy were to take my place. I stood, shivering until he moved and looked through the viewfinder. There was nothing for him to adjust. The shutter clicked.

*   *   *

Karelia had been home for a week, and still Mr. Hallgarten hadn't come by. "Maybe he's forgotten about us," I said to Karelia one morning at breakfast. I worried more that he had decided my father's project was absurd, that after we left, he and his wife had burst out laughing. I was now very glad that I'd hidden the Book of Months.

"I'm sure he hasn't forgotten," Karelia said.

"I wish you could have seen his house. What if he doesn't invite us again?"

"You'll see Thomasine again, I'm sure."

I denied that Thomasine had anything to do with it. I had told her about Thomasine, described her room and her game of dissimilarities, but I'd stopped short of telling about Thomasine finding the portfolio—the memory made me blush. And I hadn't mentioned that my father had told Mrs. Hallgarten about the project, or that I feared her skepticism would infect her husband.

Mr. Hallgarten finally arrived late on a Thursday afternoon. The weather had turned cold and rainy, and he stuffed his umbrella in the bucket by the door and gazed mournfully at his drenched shoes. He had a lavish bouquet of flowers with him, which he presented to Karelia. "I'm so sorry about your brother's death," he said.

I went to the operating room to tell my father Mr. Hallgarten had arrived. When I came back, Mr. Hallgarten and Karelia sat side by side in the waiting chairs. "They thought I would come back from San Francisco after a year," she was telling him in a low voice. He leaned toward her, watching her face with sympathy. "I abandoned them—I thought they didn't want me."

My father appeared, carrying a large frame before him.

"What's this?" said Mr. Hallgarten, standing up.

My father had printed all 24 photographs of Mr. Hallgarten's house—each one about two inches high—laid them out in four rows, and matted them all in one frame, with the hour written in neat capitals beneath each image. Eight of the shots were featureless, completely black, and in three of the other photographs, only the house's lamp-lit windows dimly registered in the gauzy dark.

Mr. Hallgarten looked taken aback. "I didn't think you'd bother developing them, because of the fog," he said.

"It would be irresponsible of me not to complete the commission you gave me," said my father. "And it's not about capturing light and shadow, it's about recording the passage of time. What use can photography be if we use it to preserve only what we see?" He waited, expressionless, as Mr. Hallgarten held the frame before his eyes, tilting it this way and that to evade the glare.

At last Mr. Hallgarten gave a short laugh. "Arthur, you are an excellent salesman, in your own way." He set the frame down, reached inside his jacket, and pulled out his checkbook and a golden pen. With a flourish, he wrote a sum, signed his name, and handed the check to my father. Then he turned to Karelia. "Tell me," he said, "about the snow—I miss it from my youth."

*   *   *

In early February, Mr. Hallgarten invited us to go with him on a Saturday morning to the Guild of Arts and Crafts exhibition at the Saint Francis Hotel. My father said that the prints he had made the day before were preying on his mind; he had gone too far in correcting for underexposure in the images of November 12 through 15, 1899, taken during a particularly rainy week, and he must destroy them and spend Saturday in the darkroom making new versions.

"You must stop second-guessing yourself, Arthur, or you'll never finish," Mr. Hallgarten said. "Come—there will be photographs as part of the exhibition, and though they may not be to your taste, you can satisfy yourself examining the technical aspects."

Reluctantly, my father agreed.

Upon entering the exhibition, we were handed a list of the artists and their works. Among etchings and ivory miniatures, lamps and laces, one wall had been given over to works by photographers that Mr. Hallgarten said were among the bay region's finest. Karelia examined each print with the avidity of a bee collecting pollen. A shot of Yosemite showed the tips of mountains along the bottom edge, pine branches at the top half of the frame, and a startling blankness of white clouds in between. In another photograph, a young woman robed in bright white linen, head bent demurely, a naked toddler in her arms, stood on a steep, shadowed slope of grass, a grove of thin-limbed trees tilting ominously toward her from behind in the top left corner. In another, a man dressed in flowing robes sat on a large globe, which was apparently suspended in the cosmos to judge by the murky swirl around him. He held a wide bowl from which cascaded a long trail of bubbles. Beneath the print was a quatrain from the *Rubáiyát of Omar Khayyám:*

> *And fear not lest Existence closing your*
> *Account, and mine, should know the like no more;*
> *The Eternal Saki from that Bowl has pour'd*
> *Millions of Bubbles like us, and will pour.*

"How was this made?" she said in a hushed voice.

"The bubbles have all been drawn in by hand," my father observed, leaning close. "It must have taken many hours."

The last photograph on the wall, by a photographer named Anne Brigman, depicted a nude woman crouched high in a pine tree. One arm stretched out to clasp a branch tenderly, as if steadying a lover. "Look," Mr. Hallgarten said, pointing: a smaller branch continued the line of her arm; the soft-focus quality of the image blurred the boundaries between woman and tree, so it seemed the branch was an extension of her body. With delight, Mr. Hallgarten watched Karelia study the image; she didn't even notice that she was crushing the exhibition's program in her hands. Gently, he took it from her.

"The first time I saw this one," he said, "I said to myself, I must show this to Karelia."

"They pulse with life," she said. "Do you mind if we sit? My head is whirling with everything I've seen." She headed for a nearby bench. I sat on one side of her, Mr. Hallgarten on the other. My father, restless, walked into the room behind us, which contained sculptures.

"At least two of the photographers live in Berkeley," Mr. Hallgarten said. "Laura Adams Armer, who made the image of the young woman and her infant, and Adelaide Hanscom, who has illustrated an entire

edition of the *Rubáiyát* with her photographs. I have a copy at home—
I'll show you next time I come to the studio."

She looked at him. Slowly, seriously, she said, "You're our angel."

I had just stood, intending to go over to the *Rubáiyát* photograph
again, when something spurred me to turn around. I saw her reach her
hand out and clasp his.

It was such a natural gesture; for a moment, they sat like that,
regarding each other, their shoulders nearly touching, Karelia radiant
with the same happiness with which she had studied the Brigman photo,
Mr. Hallgarten meeting her gaze with a gratified joy.

Then they both withdrew their hands and faced forward.

The other people in the gallery showed no sign of having noticed
anything amiss, and I wasn't sure if anything amiss had occurred.
Anyone watching might have assumed Mr. Hallgarten and Karelia were
married, and that I was their son. The thought made me blush.

My father appeared at my side. "It may rain this afternoon," he said.
"We should return before it does."

Karelia insisted on looking one more time at the photographs.
Although Mr. Hallgarten attempted to engage him in conversation, my
father drummed his fingers against his legs. "I've decided to reprint
those photographs from 1899 today after all," he said.

Mr. Hallgarten walked us back to the studio.

"We'll see you Monday, then," said Karelia, because that was one of
his favored days for visiting us, as were Wednesday and Friday; all days,
it occurred to me, that Karelia worked at the studio; I couldn't remember the last time he had come on another day.

"I look forward to it," he said, and raised his hat to us.

My father disappeared into the darkroom. Karelia busied herself with tidying the reception area; soon, however, she began paging
through the latest *Camera Work*. I sat in my father's office to read.

After about half an hour, my father passed by on his way toward the reception desk.

"Some attachment is beginning to develop between you and Thomas," he said.

I stood inside the office doorway. She didn't look up from the magazine, but I could see her grip tighten.

"To take each other's hands—" He broke off and began pacing. I ducked back a few steps, although he must have known I was somewhere about.

Still Karelia kept her head bent over the magazine. She even turned a page.

"It's natural, I understand, for individuals to become drawn to each other, and if one reads the newspapers, one knows that for all the centuries of priests arguing against impropriety of this or that sort, human nature is wayward. As you know, I believe it's best not to be ruled by passions, but to temper them with reason. Yet I also believe that we must see things as they are. I've tried to raise you and Joseph in this spirit."

Now she put down *Camera Work* and looked straight up at him. He stopped pacing and leaned over the desk. "I wasn't aware you were raising me," she said.

"I understand this is upsetting. I make no moral judgments. I've only a simple request. For the sake of your future, I beg you to set aside any feelings you have for Thomas, and to discourage any feelings he may have. And I will tell him the same tomorrow."

I edged forward, forgetting my plan to stay concealed, but neither of them showed any sign of noticing me.

"All you care about is not jeopardizing the project," she said. "If you speak of it to him, you'll only embarrass yourself. What you must have seen was only me brushing his hand, accidentally, while pointing at a photograph."

My father looked at her tenderly, sadly, fearfully. "I'm glad to hear it." He straightened several of the photographs on the wall behind her, walked into the darkroom, and closed the door.

Karelia fell back into her chair and put her head on the desk, her hair spilling over its surface. Presently she straightened up and, catching sight of me, crooked her finger.

She touched my cheek. "I take care of you, I cook our meals, I make his customers happy, I've done everything he wanted me to. Am I not to have any happiness of my own? What should I do, Joseph?"

I pressed her hand to my face. Her palm was warm and a little moist, the fingers cooler and drier. I remembered all the nights she went to the opera, saying she was going with Violet and her brother, though we hadn't seen much of either recently. I remembered the joy that had leapt into Mr. Hallgarten's eyes when she touched his hand, and the way the two of them had broken away and looked forward almost at the same instant.

For the rest of the day, Karelia and my father spoke less than usual to each other, but they were not uncordial. It seemed the crisis had passed.

Monday evening, when Mr. Hallgarten arrived, my father immediately asked him to come to the main operating room. "I've a matter to discuss with you," he said, and Mr. Hallgarten, perhaps believing that my father had reached some milestone or had even finished printing the entire series, smiled and followed. The door shut behind them.

Karelia stood, trembling. I hurried, soft-footed, to eavesdrop, but she hissed my name, and I stopped midway.

Every moment passed like a grain of sand down the throat.

I turned. Karelia had put her coat on. She seemed to be talking to herself.

On the desk stood a vase with an exuberance of dried flowers that she had arranged at the beginning of winter. Customers had often praised them. Now she rummaged in the desk, pulled out a pair of shears, and lopped off the tops of each one. The shears clacked drily. Some of the stems proved tough, and she had to apply both hands. Soon the vase held nothing but stubs. Petals and leaves, wan and crumbly, littered the desk and the floor.

"Let's go home," she said. She held out my jacket. I wanted to wait, in case my father was in fact discussing some other matter, or in case Mr. Hallgarten emerged laughing and saying to Karelia, "Your uncle has the strangest idea about us!" Or even if his face was grim beneath a polite veneer, and he said only a few friendly words to us before leaving, I wanted to see it.

But she was on her way out, still holding my coat, and so I followed. As we left, I thought I heard the door to the operating room open. I hurried after her down the stairs. We didn't look back the whole way home.

"You feared that I might distress him by bringing up the matter," my father told us when he joined us at dinner, "but I put it very delicately to him, and he assured me that I was right to mention it, as your guardian, Karelia, and that I had nothing to worry about on his account, because he sees all three of us as among his closest friends."

She said nothing. She ate her soup in silence and didn't touch the bread. I wondered what he had said to Mr. Hallgarten when they'd emerged to see the beheaded flower arrangement. As he left the table, I saw a thistle fragment clinging to his pants leg, a curled leaf on his sleeve. Presumably he had cleaned things up.

A few days later, my father showed us a letter from Mr. Hallgarten, saying that his business was acquiring another paper wholesaler, and so he wouldn't be able to visit for a while. "See, there is nothing to worry about." A week passed without a visit, then another. All three of us moved slowly when closing the studio. I took extra care polishing the display cases, and the reception desk had never looked tidier.

My father still seemed to believe that nothing was wrong. He wrote to Mr. Hallgarten describing a new project he had in mind: a photographic panorama of the city from the top of the Hopkins Mansion on Nob Hill. Muybridge had created such a panorama long ago, before my father knew him. But my father proposed to create a panorama once a week, at the same time each day, and in this way he would document the slow change of the city. Of course this would have to wait until he finished developing the final two years of my portraits—he was very close. He received no reply.

In March, Violet eloped and moved to Minneapolis, much to our surprise. Karelia ceased going to the opera. Instead, she attended lectures at the California Camera Club several evenings a week, and spent Saturdays photographing and long Sundays developing. One of her photographs—a more recent version of the cliff-top dryad that had caught Mr. Hallgarten's attention the year before—was accepted for inclusion in an art salon to be held in May. She danced around the room when she received that letter. My father, who had helped her with the printing, congratulated her with real pleasure. It was the first time I saw her happy since the afternoon at the exhibition.

My father ran through the money from Mr. Hallgarten's last check, but he continued developing prints for the project in expectation of reimbursement. Sometimes, no one came to the studio for hours. The surge of customers brought in by "Man Laughing" had already faded, and our rival, the portraitist with the Vandyke, had countered by filling his display case with the portraits of famous actors, whom he'd inveigled into his studio when they came through San Francisco. Now even my father's older customers seemed to come less often; holes opened in his schedule, and sometimes I would enter his operating room to find him in the chair reserved for clients, unmoving, dull-eyed, and if I called to him, he turned his head as if heavy weights hung from his beard. He seemed as discouraged as he had been right before Mr. Hallgarten came into our lives, and nothing Karelia or I said could bring him out of it.

Once again, I brought bread and butter sandwiches to school for lunch. For supper, we had bean or cabbage soup. On the streets, we took labyrinthine routes in order to avoid passing shops where we owed money. If I saw our landlord on the street, I was by no means to talk to him.

By the end of March, I decided to take matters into my own hands. Without telling Karelia or my father, I wrote a note to Mr. Hallgarten, telling of my father's progress in printing of the project to date—he had reached the middle of 1904 already—and also reminding him of my father's new idea of the panorama. I added a postscript: "Time—round or square?"

No reply came. One night, though, when Karelia returned from a Camera Club lecture, I caught a whiff of something that reminded me of his pipe smoke. I told myself she must have run into him by chance. She volunteered nothing, and I was reluctant to ask.

*   *   *

Early in the morning of April 18, 1906, I woke to a deep vibration. Above and below me, wood joists groaned and cracked, while church bells clanged wildly in the distance. From across the room, my dresser slid toward me. Empty bottles that I'd collected and jammed with candles toppled from my windowsills, smashing onto the floor. A jolt tossed me out of bed. The floor and ceiling seemed to twist east to west. From the ceiling came a final crunching, and then silence drifted down.

Karelia called out my name and sprang to the doorway of my room. "I have glass in my eyes," I said. She ran to kneel beside me. But all I meant was that pieces of glass had fallen so near me they filled my vision. When I managed to convince her I wasn't injured, she shook me a little. "Find your shoes," she said. I ran a hand through my hair and heard tinkling.

"*You're* barefoot," I said. My shoes were under the bed where I usually threw them.

The earthquake had wedged my father's bedroom door in its jamb. We heard him yank on the doorknob until it came off. Karelia threw herself against the door, and when it didn't budge, he called out that he would climb out the window. We begged him not to. He might fall or hurry off to check on the studio without us. Karelia and I hurled ourselves against the door at the same time, and it flew open. My father emerged, pale and stroking his beard as if to reassure himself it was still there.

I found Karelia's shoes under the writing desk in the front room, under a mass of fallen papers. When I brought them to her, she was holding her foot, from which she drew a glass sliver. A few drops of blood appeared on the floor next to her. I offered to find a bandage, but she said never mind and thrust her feet into her shoes.

The other tenants were already rushing down the staircase. No one spoke until we reached the street, where we all turned around to look up at the building. From the street, at least, it looked as it always had.

Stars faintly held their light in the dark blue sky. Karelia sat on the sidewalk and examined her foot. A man brought a gas lamp near; another ducked into his first-floor apartment and came out with tweezers and alcohol; a woman tore cloth into strips for bandages. Karelia said, "You would think I had broken both my legs from the way everyone is standing around me." I held her ankles in case the alcohol stung terribly, but she only grimaced a bit.

An aftershock sent a brief wave through the ground; those who had gone back inside scurried out again.

My father said he was going to the Murchison Building to make sure that everything in the studio was all right. When I started to follow, he added, "Stay here and look after Karelia."

"Wait," Karelia called, but he was walking away, bent forward with urgency.

One of our neighbors shared with us some bread smeared with butter and brown sugar. People filled the streets, some in night-gowns, a few in evening clothes, one man wrapped in a blanket, his bare shoulders gleaming. A family passed by, father, mother, and three children, the parents holding covered birdcages before them like lanterns.

One apartment house had lost its facade, exposed like a dollhouse, doll-people on the third floor throwing bundles of their belongings down to the ground. Still other buildings stood as straight as they ever had, not a windowpane cracked. It was as if the earthquake had shaken the city loose from time, so that some buildings crumbled as if eons had passed while others looked the same as they had the day before.

More and more people moved about the streets, with surprising calm it seemed, many with their birds, or cats, or dogs. Some pulled wagons piled with belongings, some had nothing in their hands; some walked stiffly because they were wearing much of their wardrobe in layers. A passing man offered an elderly lady his arm so she could traverse a large crack in the pavement. A group of small boys kicked a ball back and forth among them. We heard reports of collapsed buildings, small fires. We heard that City Hall lay in ruins.

A man in a bathrobe said he was certain there would be no more tremors, and he went back into his building.

"What's all the rush?" one of our neighbors called out to a man with a tuba on his back. For answer, he only tapped his nose.

Then we could smell it too: smoke. Some trick of the breeze had kept it from our area until now. I spotted a plume of gray unfurling into the air a few blocks away.

"The firemen will put it out," said one of our neighbors. A few flakes of ash drifted down. The last big earthquake had struck almost forty years ago, and it had been even longer than that since the last big fires in the city. Everyone said that we had the best firefighters in the country.

I began to worry that my father might not return. Suppose a building had collapsed on him. Or suppose he climbed the stairs to his studio, and the stairs dropped away beneath him.

The plume advanced toward us rapidly. Some people went back into their places to bundle up their belongings. The screech of heavy trunks dragging across the asphalt filled the air. A pair of young men said they knew where they could find long pieces of lumber with which they could make a stretcher and carry Karelia. She said that wasn't necessary.

"Karelia," I said, "what about our things?"

"Don't worry about them," she said.

But I felt it was my fault that she had stepped in glass, and that I had to redeem myself. Before she could object, I darted into our building.

At that time we lived in a railroad flat, all our rooms opening off of one long corridor. Inside, an eerie quiet reigned. The floor had warped, as if a giant had wrung the building like a washcloth, and it hadn't yet sprung fully back into shape. Although I could see the floor sloped, I stumbled, because my feet remembered it otherwise. The air was hot and smoky.

I went first into my bedroom and was momentarily puzzled by its disarray. My father's photograph of my mother, the first one he had taken, lay on the floor in front of me. I withdrew it from its shattered frame. To keep it safe, I tucked it into Volume One of the *Kalevala*, stuffed both volumes into the satchel I used to carry books home from the library, and slung the satchel over my shoulder. The watch that Mr. Hallgarten had given me still ticked steadily within its cotton-lined matchbox. I slipped it into my pocket.

The sight of my dresser with its drawers open inspired me to snatch up my bedspread and drag it from room to room, flinging in whatever items of clothing were closest to hand. In the realm of Karelia's undergarments, I felt confused, and so tossed in all of them.

In the kitchen, I gathered a tinned ham, a bag of onions, and a ladle and a pot. On the way out, I tipped in a blue and white vase too, because I knew Karelia loved it. The air had an astonishingly dry heat, a new kind of dry, as brittle as paper.

I hesitated. My father had hung all the portraits of my mother in a cluster in the hallway, and though a few of them had fallen, most miraculously still clung to the wall. My head throbbed, and breathing had grown difficult. But even though the light seemed hazy inside, the top of the stairs was only a few feet away. So I began stuffing portraits into the bundle, swaddling them with clothes to protect them.

Then came a crashing sound, like a redwood toppling, breaking the branches of all the trees in its path.

*   *   *

I woke on the pavement coughing. Karelia wiped my damp forehead with her sleeve. My satchel lay on the ground beside me. I asked raspily where the rest of our belongings were. She said the only thing I had run out with was the satchel. She ran her fingers through my hair. "Are you well enough to move? We can't stay here." Behind her, orange shimmered in the windows of our building.

Had I even picked up the bundle? Had I dropped it on the stairs? Another fit of coughing seized me, and I began to cry. "My mother," I said.

"Shhh," Karelia said, and embraced me. "It's all right." She didn't understand.

My father reappeared. I half-hoped he would dash upstairs to rescue our things. But he strode to the side of the house, opened the crawlspace hatch, and yanked out our landlord's ladder. This he hoisted, hurrying back the way he'd come.

"Can you walk?" Karelia asked. I nodded. She lifted me to my feet, and we followed my father. I was convinced that if we let him go out of our sight, we would never see him again. Aside from a whistle in my lungs, it was not as hard to walk as I'd feared. I couldn't help turning back to look at our building, the ominous glow inside.

Later, we learned that, after he'd left us to go to the Murchison Building the first time, he had run, convinced he would find it in pieces and his life's work destroyed. When he reached Market Street, he found the structure still standing, tilting out of true by only a few degrees, though all its windows had cracked. When he tried to enter, a militia-man blocked his way. "This building is unsafe," the man said. Nothing my father said could persuade the man to let him through. He suspected that the owner of the dry goods store on the ground floor had paid this person to keep others out, for fear of looting. He circled, gazing up at the tenth floor, where thousands of his negatives and prints were stored, each negative neatly in its sleeve, numbered and organized in boxes. When he thought that the militiaman was distracted, he slipped into the alley and unlocked the back door with his key. But the door would not budge.

As he circled the building again, a policeman commanded him to come with him. Two blocks away, a dozen men were attempting to dig survivors out from under the rubble of a collapsed boarding house. For hours my father worked alongside them, smelling smoke on the air and casting anguished glances toward his studio. Later, he wouldn't be able to remember how many they managed to rescue, three, a dozen, it was impossible to think clearly.

When they had finished clearing rubble, the workers wandered away, dazed, their hands scraped and bloody. My father thought of our apartment building's ladder, which he could use to enter the stairwell at the second floor.

I calculated the days since I'd been born—5,374, I believed. I tried to recall when my father had first employed the Tetrascope, because from then on, he took four images of me each day. Although I was uncertain about my math, it seemed that there must have been nearly 20,000 images of me in my father's files, both as negatives and as prints. They filled a large closet in the studio in birchwood storage boxes, stacked higher than my head. How would my father carry them all down the ladder? And how would we transport them once he'd retrieved them? And where would we take them?

As we hurried back to the studio, smoke rose ahead of us. My father quickened his pace. A hundred feet from the building, a fireman ordered us to keep back. Several other firemen stood at a distance in a rough semicircle around the Murchison Building. It seemed to me that they should be concerning themselves with the flames advancing toward us from the south, only half a block away.

"We must get through," said my father. "I have to perform a rescue."

"There's nobody in any of these buildings," said one fireman. "We checked."

"We've just set kegs of black powder inside that one," said another. "I don't guess you'd like to be there when they go off."

"Which one?" my father asked.

A pair of firemen hurried out of the Murchison Building. I remember feeling relief that they had broken down the door already, and so my father would not have to climb the ladder. My father must have thought so too, because he put the ladder down.

"Which building?" he said.

The windows of the Murchison blew outward, and a mighty boom shook the air. But the structure held. "Not enough," commented the first fireman.

"I've always observed that in some situations, economy is not the best idea," said the second. "In love, and in explosives."

A moment later, flames appeared in the lower floor windows.

Sweat glowed orange on my father's forehead. The fire to the south, a few buildings down Sixth Street, pressed a wall of heat toward us.

He pelted toward his studio.

Karelia shouted at him to come back. The firemen, who had been looking expectantly at the building, were caught off guard. It was not until my father had nearly reached the door that one of them grabbed hold of him around the middle and wrestled him away from the entrance.

My father's display case had fallen from its post by the door, but miraculously remained upright, the portraits of his most handsome customers gazing calmly as several firemen struggled, finally pushing my father to the ground.

A second explosion shook the Murchison. Karelia seized me as a hail of particles rattled down. Two firemen dragged my father to his feet and escorted him back to us. My father kept twisting to look behind him.

"It's not safe here," one of the firemen shouted. "Keep out of our way. Head north!"

My father looked as if he were going to make another run toward the Murchison, but the firemen stood fast. So my father dusted his shirt off, picked up the ladder, and headed back toward Market Street. We struggled to keep pace as he turned onto Taylor Street. His ear was bleeding. Karelia dabbed it with her handkerchief, but he showed no sign of noticing. At Turk Street, he unexpectedly veered right, back toward Market Street.

"I'll go in through the back," he said.

"That's too dangerous." Karelia asked me with her eyes to stop him. But my father spoke with such authority that I believed he knew what he was doing.

He led us down Market Street to Fifth Street and we turned onto Stevenson, a narrow alley strewn with rubble.

As we neared the Murchison again, columns of yellow and white and black and gray smoke streamed from our top floor studio, winding around each other, and fire licked our curtains. Our eyes stung, our skin prickled with the heat. The back door had been blown off its hinges. My father threw down the ladder and broke into a run.

I called out after him, but he disappeared into the building.

CHAPTER SEVEN

One winter, when I was eight years old, I came down with influenza. This was not one of influenza's most devastating years, when thousands died, but the disease had escorted a schoolmate of mine out of the world the week before, and my fever was high. Karelia told me later that, on the worst night, I apparently believed there were two of her, because I kept asking for the "other Karelia" to bring me water. As I slept, the ceiling folded upward like trapdoors, and dangling ropes of red light thudded onto the bedspread; I knew I was supposed to climb them, but I lacked the strength. The next morning, my fever broke, I felt better, and the extent to which my father had been concerned for my life became evident.

I expressed a longing to go outside, though I was still not strong enough. My father said he had a solution. It must have been a Sunday, because it was early afternoon and he was home. He left the apartment and returned with a roll of heavy black fabric with which he sealed the window in my room. He cut a hole in the center of the fabric and affixed a camera lens. Once our eyes accustomed to the room's complete darkness, the street outside my window manifested itself upside-down on the wall opposite. The hooves of horses and the feet of people fell near the ceiling, their heads glided along the floor. It was such a marvelous transformation that I laughed, and my father smiled.

This was a *camera obscura*, he explained, which meant "dark chamber" in Latin. It had been used for centuries before anyone devised a way to fix an image by chemical means; my old pinhole camera had operated on the same principle.

At first, I loved how the lens upended the familiar street outside, turning it into a stage where every gesture between people was mysterious, not least because the image was slightly out of focus. If I'd had a crank to move the wall of my room a little farther from the window, I could have found the spot that allowed a sharp image, but I preferred the glorious blur. Did the dog lick that young man's hand, or snatch his newspaper? Did that top-hatted fellow shake hands with the limping woman, or hand her a package? Did the lovers come close to speak sharply to each other, or to kiss? I would roll the fabric down over the window each afternoon. I would imagine leaping into the image, where I would be swept upside down myself.

Yet when I recovered from my illness, the *camera obscura* came to fill me with a kind of vertigo—not because the image was inverted, but because it threw into high relief the irretrievability of everything. After a *camera obscura* session, whatever I looked at seemed ephemeral, a trick of the light, nothing but an image projected onto on my retinas. Karelia eating a biscuit or bending to kiss me goodnight, my father beckoning customers into his studio—they were already ghosts.

A few months later, we moved to a new apartment. The fabric and its lens disappeared. I forgot about the experience until my father stumbled from the Murchison, empty handed, clutching his right arm, and I felt the same vertigo. It seems to me now that the man who stepped out of the Murchison was not entirely the same person who went in, but rather a *camera obscura* version of himself, a figure from a shadowy, inverted world.

*   *   *

Karelia let go of me, and I realized how tightly she'd been holding me. "Arthur, you fool," she cried. I'd never seen her so frightened. A falling beam or collapsing wall might have struck him, or the staircase might have crumbled beneath his feet. He could have been killed or pinned somewhere inside. But now he was staggering toward us. Sweat and tears streaked the ash on his face.

"I'm sorry, Joseph," he said. "I couldn't rescue them."

All at once I was angry—he had risked death to try to save his photographs. He hadn't been thinking of us at all, or what it would mean to us to lose him.

Karelia helped him put his good arm around my shoulder, and we took turns supporting him as we followed the others fleeing, pushed by the unbearably hot wind at our backs. In places, the sidewalk had shattered like toffee brittle, and we had to pick our way around shards of masonry. Motor cars hurtled along the street, dodging bricks, sounding horns. A wagon passed, carrying figures who lay still as dolls. None of us spoke. A hand-sized flake of ash wafted onto my father's beard, and Karelia brushed it away.

City Hall's stonework had slid from the walls of its dome, leaving a cylindrical frame of metal exposed to the air, and some of its pillars had embedded themselves in the pavement. But the dome itself remained, which I found reassuring.

A battalion of the National Guard had just moved its temporary hospital from the Mechanics' Pavilion, which was in the flames' path, to Jefferson Square. There, doctors cleaned and bandaged my father's right hand and bound the arm in a sling. They cleaned and bandaged a wound on his leg, and they treated a small burn on his temple. They said it was possible the arm might have been fractured. They returned him to us and took in the next patient, a woman on a stretcher who rolled her head from side to side and cried out that she couldn't see.

The square was filled with people and their belongings—their armchairs, their sofas, their pianos, their sewing machines. Some women wore plumed hats, or flounced silk underskirts, or veils. To our left, a family of six sat in a row in dining table chairs, flanked by two birdcages, one containing a canary and the other a calico cat. Karelia convinced the family to let us sit on their trunk. On our right, a young couple knelt on a blanket, tourists who had arrived a few days ago from Vermont; a five-year-old girl had attached herself to them, having become separated from her parents. She clutched a canvas bag to her chest and said that she hoped the fire wouldn't get her roller skates.

Someone told us all of the city's water mains had broken, and so far the fire department's attempts to create fire breaks had failed. When the earthquake struck, the city's fire chief had run to the next room to look for his wife and dropped three stories through a hole in the floor. She lived; he lay in a coma.

My father sat unmoving on the trunk. Karelia cleaned his blackened face with her handkerchief. When she had finished, he closed his eyes; agony rose off him like a steam. The doctors had given him whiskey for the pain, and its unaccustomed odor hung about him. His mangled hand hung from its sling, the fingers puffy and red.

"Would it help to lie down?" Karelia asked. He shook his head.

The sky's brilliant red kept darkness at bay all night. Bright enough to read by, someone said. At times the sky took on a terrible beauty, as if several suns had tried to set at the same time and jammed together like typewriter keys. The fire went about its business little more than a block's distance from Jefferson Square on two sides. Fortunately, the wind was from the west now, not pushing it in our direction.

Someone gave us a Moroccan rug, which Karelia wrapped around us; it had sequins sewed in rows across its length, flashing red. Whenever we started to doze off, a rain of cinders woke us, or aftershocks, or dynamite, or collapsing buildings, or the constant argument of the flames. My father lay so still that I found myself watching to make sure he was still breathing.

*   *   *

By morning, everyone had grown hoarse; I had the voice of an ancient goblin from the smoke I'd inhaled in our apartment, and my father wheezed. He ate or drank what Karelia thrust into his hand. He alternated between two states: deadness—with his eyes only slightly open, as if the lids were too heavy—and agitation, in which he fidgeted, picked ash from his clothing with his good hand, moved his lips, and from time to time yanked a hair out of his beard or eyebrows. Mercifully, the periods of agitation were brief.

The fire hadn't come nearer to the park, but it was advancing along our eastern flank. We stood in a long line to be handed a thick, sooty slice of bread and a few mouthfuls of coffee. Karelia said we had to find our way across the bay so we would have fresh air and get another doctor to look at his arm—she worried that it had been hastily worked on. My father nodded. His docility disturbed me.

Boats were picking up passengers near Fort Mason. Karelia found a young man with a donkey cart who agreed to haul us north to the bay for twenty dollars, a phenomenal amount, but my father paid without complaint, and we set off through the rubble. I felt proud of Karelia for leading us. If the studio had in fact burned, then all her photographs, too, would be gone. I wondered if the one she had sent to the art salon had survived, and whether the exhibition would have to be postponed on account of the fires.

At the wharf, a barge pulled up, and after the sick and the injured and the women with babies had boarded, we climbed on and arranged ourselves on the lower deck near an open porthole. I had thought my father would continue gazing in the direction of our lost studio, but he studied the surface of the water below as if trying to see through its dark green. The mortal remains of his parents lay in the silt of the bay's bottom, I remembered, and fearing that he wanted to join them, I pulled him back from the porthole.

Out in the bay, we could see how far the fires ranged, all the way from Van Ness Avenue to the eastern edge of the city. Telegraph Hill remained untouched, but flames poured from the windows of the just-built Fairmont Hotel on Nob Hill. On the hillsides between fires, refugees clustered. We disembarked near the Ferry Building and marched toward it, keeping our heads low to protect our faces from the choking wind and the fine white dust that seeped into our clothing with a slithery feel. The city had become a landscape of solitary columns, jagged walls, distorted steel frames of former buildings.

The clock on the Ferry Building tower read thirteen minutes after five; the earthquake must have jammed the clock's gears on Wednesday morning, as if to stamp the city with the time of its arrival.

We boarded another ferry to Oakland. Almost no one spoke, and so my father's silence did not stand out. On arrival, we were ushered into a long line. Eventually we approached a series of tables where men and women stood talking to refugees and directing them one way or another. From the murmurs that came down the line, we gathered that the cities of Oakland and Berkeley had set up camps for refugees.

When we reached the tables, a man asked, "Are there any family or friends in the area you can stay with?"

"No," said Karelia.

My father pushed forward, startling us like a music box that resumes its tune of its own accord days after its last winding. He laid his left hand on the table and said, "We have friends in Berkeley." He gave an address, and the man directed us to the Berkeley local.

"What friends?" Karelia said, hurrying after him. "Who would put us up?"

"Hallgarten," my father said. His voice was crusty, raked with ashes, as if a fireplace spoke.

At the sound of that name, there sprang up for me a vision of the

Hallgartens' house, spacious, warm, brass lanterns burnishing the red-wood walls with an orange glow. Thomasine lounged in one of the tan leather-upholstered chairs in the Hallgarten living room, next to the fireplace. She smiled to see me and jumped up to take my hand. She led the three of us to our rooms, rooms they hadn't known about on our first visit, but that had appeared just for us, grown like mushrooms.

It took me a moment to realize that Karelia had stopped walking, that my father and I had left her behind. Calling her name, I plunged back in the direction where we had come.

Immediately I collided with someone and fell to the ground. So many legs surrounded me, all moving at an animal pace. Someone roughly hauled me up by the collar, and Karelia appeared through a brief parting in the crowd. I ran to take her hand. It hung like a glove filled with sand; then she clasped my fingers.

"We shouldn't bother the Hallgartens," she said when we found my father on the platform. "He'll have his hands full enough. And he hasn't visited since you—" she broke off, glancing at the people surrounding us. "Can't you see how humiliating that was for him?"

"You might be right. I might have offended him. If he's upset, I'll only ask him to return the Book of Months. It may be the sole remnant of my project."

This gave me pause. I would have to figure out some way to retrieve it from behind Thomasine's armoire. But in my desire to see the Hallgartens, I decided this could be easily handled. I was certain they would welcome us.

"We should go back to the tables now and let them direct us to a camp," Karelia said. "Our old life is done. We have a clean slate now. We can build our lives the right way this time. You're so smart, Arthur, you don't need to be dependent on Thomas. We already owe him so much, and to call on him again would only put us further in his debt. It would be dangerous."

The train was pulling up now. As the crowd moved, my father hesitated.

My throat was scratchy. It was not too difficult to contrive a coughing fit, and this had the desired effect.

"We need to get Joseph to a place where he can lie down and rest," my father said. He turned and moved toward the train doors as they opened. Karelia wrapped her arm around me, and I patted her back and smiled to reassure her I was all right.

* * *

How sweet Berkeley smelled. Here, wisteria bloomed, trees held their green canopies aloft exuberantly, the houses stood in orderly rows. We passed lawns where families sat around a fire or stove, their tumbled house chimneys the sole signs that the earthquake had struck here too. Some of them stopped us to ask if we came from the city. Had the St. Francis Hotel burned? Was it true that the militiamen were shooting suspected looters? Had we seen a sandy-haired man named Rufus, about six foot two?

When we reached the Hallgartens' street, we had a view of San Francisco, now less a city than a volcano, veiled with smoke and seamed with red; the swollen sun loomed over the horizon as if it were gorging itself on the flames. I looked away. We had seen our flat catch on fire and our studio fall, but still it seemed impossible that they should be gone. When we returned, perhaps we'd find the buildings black and tindery outside, like charred meat, but inside they would be all right.

Sophie answered the Hallgartens' door, a half-bitten muffin in her hand. I was conscious of our appearance: our hair matted, our eyes reddened, and our clothes stinking of smoke. Yet Sophie seemed unalarmed, studying us as if we were a tableau put together for her appreciation.

Then she turned and bawled back into the house, "Mama, there are more refugees!"

Mrs. Hallgarten appeared in the doorway. "It's quite careless of you San Franciscans, burning down your own city," she said. "You should have consulted the rest of us before lighting the match." Her tone was dry, but her voice shook. She beckoned us into the entryway and began taking our coats and hats and hanging them on pegs, as if we were Sunday visitors. She drew in a breath when she saw my father's arm, but he said it was not a serious injury.

"And you must be Karelia."

Karelia curtsied clumsily.

"You were in Canada when your family visited us, weren't you? Your brother was ill?"

"Yes," Karelia said, startled. "You have a good memory."

"And how is he?"

"He passed away."

"I'm sorry," she said. She pressed Karelia's hand in sympathy.

Karelia's gaze flicked nervously from Mrs. Hallgarten's face to Sophie's and back again. I worried that Mrs. Hallgarten would notice Karelia's discomfort, but instead she introduced Sophie as her middle daughter. I felt grateful that my father had confronted Mr. Hallgarten about Karelia: whatever danger there might have been was in the past, I thought, and now we had a clean slate. But I couldn't shake off an uneasy feeling.

"How does the city stand?" Mrs. Hallgarten asked my father.

"Everything has been destroyed."

"The business district? The waterfront district?"

"I don't know," my father said.

"Thomas left this morning. He said he had to see about his office and his warehouses. I couldn't keep him here."

Karelia's face went white. Fortunately, Mrs. Hallgarten was already heading for the kitchen, instructing Sophie to show us where we could wash up. "Two other friends of Thomas's came to us earlier today. Go introduce yourselves, and I'll bring food."

After we had cleaned up, we went into the living room, where a tall man in his mid-forties held a dollar coin high above his head between thumb and forefinger, contemplating it as if it were a piece of gold. He had a long face, a thick coppery mustache, and reddish hair swept back from his forehead. His dramatic pose was undercut somewhat by the oversized clothes that hung from his frame like a collapsed balloon. Thomasine, Sophie, and Adele surrounded him in a semicircle. Behind him on the sofa sat a stout yellow-haired man stroking a cat on his lap and ignoring the business with the coin.

The man with the coin tossed it into the air, caught it, and unfolded his fingers one by one to show an empty palm. As the girls bent closer, the coin clattered to the floor behind him.

"It was in your sleeve!" Sophie cried.

Thomasine turned toward us and smiled, as if to say how charming her younger sister was. "Look, the photographer family," she said, liquidly extending her arm toward us, palm up, as if she had conjured us. She had grown taller than I, and her face had become leaner, her eyes more hazel and penetrating. When I'd imagined her welcoming us, I had forgotten the sly mockery of her glance, which was now amplified by her new height. She seemed, in the few months since we'd met, to have become more complete. She dropped her arm and gave a little impatient bounce, as if to encourage us to perform. I blushed, which made her smile.

The red-haired man bowed to us. His name was Peter Visser, and his companion turned out to be his wife Ina. "Forgive her," he said, "she's never worn trousers before. There's a shortage of women's clothing in the neighborhood. The women of Berkeley have been too eager, they've given all their dresses already to the churches."

With a shock, I noticed that my father's and Karelia's photographs no longer hung in the living room. In their place hung a series of oil paintings, landscapes in muted colors—ocher, yellow, light brown, green, gray-blue—depicting parched California hills, mudflats, fields populated by an ox or a solitary farmer, trees crouched in a valley. The dim colors and shapes seemed to flow into each other, as if evening or early morning were laying a haze across the painting. They reminded me of Karelia's work in some way, so I liked them, but I was alarmed that Mr. Hallgarten had replaced our photographs. Karelia was right—we shouldn't have come, he had moved on.

Thomasine introduced herself and her sisters to Karelia, regarding her with curiosity. Peter was a painter, he said; he showed us five small canvases, all he'd been able to rescue from his studio; most of the paintings on the Hallgartens' wall were his as well. We exchanged earthquake stories until Mrs. Hallgarten arrived with coffee and asparagus and butter sandwiches. I'd never tasted anything better in my life. My father wolfed his down, which embarrassed me, while Karelia nibbled without appetite.

Mrs. Hallgarten dispatched Thomasine and Sophie to round up fresh clothing from the neighbors for us. They returned with an assortment of garments. I ended up with overlong brown trousers, which made a comical pairing with a pale linen shirt whose sleeves left my wrists exposed. My father put on a beige cotton sweater, in which he twitched uncomfortably. Karelia returned to the living room in trousers and a man's green button-down shirt. "I lack only a tie," she said. She demonstrated striding like a man, her arms playfully akimbo, but she gave off the metallic odor of worry.

I fell asleep for a while, waking only when Mrs. Hallgarten served us a supper of more sandwiches, apologizing for the poor fare—she was afraid to use the stove; word had spread among the neighbors that no one should use their chimneys until an inspector had checked them for soundness.

Mr. Hallgarten returned at nightfall, followed hesitatingly by a thin, bespectacled fellow with a brush-like mustache. The sleeve of Mr. Hallgarten's suit was torn, his hands and face covered in soot. As Mrs. Hallgarten and his daughters embraced him, he left black streaks on the backs of their dresses. Karelia sank back into the sofa cushions as if she wished to disappear.

When he saw us all, an expression crossed his face, so brief that I almost missed it and could hardly name it—it seemed like a mix of fear and disgust, though I told myself he was only tired. Then he smiled broadly. "Like all good rats, you've abandoned the sinking ship," he said. "Peter!" He shook Peter's hand, then mine, then my father's left hand, leaving progressively lighter smudges on our palms. He stopped short at Karelia. I hoped Mrs. Hallgarten didn't notice that Karelia gazed at him with the eyes of someone who had feared he was dead.

He stretched his hands out toward Karelia and Ina. "And who are these young men? I don't believe we've met."

Karelia gave a deep bow, as if to hide her face. The rest of us laughed as if Mr. Hallgarten had made a great witticism.

"Sir—" said the bespectacled man, still hovering by the door.

Mr. Hallgarten seemed grateful for the interruption. "Of course, Algernon. I'll be right back." He disappeared up the stairs with surprising speed.

Mrs. Hallgarten said, "Won't you sit down, Mr. Locksley," but the man murmured that he was anxious to return to his wife as soon as he could. He removed his spectacles and polished them with a handkerchief. A long time passed, in which we were too weary to speak.

Mr. Hallgarten returned wearing clean clothes, his hair wet and slicked back. He handed Mr. Locksley a pile of papers turned every which way. Mr. Locksley seemed to be contemplating whether to straighten the papers or slide them into his satchel; he chose the latter. With a minuscule tilt of his head in our direction, he went out.

"If only my father had founded a water company rather than a paper company," Mr. Hallgarten said. "Or if only my brother were still alive—he had an industrious and stalwart nature. I feel like the younger brother who has unexpectedly inherited the crown, and my kingdom is under attack. The warehouses, the office building, nothing but burned-out shells. Only the safes remain, and they are too hot to open. When they cool in a few weeks, we'll swing them open and see if anything remains. Well, Algernon will sort it all out. Arthur, your arm, it alarms me. What happened?"

"I tried to rescue the prints from my studio," my father said. "But the stairway collapsed. I believe my life's work has been destroyed. I've lost every image of the project. Except there is a remnant—I gave it to you—the Book of Months. You remember, a black leather album. Is it at your office?"

The thought of his office seemed to weary Mr. Hallgarten. "No, I believe I brought it home."

"It's only a partial record, but it means everything to me."

"Very well, I'll hunt for it. Tomorrow. Meanwhile, we should all get some rest." He instructed his daughters to find us blankets so we could spread out on the living room floor. I was disappointed—I'd been hoping the Hallgartens would all share a room again, and I would stay in Thomasine's room and move the Book of Months back to Mr. Hallgarten's study in the night.

Karelia watched him disappear upstairs. I squeezed her hand to reassure her. He had made a little joke when he saw her, and he had expressed concern for the project—surely she could see from these things that he harbored no ill feelings toward us. But she still seemed nervous.

Thomasine brought over a folded orange woolen blanket. "My grandmother knitted this," she said, and dropped it on me.

"Thank you," I said.

Her eyes widened. "Unless it's going to remind you of the flames. It's orange, I didn't think of that."

I tucked it around me firmly. "It's fine." I was touched that she had considered the possibility.

For a pillow, I had a bag stuffed with pieces of cloth. It smelled of potatoes. In the darkness, Karelia's eyes gleamed. I could sense my father's wakefulness. From time to time he shifted and gasped with pain. Peter dropped off right away and began snoring. All of us still breathed raspily. I became aware of the hard shape of each minute, its metallic taste, its coolness. It was as if I were swallowing each one, like a large pill that traveled with difficulty down the throat.

In the middle of the night, I woke to find Karelia tiptoeing out of the room. I followed as soundlessly as I could. She stood in the kitchen for a moment before opening the back door and stepping outside.

"Karelia," I called in a whisper. "Where are you going?"

"Where could I go?" she whispered back.

I followed her outside to the Hallgartens' pergola, its trellis roof half-covered with vines. Beyond, the Hallgartens' yard stretched about a hundred feet before climbing steeply up. The sky was overcast and the air still held the taste of burning. "Karelia," I said again, but she rested her cool hand on my mouth.

"Sometimes I think I should have told Fulvio yes."

"Yes to what?"

"To marrying him. And living in Florence."

I wished I could see her thoughts. Did Karelia mean that if she had married Fulvio, we would all have moved to Florence? Fulvio would have taken us to the Uffizi, the greatest museum in the world, where we would stare at Venus rising from her shell all day, as he said he loved to do. Or did she mean she wished she had left my father and me here in California?

"I'd like to sleep out here tonight," she said. "I can't in the house. Would you fetch my blankets? Quietly."

I hesitated, fearing that I would return to find her gone. But she hadn't moved when I returned and handed them to her. I'd brought my own as well. We each lay down on a bench in the pergola and stared up at the vines intertwining above us, a few stars visible in the purple sky.

"I can't stay with the Hallgartens," she said.

"Where else is there to go?"

She didn't answer. I wanted nothing more than to stay with the Hallgartens as long as we could. Thomasine and I would become friends, my father would set up a new photographic studio in Berkeley, we would find a new place to live nearby, and we would no longer be so alone.

*   *   *

On Friday morning, Algernon arrived with two of Mr. Hallgarten's managers, and Mrs. Hallgarten insisted they join us for breakfast before they all drove to the paper company's temporary headquarters in Oakland. The men helped Mrs. Hallgarten carry the stove outdoors so she could cook in the open air; the chimney inspector wasn't expected until afternoon. Mr. Hallgarten and Peter removed two doors from their hinges and laid them on barrels in the backyard. Mrs. Hallgarten floated tablecloths over them, the doorknobs forming awkward lumps. She and the maid—a new one, Delia, who seemed much more nervous than the previous one—brought out rye toast and butter and jam, and we ate in silence under a rough gray smear of sky. At least in the backyard, we couldn't see the city still on fire.

My father had hollows under his eyes. Karelia, too, looked listless and uncomfortable. Only Peter Visser seemed cheerful. From time to time, when a bird flew near, he would rise to peer at it and tell us its name. "Red-shafted flicker," he said, or, "Bullock's Oriole."

"I've not forgotten about your Book of Months, Arthur," Mr. Hallgarten said. "Immediately after breakfast, I'll search for it."

I busied myself eating the crusts of my toast.

"What is the Book of Months?" Peter asked.

Mr. Hallgarten cocked an eyebrow at my father, who shrugged. Mr. Hallgarten explained the project, how I had stood for the camera every day of my life. Mrs. Hallgarten set before Karelia and me plates of soft-boiled eggs on a half-slice of rye. "There are only a few eggs left—they go to the women and children."

Karelia turned pale at the sight of them and swallowed. Mrs. Hallgarten said, "Are you all right, my dear?"

Karelia tried to smile at her. "Thank you, it looks delicious."

I poked at my own egg. Accustomed to hard-boiled, I didn't know what to do with this quivering substance that threatened to spill from its perch.

"You have to eat it like this," Thomasine said. She lifted her own off the plate, and with a swoop of her head, bit savagely. I imitated her, and her sisters giggled.

"Thomasine!" her mother said.

Head still bent, Thomasine flashed me a mischievous look, and I couldn't help but smile.

After Mrs. Hallgarten went back into the kitchen, Karelia said she would give me her egg if I promised to eat it normally. She nearly didn't wait for my reply to swish it over to me with her knife.

My father recounted his efforts to retrieve his negatives from the studio. Peter repeated his story of how he'd recovered some of his paintings;

Mr. Hallgarten told of hurrying toward one of his stationery warehouses only to see, even before he reached it, singed scraps floating down.

"And what about your photographs?" Sophie asked Karelia.

"My photographs?" she said, startled.

"Like the one *Papa* had hanging in the living room," she said. "We like it very much."

Karelia straightened a little. "All of my photographs and prints burned too," she said, waving her fork in a little upward spiral as if to sketch their disappearance in smoke, as if the loss were not great. I hoped Mr. Hallgarten would extol her work, but he was listening intently to Algernon Locksley. He wiped his mouth with his napkin and said he would go look for my father's portfolio.

Algernon looked at him with anguish.

"It will take only a moment, Algernon."

As we carried our plates to the sink, someone banged at the door. Thomasine answered it and said, "Father, two soldiers have come to see you."

The soldiers told him they needed his help in transporting dynamite in San Francisco; he was one of only two people in Berkeley to own a car at that time, and automobiles were badly needed.

"I'm a businessman," he protested, "and I have so many affairs to look into today."

"We'll borrow your car, then, and return it when we've finished," one of the soldiers said.

"Hang on." Mr. Hallgarten grabbed his coat. "Algernon, I'll have to leave you in charge of our efforts today," he said almost happily, as if relieved to escape his responsibilities. "I place every trust in your decisions, and you have the authority to do as you see fit."

Peter asked if he could accompany Mr. Hallgarten to the city, so he could find out if anything remained of his studio. My father wanted to go, too, but Mrs. Hallgarten insisted that her husband drop him off at the hospital in Berkeley instead. Mr. Hallgarten searched his pockets until he found his driving gloves, wriggling his fingers into them with pleasure.

As the men went out, Mr. Hallgarten said, "But must it be dynamite?" He began negotiating with the soldiers, to see if he could be a carrier of water or medical supplies instead.

*   *   *

Thomasine motioned me out onto the narrow balcony off the living room. She pulled two chairs next to each other for us to sit on and tucked the back of a third underneath the doors' latch handles. "I'm keeping my sisters out," she said. "I get so tired of them sometimes."

Happy that she wanted my company, I traced the apple-shaped cutouts in the balcony wall's wooden boards with my fingers, trying not to look across the bay to the blackened stubble of the city.

She wriggled her feet out of her shoes and stockings and tucked them beneath her on her chair, massaging her toes, gazing across the bay pensively. "What was it like?" she said.

I described the destroyed buildings and the things I'd seen people rescue: pianos, sewing machines, canaries in cages. Wanting to impress her, I began to embellish, adding a woman with a panther on a leash, men hoisting a suit of armor above their heads.

"Did you see your father's studio blow up?" she said.

In my telling, the explosives shot flames fifty feet in the air and left us deaf for hours. I described my father running into the Murchison Building, the terrible moments when it seemed he might never come out, his emergence with an injured arm. I didn't look at her, afraid that she might find my father's actions crazy.

"What about his business?" she asked. "Did he have insurance on it?"

I shrugged. "I don't know, I suppose so."

"With one company?"

I spread my hands in the air, baffled.

"My father's business is insured with several German companies, but they haven't responded yet," she said. "I heard him talking about them with Algernon this morning before breakfast. It's going to be a disaster."

"Why?"

She shrugged and was silent for a while. I became aware of her arm on her chair's armrest next to me, the fine down above her wrist where her sleeve had ridden up, the faint blue rivers of her veins beneath the surface of her skin. I had been a little wary of her, of her confidence, her capacity for mockery, but now I saw that she was also vulnerable, that the earthquake had disrupted her sense of safety, too. I wanted to rest my hand on hers.

Then her mother rattled the doors and beckoned us to come inside.

*   *   *

A little later, when Thomasine had settled into the pergola with a book, I decided to retrieve the Book of Months; Mr. Hallgarten was still in the city, Sophie and Adele were sewing, and Mrs. Hallgarten was meeting with members of her Hillside Club committee in the living room. So I asked Thomasine if I could borrow one of the books in her room. Without looking up, she waved her hand toward the house and turned the page.

Her room looked much the same as it had in January, except that she'd acquired a globe for her desk. It was so finely balanced that it rotated on its axis at the slightest touch. Once again, I felt something enchanted about her room. How I envied her for having a bed, curtains, a soft rug on the floor, a desk with a neat bookshelf above it.

The walking stick, however, was missing. How would I push the Book of Months out? I hunted under the bed and in every corner

of the room. Nothing. I would have to find some other way. I heard
steps in the hallway and ducked out of sight on the other side of the
armoire. Even though Thomasine had given me permission to go into
her room, I felt that one look at me would reveal that I was up to something. I listened while the steps went down the hall, then returned and
descended the stairs.

I opened the armoire and felt around at the back. The walking stick
leaned diagonally behind Thomasine's clothes. Relieved, I used it to fish
behind the armoire, careful to make as little noise as possible.

The stick slid freely along the baseboard.

Panicking, I pushed it back and forth. Had the Book of Months
somehow slipped underneath? I knelt in front of the armoire and swung
the stick along the small gap carved out at the base, retrieving only dust
fluffs and a miniature wooden pig.

Perhaps Thomasine had found the Book of Months and returned
it to her father's study. If so, then Mr. Hallgarten would find it
and I needn't worry. Thomasine had said nothing of it to me, but she
may have thought it best to conceal her discovery. Or possibly the maid
had given the room a thorough cleaning and come across it. If she had,
she would have read the dedication my father had written to Mr. Hallgarten and known to return it to him.

I returned the walking stick to its place. When I closed the armoire,
I was startled to see Thomasine watching me from the doorway, amused.

"What are you doing?" she asked.

"I was—I was envying your armoire," I said.

She came into the room. "I thought you might be trying on my
dresses."

I shook my head, blushing.

"What book did you pick?"

A copy of Jack London's *Call of the Wild* was the only one visible on the bookshelf from here, so I named it.

"Then come down and read it beside me," she said. "Why else do you think I was sitting in the pergola?"

I grabbed the book and followed her down, happy that she wanted my company. If she'd been the one to discover the Book of Months, she was concealing it very well.

*   *   *

My father returned from the hospital before lunch, his right arm bound in a cast, the tips of his fingers emerging like little pigs in blankets. At least three bones had been fractured, they'd told him. The doctors had given him a bottle of Aspirin, but he looked, if anything, more miserable than ever. He could be persuaded to take only a few bites of food. Afterward, Mrs. Hallgarten and her daughters headed to the church to sew garments and sheets for the refugees flooding the city.

The three of us were left alone in the house. Karelia motioned me outside, and we stood on the back step, looking out into the Hallgartens' yard.

"She isn't as I'd imagined her to be."

"Who?"

"Celeste. I *like* her. To hear him talk of her, you would think she never said a kind word to him. But she seems to love him. Perhaps realizing her husband could have died reminded her of that."

I wondered how Mr. Hallgarten had described his wife to Karelia. "I like her too," I said, which was true, although I also remembered her laughing when my father had described his project, the neutral way she'd said that he was either a genius or a madman, as if either were a possibility.

"And their children," Karelia continued. "I never thought about them before. It's almost unbearable to see them. This morning, the little one—Adele, is that her name?—gave me a pressed red poppy she'd been keeping between the pages of a book. She wanted me to have it, she said. I told her I had no place to keep it safe, and she said she would keep it for me in her book until I did."

Probably Adele was looking for an ally, tired of always being bossed around by her sisters. But I didn't say this.

"It has to stop," Karelia said, so quietly I almost didn't hear her.

I remembered the many nights she'd spent at lectures at the Camera Club, the time I thought I'd smelled Mr. Hallgarten's pipe smoke on her. I'd wondered if she'd run into him, but I hadn't considered they might have deliberately arranged to meet there. Or she may not have attended lectures at all.

"What do you mean?" I asked.

She looked around, as if neighbors might overhear. Inside, the Hallgarten's maid was sweeping the kitchen floor. "We have to make plans. There's no place to talk here."

I offered to take Karelia to the canyon the Hallgartens had showed me. When I went to tell my father we were going out, the living room was empty. I called for him. Had he gone to cross the bay? I ran out but didn't see him on the street.

I found my father outside the door to Mr. Hallgarten's study, gazing in despair at the heaps of papers and objects crowding the little desk. The room was in even greater disorder than I'd last seen it; some of the piles rose higher than my knee, and they all slid into each other. The small bed's sheets and coverlet were thrown back and twisted. My father didn't seem to be aware that his left hand was opening and closing. The strange quality of silence that I'd noticed when Karelia was away in Canada hung around him like a cloud, so thickly that I found it difficult to speak myself—it was as if he were a distant figure on the horizon, so far away that there was no possibility of reaching him.

I shut the door. "Karelia and I are going for a walk in the canyon,"

I said. "Do you want to come with us?" Karelia would be upset with me, because she wouldn't be able to talk freely in front of him, but I couldn't bear the thought of leaving him alone.

He shook his head. He did allow me to lead him downstairs to the living room, where he lay on the floor and arranged his blanket over himself. When I moved to leave, he grasped my hand. "I tried to save them," he said. "I may have made it as far as the third floor. I don't remember everything yet—I was on the landing, and a beam fell, or some object—"

"It's all right," I said.

He sat up and looked me directly in the eye, which was unusual for him. "How long was I in the building?" he asked.

He wanted an exact number from me. Usually I would have been able to supply it, but I realized that I had no idea. My sense of time appeared to have slipped for the length of his disappearance, which alarmed me—I had thought it an ability I could rely on always. "Eleven and a half minutes," I said firmly, though it had seemed much longer and was likely much shorter than that. The precision seemed to reassure him.

"Thank you," he said, and lay down again.

I was still worried that once I left, he would spring up to go hunting for the Book of Months. But I couldn't think of anything to say to stop him.

Outside, it was overcast. Karelia and I walked eastward, not looking behind us at the city smoldering. If we had, we might have noticed rain clouds gathering on the horizon, but we might have thought they were only smoke. Bees drew lines through the air, vireos flitted.

I told her that I'd found my father standing outside Mr. Hallgarten's study, that I'd led him away.

"We need Arthur to pull himself together," she said. "We have to find another place to stay. You understand, don't you? I made a terrible mistake."

I didn't want to hear more. We had had such good fortune in having Mr. Hallgarten as our patron. If she had remained friendly and cordial to him but not allowed love to bloom, we would never have lost his support. And now it seemed that all those months when my father had glumly forged on without his backer, Karelia had been meeting Mr. Hallgarten secretly, no doubt eating wonderful meals with him, talking about the nature of time and art. Why hadn't she confided in me? She had never kept secrets from me before, or if she had, she kept them so sloppily that it was as if she wanted me to know them.

"Where would we go?" I asked. At breakfast, one of Mr. Hallgarten's managers had described the rumors about the camps at the university—crowded and noisy, long lines to obtain food and blankets. I didn't want to leave the Hallgartens. "Why don't you just both keep pretending?"

It must have come out a little more harshly than I meant it to, because she winced.

I wondered where she and Mr. Hallgarten had been meeting. At school I'd heard rumors that certain French restaurants in the city—the Maison Dorée, the Maison Riche, the Poulet d'Or—provided places for assignations on their upper floors, above the ground-floor dining room. A separate entrance on a side street led up to small private dining rooms and suites on the second floor. The restaurant's food was so delicious, the service so sophisticated, that even the most upstanding citizens ate there, even though they knew what went on above. But I couldn't imagine Karelia and Mr. Hallgarten there. I felt I didn't know her anymore.

A gust of wind blew off the ill-fitting hat she wore. She chased it down and came back. "I'm sorry," she said. "I never thought—I'm sorry I've kept secrets from you. Thomas and I—" She wiped her cheeks and seemed to grow calmer. "I'll make a true break now."

She stopped and took my hands in hers. "I wish we had relatives who lived nearby who could take us in. You've been too alone all your life without a proper family, without even anyone your age for companions. The three of us—we haven't managed to take root yet, somehow."

"Thomasine is my age," I said.

She made a face.

I pulled away from her and kept walking. "We don't even know for certain if our apartment burned down or not."

She shook her head. "It's a good thing everything has been destroyed and lost—we're all freed now. Arthur can let go of his project. He'll recover and be able to build a steady life. I've always feared what would happen for you if he became famous for this project. You'd be known as a scientific specimen."

At the canyon's rim, she drew in a breath at the rolling grassy sweep of the canyon below. The creek wound along the bottom, just as I remembered, and the only trees were those along its banks, as if drawn to the water like bees to pollen.

"It's one minute to three," I said. "The last two days, I didn't feel it approaching."

"What does it feel like?"

"Like a pressure, here." I touched the back of my neck. I'd never told her before.

We waited. I considered what Karelia had said, that my father would recover, as if the project were a kind of disease. Whenever illness had kept me from a session, I had felt guilty and disappointed. Even after Karelia refused to act as his successor, I had assumed another photographer would carry on the project. Or I would click the shutter myself. I imagined gray streaking my hair, my wrinkled hand reaching for the trigger, day after day, until one day when I could not. The chain of photographs linked me to the far end of life. If the project never resumed, that chain would be broken.

"Now the feeling is gone," I said.

"It's not natural to feel the approach of an hour. It sounds a lot like dread."

"I don't know."

"What does it feel like, not to have been photographed just now? Are you sad?"

I considered. "I feel lighter." It was true—it was as if I'd been carrying around something heavy and precious all my life, like a gold crown, and when I finally set it down, I felt as if I could float. Now that everything was lost, anything was possible.

She put her arm around me. "I'm glad you told me," she said. "It's time for us both to find our freedom."

I wanted to ask her what that might mean, but the sky darkened further and rain began to pelt down. We put our jackets over our heads and ran back to the Hallgartens.

CHAPTER EIGHT

Rain fell all evening. While we waited in the living room for Mr. Hallgarten and Peter Visser to return, my father kept trying to reconstruct what had happened in the Murchison Building, turning images over and over as he told us about the thick smoke, the noise of glass shattering from the heat. He had skidded on an unexpected scattering of pennies on the second floor landing—where had they come from? What he found the most terrible was the disorientation that came over him the higher he went. "At one point, I found myself thinking I had climbed too far—which is absurd, because my studio is on the top floor." He sent a look of appeal toward Mrs. Hallgarten, whose expression was a mixture of sympathy and unease, or perhaps impatience, because my father had repeated this sentence several times in the past hour. He shook his head. "I don't even remember deciding to turn around. I came up to a wall of fire—but was it ahead of me on the stairs, or to the side? If I had continued going up—"

"You wouldn't be alive now," Karelia said gently, for the fifth time.

Mrs. Hallgarten said she had delayed dinner as long as she could, and that we would begin eating without the men. When we were halfway through our sandwiches, they returned, sodden and depleted. In place of the soldiers, they brought two refugees.

Mrs. Hallgarten seemed taken aback to have more people to look after. But she recovered quickly and greeted them both, sending Thomasine to fetch some clothes from upstairs so they could change into something dry. Peter introduced them as Sebastian and Bee Crowley, brother and sister, both artists, former students of his at the Mark Hopkins Institute. He had run into them while searching the ruins of his studio, he said, which hadn't burned but instead collapsed in an after-shock. They'd helped him recover a few paintings. "And look," he said, holding up a little Delft vase. "This used to stand on my windowsill—it's unharmed save for a little chip on the rim." He gazed at it in wonder. "We weren't so lucky," Sebastian Crowley said. "We lost everything." When Thomasine returned with an armful of garments, he lifted them mournfully, as if expecting them to vanish, too.

Because she still couldn't cook indoors, and the rain was too heavy, Mrs. Hallgarten served a cold potato salad she'd made earlier in the day, as well as cold asparagus, with bread and jam for dessert. She apologized for the mediocrity of the dinner. Karelia noticed me watching her eat desultorily and made a show of forking a potato into her mouth.

Hungry all the time, I took a third helping.

*   *   *

The soldiers had requested that Mr. Hallgarten meet them in the city the next morning. The fires had been beaten back almost entirely, so he agreed to let my father and me accompany him, to see if anything remained of our studio or our home. Karelia insisted on coming too. Mr. Hallgarten seemed to have decided not to look Karelia in the eyes.

Next to me in the back seat, Karelia stared at Mr. Hallgarten's head as if trying to see his thoughts. In light of what had happened to the city and its people, everything seemed frivolous: Karelia's affair, my father's project.

Mr. Hallgarten dropped the three of us off in the general area where we believed the Murchison Building had once been, and we walked through the blasted plain that stretched from the Ferry Building all the way to Van Ness Avenue, the air a haze of steam and partic-ulates. A muck of damp ash clung to our shoes and gave off a burnt odor. Streetcar wires had melted into the asphalt, looping up in places like segments of a sea monster. The fire had picked this part of the city clean—nearly 500 blocks consumed, according to the newspaper. Here and there, skeletal fingers of steel and masonry pointed to the sky, but all the buildings were gone.

It took us an hour to find the cornerstone with the Murchison Building's name on it, the letters' grooves nearly filled in with ash. People walked past us with curiosity as we dug through the rubble. Eventually I unearthed an object like a small log. I brushed it off, revealing what seemed to be fused iridescent glass, its surface rippled like hardened lava. It was warm to the touch, as if alive. I knelt and pulled out two more shapes, all made of the same substance.

"What are they?" I asked.

"They were my glass plate negatives," my father said.

Karelia put an arm around both of us.

My father lowered himself onto the rubble and cradled the shapes in his lap, staring at them in disbelief. Here were the remnants of all my days.

After a while, my father placed them one by one into a suitcase.

"Why are you taking them?" Karelia asked, alarmed.

Did he hope he could reconstruct them somehow, unmelt the melted? How I had admired his persistence all my life—I had adopted it for myself, as a badge of honor, knowing that the great never gave up.

He closed the suitcase and fumbled with the latch. "They will serve as a reminder to me that time always seeks to outwit us, that even the very record of time is not safe from permutation."

When we found the place where our apartment building had stood, he seemed not to see it, lost in his dreams. I realized that every one of the apartment buildings we'd lived in around the city must have burned—seven or eight of them. I tried to picture each one in relation to where we sat, to remember what it was like to step out onto the street from each one. It was as if the numbers on a clock had been removed, and the hands, too.

*   *   *

On our return, the Vissers and the Crowleys were in the backyard. Members of Berkeley's relief committee had dropped off tents and boxes of clothing and food that had been donated from all over the country. My father disappeared into the house.

Sebastian Crowley helped Peter unroll the tents on the damp grass behind the Hallgartens' house. They regarded them with bafflement. "These were designed for military minds," Sebastian said. "We'll have to think like soldiers to assemble them." He threaded rope through holes in a pair of wooden pegs. Soon, having knotted the ropes into an unusable tangle, he threw them to the ground.

"My father is good at putting things together," I suggested.

"Then where is he?" Sebastian said. "People like that usually love to start right in and show everyone else how to do it."

I had to admit I didn't know where he was. I worried that he was lying on the Hallgartens' living room floor.

Bee Crowley seemed to have an instinct for untangling. By the time my father emerged, the men had managed to erect four tents, each one large enough for two or three people.

Ina, Karelia, and Bee cooked dinner on a bonfire, and we lined up to receive a pile of beans on a carefully washed scrap of tin, its sharp edges folded in on themselves to make a sort of plate, which one had to hold carefully, because it conducted heat well. We sat on rocks. Ina found a note in a loaf of bread she was slicing—it asked that if anyone knew of the whereabouts of John Tierney, they should send him to Arvid's Bakery, 1120 Gough Street. We ate gingerly, in case of another message.

My father seemed less agitated now, lost in thought, but I watched

Karelia with concern. She fiddled with her hair, ran her hands over her face. Soon, she scraped half her plate onto mine, saying that as a growing young man, I needed it more than she.

She said, "I should write my family in Canada to tell them we're all right. I'm sure everyone else has letters to write. I'm going into the house to ask for stationery and ink." She walked quickly away, as if worried someone might call out that they had plenty of stationery to share.

She reappeared, hands full of supplies, too soon to have had a talk with Thomas, and in any case it was hard to imagine where she could have conducted such a conversation in the house. But she must have contrived, then or soon after, to get a message to him, because the next morning, when I was eating toast with the others, Karelia came down the hill through the grass, the hem of her dress wet with dew. "Where were you?" I asked. She had a radiance about her that I didn't trust.

"I woke early, and the morning was so beautiful I couldn't help going for a walk," she said. "I saw a family of deer gliding through the canyon—a doe, a buck, and three small ones."

"You shouldn't walk there alone," Sebastian said. "What if you met a mountain lion?"

"I never felt alone," she said.

I offered to make her toast, but she told me she'd already eaten.

*   *   *

The next morning, Mrs. Hallgarten brought us a box of old shoes some of the neighbors had gathered. She chatted for a while with Ina and Karelia while they shelled peas for lunch.

When Karelia stood to bring her bowl over to Ina, she sat down again quickly, her jaw clenched.

"What is it?" Mrs. Hallgarten asked.

"I think I have a bit of an inner ear infection—it's really nothing."

"Why don't you come with me into the house? I might have something for that."

Karelia hesitated, then agreed.

What if Karelia had a terrible disease and was concealing it from all of us? Perhaps Mrs. Hallgarten had guessed what it was. Karelia so rarely suffered from any ailment—she always claimed that growing up on a farm had made her immune to everything—that her behavior recently alarmed me. Sometimes when I was a child, I had lain awake in the middle of the night fearing that she would die, like my mother.

When they had gone into the house, I followed them inside. Mrs. Hallgarten led Karelia into the pantry and shut the door. It was a small room, I knew, dank with the smell of potatoes. A large glass jar on the counter held pickles. I pressed my ear to the door, watchful for the appearance of the family or any of the artists.

"Your mother died when you were very young, is that correct?" Mrs. Hallgarten said.

"Yes."

"I'm sorry—that must have been terrible. I hope you'll think of me as a mother. I'm concerned that your uncle may not have been able to provide the guidance that a young woman needs."

"My uncle has taught me a great deal," Karelia said.

"Please don't take offense. But there's more going on with you than an ear infection, isn't there?"

"It's only a cold, I'm sorry to alarm you," Karelia said, sounding suffocated.

"I've carried three children myself, Karelia—I know the changes the body undergoes."

There was a long silence.

"Thomas and I feel that all of you are under our care, and I'm very concerned about your uncle. I should talk to Thomas and see what kind of solution we might devise."

"Please don't speak of this to anyone, not even your husband," Karelia said. "Please promise me, I couldn't bear it. And it may be that I simply have a touch of something."

Mrs. Hallgarten asked, "Who is the young man? Is marriage a possibility?"

Another long silence. Finally, in a voice so low I could hardly make out the words, Karelia said, "I'm so ashamed." Kneeling outside the door, I held my breath, afraid to hear more, afraid to leave. "I was in love with an artist who'd come from Florence to study painting, and he said he would marry me as soon as he'd established himself and could support us. I knew Arthur didn't want me to leave him and Joseph, so I kept it secret. He made me many promises, all with such passion that I believed him. I let myself be—carried away." She said again, "I'm so ashamed."

Fear took hold of me. My mother had died giving birth to me. Now Karelia could be in danger.

"And where is this man now?"

"A couple of weeks before the earthquake, he returned to Italy where—so he said—he was engaged to his childhood sweetheart."

Mrs. Hallgarten made a noise of disgust. I glanced behind me, hoping no one else would enter the room. If they did, I would say I had come in for a drink of water.

"Does he have relatives?"

"His relatives all live in Italy, and even if I knew where to find them, I couldn't make any claim on them."

"This camp is not an ideal place for a woman in a delicate condition. The men can be rowdy, there's a chance you might catch something. If you don't feel able to go to your relatives in Canada, you would be much better off in the main camp, where there's a separate place for pregnant woman. Or in a home for unwed mothers—the Salvation Army has one in Oakland. Afterward, your child would go to a family who yearn for children, a family who can provide a good home."

Karelia was quiet. Then she said, "I've thought about the other possibilities, of course. It might be easier for me to give up a child if I hadn't already raised one. Would you care to have one of your daughters growing up among strangers? Wouldn't you be haunted your entire life?"

"I fault your uncle. This wouldn't have happened if he weren't so absorbed in his strange ideas. I don't see how he'll be able to support you and Joseph, let alone a new child. If you stay here, it will be impossible to keep your secret for long. What will my daughters make of it, do you think? How should I explain your condition to them, to my neighbors?"

I could barely hear Karelia's reply: "Please, let it remain a secret for as long as possible. I'll leave rather than disrupt your lives. Shall I write to my relatives in Canada?"

"I'm sorry to press you," Mrs. Hallgarten said, softening her voice. "I don't mean to be harsh. You look pale now, you should lie down. I'll give you the name of my doctor. See him as soon as you can. Tell Bee and Ina that I said they should make appointments, too, that way no one will think it unusual. Women must take special care to look after their health. In the meantime, I'll think about your situation. And we'll talk again. Will you promise me to do nothing rash?"

"Yes," Karelia said. "I promise, but please don't tell anyone, not even your husband. I can't bear for anyone to know."

I backed away as swiftly as I could and fled the kitchen. I ran to the canyon and threw myself onto a slab of rock near the grove of alders. The stone was hot from the sun and crossed by a line of ants. I let them crawl over me. I couldn't picture Karelia in Canada. But I couldn't say anything to her about what I'd overheard. It seemed unfair to me that she had blamed Fulvio for her condition—he had offered to marry her, after all, and she had turned him down. But of course she couldn't have told Mrs. Hallgarten that her own husband was the father. How foolish I was to have admired Mr. Hallgarten so unguardedly, how naive I was not to have noticed that she kept meeting with him long after we thought he had abandoned us.

I told myself that Karelia was young and strong, that she would be fine. Soon I would have a brother or a sister. But then I corrected myself. The baby wouldn't be my sibling, because Karelia was not my mother.

*   *   *

The men built a bonfire in the evenings, and we huddled around it, trying to soak up as much warmth as we could before turning in. The artists lamented the loss of their work and speculated about the fate of their favorite haunts.

"We used to go drink at Coppa's and vie to be wittiest," Sebastian said. "We're not going to be able to go on painting dreamy landscapes the way we used to. We were pretending we wouldn't die. Or at least I was."

Sebastian and Bee Crowley both had straight hair as shiny and black as onyx. I found Sebastian a little intimidating; his icy blue eyes flicked here and there, as if licking everything he saw and finding the taste bitter or flat. But he treated his sister with tenderness, so I had some grudging liking for him. Bee was short and birdlike, her hands smaller than Thomasine's. She moved delicately, as if she had to be careful lest she snap a bone through too much vigor. She signed her work "B. Crowley," she told Karelia. "You have to use an initial, if you're a woman and want your work taken seriously."

Tuesday night after dinner, Thomasine invited me to sit on the balcony with her to watch the stars come out. It was six days since the quake, and I hadn't seen much of her or her sisters—Berkeley parents were keeping their children indoors, as if lawless refugees stalked the hills looking to kidnap anyone they could. Or perhaps it was just due to an awareness of the instability of everything, the way the earth might flex and warp beneath a family at any minute, and it was important to stay close together.

Thomasine seemed content to sit with me, and so we stared at the city across the bay as its blackened ruin slowly disappeared in the twilight. It seemed to me we were bound to each other in some way. That she had seen me as no one else my age had—unclothed from infancy to my present stage of youth—meant something important, though I couldn't have said what. It was only one of several imbalances between us—her family's greater wealth, our presence on their property, our dependence on their help—yet it struck me that this one was in my favor, that she was aware she still owed me something in the ledger of intimacy. I wanted her to know that she could trust me, that we had much in common. I leaned closer to her, as if to get a better look at the city, but it was her profile that I studied. How had I not seen before how beautiful she was?

"Do you ever wonder—" she said, then stopped.

I was trying to formulate some sort of compliment about her eyelashes when a noise came from the yard below. We stood. A figure approached the house, moving uncertainly, tracking back and forth, as if correcting course. A man I didn't recognize. Right before he was about to go out of sight beneath us, he stopped, swayed, and fell.

"*Maman*," Thomasine cried, bolting into the living room. I followed her down the stairs and out the door.

She leaned over the man lying with his face in the grass and turned him over. His eyes were closed. He wore a long greatcoat with a singed hole in the front large enough to put a hand through. His hat had fallen off, revealing a considerable mass of long, black hair. Mud caked his shoes and trousers, and the reek of earth and whiskey came off him.

Thomasine ran into the house, I thought to get her mother, but instead she returned carrying a vase of flowers. She yanked out the bouquet and upended the water over his face. I admired her quick thinking.

He sputtered and gave a shout, half rising on one elbow. A flower stem, blackened and flattened by rot, clung to his stubbled cheek.

He wiped his face and looked around, groggy. After a moment he extended his fingers toward Thomasine. She set the vase down, as if she thought he wanted her help getting up, but instead he grasped the flowers by their heads. She let go, and their stems reluctantly released from her palm.

"You need to get that hand looked after, darling," he said. She held up her palm in the moonlight: beads of blood appeared where thorns had dug in.

"I didn't notice they were roses," she said.

Mrs. Hallgarten came out and sent Thomasine back into the house, eying the vase as if the man had been caught thieving. I explained what had happened, irritated to have my moment with Thomasine broken.

"You smell of whiskey," Mrs. Hallgarten told the man.

He struggled up. "My name is Nicholas Forrester," he said. "And the whiskey is, in this case, more medicinal than diversionary." He lifted his hands in the air, showing us they were scraped and swollen. Under Mrs. Hallgarten's scrutiny, he seemed to sober up. He said that he'd crossed to Berkeley on Friday and spent a damp night in the university baseball field, jammed in a small tent with five Scotsmen. He'd come across the newspaper's list of refugees staying in Berkeley and saw his friends the Vissers and the Crowleys were at the Hallgartens'. Before he could leave, soldiers commandeered him to help them dig latrines for the camp. Three hours later, they let him go, and the Scots shared some of their whiskey. "I'm sorry to have collapsed of exhaustion on your lawn, and I'm grateful to the girl for the dash of fetid water to the face."

His voice was a raspy baritone. At the time, I assumed the inhalation of smoke had changed his tone temporarily, but as long as I knew him, he never lost that slight vibration in his vocal cords, which seemed to give his voice an extra timbre. He stood, dignified, unpleading, his wet head cocked as if listening to a far-off music. Mrs. Hallgarten sent me to fetch Peter, who expressed delight to see him. "He's an actor," Peter told her. "You have to forgive him if he can't help making a dramatic entrance."

After he had settled around the bonfire, Peter and Sebastian bombarded him with questions. First Nicholas asked for a basin of water, into which he plunged his head, holding back his long dark hair with one hand. I had thought him older, but now, clean-faced, he appeared to be in his late twenties. Ina poured him a cup of cold coffee and sliced him some bread.

Nicholas told us his story between mouthfuls. He had been writing a letter at five in the morning, for reasons he couldn't recall. Then all his furniture jerked about and snow fell. "I said to myself, 'I can't be that drunk!'" But the snow turned out to be flakes of ceiling plaster. He flung himself under his desk. A tremendous ripping noise came, followed by silence. "When I looked out, one wall had vanished, and my bed had slid right out like a biscuit from a tin. It landed on a pile of bricks, three stories below."

We wrapped ourselves in blankets against the cooling air. Nicholas attempted to cheer us with stories about his acting career, which was still young—he had left Los Angeles six months ago in the hope of finding better roles in San Francisco. We learned of actors who had had a breakdown on stage, or drank themselves out of a role, or punched or cuckolded a director. He tried to draw out some of the rest of us, handing around a flask of whiskey, which he said the Scots had insisted he take as a parting gift. The artists drank from it and seemed to brighten a little. Karelia hugged her knees, and my father remained as still as a stone.

"What do we have to keep our spirits up?" Nicholas said. "Cards? Musical instruments?"

Sebastian shook his head glumly. But Bee pulled out *Leaves of Grass* from the donation box and recited several poems in her beautiful contralto. Peter told a story about his time in Paris and said he still remembered the *chansons* taught him by a group of students he met in a bar. He drew a breath as if about to sing one, but a look from his wife silenced him.

"A song has been assembling itself in my head tonight, inspired by this remarkable bonfire before us," Nicholas said. "It may help, if my untuneful voice doesn't raise the hair on your heads." He sang in his ragged (but on-key) baritone:

> *Oh we like smoke and that's no joke*
> *We made our homes a pyre.*
> *We didn't die and that is why*
> *we gather round the fire.*

> *The flames of Hell are pretty swell*
> *But won't make us perspire.*
> *Once you're torched, you can't be scorched*
> *so gather round the fire.*

"Those are the only verses I've come up with so far," he said.

We clapped, and Peter stood, eyes glistening; he had helped himself several times to the flask. "Teach it to us, we'll sing it every night, and invent new verses, some of them obscene." He stopped short. "When there are no children around, of course."

We sang it three times, and for the first time since the earthquake—the first time in a long time—I felt happy. I remembered the plays Karelia and Violet had taken me to from time to time, how the actors had seemed another species of being entirely: they could change their very selves. Watching him among us, laughing in that easy way he had, I wanted nothing more than to be like him.

I dozed off. When I woke, my father was telling Nicholas about his project. "My goal is to document time's inscription on the body, to create a record that will endure long after the subject has passed on," he said.

It irked me that my father could refer to my death so lightly.

"But why once a day?" Nicholas asked.

"Yes, I see what you mean. Taking the photograph once a week or once a month would reduce the data to sort through and maintain."

Nicholas shook his head. "No, it's that I can't imagine doing the same thing at the same time each day for a week, let alone for years on end."

"Even after fourteen years of it, I can't imagine it myself," said Karelia.

"The month is an irregular unit marked by the vagaries of the moon," my father continued. "Seven days is as arbitrary as thirteen. Only the day is a true unit of time, representing a complete rotation of the earth. If the earth did not rotate or revolve about the sun, we would never have developed a sense of time, only of space. You would set sail for night, and you would get on the train to travel into day, but that would not be a matter of time."

"Yet isn't your project, at its heart, an artistic one?" Nicholas asked. "Isn't the painter also trying to capture the true essence of the person before him?"

"A photographer can be an artist as much as any painter," said Karelia.

Nicholas tipped his hat to her. My father, however, refused to be distracted. "For thousands of years, painters falsely portrayed the gallop of a horse, until Muybridge showed them they were wrong."

Nicholas pondered this a moment. "The camera will never be able to show us the soul," he said quietly.

We heard footsteps and saw Mr. Hallgarten approaching in the half-light of the fire. "I've come to look over the newcomer, the actor." He folded his arms.

Nicholas bowed grandly. "I'm Nicholas. You must be the lord of the manor." As Mr. Hallgarten inspected him, Nicholas returned his gaze with an aggressive cheerfulness. "The company you've assembled here couldn't be better," Nicholas continued. "Esteemed artists, provocative philosophers, beautiful women." He gestured toward Karelia, who rolled her eyes.

Mr. Hallgarten looked at Karelia and then away. "And where do you place yourself among these categories?" he asked Nicholas, his voice thin.

"Simply a humble appreciator of all three."

"As a friend of Peter, you're welcome here—I esteem him highly," Mr. Hallgarten said. "I understand that men appreciate their liquor on occasion, and I'm not one of those clamoring for the saloons to be closed for good. Yet please reassure me that you'll exhibit good sense when on my land." He collected himself and gave a wry smile. "My little fiefdom."

"No man can claim to have good sense, unless he lies or is in error," Nicholas said. "But if you're afraid I turn to liquor as a solace, then let me proclaim that I won't need any solace as long as I have such wonderful companions as these."

Mr. Hallgarten gave an irritated smile. "I'd urge you all to make good use of your time here, however long it may be. You are displaced, but you must continue your work. As your 'lord of the manor,' if that's what I am, I expect the painters to paint, the photographers to photograph, the actors to act, and in short for you to take this not as a holiday, but as a spur to greater efforts. Good night." Flinging a wave above his head as he turned, he walked back to the house.

"I hope he thinks to give us paint and canvases," said Sebastian.

"I haven't found a better patron," said Peter. "We should all be grateful that we're here and take the trouble to let him know it."

"I'm always grateful for a place to lay my head," Nicholas said. "Now whose tent will have me tonight?"

* * *

The next morning, on her way to fetch water, Ina let gave a shout; a man was bathing in the creek. It was Nicholas. He volunteered to sing while washing from then on. Once shaven and dressed in fresh clothes, he looked much better than he had on his arrival. He pulled out a pencil stub and paper from his greatcoat and quizzed everyone on what they would need to fulfill Mr. Hallgarten's mandate: paint, brushes, canvases, canvas stretchers, basins and palettes, cameras, film, a darkroom, chemicals, printing paper. For good measure, he added a cooking stove, pots and pans, a mirror, a bathtub, crates that we could use as furniture, and a cot for himself. He gave the list to me to take to Mr. Hallgarten. "When making requests of management, send the youngest in the company," he said. "Rule of thumb for actors." I found the kitchen empty, left the paper on the table, and hurried out, uncertain that Mr. Hallgarten would welcome such an extensive list.

We hardly saw Mr. Hallgarten—reestablishing his company in Oakland demanded all his time, and when my father ran into him on the street and asked if he'd had a chance to search for the Book of Months, he'd snapped that he barely had time to search for his next breath of air.

At the end of the week, the U.S. military officially took over the running of the camps at the university. Now, according to the newspaper, the refugees living there had to show a medical inspection card even to use the baths. They couldn't leave the camp after nine o'clock in the evening, liquor was banned, and all able-bodied men had to work whenever asked to, or else be banished from Berkeley. "I hear refugees are fleeing that camp in droves," Nicholas said. "But that may be the military's intention."

That Sunday, eleven days after the earthquake, Mr. Hallgarten set aside the afternoon to search for the Book of Months. My father watched the house intently. Mrs. Hallgarten had taken Thomasine with her to run errands, so Sophie and Adele commandeered me for a game of dominoes under the pergola. "Ordinary rules," Sophie said, shuffling the ivory tiles with authoritative clacks. With the air of a mother hen watching her chicks peck at corn, she watched us choose our seven bones; I understood how much Thomasine usually checked her, how much Sophie relished her power now, which in this case came from knowing the rules exactly as they had been handed down by tradition.

At last, Mr. Hallgarten emerged from the house; the slow drag of his legs betrayed that he hadn't found the album.

"I must have left it in my office in San Francisco after all," he said. "I'm sorry, Arthur. It's gone."

"You said that you had yet to open the safe in your office," my father said. "When it cools—"

"It was damaged in the earthquake—breached by a falling beam. All its contents are ash."

"I suggest that I look myself in your study—" my father said in a low, reasonable voice.

"Arthur, that will not be possible."

"—perhaps you set it down on a table and it fell behind, or slipped it by mistake into a trunk—"

"We've looked everywhere. That is all."

My father moved close to Mr. Hallgarten and dropped his voice. "The Book of Months represents the essence of my project. I selected each image to show the project at its best advantage—the loss of everything else is not important if I still have this to build on, as a foundation, as evidence at the very least." He seemed to have forgotten his assertion that the day was the only valid unit of time. His left hand clenched and unclenched, and he looked at the house as if disassembling it in his mind. "Time will take everything from us, in the end," he said. "To misplace things, to forget them, to allow oneself to cease valuing something one has valued, these are the marks of a fool."

He headed past Mr. Hallgarten toward the street. Mr. Hallgarten gave a venomous glance at my father's departing back. When my father reached the street, he turned and disappeared from view. I watched him go in anguish, knowing it was my carelessness that had caused this, and my cowardice that led him to blame Mr. Hallgarten.

"What an impossible fellow," murmured Sebastian.

Mr. Hallgarten closed his eyes. When he opened them, he smiled, though his eyes remained still. "A man who attempts the impossible will have a difficult time in this world," he said. He met Karelia's gaze for a moment; she lowered them, and her color deepened.

Sophie swept the dominoes into their bag, handed this to Adele, and picked up the little table; the two sisters followed their father into the house, and the door closed behind them.

*   *   *

By suppertime, my father still hadn't returned.

"It's not the first time he's gone for a long walk so he can be alone and think," Karelia said. "He's probably having dinner right now in a restaurant. He'll be back soon enough. It's not good for you to worry about him or feel responsible for him all the time."

I was worried about her too. She'd eaten only a mouthful of Ina's Spanish bean soup. I worried she was losing weight. Like all the women in the camp, she wore long, flowing gowns, following the custom of Berkeley, so it was hard to tell.

"I'll finish it in a while," she said. "I had too much lunch." But she had only nibbled on a potato then, as far as I remembered.

Peter mentioned that the relief committee had set up a job bureau for refugees, and the men began discussing their trepidations and their desire for money. Then it began to rain, first light pinpricks of water, followed by thick drops that left dark, coin-sized patches on the ground. We set our dishes out to let the water rinse them clean and dove into our tents. I joined Bee and Karelia, because I couldn't stand the thought of waiting alone in my tent. I left their tent flap open a crack so I could keep an eye out for my father's return. Meanwhile, I pondered what might have become of the Book of Months. Could Mrs. Hallgarten have discovered it? If she had, why wouldn't she have brought it to her husband? Could Adele or Sophie have stolen it? Every option seemed unlikely—I'd concealed it so thoroughly. If not for the downpour, I would have run to the house that very moment and found some way to look again in Thomasine's room. Surely it must still be there, behind the armoire.

The rain pattered constantly on the fabric above us. While Karelia and Bee played cards, I read the *Kalevala*, finding some comfort in the loping rhythm of the words. I'd never tried to read it straight through before, and now it seemed more brilliant and strange than ever. Twice I reread the tale of Lemminkainen, who is killed by a serpent during an adventure and then, in the underworld, chopped into five pieces and scattered in the river of death. Far away, at home, his aged mother sees blood oozing from his hair-brush and knows this means he's been killed. She hunts everywhere for him. At last, she rakes his pieces out of the river and restores him to wholeness and to life with her magic. What if Lemminkainen's mother had been unable to find every piece? What if the currents had taken her son's head or heart out to sea before she could retrieve it? Yet he seemed good as new, just as reckless as before.

By nightfall, not even the *Kalevala* could calm me. I hoped my father was sheltering under a tree, waiting for the rain to lessen. Perhaps he had been caught by police after curfew and put in jail. Or some Berkeley resident had taken pity on him and invited him to stay on their porch. He would return soon, I told myself. I drifted into an uneasy, dreamless sleep, woken at intervals by a feeling that the ground was shaking. "Should we go looking for him?" I asked Karelia. "Should we tell the Hallgartens?"

"No!" she cried, with such vehemence that she startled even Bee. "No," Karelia repeated, laying down a trio of cards. "The last thing we should do is bother Thomas about Arthur."

"Not all of those are clubs," Bee observed, watching her with curiosity.

Karelia thrust the cards back into her hand. Now I was afraid she suspected that something terrible had happened to my father, or that he was even now trying to end his life.

The rain seemed to have stopped. "I'm going to go look for him," I said.

"It's too dark in here for cards anyway," she said. "I could use a walk."

I followed her out and down the street, passing a couple of half-built houses until the road turned into a dirt path. "What if thieves robbed him?" I said. "What if he was hiking along the canyon and fell and injured himself? Or a mountain lion attacked him?"

"What if he was invited to supper by a lonely widow?" Karelia said. "What if he found a camera lying on the ground and began photographing the dark?"

After a moment, she said, "Why are you walking like that?"

I hadn't realized I'd been moving differently. When I was agitated, it sometimes comforted me to practice imitating. Peter moved with a kind of leisurely drawl, a hesitation at the knee, which I'd mastered, but as I'd watched him more closely, I'd realized I'd missed that he splayed his feet. To perform both at the same time was harder than I'd suspected.

If I was walking with Peter's gait, as I was now, then I didn't have to be myself.

"You're often moving strangely. And many times when I look over at you, you're contorting your face. I'm afraid we raised you all wrong," she said.

After an hour of walking through the hills, calling for my father, we returned to the camp. The rain had started up again and continued all night long.

*   *   *

My father was still missing in the morning. Peter suggested that we organize a search party, but no one could think of habitual places my father tended to go. Ina insisted on telling Mr. Hallgarten so that he could notify the police.

Early in the afternoon, a policeman came to the camp. The owners of one of the ranches in the canyon had found a man sleeping on a pile of straw that morning, and when they'd approached him, he'd seemed confused and couldn't or wouldn't tell them his name.

I leaped up and said I would go. Karelia told Nicholas to accompany me. "You're the most charming of us," she said, "in case charm is necessary."

"My charm doesn't tend to cast its spell on policemen," Nicholas muttered. But he agreed.

In the marshal's office, my father seemed both embarrassed and relieved to see us. Marshal Vollmer scrutinized us when we introduced ourselves. "A little food and coffee seems to have revived him," Vollmer said. He was perhaps in his early thirties, with a long, narrow face and green eyes that seemed to observe searchingly, as if he were memorizing everything and everyone he looked at.

"How are you doing, Arthur?" Nicholas said with too much brightness, as if they were old friends meeting on the street after many years. The marshal seemed to make him nervous.

My father got to his feet. He was old, it occurred to me. He'd been nearly fifty when I was born, and now he was in his sixties. His hair had receded, and a fine network of wrinkles had branched across his face, and he was thin.

"I'm fine," he said. He nodded to me in greeting.

"He was telling me his theories of time," Vollmer said, speaking to Nicholas, who looked out of place in the office, with his wild hair and beard, like a prospector or mountain man. "May I have a word with you before you go?"

As we left, my father said to Vollmer, "If time is a current, and we are swept along in its pace, then we can't expect to feel its motion. That's why no sense organ has evolved to detect the passage of time directly. We are like those fish at the depths of the ocean, where no light ever penetrates, and so they have never grown eyes."

The marshal's eyes glittered with interest.

My father and I waited on the street. If he was upset with me, he didn't show it. He seemed lost in thought. "What were you telling the marshal?" I asked.

"I told him I'd been considering the way each of the five senses apprehends time. Only images and sounds can be recorded, allowing us to compare one moment with another. Not far in the future, some inventor will devise a way to record odors, tastes, tactile sensations, but until then, we have to judge sight and hearing as superior—" He broke off. "I'm sorry, I'm carried away again, aren't I?"

Nicholas joined us after a moment, his face solemn, and we walked back. While the women fed my father lunch, Nicholas said the marshal had asked him numerous questions, which he'd answered as evasively as he could. "He seemed concerned that your father might not be—" he hesitated—"capable of looking after you and Karelia once this camp disbands for the winter. I told him that Arthur may be eccentric, but he'd made his living as a portrait photographer for many years, and I expected he would again. Has he talked to you about any plans?"

"No."

"I wish we hadn't come to the marshal's notice. He said he would keep an eye on us."

When I entered our tent, my father looked at me with a muffled tenderness, as if seeing through cotton. "I'm sorry to have worried you." With his good hand, he touched my arm as if I were a ghost. He seemed unable to recall where he had been. "I did walk for a long time." He finished the apple he was eating, crunching up even the seeds and the core, as he preferred to do in order to avoid waste. "I'm sure I must have slept a little somewhere."

The newspaper said the downpour had drenched the five thousand people camping in Jefferson Square, flooding their makeshift shelters of carpets and bed sheets and salvaged wood. We had a few leaks, and the edges of our tents suffered some dampness, but we were much better off than they, here in our safe aerie in Berkeley.

Still, that day I brought up the marshal's question. What were his plans? Was he thinking he might start his portrait business again soon?

"I'm sorry. I forget to tell you things, Joseph, or I come to believe I've already told you something, or that you must know what's in my mind." It was touchingly eerie that he had created a Joseph in his mind, someone he felt he had to apologize to, or rather wanted to apologize to, who was nevertheless not quite me. "I've been in correspondence with the insurers for my portrait studio in San Francisco, and it looks like it will only be a matter of weeks before they send my reimbursement. We don't have to worry about money for a while yet."

The next day, Karelia and Peter took my father to the hospital to tend to his arm. When they were gone, Mrs. Hallgarten emerged from the house and pulled Ina to the side of the yard to speak with her. I hovered as near as I could, behind Sebastian and Nicholas's tent, pretending to be idly drawing patterns in the wet dirt with a stick. The wind took most of their words away. I heard, "...seemed confused..." "...what did he...?" "...should take him to Stiles Hall...."

I knew from the newspaper that doctors had set up another temporary hospital at Stiles Hall near campus, this one for those suffering from nervous insanity. One man was taken there because he had slashed himself with a razor and fought off six men for a quarter of an hour before he was subdued. A woman had been taken there after she refused to eat or sleep and would not stop calling out the name of her son, who'd died in the earthquake. It alarmed me that Mrs. Hallgarten—for it was she who had said the words "Stiles Hall"—might think that my father belonged in their company. Surely she could see he posed no danger to anyone.

Berkeley's schools had reopened the day before. I told Mrs. Hallgarten that I wanted to return a book that Thomasine had loaned me, and I used the occasion to search her room again, to no avail. I even asked the maid if she'd come across the Book of Months anywhere, but she had not. It had vanished.

I was relieved when my father returned with Karelia and Peter. He was to rest and drink small amounts of water often, the doctors had told him. I helped him into bed and told him I would look after him. He thanked me and closed his eyes.

CHAPTER NINE

Mr. Hallgarten visited that evening. He spoke with my father briefly, then lowered himself with a groan onto one of the stones next to me and Karelia. She studied the grass.

"Your father is in poor condition," he said.

"He needs to rest," I said.

"He needs more rest and help than I can give him." He raised his arms as if to fend off my look of panic. "But it may be that he only needs something to occupy his mind. Karelia, I've found a studio and a darkroom for you and him to use." He seemed pleased with himself. He told us that Anne Brigman, the woman whose work we so admired at the exhibition last February, was out of the state visiting family. She had written to some of her friends in the area that her Oakland studio should be opened up for burned-out photographers to use until she returned. Mr. Hallgarten had found out and put in a good word for us. "It's small, I hear, but a delightful space. And I'll provide funds for the cameras and printing paper and chemicals you want." He regarded Karelia with an eagerness that alarmed me.

Sebastian asked, "What about canvases and supplies for the painters among us?"

Mr. Hallgarten's expression grew stern. "I'm afraid I don't have the funds for that. My business is greatly challenged at the moment. However, the relief committee has set up an employment bureau for the refugees, I'm sure you could find work and earn enough to buy supplies." He glanced at his watch, though it was too dark for the numbers to be visible. "Now I must be off to bed."

"You needn't extend yourself for the cameras," Karelia said. "I can't think of photographing in these times."

"Not here in the chaos of the camp, no, how could anyone think? But if you spend some time in the studio, at the very least you'll be able to see more of Brigman's work, that will inspire you. I've reserved Wednesday afternoons for you and Fridays for your father—here, I've written down the addresses of her studio and the camera store in town—and they'll supply your needs, within reason." He handed her an envelope, which she quickly took and folded. It looked too thick to contain only an address. "Promise me you'll go."

My father greeted Mr. Hallgarten's news with excitement. He told me the next morning, "My project has always been to show the continuity of time, as if it were incremental in nature, like the growth of a single body. Yet the earthquake has shown us that events can be ruptured, that time is more wily than we suspected. To give an accurate picture of time's true nature requires capturing the discontinuities and incongruities. While one body is growing, another is wasting away. I have to rethink my approach." We went to the camera store, where he selected one of the most expensive models, to my anxiety, as well as so many supplies that I had difficulty carrying them back up the hill.

He marked four points around the yard and had me carry the camera on its tripod from one to the other. Starting at three o'clock, we took five shots of the camp from each spot at intervals of a minute each. When I asked him what his purpose was, he said, "When Thomas proposed that I photograph his house in January, he said that we could think of the inhabitants of a house, moving back and forth behind the windows, as the thoughts of a house," he said. "This is absurd, of course. But we can think of the movement of people in a given locale as the thoughts of time itself, and if we take photographs from the same angle at the same time each afternoon, we may gain some sense of them."

"I don't understand," I said.

"We'll understand more as we continue."

"I wish to be absent from any photographs," called out Sebastian as he walked past.

"I'm not taking portraits." My father was studying his watch while he waited to take the next photograph. "I'm capturing time itself. No one should attempt to pose."

"I'm not attempting to pose." Sebastian came and stood within an inch of the lens, so that nothing would be visible.

My father didn't look up, and when the second hand passed the twelve, he clicked the shutter. "Everything that happens is a trace of the mind of time," he said.

The next day was Wednesday. I insisted on accompanying Karelia to Anne Brigman's studio, telling her that I wanted to be sure she navigated through Oakland safely. To my surprise, she said yes right away. I hadn't had much time to be alone with her since the fire, and I was longing to talk with her. But she seemed preoccupied and fretful on the streetcar, and as we walked. I wanted to tell her that I feared my father was losing his mind. I wanted to tell her I knew she was going to have a child. Everything felt like something I shouldn't say.

The studio was a small shack shingled in redwood next to the Brigman's house. Karelia paused at the threshold, breathing deeply, and for a moment she seemed almost happy, looking up at the wisteria draping the doorway, petals mostly blown.

Inside, it smelled of lavender. A writing desk and a low table divided the room, with a sitting area on one side and a piano and small bed on the other. Karelia walked through it, taking in every detail as if she might never see it again.

The darkroom in the corner was barely big enough for one person. The bathroom had been built out around a tree, which disappeared up through a hole in the ceiling. A showerhead dangled from one of the lower branches; mosquito netting discreetly veiled the john.

She sank onto the bed and said, so quietly I almost didn't hear, "Oh, if only I could live here."

I wished I could put my arms around her.

A knock came, and she bolted upright.

I ran to the door and opened it to see Mr. Hallgarten, as I'd expected. He seemed disconcerted to see me, possibly even angry. He made an attempt at a smile. "I wanted to see how Karelia was settling in," he said.

He dropped into the wicker love seat, which creaked alarmingly. For a while no one spoke. I was determined not to leave. But I hadn't imagined he would be so upset—he kept gripping the armrests of the love seat, whitening his knuckles. The eagerness he'd been trying to conceal the other day had dropped away entirely. Karelia looked ill. He asked after my father's health, and she responded dutifully. He asked if she was comfortable in the camp, and she said yes.

"You must find it a burden," she said, "to have so many dependent on you."

"No one could be happier than I to help those who've been distressed by catastrophe and don't know what to do."

I'd never seen him look so unhappy.

"The Vissers are estimable people," he continued, "but I hardly know the Crowleys, and this Nicholas not at all. Are they treating you respectfully?"

"Yes, of course."

"The young men are both in love with you, I fear."

She made a dismissive noise.

"You must be careful."

"You needn't worry."

"You haven't given me a tour." He walked to the darkroom door and pulled it open.

Karelia laughed. "Did you expect to find someone hiding in there? Have a look in the john, too. It's the most charming you'll ever see—not even yours has its own tree."

His face darkened, and he walked outside without closing the door and stood in the little garden for a minute. Karelia stared at the floor.

He came back in, and this time he seemed to have reached a decision. "My wife worries about you as well, you must think of her, too."

Karelia went pale.

"She told me some interesting news this morning," he said.

Now Karelia seemed preoccupied with the large Japanese paper lantern hanging opposite her. It was all I could do not to jump up and run out of the room. I'd come with the idea of protecting her from him, somehow, but I hadn't foreseen this.

"In her volunteering for the relief committee, you know, she helps many young women. I heard of one this morning who is with child, but the man responsible had already deserted her. Isn't that cruel?"

"It would be cruel," she said.

He turned to me. "Joseph, I suppose you came to know all of the suitors who came courting Karelia in the old days, didn't you?"

To hide sudden fear, I pretended his remark baffled me. "Suitors?"

"Your cousin is a beautiful woman—every beautiful woman has suitors, whether they want them or not." He began pacing the room. "Sometimes I think the woman chooses one to marry only to put an end to the encirclement. Yes, I believe Karelia mentioned some of them in our afternoons together, the four of us, didn't she? I remember her describing a young Spaniard, for instance, or was he Italian?"

As far as I could remember, Karelia had certainly never mentioned Fulvio to him, at least not in my earshot.

Slowly, as if I had to think for a while, I said, "Yes, an Italian artist, for a while, would visit us. We went to his studio once—I liked his paintings of moonlight on the water."

"Thomas," Karelia said warningly. "Why are you interrogating Joseph? Are you concerned I'm not virtuous enough to live in your backyard?"

He ignored her. "What became of this man?"

"He decided to go back to Italy," I said.

"And when was this?"

I watched Karelia, but she gave no sign as to how she wanted me to answer. "A few years ago."

"But if there is another young man, someone Karelia perhaps thought well of, should we see if this man can be found? Is there a young man worried about Karelia, believing she's lost or dead? I feel it's my duty to put his mind at ease, but I'm afraid Karelia might be shy to tell me. Young women can often feel reluctant to discuss the person they love with someone who is a—friend, not a relative." He had come close to me by now. "But now that I am in a position of responsibility, I'd like to know."

Karelia bowed her head.

"No," I said. "Karelia grew tired of suitors and stopped letting them come near years ago." I spoke as innocently as I could, giving Mr. Hallgarten a childish expression.

"I'm sad to hear Celeste is worrying about me and my *suitors*," Karelia said. "The last thing I want is to be a burden to anyone. I've been thinking I should visit Violet."

Mr. Hallgarten crumpled into the love seat. He didn't seem to have heard Karelia. I assume he'd suspected that he was the father as soon as his wife told him, but he couldn't ask her directly, and he had worked himself up into a state of jealousy.

"No," he said eventually, his voice quiet. "Now isn't the time for traveling great distances. It wouldn't be wise. Joseph, tell her, it's too physically demanding—for Arthur, of course. Isn't it? And you could hardly abandon him here."

I was stuck in innocence, I couldn't get out. "I'm worried about him," I said.

"Of course you are." His voice was barely audible, though, and he seemed to have forgotten what he was answering. "In any case, Celeste wouldn't forgive me if I let you go far away." Speaking his wife's name seemed to terrify him. He opened his eyes and stood.

"I'll think of something. In the meantime—Celeste also worries about your health, Karelia. You will take care of yourself, won't you? You won't do anything foolish. You won't go to some other doctor? Her doctor is very good."

"He'll keep me sound," Karelia said. Now her voice had softened. They looked at each other for the first time, and there was a tenderness to their gaze.

He went out, shutting the door this time.

I felt the hour of three o'clock pass, darkening the moment like a bird flying across the sun.

"Couldn't we just move in here?" I asked. "We could put a curtain down the middle. You could sleep on the bed, and Father and I would sleep on the other side."

She shook her head, still watching the door. "Anne Brigman will return in a few weeks. Anyway, I only have Wednesday afternoons. Don't worry about me. Everyone wants to worry about me."

"I'll come with you every Wednesday. I can help you with developing."

"I don't need an escort. If you want to help me, be quiet for a while. I want to think now." She went over to Anne Brigman's desk and found a pencil and paper, but she didn't write a word.

* * *

Our situation seemed impossible. I'd thought it would be an adventure to live in tents in the Hallgartens' backyard among a group of artists, with Thomasine for a friend. But now that she and her sisters had returned to school, they seemed to have little time for me. My father's photographing irritated the artists, and he often seemed disoriented and distracted, still thrashing in the middle of the night. Karelia had sunk into a gloom punctuated by moments when desperation clouded her face. Each morning I feared I would wake to find her gone. If I told my father she was with child, would he pull himself together, would he be able to look after her? Several times I opened my mouth to speak to him, but did not. Was she still in love with Mr. Hallgarten? What would he do now that he knew she was bearing his child?

Perhaps to distract herself, Karelia embarked on a project of photographing refugees in the afternoons. She knocked on the doors of neighbors' houses to find them. She photographed a couple who had moved in with their aunt and had brought with them seven cats. She photographed a family of twelve—grandparents, parents, children—who shared the attic and basement of the house of a relative. Once she'd developed a few of these photographs to her satisfaction, she planned to ask the army for permission to photograph in the university camps, too. "So many photographers are in San Francisco, taking pictures of the ruins," she said, "but I'd rather focus on the people whose lives have been cracked open."

*   *   *

One evening, after my father had retreated to our tent, Peter asked Nicholas to recite a soliloquy or two to entertain us. Nicholas handed his flask around to the other men and said, "Instead, I thought Karelia and I would perform for you a little sketch."

Karelia looked up, startled. "You did, did you?"

"You know the story of Odysseus?"

"Of course," she said. "A man is declared a hero for getting lost on his way home."

He laughed and beckoned to her. She sighed, got to her feet, brushed the leaves off her dress, and followed him out of earshot of the rest of us. They spoke in low voices together for a few minutes. Then Nicholas announced that they would act out the moment when Odysseus, having slain all Penelope's suitors, removes his disguise and reveals himself to his wife.

In this version, rather than being happy to see him, Penelope scolds Odysseus for spattering the house with suitors' blood. "Why couldn't you have lured them outside?" she laments. "Even the ceiling, husband. How will we ever get it clean again?" We laughed to the point of tears at his crestfallen face, his useless boasts: "But didn't you see how I vaulted over the dining table to dodge their spears? How I killed two with one ax-blow?" We laughed hard enough to forget the mosquitoes, the hard rocks we sat on, the smell of the outhouse that wafted by when the wind changed. When we applauded, Karelia bowed, flushed with pleasure.

Later, I helped Nicholas rake over the fire for the night. "Your cousin has been with you since you were born?" Nicholas said as we worked. "It's unusual for a young woman to raise another man's child, unless she marries the man."

"She was only twelve when she arrived."

"All the more generous of her, then, and patient."

I said that she was not known for her patience.

He laughed, and I liked him even more. Karelia would do far better to fall in love with him, I thought.

* * *

That Sunday, the first Sunday in May, Karelia declared that she was taking her camera on an expedition into Wildcat Canyon to photograph in nature; photographing only refugees left her sad and worried for them, even though so many of them were optimistic. When Nicholas saw her pick up the camera and tripod, he said, "What you need is a donkey," and knocked his fist against his sternum. "I am that donkey."

"Joseph will help me carry," she said.

"Then let me accompany you anyway, and I'll be entirely useless."

In the end, she let Nicholas hold the tripod. I had a sack of sandwiches, and Sebastian, who insisted on accompanying us, carried his sketching pad. The air, warm and a little breezy, rippled through the long swishy grass that covered the hillside as the three of us made our way to the rim of Wildcat Canyon. From there, we could see the undeveloped land stretching to the north, where a few tents and makeshift shelters dotted the grass. There, in the tin can camp, as it was called, lived refugees who did not have friends or family and who had been kicked out of the large organized camps for one reason or another, or who did not want to follow the rules. The residents of Berkeley said they were lawless men, who kept aloof from each other and were half-crazed with hunger.

I watched Karelia carefully. Ever since Wednesday's encounter with Mr. Hallgarten, she'd seemed haunted, and I hadn't slept well. In the afternoons, she often napped, and food sometimes still revolted her. But now, she seemed brisk with energy, if a little tense. I wondered how long she could keep up with her photographing, given the infant unfolding inside her. And when she did have her child, would she still think of me the same way, or would all her attention turn to her own baby? It was absurd to feel jealous, but I felt another loss traveling toward me. For her to have a child without being married would turn many people against us, too. Once, a customer at the studio said that she had to find a new hairdresser, because her former one had given birth out of wedlock. My father might have trouble starting a new portrait business.

We followed Karelia down a thin winding path where animals or people had worn through the grass, toward the loose row of alders that grew along the creek at the canyon's bottom. While we walked, Nicholas got out of Karelia the story of her arrival at my father's doorstep, which made him laugh.

When he was a boy, Nicholas told us, his father inherited a fortune. He bought fine clothes and a house in Pacific Heights, and the family summered in Europe. At one party, his father planted torches in the backyard and set loose peacocks, one of whom caught fire and flew at the mayor, singeing his jacket. When Nicholas said he wanted to study acting, his father sent him to college in New York. But after a year, his father lost all his money in a Ukiah silver mine that had come to nothing. When Nicholas returned from school for the summer, his father had disappeared, and his mother and sister were living in a cousin's basement.

"I couldn't stand it, our fall in fortunes," he said. "So in the autumn I went back to New York and worked here and there and paid my own way through school. I should have stayed to look after my mother—she wasn't well, and their circumstances were pinched. She died a few months before I was to complete my degree. I came back and my sister wouldn't speak to me. I've never forgiven myself."

"I'm sure you sent money back," Karelia said.

"Some, not enough. Now you know the worst thing I've ever done." He said this lightly, but his face was grave. "You're lucky in your father, Joseph. He won't abandon you, and he has a brilliance about him. If we opened the top of his head, I believe we'd see a scale model of the universe composed of crystal and set in motion by tiny gears. I'd like to talk more with him about photographing the soul."

"Painting can show us the soul," said Sebastian. "Because the artist interprets every detail through the medium of his own soul—musicians and actors do so as well. But with photography, the machine records everything in front of it. The hand of the artist is nowhere to be found."

"That's not true," Karelia said. "The photographer seeks images or figures or landscapes that have some dialog with the drama of her inner life, and if she is inspired and skilled, she can bring out something that has to do with soul. In the darkroom, she can brighten or darken, superimpose images from one photograph to another, even paint or etch the image to make it harmonize with her vision."

"I'd like to watch you work in the darkroom," Nicholas said. "It sounds like a sort of magic."

We reached the creek, and Karelia scanned the water. Sebastian said he'd stop here. "I don't mind the presence of others, so no one need feel constrained by my choice—you may set up here if this glorious fallen trunk appeals to you as it does to me."

"I'm interested in that stand of alders on the other side," Karelia said, pointing. She began casting about for an easy way to cross.

"No trouble," Nicholas said, and without pause hoisted her on his back and forged through the shallow water, his boots kicking up glitter. Karelia laughed, as she rarely had since the earthquake.

Sebastian heaped himself on the trunk. I glanced at him, then followed Nicholas into the creek. The water was exhilaratingly chilly. When I reached the other side, Karelia was setting up her tripod by the alders. "I thought at least one of you would be sensible enough to take off your shoes first," she said.

"Sensible!" Nicholas said. "I don't know what the word means."

Karelia asked me to pose for her. Reluctant, I hid behind a tree. Karelia clicked the shutter. I put my ear to the rough bark, straining to hear sap move. After a while, I reached out so the fingertips would be barely visible. She shot several more images, one with my elbow emerging, one with my bare foot curling forward around the roots.

When she had finished, Nicholas asked, "Do you think it's possible to photograph the soul?"

"I don't know," she said. "The soul may be easy to photograph, but just as hard to see on film as it is in person."

"Would you photograph mine?" He shut his eyes and stood still, as if awaiting an execution. "I feel a little fear. It might prove flimsy and light, like a feather."

"You've lived a light life, then?" she asked. She had him sit on a flat rock and began to load fresh film into her camera. Across the bank, Sebastian seemed to be concentrating on his sketch pad.

"No one's accused me of having great substance."

She took a few shots, then asked him to stretch out on the rock. He kicked off his wet shoes. The tops of his feet were covered with black hair. I remembered the times when I sat before my father's lens, imitating the expressions of his customers, trying to relax into my own true face. Nicholas seemed enviably unplagued by this difficulty.

"I'm out of film," Karelia said.

But he had fallen asleep.

After a while, I said it was time for lunch. She ate her sandwich with gusto, which relieved me. Now, in the sunlight, with Nicholas sleeping calmly next to us, it seemed possible that everything could be all right.

Her eyes rested on Nicholas. "He plays the fool an awful lot, doesn't he," she said.

"Don't you like him?"

She considered his prone body, one hand tucked under his cheek, breath flexing his lips as he snored lightly. "He's asking you to like him with every breath, when he's talking and even when he's sleeping."

"Still," I said, "that doesn't mean you shouldn't like him."

She settled her camera back into its case. "He's merely a boy," she said. "I want to make use of this time, as impossible as it is, to find out what I can do as a photographer."

I tapped Nicholas on the leg to wake him. When we turned around, Karelia was wading across the water, barefoot, her shoes in one hand and the camera in the other.

On the other side, Sebastian was still contemplating his sketch pad, a page with two curving lines, each about an inch long. "I could get no further," he said. "You seem to have been much more successful."

"That's the strangeness of being a photographer," Karelia said. "You can shoot all day, excited by what you're capturing, but not know anything until you get into the darkroom."

As we walked back, I told Nicholas about the *Kalevala*, that it was the epic poem of our ancestors, that Karelia had brought it with her when she first came to San Francisco. He sounded interested, so I said I would loan him the first volume. I was sure that he would love it, and that this would endear him to Karelia.

That night, however, Nicholas went out drinking with Sebastian and Peter in Oakland; the city's officials had finally allowed the saloons to reopen since their closure after the earthquake. The men returned late, after the rest of us had turned in; I heard their drunken voices, interrupted by Peter telling everyone to be quiet, giggling when they could not. Then there was a shout and a crash. I scrambled out. Peter and Sebastian were lifting Nicholas off of the tent he and Sebastian shared; he had fallen on it, or he had mistaken the wrong part of the tent for the entry. They dragged him away and set about trying to right the tent poles that had lurched out of the ground. By the time they had made a passable job of it, Nicholas had fallen asleep, so they dragged him into the tent, laughing. To my dismay, I saw Karelia had woken too and watched the proceedings, and though it was too dark to make out her expression, something about the way she turned around and went back inside suggested she was not as amused as the participants.

Nicholas stayed in his tent most of the next day, reading the *Kalevala*. "How wonderful it is," he told me that evening. "But these aren't like the heroes of Greek mythology, who at least managed to carry out some feats of greatness before their hubris or carelessness brought them down. This Wainamoinen, for instance, who's stuck in the womb for 700 years. A great singer and enchanter, so we're told, but he mostly uses his power for fixing broken sledges or winning petty duels. Please tell me he at least woos a wife successfully by the end."

"No."

"What about Lemminkainen, then?" he said.

"Never marries."

"The blacksmith Ilmarinen, who tries to build a replacement out of gold when his wife dies. Surely he finds love?"

I slowly shook my head. I couldn't bear to mention that, later in the *Kalevala,* Ilmarinen becomes so desperate with loneliness that he kidnaps one of his wife's sisters to take her place. She insults him with such fury and deftness that he casts a spell that transforms her into a seagull.

"There's something so poignant about them all." He ran his fingers through his beard.

"Why don't we make a play out of one of the stories?" I said. "We could surprise Karelia with it. She'd be happy. I could be one of the actors."

He regarded me thoughtfully. I had believed I was thinking only of Karelia, but my enthusiasm surprised me. Belatedly, I feigned indifference by shrugging.

"If there's an opportunity to make someone happy," he said, "it would be churlish to pass it up."

*　　*　　*

Although we slept on narrow cots, although we were often cold and pricked by mosquitoes or fleas, although our clothing and hair harbored the smell of smoke and reminded us always of the very thing that had razed our city, to live among artists thrilled me. I drank in their gossip about fellow artists. I practiced their mannerisms—the way Sebastian had of darting his eyes to the side when he said something sarcastic or despairing, the little explosion Bee made with her fingers in lieu of saying the word "gone" or "lost" or "disappeared."

Berkeley's schools couldn't handle the influx of earthquake refugees, so I had too much time on my hands during the day. With everyone else working, the camp was deserted. And our insurance money still hadn't come in. To contribute to the camp's purse for meals and supplies, I began to run errands and perform small tasks for Mrs. Hallgarten and some of the neighbors. I painted a fence, chopped firewood, planted a tree, posted letters, and waited for evenings.

My whole life had been spent in what now seemed like close confinement with the only two people I loved, my schoolmates no more real to me than the shadows cast by my father's camera obscura. For the first time, I was more than a scientific object to be photographed; I was part of a company of artists.

Yet late at night, whenever any of the artists laughed or shouted too loudly around the bonfire, I imagined Mrs. Hallgarten lying in bed cursing our presence on her lawn.

On the first Friday in May, a string quartet came to play at the Hallgartens' house for their neighbors and friends, and Mr. Hallgarten invited the members of the camp to come too, saying it would inspire us. We bathed and put on our best, cleanest clothes. I had taken to washing my armpits and feet every day, because my body had developed a new rankness since the earthquake, as if the smoke had sunk itself into my skin. My father wanted to put on a tie, but couldn't manage it with his injured hand, so I followed his directions and eventually managed to tie it.

"Thank you," he said. When I held up our mirror for him, he even smiled a little. He was coming back to himself after all, I thought.

It was strange to return to the Hallgartens' living room, where the light of the lamps warmly burnished the redwood walls; we had grown acclimated to the fragmentary, leaping illumination from the bonfire and our few scattered lamps burning, their light going outward into the unwalled darkness, reflected only by our bodies.

Mr. Hallgarten and Karelia never occupied the same side of the room—somehow when one moved, the other would glide elsewhere. Karelia seemed tired and kept close to Bee. Whenever I wandered near, trying to eavesdrop, she was asking Bee questions about painting, about art school, about growing up in Seattle—ordinary questions that Bee answered with an air of amusement, under which lay an air of delight in having her history inspire so much interest.

Nicholas watched them from the other side of the room, puzzled that each time he tried to talk to Karelia, she responded briefly and turned toward Bee. I hoped that he wouldn't be discouraged, that as soon as we returned to camp, out from under Mr. Hallgarten's eyes, she would be friendly with him again.

The musicians began tuning their instruments. Mr. Hallgarten sat next to his wife on the couch and called his daughters to settle themselves on the floor by their feet. When she saw me, Thomasine patted the floor next to her, and I gladly settled there, though she proceeded to play an intricate variation of cat's cradle with Sophie for the rest of the evening, chiding her each time the strings knotted. I'd seen little of the sisters since they'd started school. And because the artists had found work—Peter selling ceramic building materials in San Francisco, Sebastian and Bee tutoring pupils, Nicholas working as a carpenter building new houses in Berkeley—I'd been at loose ends during the day. Even Karelia had gotten a job, as a receptionist for an optometrist in downtown Berkeley three mornings a week, and when she wasn't working, she was often off photographing refugees or developing prints.

Now Karelia led Bee to a pair of dining chairs at the back of the room. As she edged into her seat, she stumbled and caught herself clumsily, bending her wrist back. She sank into the chair and closed her eyes, looking pale. Mrs. Hallgarten asked her if she was all right. Embarrassed, Karelia kneaded her hand and said she was fine, just a little dizzy today, she had slept poorly, she'd had a headache that morning. Mrs. Hallgarten returned to her seat at the front of the room as the musicians finished tuning.

During the concert, Mr. Hallgarten sat in the front row with Adele on his lap. Karelia's hand twisted a fold of her skirt, and she watched him with a look I had never seen on her face: wistful, anxious, considering. Her eyes moved on, resting searchingly on Nicholas, on the Vissers, and on my father, who held himself very still in his chair, as if the music had sharp edges. I wished I knew what she was thinking.

* * *

The next afternoon was unusually hot. Thomasine and her sisters hadn't returned from school. Only my father and Ina were in the camp, and she looked up with hope in her eyes as I came into view; she had a basin mounded high with carrots, from which she was trimming the tops. When they weren't at work, Peter, Sebastian, and Bee spent every free moment they had painting watercolors, so often I was drafted to help. I ducked quickly into the tent and then, when her back was turned, scuttled away again. I decided to take the streetcar to Oakland and visit Karelia at the studio—it was her last session before Anne Brigman returned, and she'd said she had much she wanted to complete. She would rework the same images over and over, trying different methods to capture the scene she saw in her mind's eye.

I was about to knock on the studio's door when I heard a man's voice and realized Karelia was not alone. It took me a moment to recognize Mr. Hallgarten. He spoke in a wheedling way that I didn't associate with him. Karelia's voice remained cool and even, though it grew louder as I listened.

"Please don't talk about going to live with Violet anymore. Unless they've found larger quarters than the tiny apartment you described to me, downwind of the—was it a tannery?"

"I'll go back to my family in Canada, then."

"They aren't your family. They don't know you, they don't understand you, and you aren't suited for those freezing winters, you've told me yourself."

"I could live there."

"And what about Joseph? Do you see him pulling a plow?"

"The animals pull the plow."

"He's as unsuited for farm life as I am."

"So where does he live in *your* scenario? And Arthur, for that matter?"

"Arthur is a question. I can see his path forking in two directions. In one direction lies Stockton. There is a place there where he would be well looked after—"

"The asylum."

"The other direction," Mr. Hallgarten said hastily, "should he choose to travel down this path—and this is the one we both wish for—is to put aside his wild projects and take up his yoke as a businessman again. Open a new studio, or hire himself out as a photographer, or find some new way of earning a living. I'll offer help getting back on his feet, and he and Joseph can stay in a boardinghouse in Oakland."

"And how would you explain to them that you've cooped me up in an apartment in San Rafael, to be your secret second wife and have your secret child—"

"They'll know soon enough you're having a son anyway—so you'll say that your Italian lover came back, seduced you, abandoned you a second time. Your father isn't pious, and Joseph adores you and will think nothing of it. In *your* scenario, what are you telling them?"

"They don't ever know, because I disappear."

"You'd break Joseph's heart. And what do you mean by 'disappear?'"

"You don't know the child will be a boy."

"I think that after three daughters," he said dryly, "I'm at least assured that."

"It's too soon to count on anything," she said. "I want to have this child—don't look at me like that—but it's too soon to know for sure what nature has in mind for me."

"If you disappear," he said grimly, "I won't play host anymore. Joseph and Arthur and all the rest, they will have to make their own way. Don't think you assure them anything by disappearing."

The hardness in his voice repelled me. I backed away and ran down the path to the streetcar. Was Karelia really planning to abandon us? If she stayed, how long until her condition was obvious to the camp, even to my father? At least Bee already knew, I thought. Probably Karelia had told her the same story she'd told Mrs. Hallgarten. One afternoon, when Ina summoned the two younger women to peel a large sack of potatoes, Bee had volunteered to do them all so Karelia could rest. "You look exhausted, you spend too much time in the darkroom," she said. If Ina knew, she gave no sign—she spoke rarely and her face made few movements.

Once winter came, and the weather turned cold, and the rains came, we would have to find some other place to live. My father's insurance money still hadn't arrived, and what little money we had came from Karelia's salary at the optometrist's and my errand-running. I had no idea how long Karelia would be able to keep working. I didn't even know when her baby would be born. And if she refused the Hallgartens' help, and my father could not pull himself together, then how would we live?

These questions tormented me the whole way home. When I reached the Hallgartens' house, Thomasine's violin through the window was the first thing I heard, and it was so sweet to me I went upstairs and stood at her doorway to listen and to watch her serious face. She was playing by memory, living inside the music, all of her masks discarded. Gradually my heartbeat began to slow. At the end of the song, she set down her instrument and seemed to see me for the first time.

"Come here," she said. I obeyed, and she passed her hand over my eyes to shut them. I stood like that for a long while, waiting. When I opened my eyes, she had left the room.

CHAPTER TEN

Friday night at dinner, Sebastian turned to my father and said, to my surprise, "Tell us, Arthur, how your latest attempt to capture time is faring. Are you pleased with the results to date?"

"The patterns of time are more complex than we can know," my father said. "I've only collected a little more than a week's worth of photographs so far, and any conclusions I might draw would be conjectural at best."

"May I see them?" Sebastian asked.

Sebastian's tone was exceedingly polite, which raised my suspicions, and perhaps my father's, too, because he hesitated a moment.

"After all, we've all been collaborators in this project of yours, haven't we?" Sebastian said. "I feel invested in it, and I'd like to see what your results are."

Reluctantly, my father asked me to fetch the prints from the tent, and I did so. I told myself that the negatives, at least, were safe, so if Sebastian threw them into the fire, my father's work wouldn't be lost. I brought a towel with me as well, which I spread out ostentatiously before Sebastian, so that he wouldn't lay the prints out on the dirt.

My father had made ten prints, one for each day since the beginning of the project, and each contained four views of the camp, one from each quadrant. Certain elements were fixed, such as the position of the tents. Most of the photos were devoid of people. Ina appeared a couple of times, carrying a pot or a basket of vegetables, and Nicholas's left arm appeared once at the edge of a frame. I'd avoided being photographed entirely, preferring to be invisible now.

"I remember you saying that the people in a given locale could stand for the thoughts of time, didn't you?" Sebastian asked. "But there are hardly any people in these shots."

"The project is quite preliminary still—"

"It may take you years at this rate, and the camp won't be here for more than a few more months," said Sebastian. "If you wish to photograph the way the earthquake has disrupted the continuity of time, you might choose a location more disturbed than this one. So many of us are at work in the afternoons, in any case. Think of the tin can camp, for instance." He said this as if it had just occurred to him. "I walked near that camp the other day while looking for a new place to sketch, and I was struck by the numbers of people there. They've no support, you know, and some of them seem in rough shape, but they're making do. If you were to transplant your project there, you would see many more of time's thoughts than you do here." He slid the photographs together and held them out to the others, who demurred, except for Nicholas, who took them and looked them over.

"Thank you," my father said. "I haven't seen the tin can camp. Where is it?"

The next afternoon, my father and I headed down the hill and then north to the edge of Berkeley, past the houses under construction and into ranch lands. Karelia and I had once come as far as Boswell's Ranch, where there was a popular picnic spot sheltered from the wind by a boulder, but we'd stayed away from the tin can camp, despite Nicholas's reassurances that the rumors of their lawlessness were exaggerated.

A family of quail, startled from a bush, hurried away in a line along the ground. The sky was overcast, as it had been all week, and the air had an unusually dank feel.

As we walked, I pressed my father about his insurance money. When would it arrive, how much would it be? Would it be enough to rent a portrait studio? After all, I pointed out, houses were going up all over in Berkeley, and the number of residents who would need portraits would only increase. "Think of all the people for whom the passage of time will go unrecorded if you don't help them," I'd said. I winced. I'd abhorred Sebastian's false concern for my father's project—he clearly only wanted my father to stop photographing in our camp, as if the very project offended him. Now I was the one leveraging my father's obsession to try to influence him.

"I'm not sure the portraits I take help people," he said. "Sometimes I think these portraits, taken once every few years, are worse than nothing. They give a fixed impression, the opposite of what I hoped to achieve."

"We can't stay on the Hallgartens' land forever," I said. "How will we live?"

"I don't know," he said, with a slight quaver in his voice.

I wanted to put my arms around him and also to strangle him.

The improvised hovels of the tin can camp came into view, two dozen of them, most not tall enough to stand up in, constructed of scrap wood, corrugated tin, canvas, and even empty flour sacks sewn together. Unlike our tents, these were set at some distance from each other, a community of loners—people without money or family or friends, unable or unwilling to follow the army's rules. The odor of an open latrine wafted toward us.

Outside one dwelling, a woman hunched over a small fire, roasting a meager piece of meat that could have been a squirrel. A cat with matted fur watched intently.

"This is unfortunate," my father said. "The town should give them food."

Perhaps the camp's occupants had refused help, or accepted it in a surly fashion, or the town considered them beyond its borders.

My father moved closer to the woman cooking the meat. A head scarf concealed her face from us. On the ground next to her dwelling, in the shade of a bent cardboard awning, a sleeping infant lay in a wicker basket, almost completely wrapped in cloths, as if in a nest. Its eyelids were scarcely bigger than fingernails.

"Would you mind if I take photographs of the camp?" my father asked.

The woman looked at him uncomprehendingly. My father indicated the camera I was holding and mimed photographing. She responded with a string of words that were not English, ending with a shrug that we took to mean she was not opposed.

"That baby," I whispered. "Is he breathing?"

The woman followed our gaze and, with irritation, flicked a fly away from her infant's forehead. As if sensing the movement, the baby flexed his fingers feebly and moved his lips in a discontented fashion.

"Tomorrow, when I return, I'll bring you some food," my father said.

He set up the tripod some distance away and had me place the camera on it. "We're very lucky to have the Hallgartens," he said to me, adjusting the focus. "Sebastian was right, we've been spared the worst of the disruption, our lives proceed with a semblance of their old order, and we are able to retain our complacency, as the occupants here may not. I see now why Karelia is taking portraits of the refugees—while her work is different from mine, I believe there are—"

He stopped, because a portly, muscular man with a terrific sunburn and a battered cap was approaching us with some speed.

"What are you doing here?" said the man.

My father indicated the camera with his hands.

"None of that," said the man. "You people come around taking our pictures so you can sell them, no one gives us a share."

"I'll bring food tomorrow," my father said.

The man laughed, standing too close to my father. "The last one said he'd bring money. You aren't even promising that."

"I have a few coins on me now," my father said. He pulled out a handful of dimes and two quarters and held them out.

The man took the coins and spat in the dirt. "The earthquake is your bread and butter, isn't it? You'd love for there to be another. One guy, I heard, came across a man dying, trapped under a steeple—yes, a steeple fell on him, sheared right off the church, that's the church for you—and instead of calling for help, the guy set up his camera and snapped him, trying to get the last breath because it would be worth more."

"We all hear rumors," my father said. "I'm sure no one—"

The man snatched the camera off the tripod without taking his eyes off of my father. Flakes of dead skin furred his massive, sun-reddened arms. "This is a fancy camera," he said, holding it to his side. "I'd like to sell it."

"Let's go," I said, taking hold of my father's shirt. To my alarm, he was looking at his camera with desperation, as if the man had stolen a part of his own body.

"Like you, I've lost a good deal," my father said. "Time didn't proceed the way we thought it would, and it took the comforts we were accustomed to, but—"

"I never had any comforts." The man shoved my father, as if to walk right through him, and my father fell to the ground. The man proceeded past the woman roasting her food and disappeared down the path without a backward glance.

I helped my father up. He gritted his teeth—he'd landed on his bad arm. "Don't try to stop him," I said. "We can tell the police later."

He shook his head and leaned on me to steady himself. The young woman regarded him with a mixture of tenderness and pity before turning back to her cooking. "We can always get another." He picked up the tripod, and I took it away and held it under my arm. Still holding onto each other, we made our way back to the camp. At any moment I expected the man to return and grab the tripod as well, but we never saw him again.

*   *   *

The following afternoon, after I returned from mailing some packages at the post office for a neighbor, I learned Mrs. Hallgarten had barred my father from her house. Adele had spotted him in the living room, first peering beneath the sofa and armchair, then tilting books forward in the bookcase to check behind them, which is where Mrs. Hallgarten, alerted to his actions, found him. "What are you doing?" she asked, and he explained that he was looking for the lost photographs. She told him that it made her nervous to see him rummaging through her house, and he apologized. "Sometimes a thought occurs to me and I carry it out without thinking," he said.

It was Thomasine who informed me of this, to my embarrassment.

"Later, *Maman* also found her hairbrush underneath her dresser in the master bedroom," she said. "How did it get there? She always keeps it in her nightstand."

"He wouldn't have touched it," I said. I'd been reading in the shade of the bay tree at the side of the house, hoping she would come out to find me.

She narrowed her eyes, as if considering how much to believe me. She had drawn her hair up in a bun that day, and the narrow splendor of her neck dazzled me. I patted the grass next to me, but she remained standing. Another girl, with long ringlets and a plump face, walked toward her from the street, and Thomasine greeted her. They started gossiping about schoolmates. I tried to read, annoyed that Thomasine hadn't introduced me.

After a few minutes, she extended her hand to me and said, "Give me that book a moment, Joseph. This is the one I was telling you about, Francesca."

"Oh, don't touch it," Francesca said. "He's a reffie, isn't he?"

"A reffie?" I said.

"They're covered in germs."

"I haven't caught anything yet," Thomasine said. "So they must not be very strong germs." She riffled through pages as if to imply that she had no fear. It was *The Hound of the Baskervilles.* She held it out to Francesca, who shrank away.

"Still, they're dirty," the girl said. "I only wanted to see the camp from a distance, I didn't want to meet any of them."

Thomasine shrugged and tossed the book back to me. I was conscious of the grime on my shirt, the frayed holes in my trousers, and I thought of my visit to the tin can camp with my father. The two girls faced the tents. Karelia helped Ina unfold a blanket from a new box of donations; Ina bunched one end to her nose, sniffed, and made a face.

"Let's go to my house, Thomasine," the girl said. And with a docility that surprised me, Thomasine agreed.

Karelia returned late that afternoon with the prints she'd just developed: a woman drying laundry on an improvised line, a man carving sticks of wood outside his tent. When Sebastian told her my father had been caught searching the house, she covered her hands with her eyes. "You have to tell your father to let go of this," she said. "He might listen to you."

That night, as we were getting ready to go to bed, my father moved slowly, as if weighed down with sadness. I couldn't bear to bring up the Book of Months. He wouldn't meet my eyes, which made me think he was embarrassed enough already.

As I was falling asleep, he said, "In the days after your mother died, I thought of following after her."

The meaning of his words didn't sink in immediately. "How would you have followed her?"

"I thought you would have had a better life if you grew up with the Hajdus instead of me."

I had no memory of the Hajdus, only Karelia's stories of them as lively, laughing people. I wished they had absorbed the three of us into their family, as impossible as that was to imagine. Was he saying that he'd been thinking of killing himself?

"Why didn't you—follow my mother?" I asked.

"I didn't foresee Karelia."

"You could have sent her back." I remembered many times when melancholy had seized my father, and there had even been stretches when he stayed in bed like this, but I had never imagined him contemplating suicide. I wanted to know how serious this contemplation had been, how close I had come to being orphaned.

He shook his head. "She was full of life even though her parents had both died." He murmured something I couldn't hear. When I pressed him, he repeated it: "She gave me hope. You both did."

"Then help her now. She's—" I stopped short.

"What is it?"

If I told him about her, he could look after her, he would stop his slide into dark thoughts. But I remembered that she hadn't even told me.

I opened up the *Kalevala* and removed the portrait I'd saved of my mother. Travel and chaos had marred its surface, as if to age her. I handed it to him. "I'm sorry it's the only one I could save."

He took it. "How did you get this?"

"I ran back in on the day of the earthquake."

He looked at me in surprise. "I didn't know that. You could have been hurt. Thank you." He tucked it into the crate where he kept his clothes.

*   *   *

Early Sunday evening, Mr. Hallgarten joined us and used two twigs to tong a live coal from the fire to light his pipe. He had lost a fair amount of weight since we'd first met him, and something of his old grace had gone out of his movements. In preparation for our *Kalevala* performance tonight, Nicholas and Peter had sunk four poles into the ground and stretched sheets between them to form a stage, and the breeze rippled the fabric.

Mr. Hallgarten sucked on his pipe as if trying to inhale his old, pre-quake self. "Algernon is pulling his hair out." He gazed around at our little encampment with what looked almost like envy. "One of our insurers, the one we relied on for most of our warehouses, is refusing outright to pay what it owes us, and it may have run out of money entirely. Well, things will turn around somehow. Or if it all goes wrong, I'll give up business, become an artist, and move into the tents with all of you!"

His eyes rested briefly on Karelia, who kept her gaze on the fire.

"How is the artistic gypsy life?" he asked her. "I'd like to see your new photographs."

Karelia told him that her work was going well but wasn't yet ready to be shown.

"Didn't you always say I had a good eye for your work? Haven't I helped you?" He spoke as jovially as he used to, yet there was something rough and over-keen beneath his tone, both beseeching and commanding.

"You have an excellent eye," she said. "And that's why I'll wait until I have something more finished to show you. Have patience. The camera shutter is instantaneous, but the making of a print can be long."

He stood abruptly. "Not too much longer, I hope. The muses must bow to the patrons, isn't that how it has always worked? We are useful that way." He clapped his hands. "What about the rest of you? Each night, before I go to bed, I look out on my little fiefdom here, and I'm impatient to know what you've been up to."

He looked over several of Sebastian's oil paintings first. "Your landscapes are less cluttered than before, which is a good direction, but you should return to watercolors, that's your natural medium." He considered Peter's. "Marvelous as always. Although your trees seem too placid. You should visit William Keith's studio again and study his trees more closely."

Bee had only one landscape to show, which she said she'd finished that afternoon. Mr. Hallgarten held it up before him with great concentration, bringing his eye close to the brushwork. Finally he said, "A masterpiece. I like it so much, I must carry it into the house with me tonight. Yes?"

Bee looked uncomfortable, but gave a nod. He laughed and said, "Well, we'll talk about it later. Meditate on a price. Now where is Arthur? Ah yes, he's lost his camera. Yet he must have something to show. Bring me your father and his latest work, Joseph."

I fetched him from the tent, where he had been lying on his cot, fully clothed. When I told him what Mr. Hallgarten wanted, he gave me an envelope of prints, then seemed to change his mind and accompanied me outside.

The sun was sinking to the horizon. His head bowed, my father handed the photographs of our camp to Mr. Hallgarten, who shuffled through them.

"Arthur, I can see why you were hoping to find the remnants of your old work in my house—there, the viewer grasped at once that you were wrestling with the nature of time, whereas these photographs seem not to speak of anything at all." He gave the prints back. "Yes, seek again, Arthur, seek again!" My father took them without looking up, and I wished he would say something sharp, or stalk off, anything but stand there meekly.

Thomasine walked toward us from the house, wearing a pale blue dress. She leaned her head against her father's arm. "It's her fifteenth birthday today," Mr. Hallgarten said. Now that his daughter was with him, his mood seemed to mellow. "When I told her that I was coming to visit you and that Peter had said you were putting on one of your plays, she begged me to let her join us."

"I hear you laughing and singing every night through my window," Thomasine said. "It's annoying when I can't make out the words." If she'd begged to come see us, she seemed bored already now. Perhaps she expected to find us all wearing elaborate costumes, or she was still influenced by Francesca's view of us as "reffies."

That morning, Nicholas, Peter, Bee, and I had gone down into the canyon to rehearse the play we'd cobbled together from the *Kalevala*. I hoped it would leave Karelia impressed with Nicholas. I hadn't expected that Mr. Hallgarten would join us for the performance.

I stood and recited from memory the opening of the *Kalevala's* preface:

> *Mastered by desire impulsive,*
> *By a mighty inward urging,*
> *I am ready now for singing,*
> *Ready to begin the chanting*
> *Of our nation's ancient folk-song*
> *Handed down from by-gone ages.*

As I uttered these words, so familiar to me from my childhood, I feared that the rhythms of the poem would sound ridiculous, that the repetitions would perplex and bore the audience. Nicholas had cut the preface in half, but even so it was sixty lines long. I fixed my eyes on the Hallgartens' house beyond us so that I wouldn't have to see my audience.

As I continued, my voice grew stronger, however, and I heard the original Finnish beneath the translation, the talismanic force of the names of heroes and places:

> *These are words in childhood taught me,*
> *Songs preserved from distant ages,*
> *Legends they that once were taken*
> *From the belt of Wainamoinen,*
> *From the forge of Ilmarinen*
> *From the sword of Kaukomieli,*
> *From the bow of Youkahainen,*
> *From the pastures of the Northland,*
> *From the meads of Kalevala.*

As I finished, I felt an elation that surpassed anything I'd ever felt when the Tetrascope came into focus. Even Thomasine seemed caught up.

Bee and Nicholas enacted the tale I had selected, one of Karelia's favorites: the ancient singer Wainamoinen encounters the Rainbow Maiden in the woods, weaving thread on a shuttle. Struck by her beauty, he asks her to become his wife. She tells him she prefers the freedom of maidenhood: "Married women, far too many, are like dogs enchained in kennel, rarely do they ask for favors, not to wives are favors given."

When Wainamoinen insists that she will be treated as a queen, as the wife of a hero, she sets him tasks: to split a hair using a knife with no edge, to snare a bird's egg with an invisible snare, to build a ship from the splinters of her spindle.

The first two tasks he handles with ease. But in the middle of the third, he cuts his knee with his hatchet, and streams of blood pour out, signified by red handkerchiefs knotted together. After a long journey, he finds a healer—played by me—who mends him. The play ends with

Wainamoinen limping back to the half-built boat and picking up the hatchet triumphantly.

I disapproved of the way Nicholas changed the ending—in the *Kalevala,* Wainamoinen doesn't return to finish the boat, but instead gives up, and the maiden never appears in the story again. Still, I felt proud when everyone burst into applause at the end, even my father, though he began a beat after everyone else.

Mr. Hallgarten clapped vigorously. He may have enjoyed the sight of Nicholas wooing Bee. "A good beginning," I heard him tell Nicholas. "You could do more with these tales."

Karelia hugged me hard, tears in her eyes. "That was beautiful," she whispered.

She had scarcely let go when Thomasine seized my arm. "How did you memorize all those lines?" she asked, almost accusingly, as if I'd cheated.

"It was easy," I said. I'd told her about the *Kalevala* when we'd first met, in January, which seemed like ages ago. But she had forgotten all about it, and asked me to describe it to her again now. Baked by the bonfire's flames, she gave off an aroma of sage and hickory. "You were good tonight," she said, almost as an afterthought, but I was pleased. She quizzed me on how often we performed these sketches. "Tell Nicholas I want to act in them too."

I pointed out that her parents wouldn't let her be in our camp at night on her own, but she said she could persuade them otherwise. "After all, I'm fifteen now," she said. "And I'll have you to look out for me."

"Come, Thomasine, I can hardly keep my eyes open," Mr. Hallgarten called out from the other side of the bonfire.

After they left, Peter strummed his guitar, and Nicholas asked Karelia to dance. She had often told me she disliked dancing: "You have to follow patterns rather than step where you like," she always said. But to my surprise, she accepted his hand.

An hour later, when I could no longer keep my eyes open, I went back to our tent. As I climbed into my cot, my father said, "You did well." I had mostly avoided him since his escapade in the Hallgartens' house.

"Thank you." After a moment, I said, "Mr. Hallgarten seems to have changed."

"We've all changed," my father said. "I wish I understood theater—the enactment of events that didn't happen. There are already so many interesting facts in the world, more than mankind will ever record or share with each other."

I didn't know what to say.

"I'm worried you aren't getting enough sleep," he continued. "You stay up late so often around the bonfire."

"I don't like to sleep. I have nightmares."

"They will pass eventually," he said, though without certainty. "And it's restful to lie still and quiet. The artists are well meaning, but they drink too much. I worry about their influence on you."

It was true that sometimes I stayed up with the men after the women had turned in, and if Nicholas had managed to refill his silver flask, I'd watch them pass it among them, interested in the way drink loosened their talk and their laughter.

All at once I became angry. "Some of the best moments I've ever had have been around the bonfire."

He looked away. I remembered my childhood expeditions with him and Karelia, his careful explanations of the natural world around us. Perhaps he was lonely without my presence in the tent—not only because I wasn't there with him, but because I found warmth in the company of the artists, which he did not.

"Adolescence is a new birth," he said. "The rate of growth increases rapidly, in height, in weight, in strength. The senses undergo reconstruction, and new sensations arise; the senses of smell and taste modify, the voice changes, vascular instability increases susceptibility to blushing. Sleep is essential to this work of the body."

It was true that my body felt alien. I was clumsy, stumbling over my own feet, which had rapidly grown larger, and even my own voice had become unstable. To hear him describe what I was going through as natural gave me a brief sense of relief. But I thought Mr. Hallgarten's evaluation had wounded him in ways he was trying to hide from me. My dreams that night were uneasy.

* * *

In the morning, I woke to find him gone. I was concerned until I heard him talking with Ina outside. After a long quiet came the sound of pouring; I guessed that someone had carried back a bucket of creek water to fill the largest pot on the stove. If he was up this early, maybe his despair had lifted.

Peter's voice, broken by a yawn, wished Ina and my father good morning. Shortly, the large pot's metal handle rasped as it was lifted from the stove—when filled, it was heavy enough that it took two to carry. The men had set up a small tent next to ours for bathing, and I could hear the water splashing into the tub. My father asked Peter if he would sharpen the straight razor so he could shave. His voice had a slight echo, which suggested to me that I was on the border of slumber, where voices in the distance acquire a comforting dreamlike roundness. Peter himself was always clean shaven. He murmured that he would be glad to. Next came the striking of a straight razor against a whetstone.

"Thank you," my father said.

A rippling announced that my father was lowering himself into the few inches of water.

All at once, I came fully awake, and the comfort fell away. Something felt odd about the way he'd said "Thank you," dropping the words quickly as if they were hot coals. I was seized with the notion that he planned to draw the razor across his throat.

I ran out and burst into the bathing tent.

From the tub, my father looked up, his hair plastered to his face, giving him an otterish appearance. "Yes, Joseph?" he said.

"Nothing," I stammered. The air was humid and smelled of the creek. The tent was not much larger than the tub, and the fabric was clammy as I backed into it.

His whole face was suffused with a terrible exhilaration. He lifted the razor to his cheek left-handed and scraped the stubble with one wobbling sandpapery stroke. The line of his jaw emerged, shining and pink. I hadn't ever seen him beardless before. I remembered the story Karelia told me of the end of my father's long gloom after my mother died, how he rose and shaved himself clean, and hurried me and her off to the portrait studio with him, full of the energy of an idea no one had come up with before. Hope sprang up within me.

He shaved below his jaw line with clumsy, impatient strokes, nicking himself several times; a thin thread of blood descended his wet neck. "I've decided it's time to start the project again. We will rebuild the Tetrascope and begin as soon as possible."

He smoothed his jaw with his hand and then, satisfied, poured a bowlful of water over his head. He gestured for me to fetch him his towel.

I threw it to him and turned away. "Where will you find an infant?"

He looked startled. "We'll start where we left off, you and I."

"But it's all been destroyed."

The hair on his chest was gray and matted, the skin dappled with liver spots, the ridges of his ribs prominent. The water sloshed as he stepped out of the tub. "We don't know that. In any case, the photographs are only the physical embodiment of the project. Our project takes place in time, not in space."

"You missed some days, even before this year," I said, angry that he had worried me—though he'd done nothing but take a bath—angry that he had once wished to die.

His trousers rustled as he pulled them on. His keys—to his studio, to our home—still jangled in the pockets. "The act of taking the photographs, of fixing a small moment, is a victory, even if an image endures only for an instant. By photographing you from the moment you were born, once each day, in the same position, recording the progress of your development, we are marking the very surface of time. Each session is a dot, and by means of these dots we score time's surface with the straightest line possible, bringing order to chaos."

I heard a soft sound, as if he had pulled on his shirt with such vigor that a sleeve or shirttail struck against the tent canvas. "The nature of time—I see it now. Nothing endures. That is the pitiless side of time. And yet there is a consolation, Joseph." Now he was whispering, as if to prevent anyone from overhearing.

He stood close behind me, the damp smell of his hair faintly detectable in the air, and snapped his cuff links into place. "There is this consolation: no action can be undone."

For me, this was no consolation; it cut me to the quick.

* * *

Late in the next afternoon, Thomasine appeared in the camp wearing an old brown corduroy coat—I suspected she had taken it from one of the boxes of donated clothes—and asked Nicholas when our next play was to be performed and what role she might have.

"You know the myth of Daedalus?" he asked. "Say Ariadne comes to Daedalus to discover the secret of the Minotaur's labyrinth, so she can help her lover Theseus find his way out after he kills the Minotaur. But first she has to persuade Icarus to let her see his father. Thomasine, you will not give up until he lets you pass. Joseph, Daedalus has told you to let no one see him today except the king."

"But where is the script?" Thomasine asked.

"There is none—you must make it all up."

"And what about you—are you Daedalus, or Theseus?"

"Don't worry about what may or may not happen next," he said. "For now, you have one goal, to convince Icarus to let you through. Now begin."

Nicholas seated himself on a rock and watched us while we awkwardly began improvising lines. After a moment, she tossed her coat on the grass. Underneath she wore a green summer dress, not new, but made of fine cloth, and it left her shoulders bare. She stepped close to me. "Icarus," she said caressingly. "Haven't we always been good friends?" The curve of her neck, the tender rise of her clavicles above the top of her dress, distracted me.

"If you bring your father the king with you, then you may accompany him," I said, backing away slightly.

She undid the clasp that bound her hair in a ponytail. It cascaded down as she pressed the clasp into my hand and folded my fingers around it. "This is encrusted with diamonds and emeralds," she said. "Take it as a gift."

The warmth of her fingers stirred me. It was made of wood, but in that moment I thought it more valuable than if it had actually been encrusted with jewels.

"Don't look my way, Thomasine," Nicholas said. "The audience doesn't exist in the world of the play."

She turned her gaze back to me. "Icarus," she said again. The strange hazel of her eyes kept changing in the light as she ran her fingers slowly down the front of my shirt.

Then her mother called her in for dinner. She held out her palm, and as I laid the clasp in it, she smiled in a slow, possessive way.

On her way back to the house, she dipped a spoon into the stew Karelia was stirring on the stove and tasted it. "I wish I could eat with all of you," Thomasine said, and then was gone.

"You should be careful around that girl," Karelia said. "She troubles me."

"She's my friend," I said.

"I believe that's just her manner," Nicholas said. "If she wants to act with us, who am I to say no? Her father's our landlord, and he charges us no rent. It's the duty of the rich to look after artists, and in return we can corrupt their offspring." He picked up another spoon, and she plucked it from his fingers before he could have a taste.

"Not fully cooked yet," she said sharply, and he grinned.

CHAPTER ELEVEN

On May 18, exactly one month after the earthquake, we went to see the great Sarah Bernhardt, who came to Berkeley to play Racine's *Phèdre*. She had sold out all 7,000 seats of the university's outdoor theater; we spread out blankets on the grassy hill above. Bernhardt and her fellow actors would speak their lines in French, so Nicholas summarized the plot for us beforehand: Queen Phèdre falls in love with her own stepson, Hippolytus; he rejects her; Phèdre lets her servant falsely accuse him of trying to seduce the queen. When King Theseus returns, Hippolytus, exiled by his father, dies offstage at the hands of a creature that is half bull and half dragon; Phèdre kills herself in remorse. "In other words, a thoroughly lighthearted play," Nicholas said.

As the play began and Prince Hippolytus stepped onto the stage, Nicholas moved toward Karelia, leaning close to translate lines. Thomasine had said she would translate for me, but she seemed distracted, twisting to get comfortable, biting her thumb. Sometimes she tapped Nicholas to ask questions about the unfamiliar words. "*Qu'est-ce que le Ténare?*" "*Qui est le géant d'Epidaure?*" My father sat by himself, seemingly lost in thought, as he often was these days. Mr. Hallgarten smiled as if we were all his children, but anger came into his eyes when Nicholas whispered into Karelia's ear.

Then Bernhardt, clad in an ivory gown, whirling her purple and crimson train, staggered onto stage. It was as if a thunderstorm had compressed itself into human shape. When she threw herself onto the divan and stretched her arms imploringly to her elderly servant, I wanted to rush onto the stage and bring her whatever she needed—a drink of water, the pyramids, the Roman empire. When Bernhardt knelt at the scornful prince's feet, and pleaded with him, and drew the sword that hung at his waist, and held it unsteadily to her white neck, Thomasine clenched my arm hard enough to bruise. How quickly the play wound into tragedy and death. In life, the bull-dragon doesn't always come right away, the hand hesitates to bring the toxic cup to the lips. As the sun dropped behind the columns, Phèdre guzzled the poison and sank slowly to the ground, her hands trembling like little birds, woe and banked passion riding the ebb of her cooing voice.

For a long time the crowds lingered. As Bernhardt climbed into her carriage, dressed in rose-colored silk, a large contingent of admirers pursued her down the hill.

Our party walked back toward the Hallgartens' house. "Don't take Bernhardt as a model for an actor," Nicholas told me. "She doesn't disappear into her roles—every role disappears into her. Yet I wouldn't want to live in a world without her."

The streets were empty at this hour. Mrs. Hallgarten seemed to be weeping, though she made no noise, and Mr. Hallgarten rested his hand on her back. "She misses her home country," he said.

"I miss it too, and I've never been there," Karelia said.

"You would love it," Nicholas said. "The cafés…the climb up Montmartre to the basilica…the evening light on Notre Dame Cathedral as you walk toward it along the Seine…someday I will take you and be your tour guide."

Karelia smiled and was about to speak, but Mr. Hallgarten looked back at the two of them fiercely, and she fell silent and looked away.

"King Theseus is the most wronged figure in the play, don't you think?" Mr. Hallgarten said. "The women lie to him, he's driven to cast out his beloved son, and he loses his wife as well, when she would have done better to have remained loyal and tamped down her misbegotten passion."

"Theseus is as much to blame as anyone," Nicholas said. "He spent little time looking into the matter before banishing his son. I find him as impetuous as the others."

"A king shouldn't have feelings? Is that what you believe?"

"A king can't help but have feelings, same as any man. But what we look for in a king is a willingness to act very carefully, to look after the kingdom in his charge, to balance and weigh the evidence."

"If those in the king's care can't be bothered to look after his interests, then the kingdom is lost. That is what the play is telling us."

Nicholas seemed bewildered by Mr. Hallgarten's keen interest in this point of the drama. "What do you think, Karelia? Tragic plays endure because they're true, they show us how people behave, and the dangers that can befall any one of us. After the fact, it's easy to say, Phèdre should have done this, Theseus should have done that. But when it is us in the thick of things, all of those shoulds are out of sight, and we act with our hearts, for good or ill."

"You ask me what I think, but you don't give me room to answer," Karelia said wryly.

"Tell us now, Karelia," Mr. Hallgarten asked. "What rules your heart? Loyalty? Or some new passion? If you were Phèdre, that is."

"Loyalty, of course," she said. Mr. Hallgarten seemed mollified by this and took hold of his wife's arm again. I thought Karelia gave her answer with surprising ease, but her smile had the curve of mockery, and when Nicholas began to earnestly take up the subject of Theseus again, she smacked him lightly on the arm and said, "Just admire the beautiful twilight, you fool."

*   *   *

Our next Sunday evening play drew more than a dozen people—somehow, word of our performances had spread, and everyone was still in the mood for theater, no matter how amateur. They arrived with picnics and set out blankets in a semicircle before our improvised stage, the young men and women flirting with each other, the older ones sharing complaints or asking advice. When Nicholas clapped his hands to announce the start of the performance, they hushed and turned to face us. It astonished me, their hunger for the little dramas we presented.

Acting flustered Thomasine. Even in rehearsal, she seemed a different person. She finger-twisted her hair on her first read-through, flushed when she flubbed lines, laughed in a skittery way at odd moments. If Nicholas suggested she give a line a different emphasis, or perform an action in a different way, she often as not botched the line. But after Nicholas called me a natural actor who needed to learn not to ham, she lost no time in noting whenever she felt I had overdone it. "You sound like you're gargling blood," she would complain when I died with too much emphasis. Or, when I expressed horror at the news that my beloved had been kidnapped, she broke character to whisper in my ear, "Careful, you don't want the audience to worry you've soiled yourself."

She was rarely mistaken in her assessments, however. And when she gave me approving looks after I'd finished a scene, I was much happier than when Karelia praised me, because Karelia did so routinely and without thinking.

That night, Thomasine played Pallas Athene. She had an electric way of pivoting or darting. She poked my chest hard with the blunt end of her spear, her helmet gleaming in the setting sun, and I felt the goddess flicker behind her eyes.

She often confounded me. In her company, I lost track of time, or more precisely, I lost track of myself in time. The lens of my perception narrowed.

Many years later, when I saw A *Midsummer Night's Dream* for the first time, the actress who played Titania was commanding and mysterious, and her scenes outshone all the ones with the young lovers. She made me wish Shakespeare had dispensed with the others and written the play entirely about the power struggle between the fairy king and queen. The audience laughed at the young lovers, so passionate in their love, whichever direction it pointed. Now Lysander was wholly in love with Hermia; now, under the influence of the magic flower's juice, he was wholly in love with Helena and despised Hermia. They don't behave any better than people in real life, but their affections are undivided. In our own midsummer night's dream, it was less straightforward.

Sometimes Thomasine would ask my advice on her acting, paying close attention to what I said. Other times, she would touch my cheek and say, apropos of nothing, "Poor Joseph, you haven't a home."

Walking in the canyon together, I would touch her hand and she would clasp it in hers. Once, I ran my fingers lightly down her arm, and she scratched my bare arm in return with her thumbnail, leaving a long, nearly invisible thread of red. She hadn't meant to scratch, she said. "I was thinking."

When she joined us in the camp, she would throw her arm around Bee, rest her head on Sebastian's shoulder, tug on Nicholas's jacket to ask him a question about a scene we were practicing. She never put her arm about Karelia, I noticed. When Thomasine would fling open a window at the back of her house and call, "Joseph," waving me inside, and I would drop the book I was reading or the apple I was eating, Karelia might sigh, or mutter under her breath.

"What?" I asked.

But she only shook her head.

At times, I felt jealous of Thomasine's attentions to the others in the camp, especially Nicholas. Sometimes she would speak French to him, and he would answer in kind, although if she persisted too long, he would tell her it was rude in the company of those who spoke only

English. *"Merde!"* was one of her favorite expressions when she made an error, and it always made him laugh. She would pepper him with questions—Is my character angry when she drops the vase? When Theseus frees me, what if I faint? What if I came in with my hands behind my back? I started inventing questions for Nicholas myself, which he answered with slight puzzlement, probably sensing their slapdash quality.

Our next play was based on the bloodiest of the *Kalevala* stories: the tale of Kullervo. Two brothers quarrel until one slays the other. The victor sells the other's son, Kullervo—his own nephew—to a blacksmith as a cattle-herd. The blacksmith's wife treats Kullervo cruelly, and in retaliation, Kullervo drives home wolves and bears instead of the cattle. They tear apart and kill the wife. Kullervo then murders everyone at his uncle's farm, burns it to ash, and returns to his home, where remorse eats away at him and he ends his life with his sword.

"Here the *Kalevala* rises to the heights of a Greek tragedy," Nicholas said. "What I could make of this story, if only I were Sophocles."

At the end of the performance, when I cried out in misery right before stabbing myself, I thought of Sarah Bernhardt, yearning to capture her intensity.

The day after, the *Berkeley Gazette* published a review of the play dubbing us the "'Hallgarten Players,' talented painters and photographers who have refused to let calamity halt the flow of their artistic production." The reporter praised Mr. Hallgarten as an exemplar of compassion and as a patron of the arts, "the sort that Berkeley needs in order to fulfill its potential." I thought that now Mr. Hallgarten couldn't turn against us, because we raised his profile in the city. I thought that he might come out to congratulate us, but he didn't.

After the *Gazette* article, some members of the Hillside Club approached Nicholas about putting on a special performance for them. The club was having a new building constructed for its headquarters, and it would have a stage and enough seats for an audience of more than a hundred. Although the official opening wouldn't be until September, they thought the stage would be ready by last weekend of June, and they wished to inaugurate the space by showcasing some of the brilliant artists and Bohemians who had found a home in Berkeley, to better establish the town as a new art center. There would even be a gallery space where Peter and Sebastian and Bee and Karelia could show their artwork.

Nicholas told us excitedly of his meeting. "Why shouldn't Berkeley become the new home of California's Bohemia?" he said. "If our performance and exhibition catches the hearts of the Hillside Club members, we could establish a permanent theater company in town, even buy or build our own theater. Upstairs, we'll have artists' studios and darkrooms and a rehearsal hall. All we need is the right tale." He looked at me.

Before I could speak, Karelia said, "The story of Aino."

"What?"

"We should tell the story of Aino." Her eyes shone in the firelight. Recently, she had begun photographing us in our costumes; she wanted to create an illustrated edition of the *Kalevala* someday. I remember one of Bee in soft focus, dressed in a white robe, peering into a pool of water; another of Peter, dressed as Wainamoinen, binding his bleeding knee with cloth, the bloody hatchet on the ground; one of me as Kullervo gazing in astonishment at the broken loaf of bread in my hands, a large black stone gleaming from within the crumb.

Now she said, "A young wizard, Youkahainen, challenges the ancient wizard Wainamoinen to a duel of chanting legends and loses. To win his freedom, Youkahainen offers his sister Aino in marriage. His mother is delighted to have a man as illustrious as Wainamoinen as a potential son-in-law, but Aino is inconsolable. After encountering Wainamoinen in the woods, she runs away and drowns herself rather than be married to him."

"Too gloomy," said Sebastian.

"Tragedy consoles," Nicholas said. "Was *Phèdre* uplifting? It's a warning to us all not to despair like the queen."

"I want to be Aino," Thomasine said.

"Karelia will be Aino," Nicholas said. "And it would be unsettling to have you play Aino's mother, so we had better invent a younger sister for Aino for you to play."

Bee agreed to be Aino's mother. Sebastian would play Youkahainen, Peter would be Wainamoinen. I would be the fox that witnesses Aino's drowning and tells her family.

"In the *Kalevala*," I said, "it's a hare who tells the family."

"Yes," Nicholas said, "but dramatically speaking, at such a bleak moment, there's something ridiculous about a hare on stage. And wouldn't you rather play a fox?" I had to admit I would. I began to ponder how a fox might walk. The story of Aino had always been one of Karelia's favorites, and mine, and I was certain that our drama would impress Berkeley's wealthiest so much that they would open their wallets, and we would make the town into an art colony known far and wide.

* * *

On Wednesday afternoon, Nicholas told me to practice lines with Thomasine before rehearsals the next evening. The day was unusually warm. My father was drawing up a plan for a simplified version of the Tetrascope. Karelia had gone into Berkeley: now that Anne Brigman had returned, she sometimes rented a darkroom by the hour from Rose, a photographer who lived downtown.

I found Thomasine at her desk, fanning herself with a folded paper and staring at the wall before her, lost in thought. She seemed pleased at the idea of rehearsing, though she wasn't enamored of our current play, based on the myth of Narcissus and Echo. "Why would I fall in love with someone who's in love with his own reflection?" she asked.

We couldn't stay in her bedroom, she said; Sophie or Adele or both would invade. I suggested we practice among the trees along the canyon's creek, although their shade was sparse.

"I want somewhere out of the sun," she said. "Let's try the cave instead."

"What cave?"

She crooked her finger. As I followed her out of the house and up to the canyon's rim, I imagined a vaulting cavern, glittering with rough crystals, its entrance concealed behind vines. I wondered why she'd never spoken of it before.

Once we reached the canyon's bowl, we headed northeast. She walked cat-like, her bare sun-browned feet hardly raising dust on the trail. I wished my feet were as tough as hers, so I could go barefoot too. Whatever she'd been brooding about in her room still seemed to preoccupy her, and she answered my attempts at conversation tersely until I gave up. Even the dust seemed so enervated by the heat that it barely rose. The canyon's grassy flanks were golden from lack of rain.

We followed the creek for a while until we came to a spot where caves riddled the side of a steep slope, stacked vertically. Most were too small for a person to stand inside. Thomasine clambered up until she reached a larger one that wasn't visible from below. She beckoned to me. "This is where I like to come sometimes to be alone," she said. "Not even my sisters know about it." I was flattered to be invited, yet also disappointed that she hadn't invited me until now.

We stepped inside the cool, dim space, the ceiling a few inches from our heads.

"Where's your script?" she said sharply.

"I've memorized my lines," I said.

She threw her script down and sat against the cave wall. "Sometimes you make me sick."

"Your lines are easy," I said. "You only have to repeat the last few words of what I say."

She closed her eyes. I sat across from her and tried closing my eyes, too, but the walls of the cave seemed to come closer when I did.

"In a way, you're lucky," she said, in a soft voice.

"Lucky?"

"You've already had the worst thing happen to you," she said. "Your home was destroyed, your father's work and his studio was destroyed, your school—everything. You don't have to worry about anything anymore, because the worst has already happened."

"We have worries," I said. "We don't know where we're going to live or how. Your parents could kick us off their property any time."

"Why would they do that?" She picked at her fingernails. "I don't think my father is going to get his insurance money. They say the fire was caused by the earthquake and so they're not liable. Whenever Algernon is here, he looks paler than he did the time before. And Papa says that the people he works with wish my uncle were still alive and running the company. I think the business isn't going to survive, and we'll have to sell the house." She threw a pebble at my leg.

We were quiet for a while, listening to the trickle of the creek below. The thought that they would have to give up their house alarmed me.

"And there's something else," Thomasine said.

"What do you mean?"

"It drives me crazy, all the time. I can't talk about it."

"Why not?"

She tossed another pebble at me. "Don't you understand anything?" Her eyes were fierce and she leaned toward me as if to strike. I grabbed hold of her and pulled her toward me.

Her nostrils sucked in breath, and she pushed into me so that the cave's rocky wall dug into the back of my skull. After a moment, she shifted and placed my palm between her small breasts, the warmth radiating through my arm into my chest. The tang of dust mingled with the scent of her hair. A slow flood of heat overcame me. Time curled away from the orderly march of minutes and dispersed like ash.

She drew back, and I opened my eyes. It was hard to tell in the cave's dim light, but it seemed that tears streaked her face. She slumped against the wall, pressing her fists into the dirt. "Why couldn't you be older, and taller, and more—" she hesitated, then, giving it the French pronunciation, "*insouciant.*"

"What are you talking about?" I asked.

"You think you own me, but you don't."

I shook my head.

"No." She paused for thought. "You think I *owe* you—that's it."

Abruptly she stood—I started to jump up after her, in case she was going to leave, but she pushed me with both hands, and I fell back. She pointed her finger in my face, laughingly, as if I were a dog she were commanding to sit. Then she stretched her arms out, presenting herself. She stooped. At first I thought she was bowing, but instead she hoisted her dress over her head, her fingers grazing the cave ceiling.

I must have made some motion to speak, because she pressed her finger to her lips. She met my gaze with a mocking look as she removed her slip, her brassiere, her underpants, and held her arms out again, triumphant now, bare in the hot cave's shadow, her clothes in a heap like a molted skin. Her toes gripped the rocky ground.

I had only time to take in a bleary sense of her, the rounds of her breasts, the brown nipples, the slight flare of her hips, the scramble of pubic hair, her thighs balanced on her bony shins.

She made a sound—a breath, a kind of military hup—as she spun to her right, presenting me with her left profile. Then another breath, and she faced away from me, her long hair, the crumple of a dead leaf caught in it, the two knives of her shoulder blades, a trickle of sweat running between them toward the curve of her buttocks. Another breath, another pivot, and she presented her right profile. A fourth turn brought her to face me again, the whole of her bestowed to me and yet withheld. Her gaze held triumph and amusement, but also something wilder—exaltation and alarm and hunger.

Before I could say anything, she was dressing. Her knuckles were a little bloodied—they must have struck the ceiling. I felt she had wanted to sever something between us, but that instead it had only tangled us further. Fully dressed, she took up her script with a shaking hand. "All right," she began, and stopped short.

I turned. Sophie peered in from the side of the cave's mouth, her long hair falling across her neck in such a way that her head seemed to float, disembodied. Her eyes were wide. Thomasine barked her name, and her sister vanished.

Thomasine threw the script down and darted past me, and I hurried to follow.

She skidded down the slope after Sophie. Adele was there, too, trying and failing to keep up with Sophie, her little legs pumping. She kept twisting back in bafflement at the fury with which their oldest sister pursued them.

Thomasine flew past Adele, who all at once gave up and crouched, panting hard. To keep from bowling her over, I pitched myself to the side and tumbled to the ground hard, my right arm ramming the earth. When I looked up, Thomasine tackled Sophie and they both went down, too. The wind knocked out of me, I watched as Thomasine held her sister down, one hand on the back of Sophie's head. She was whispering something fiercely to her.

"What happened?" Adele said.

"Were you spying on us?" I asked, trying to keep my voice casual.

"We wanted to find out where you went," she said. "You're always going off together," she added sourly. I decided that she, at least, must not have seen Thomasine undressed: Sophie must have kept her back, or else the slope had been too steep for her to climb. The two sisters ahead of us still hadn't moved. I got to my feet, my arm smarting.

At last Thomasine let Sophie up. Sophie had the air of a wronged party, tinged with smugness. She dusted herself off in a leisurely fashion, gave me a scalding once-over, and called Adele to her. The two girls trotted off together toward the path that led up out of the canyon.

"I told her that if she tells Maman, then she'll never see *Aino*, because the play will be canceled," Thomasine said.

"And that persuaded her?"

"No. I had to promise her other things. That's not important. She has to keep Adele quiet, too. If Maman knew, she would scalp me."

"I don't think Adele saw anything," I said. Twigs and debris hung from her hair, but when I reached to pick them out, she batted my hand away and did it herself.

"You look a mess yourself," she said.

"You're beautiful," I said, though this seemed inadequate—she was still breathing hard, and dust speckled her cheek. I moved to embrace her.

She slid away. "Come on," she said, and followed her sisters, walking quickly. She said nothing more to me the whole way back.

*   *   *

When I returned to the camp, my father was waiting for me. Mr. Hallgarten had called the relief committee headquarters and arranged for us to pick up a tent to house the new Tetrascope we were to construct. "He's only given me enough credit to purchase four inexpensive

Brownies," he said. "I think he wouldn't have agreed even to that, if he didn't feel guilty that he lost the Book of Months. But when the insurance money comes, I'll be able to buy my own cameras."

The other refugees waiting in line for supplies regarded us curiously, as did the women behind the desk when we gave them our request. The rolled-up tent was crushingly heavy. My father lifted it onto his shoulder with his good left hand, but I struggled with my end. After a hundred feet, my father suggested we rest. When he saw how hard I was panting, he left me and went to fetch Nicholas, who hoisted the tent uncomplainingly, even though he must have been exhausted from his day of carpentry.

The Crowleys and the Vissers watched with bewilderment and annoyance as the three of us struggled with the stakes and ropes.

When we were done, and the tent was more or less standing, if listing a bit to the side, Sebastian said, "What a grand room you have for yourselves here. It must be at least twelve feet square, wouldn't you say?"

"It isn't for us," my father said. "It's to house a new Tetrascope."

"Still, it would be a shame to let such spaciousness go to waste. Were you and Joseph to move your sleeping quarters into here, then those of us who aren't fortunate enough to receive a new large tent might find a use for your old one. I imagine down in the camps something this size must sleep at least a dozen."

My father said that was reasonable. Karelia was upset with both of us when she saw the tent that evening and found out what it was for. "You told me you were done being his measuring stick," she told me. "Why are you letting him do this?"

"Because I can't tell him no, not now," I said. "And what harm is it doing me? Nothing will ever come of it anyway."

"Is that how you feel? That's almost worse. If you don't believe in the project, that's even more reason to tell him not to start it up again. He's going to waste a good deal more time and money—or Thomas's money."

I woke up in the middle of the night, worried that she was right. But the next morning, I threw myself into helping my father build a new Tetrascope. This one was simpler: we placed the four Brownies on tripods at the four corners of a square, anchored to the ground so they would always remain the same distance apart from each other. My father devised a way to connect the triggers with cords so that all the shutters would fire at the same time, but we didn't use pipes with mirrors to line up all four images on the same negative; my father would have to develop each negative separately. "If anything," my father said, "this is an improvement over the original," he said. "The mirrors added an unnecessary degree of complexity." Much of the work fell to me, because of his injured hand, but he was patient with my clumsiness.

My father asked me to stand in the center so he could focus. It was strange, after so many weeks—very nearly a month—and I couldn't sense the focal point the way I once had. It felt dull and cloudy, barely there.

"Excellent," he said. "We'll begin tomorrow at our usual time."

My father spent the rest of the morning and early afternoon inspecting and polishing the Tetrascope in readiness for our first session, taking test photographs using stacked crates, developing them in the darkroom he'd set up in the Hallgartens' shed. I read the *Kalevala* under the tree. I'd thought he would call me, but it seemed he expected me to appear, as I always had. At ten minutes before the hour, I ran into the tent. I told myself that it was a simple matter, to stand once again for the Tetrascope.

At five minutes before three o'clock, I undressed. I heard Peter's and Ina's voices as they passed by, their shadows crossing the fabric. In the studio, the world had seemed so far away; I felt doubly naked in the middle of the camp.

I stood for the lenses. The shutters clicked. For the first time, I felt as if the camera had taken something from me, as if by standing for the Tetrascope again I was stepping back into an obedient line of dead Josephs, all marching precisely in the same direction, toward nothingness, eradicating the living Joseph who laughed and lied and longed for Thomasine and could turn himself into a fox or a murderer or a thousand other beings.

*   *   *

The next afternoon, I delayed, reading the *Kalevala* for as long as I could, telling myself that it was important that I decide on the next story we might turn into a play. A few minutes before three o'clock, I went into the tent and pinned the flaps behind me.

My father was making tiny adjustments to the camera, not looking up.

I pulled my shirt over my head and stopped with my arms still in it.

An ant crawled across the trampled ground beneath me, halting and proceeding. My father once told me Zeno's paradox: for a turtle to leave Point A and reach Point B, the turtle must first reach a point equidistant between A and B—call it Point C. But to reach Point C, the turtle must first reach Point D, equidistant between A and C, and so forth, ad infinitum. Therefore, it is impossible that the turtle should ever be able to move at all. My father had dismissed the paradox, saying, "Just as a photograph has a grain, observable with a strong magnifying glass, so too does space have a grain. There are units of matter that are indivisible, and once one has reached this level, it is absurd to speak of an equidistant point. Therefore, motion is possible, as anyone who has eyes can see is true."

To have dreamed up this paradox, Zeno must have experienced something like what I felt now, because I could not move from the side of the tent to the center of the Tetrascope. I told myself that it was only one moment of the day, and that it changed nothing, but I still couldn't move.

My father waited, staring ahead. I was invisible to him as long as I remained where I was.

I yanked my shirt back over my head.

"Joseph?"

Avoiding his eyes, I thrust my feet into my shoes without tying them and hurried out of the tent. It felt to me as if an invisible force propelled me away, as if I had nothing to do with it, though I knew this wasn't true. All I had to do to give my father a sense of meaning was to stand still for a few seconds, but to my shame, I couldn't.

"Joseph," he called. I ran up the slope behind the camp and didn't slow until I was well into the canyon.

I returned to camp only when supper was almost over, grabbing a slice of bread like a thief and spending the rest of the evening in Sebastian and Nicholas's tent playing cards.

I hoped my father would fall asleep before I returned to our tent, but he began speaking as soon as I pushed aside the flap. "Your participation in the project has always been voluntary," he said. "You, more than anyone, understand the importance of the work we've done together, and so I couldn't account for your behavior until I realized that you're angry with me."

The night was moonless and clouded, the bonfire extinguished, everyone else in their beds. It was too cold outside to run away again, and I was tired. I wished I could explain, but I had no words.

"From the very start, I should have made duplicates of each negative and placed them in storage in another city. I knew that San Francisco had burned before. You blame me rightly. But I've made arrangements to store duplicates of the new negatives in San Jose. At the end of each week, I'll deliver them myself."

I took off my trousers and shirt and climbed into my cot.

"I've been careless." His voice rose a little. "But when Thomas finds the Book of Months—"

"It's gone," I said.

"We don't know that. I gave it to him in the evening after he'd already left the office, I remember this distinctly. And he himself said he brought it home. Don't despair. It will turn up, I'm certain of this." He seemed relieved, now that I had spoken. "We'll start again tomorrow, shall we?"

If I could only convince him that the Book of Months had been destroyed, he could turn his brilliant mind to something else, some new project with greater likelihood of success. Or I could tell him the truth, that I had hidden it because I hadn't wanted anyone to see it, and that it had mysteriously vanished. But wouldn't it hurt him even more to know I'd wanted the project buried as far back as January? After all, I hadn't helped him rescue the project on the day of the earthquake, I'd stayed with Karelia both times he'd attempted to enter the studio. If I'd gone with him, we could have salvaged something, we could have convinced the firefighters to let us into the Murchison Building before they detonated the explosives. Hot with shame, I mumbled something indeterminate and turned over, wrapping myself in my blankets.

The next afternoon, as the hour of three o'clock approached, I stood outside the tent. When he emerged to look for me, I didn't know what to do. Behind our stage stood a large box of old hats that some neighbors had donated for costumes, as if they hadn't noticed we set all our plays in ancient Greece or Finland. I tried on a battered Panama hat, wondering how people decided what kind of hat suited them. I replaced it with a black bowler, so large that it covered my eyes.

"Will you not stand for me?" my father said.

For whom had this bowler been made? A gorilla, perhaps. I thought of an idea for a sketch I could propose to Nicholas. If I was a gorilla in a bowler, I couldn't be expected to talk. I stood still, trembling. I believe that day I settled something for myself, though I couldn't have explained it: I was an actor. Not a person who changed by barely detectable increments from day to day, but a mutable figure who could not be marked out and plotted. To pose for the Tetrascope seemed an utter lie.

"Will you not stand for me?" My father's voice was strident now. I'd heard him be angry with others—with Karelia, with Mr. Hallgarten—but seldom with me. Now I was finally disappointing him.

"I can't," I said.

After a minute had passed, I removed the hat and turned around. But he was nowhere in sight.

* * *

I worried that he would disappear again, that the police would find him wandering and disoriented, and this time they'd lock him up or send him to an asylum. Or worse, what if he did away with himself? I cursed myself for my rebellion. After dinner, I told Karelia what I'd done, and she said she was glad. "You've been entirely too docile with him," she said. "It's time you stopped pretending that you're an extension of him."

"But what if he—"

My father appeared at the edge of camp, halting when he saw me in conversation with Karelia, then quickly glancing away and heading over to the soup tureen.

"All he wants me to do—" I began again.

"No," Karelia said. "No, you will not back down." She jumped up, and before I could stop her, went over to my father, who was scraping the bottom of the tureen with the ladle. She leaned close, talking urgently and quietly. When she came back, she sat next to me and drew me into her arms. On the other side of the fire, Sebastian smirked, and I pulled away.

"I told him he's harming you," she said. "All your life, he's treated you like a laboratory animal, and it's time for him to treat you like his son."

Her words horrified me. "What did he say to that?"

"He said he never thought of you as a laboratory animal."

Part of me wished that she hadn't interfered, and part of me was relieved. It seemed like a conversation we ought to have been able to have between the two of us, but I couldn't imagine that happening. Perhaps we would be able to talk about it when we went to bed that night. I dreaded this and hoped for it.

After everyone but Peter Visser had turned in, I finally went into our tent, having failed to think of what to say to him. It was a cloudy night, so dark I could only tell he was there from his breathing. "I don't feel like you've treated me like a rat," I said.

After a pause, he said, "I'm glad of that." His voice was too gentle, as if he were afraid of scaring me away.

"I'm just—too old now to be part of the project."

"Yes," he said. "I understand."

I felt my way into my cot. "Thank you." I knew this was inadequate. I could feel his sorrow permeating the tent, his regret at the end of his great endeavor and at the thought that I couldn't bear it anymore. I wished I could find words for everything I felt: my sadness at the way I'd hurt him, my anger at him for making me the center of all his hopes, my fear that he had been broken in some way that could never be repaired. The thought of speaking plainly to him seemed beyond my capabilities, however, and I soon fled into sleep.

*   *   *

Nicholas obtained a typewriter for his tent, and he and Karelia spent every morning that week working on the script. We sometimes overheard them talking through scenes vehemently. Then came the sound of typing. With the tent's side flaps up, their legs were visible, so we could see when Karelia took over the typewriter—her efficient pecks rising and falling in a crescendo—and when Nicholas thumped the keys, his rhythm irregular, the volume constant, while Karelia looked over his shoulder. When a breeze blew, crumpled paper scudded across the grass like overgrown dandelion puffs, and sometimes Nicholas would dart out to chase them down and throw them on the bonfire's coals to watch with satisfaction as they curled into flaming roses.

They disagreed about the last moments of the Aino story. In the *Kalevala,* when Wainamoinen hears of Aino's death, he weeps. Then he takes a boat out onto the waters where she drowned and casts a fishing line. He lands a large fish of a kind he can't identify. But when he takes out his knife to fillet the fish, it jumps out of the boat and upbraids him: "I am Aino," says the fish, "and I didn't come to be cut up for breakfast, I came to be your life companion, to make your bed with snowy linens and smooth your head on the pillow, to build your fire, to bake honey bread and fill your cup with barley water." With that, she disappears beneath the waves, never to be seen again.

"It's a strange moment, considering that Aino drowned herself rather than be married to Wainamoinen," Nicholas told me. "I take it to mean that she regrets that decision. She threw herself into the water, the gods apparently transformed her into a fish, and she's realized that she misses life, and all the little things that make up life, fixing the pillow, baking bread. Now that she's had time to swim in the cold waters of death, she wants to come back, and so she's sad and also angry that Wainamoinen didn't recognize her."

"I don't see it that way," Karelia said. "I think Aino is mocking Wainamoinen. He thought he could have her for the asking—even when she was human, he treated her like a fish he'd caught—and she's escaped him by transforming herself. It is her triumph."

Nicholas turned to me. "What do you think?"

"Why would anyone want to stay a fish?" I said.

"Because life under sea would be wonderful," Karelia said. "How much better to play among the herring and the salmon and the whales than to bake honey bread all day for an old man."

CHAPTER TWELVE

One moonless Friday night in early June, Sebastian, Peter, and Nicholas were walking back late from the streetcar, having spent the evening in the saloons of Oakland. They had drunk a lot. They were only a block and a half away from the Hallgartens', one street down, when Sebastian veered away from the others and disappeared. Peter and Nicholas waited on the street awhile, confused, and Nicholas decided they should stand still and stay quiet so as not to disturb anyone in the nearby households; the curfew was still in force, and technically they should not have been out at all.

Then they heard a gunshot and a cry.

Apparently, as I heard Peter tell it later, Sebastian had mistaken another brown-shingled house for the Hallgartens'. He'd hurried into the backyard, eager to reach our latrine, and had been surprised to find that the tents were gone, all traces of the bonfire vanished, even the very stones we sat on disappeared. Drunk, he'd considered that the Hallgartens had finally done what he'd been expecting all along and disassembled the camp, no doubt hiring a large crew to swiftly blot out the evidence in the few hours since he'd left. He decided to relieve himself in the usual spot, whether the latrine yet remained or not, and then find Nicholas and Peter and deliver the unwelcome news.

He must have knocked over some lawn furniture or made some other noise, however. As we later learned, the home happened to be owned by a member of the Berkeley police, or one of the residents empowered by the police to serve as a deputy during the refugee crisis, it was never clear. This man saw Sebastian heading back toward the house, stepped out of his back door, and fired a warning shot. Sebastian fell.

Nicholas and Peter ran around the edge of the house to see the man hauling Sebastian to his feet. Another man emerged from the house, and Nicholas and Peter overheard enough to tell that Sebastian was unharmed and that the men intended to take him to the police station. By now, lamps were lighting in the windows nearby, windows were raised, and Peter pulled Nicholas away, hissing to him that if they were caught, they would be arrested too.

"I should have defended him," Nicholas said the next morning at breakfast. "I should at least have gone with him, and if we were thrown into jail together, then we would have been company for each other."

"You were right to avoid arrest," Ina said.

"Why didn't you wake me?" Bee demanded. "You simply came back and went to sleep?" I'd never seen her so distraught. She hurried off to the police station without eating anything.

"I'm sure it will be fine," Ina said. "No one could seem more harmless than Sebastian. But you'd better go with her and explain—no, you and Peter both look like you spent the night passed out in a field. I'll go with her."

We saw Sebastian and Bee only once more. They came back that evening to collect their belongings while we were eating dinner. Two policemen waited at a respectful distance. For breaking the curfew, for drunk and disorderly behavior, for trespassing, Sebastian was ordered to leave the city limits and not return. He spoke little to us, and would be cordial only to Ina and Karelia, who had joined us for dinner. Peter and Nicholas in particular he regarded with disdain. He said he and Bee had a distant relation who lived in Sacramento, and they would see if they could find refuge with her for a while.

"Well, Arthur," he said as he staggered a little under the weight of his bundles, "you'll want to photograph the camp now that I've gone, so you can have a record of our absence. This is the way time goes, taking away little by little, isn't it?" He turned to the policemen. "I don't suppose you help carry, do you?" They shook their heads.

*   *   *

After dinner, as twilight fell, Mr. Hallgarten joined us around the bonfire. He lowered himself next to my father, who was whittling the ends of sticks into sharp points by firelight; Ina had said she wanted to roast quail the next day, and my father seemed eager these days to be helpful in the camp. He was always fetching water and wood, sometimes bringing more than was necessary. Sometimes I had the sense that he was watching me with a wary tenderness, trying to tread softly around me, which irritated me. At other times, I'd come across him standing still, and I could sense that his mind had returned to his old obsession, trying to find some way to photograph time he hadn't considered. We were polite with each other, but spoke even less than we had before.

Mr. Hallgarten cleared his throat and said, "What happened last night is unacceptable."

Nicholas laughed. He had been drinking more than he usually did for a weeknight.

"You find it amusing, but Celeste and I do not. Remember that you're our guests, your actions reflect on us—you have even gone so far to style yourselves the 'Hallgarten Players.' Mr. Stanton, the man whose lawn Sebastian stumbled into, is also a member of the Hillside Club, as is his father, and they were not amused either. Sebastian wouldn't say whether he was returning alone or not, so I don't know how many of you got drunk and made fools of yourselves. Any further incident and we will send you all packing. Your performances have made you popular among the neighborhood, but we expect loyalty and good behavior while you are living on our land."

"I'm very sorry this happened," Peter said.

"I wish I could undo it," Nicholas said. "But everyone will forget it in time, your club members, even Mr. Stanton." He stretched out on the ground alongside the fire and looked up at my father, who had stopped whittling and seemed to be lost in his thoughts. "The tragedy of time is that nothing can be undone," Nicholas said. "Isn't that what you said, Arthur? And the comedy is that nothing endures."

If Nicholas's mangling of his ideas upset my father, he gave no sign.

Mr. Hallgarten said, "I need you to reassure me there will be no more foolish acts."

Nicholas laid a hand across his eyes. "No more foolish acts—who among us has managed such a feat?"

Karelia said, "There won't be any other incidents like this."

Mr. Hallgarten stood, brushed off his trousers, and walked back to his house.

Later that night, Karelia and Nicholas had a tremendous argument. It began some distance up the slope from us, while the rest of us sat around the bonfire, and as their voices grew louder, they traveled farther up the hill. "You're too deferential to that man," I overheard Nicholas say. "Artists should never be too well behaved around their patrons, it secretly disappoints them."

"You don't know anything about patrons," she said. "And you don't know anything about him."

Peter strummed his guitar idly, but no one sang. I worried that, with only a half-moon to light their way, they might fall and hurt themselves or get lost.

Not long after the camp had fallen silent and I climbed into my cot, I heard footsteps. I strained my ears, but if they spoke to each other, they did so too quietly for me to hear.

In the morning, I found only Karelia awake, returning from the creek with her hair and face wet and carrying a pot of water. I helped her start the fire. She looked shaken and weary.

"Where did you and Nicholas go last night?" I asked.

She smoothed my hair as she had when I was a little boy. "I told him to grow up, and he didn't take it well," she said. "That's all."

A little later, Nicholas emerged from his tent dressed in his carpenter's clothes. He grabbed a piece of bread for his breakfast and left without a word.

*   *   *

For the next few days, Nicholas worked long hours at his carpentry jobs. He announced that he had decided to drink less. He and Karelia became friendly with each other again—tentatively, slowly, gently.

On Wednesday, Nicholas asked Karelia and me to walk with him through the hills, even though we all still had so much to do to prepare for our performance of *Aino*, only two and a half weeks away: Nicholas had taken over the role of Youkahainen, and Ina would play Aino's mother. Performing made her nervous, but she didn't have many lines. Peter and a friend of his from work were painting backdrops, the women sewed costumes. Peter was also painting as many canvases as he could to prepare for the exhibition. Karelia spent all her free hours in the darkroom developing and printing her photographs. That morning, my father had said to me, "If only we had the *Book of Months*, we would have something worthy of exhibition." He'd groaned, and I'd slipped out of the tent guiltily.

Now, as Nicholas, Karelia, and I climbed the hill, Nicholas seemed to come to life. "Maybe at the beginning of the *Aino* play, Wainamoinen could appear in a cloud of mist at the back of the stage when Youkahainen is complaining to the audience about the renown the old man has won. After this play, we'll have begun to make a name for ourselves and can think about opening our own company in Oakland or Berkeley."

Karelia crossed her arms over her chest. "This is another dream of yours."

"What do you mean?"

"You blow ideas like soap bubbles, and you can, because everyone loves you, and you have so many possibilities open to you, while we—"

"You're the one everyone loves. You're a brilliant photographer. We have a great future ahead of us." He jumped up onto a boulder and held out his hand. At first she hesitated. In the past, Karelia would have sprung up beside him as easily as anyone, but she must have been almost three months pregnant by now, though it still didn't show. Sometimes I caught her walking around massaging her back. What was it like to have a child inside you, to feel the weight of that life, to know that it was growing each day, that your body was all that fed and held it?

She scrambled up the side of the boulder and I worried that she would hurt herself or the child. But she seemed to be fine.

The bay stretched out below, an immense long band of fog gliding in from the ocean, slowly cottoning the sunlit expanse of Marin and San Francisco.

"We'll all be much better off when we create our own place in the world. You're right. It's time for me to grow up. You are an inspiration to me." He knelt and took her hand. "Will you marry me?"

This startled her. The wind whipped her dress, and she didn't speak.

"Joseph, you've no objection, do you?" he asked.

I shook my head.

"Is this another soap bubble?" she asked Nicholas.

This seemed to wound him, although he didn't let go. "I wanted to marry you that first evening I knew you. It's as solid an idea as this." He rapped his knuckles on the stone.

Karelia turned in the direction of the Hallgartens' house. Nicholas couldn't see the fear on her face, but I could. I looked away.

"And if this dream doesn't come true, if it can't?" she asked.

"Then we'll dream another one."

She seemed to master herself and pulled him to his feet. "I've always thought like the Rainbow Maiden," she said. "'Married women, far too many, are like dogs enchained in kennels, rarely do they ask for favors, not to wives are favors given.'"

"But I'm not Wainamoinen, and I'd never enchain you. I want us to be artists together. I would only do this if it was your dream, too, and Joseph's. We'll be a family together."

"So much has changed in the last few months. I'm not even sure I know who I am, and there's still so much we don't know about each other yet. If I'm to marry, I don't want it to be a whim of the earthquake. And the Hallgartens—they're touchy about these matters, it would be better if we didn't discuss this until we're no longer dependent on them."

"You think they would be upset to hear we were to marry?"

Karelia didn't answer.

"I feel sure you care about me," Nicholas said, sounding more puzzled now than wounded.

"I do…I love your company, I love your mind…" How distraught she looked. "Nicholas, I have a confession to make."

Was she going to tell him about Mr. Hallgarten? I wanted to warn her not to, to think about it first, but she resolutely avoided looking my way.

"Ah…you're about to tell me you're already married," he said, his voice light, though his face became grave.

She shook her head. "But there was someone."

He stiffened. "How long ago? Where is he?"

"He went back to Italy—" I began to say, but Karelia stopped me.

Her eyes were wet as she touched his arm. Again she shook her head. "Can we wait until after *Aino* to talk of this again?"

He tried for several minutes to convince her to say more, but she repeated that she wasn't ready and couldn't talk about it.

Finally, Nicholas flung up his arms and said we might as well return to camp. As we walked, he began to tell apparently lighthearted stories of backstage pranks played by actors he'd known. As he talked, he glanced at her, but didn't bring up the subject of love, and when we reached the Hallgartens', he went off to a carpentry job. I followed Karelia into her tent. "If you marry Nicholas," I said, "we can all go on together, and we can make plays together."

"Oh, Joseph," she said.

I said, "You love him now, don't you?"

"It's not that simple."

"Do you love him?"

"Yes," she said, and burst into tears.

"He's an artist, he loves you. You could tell him anything and he'd still want to marry you."

"What are you picturing me telling him?"

I dropped my eyes to her belly and back to her face. She looked at me with horror. I tried to put my arms around her, but she shook me off.

"How did you…don't say anything to anyone. Does Arthur know?"

I shook my head.

"Don't say anything," she said again. "How did you find out?"

I couldn't tell her I'd known since her conversation with Mrs. Hallgarten. "You walk differently," I said.

"Please get out of my tent, I have to think."

*   *   *

Late afternoon on Sunday, our audience began arriving as usual, though neither Mr. or Mrs. Hallgarten had attended the last few performances. We had returned to older works to save our rehearsal time for *Aino*. The week before, Thomasine and I had done *Narcissus and Echo*, and we could no longer do *The Rainbow Maiden* without Bee, so tonight we reprised *Pallas Athene*.

After we finished, Karelia rose and said she had another tale from the *Kalevala* to present. Nicholas looked up in surprise. Karelia, Peter, and I had rehearsed this one in secret: the story of Mariatta, based on one of the last stories in the book.

One day, a young woman passes a whortleberry bush. One of the berries speaks to her and persuades her to swallow it, whereupon she becomes pregnant. Her family exiles her, because she won't name the father. When the baby is born, a boy, she asks a priest to baptize him, but the priest calls in Wainamoinen to judge whether the infant is worthy. Wainamoinen decrees that since the two-week-old is an outcast, his head should be dashed against a birch tree.

Karelia—Mariatta—cradled the infant, an eerie, lifelike cloth puppet—it must have been Ina's handiwork, because only she could sew with such skill. To the audience's astonishment, the infant spoke— and why not, fathered by a silver-tongued berry? The baby rebuked Wainamoinen, reminding the ancient singer that he, after all, was not killed despite having committed worse deeds, such as when he gave away his brother to win his freedom, or when Aino drowned herself to escape his persecutions. As the priest, I mulled the baby's words, then grandly overruled Wainamoinen's judgment and baptized the boy, and the ancient singer departed in defeat.

Although we'd had little time to rehearse and improvised many of our lines, the audience applauded fervently. I realized that something in the play's very roughness was moving, something in Karelia's tender gaze at her strange infant, in Wainamoinen's sanctimonious and chilling advice. As the crowd rose to leave, Karelia watched Nicholas closely. If he read any particular meaning into the play, he gave no sign.

Afterward, I followed her into her tent and said, "If you want Nicholas to know, why not tell him?"

She shook her head and lay down on her cot, still wearing her costume. "I'm so tired," she said, and shut her eyes.

I watched her for a moment, then went out and joined the others, who were sitting around the fire eating dinner. Peter brought out his flask, but when it reached Nicholas, he handed it back without taking a sip.

"It's bad luck to break a tradition," Peter said. "Are you afraid Hallgarten will catch you?"

Nicholas shrugged. "In the next two weeks, I'll need all my wits about me."

Peter looked offended. "I've always found that a handful of my wits are enough to get by," Peter said. "But I'm only a painter. As our Shakespeare, you, of course, must keep your brain unpickled." He took a deep draught, capped the flask, and slipped it back into his jacket.

* * *

Over the course of the next couple of weeks, our anticipation and nervousness increased. After the men returned from their jobs, we would rehearse *Aino* until it grew too dark to see each other. We worried that we wouldn't have time to work out our staging at the Hillside Club, and that construction of the stage might not be finished in time, but Nicholas said as long as we practiced enough that we became our characters, we could put on the play in a pig sty and it wouldn't matter. Mr. Hallgarten no longer joined us around the fire, but occasionally he walked Thomasine to rehearsals and would ask after the progress of the play. He returned to being stiff with Karelia and remained distant with Nicholas and Peter. We made extra efforts to keep the camp quiet and to ask him for as little as possible.

The army was about to close the camps in the university's athletics fields, and soon the Berkeley relief committee would disband as well. In the back of my mind, I had always thought that if the Hallgartens decided we could no longer stay on their land, we could go to the university camps, or throw ourselves on the mercy of the committee. Now we had no safety net.

One day, I found my father kneeling before a board he had placed across the top of his cot. He clutched a pen awkwardly in his right hand. It dripped ink in splotches and streaks as he attempted to direct it with his stiffened fingers. I couldn't make out what he was drawing, but it looked like a pair of bicycles that had collided with each other and were being attacked by spears from all sides. Around him lay sheets of paper crowded with writing.

"What are you doing?" I asked.

"I'm writing a book," he said, concentrating on drawing a precise arc. "I've decided I was wrong to keep the project secret for all those years. Instead I should have described my processes, my thinking about the nature of time, even given detailed plans for building a Tetrascope. Why not share it with the world? All that matters is that humanity advances our understanding of time. Another might carry on the work as well as I."

He looked up at me with such openness in his face that I couldn't bear it.

"That's a good idea," I said.

He nodded and resumed working, painstakingly trying to draw with the fluidity he'd once possessed.

After lunch, he left to go to the post office, as he did every day now, hoping that the letter from the insurance company would arrive. While he was gone, I read portions of the manuscript, as much as I could make out. He began by describing his first efforts to photograph me. I skimmed the pages describing the construction of the Tetrascope until I reached this passage:

At the age a child can stand for himself, the project becomes much easier. Joseph was highly willing to stand still, with a little training. I was fortunate to have a child with an agreeable and conscientious nature, and not every photographer attempting to replicate this project will have the same results. It may also be that the regularity of being photographed every day from a very early age acclimatizes the subject to respond well. The project becomes a kind of ritual, as it were, and when all the elements familiar from birth onwards are present—the photographer, the cameras, the click of the shutter, the environment of the room as a whole—then it is easy to assume the role of the subject.

As the subject enters adolescence, the project both reveals more rich data and becomes more challenging. The rate of growth accelerates as it has not since infancy and never will again. In my reading on the subject, I have discovered that in the 1700s, the Count Philibert Guéneau du Montbeillard measured and recorded his son's height twice a year from birth to the age of 18. This admittedly simplistic effort nevertheless revealed many useful facts, among them the variation of his son's rate of growth depending on the season, as well as the phases of faster growth during infancy and adolescence. I have not discovered why the Count stopped measuring his son. It may have been due to the natural desire for independence that comes with this period of development, which may in fact be a hindrance to the prospect of anyone achieving a full lifetime photographic record of a human subject. How the genial child becomes a being with his own desires and views, which may depart from those of the parents, is one of the great mysteries, and it would be fruitless to speculate on the causes or any potential remedies. Nor would I wish such a remedy, because how could one wish a child to remain tractable to one's will for a lifetime? One must be glad that the adolescent still holds fast to the values of truth and curiosity, which form the bedrock of human character, and which time, one hopes, cannot alter.

I thrust the papers aside. I wondered if he could sense how much I was concealing from him, and if he wrote these words in the hope that his intuition was wrong.

*   *   *

The morning of our *Aino* performance, the last Saturday in June, was cool and overcast. To our surprise, Mr. Hallgarten volunteered to drive as many of our props as possible to the Hillside Club. The building was almost complete but still unfurnished. We had arranged to borrow chairs and had hung an exhibit of Peter and Karelia's work in the gallery.

Mr. Hallgarten seemed in a good mood. He praised Peter's beautiful, mythic backdrops: the ominous dark spruces of the forest where Wainamoinen and Youkahainen would have their magic duel, the eerie stand of silver birches where Aino would reject Wainamoinen's ham-handed wooing of her. "I hope you all will do us credit tonight," he said. I closed my eyes, hoping against hope that he would not see himself in our portrayal of Wainamoinen and Aino. The last lines of the play were Wainamoinen's, after he realizes he's lost Aino forever:

> *Fool am I, and great my folly.*
> *All my virtues now have left me*
> *in these mournful days of evil,*
> *vanished with my youth and vigor,*
> *insight gone and sense departed.*

I ran into the tent to retrieve my cap and found my father working on another of his incomprehensible drawings, surrounded by books. I told him we were about to head over, and that the performance began at two o'clock. He didn't seem to hear me, so I repeated myself.

"I'm aware it is at two. It will likely not start on time, I gather?"

"If you get there early, you can make sure you'll be able to see." I thought that when he saw all the most important people of Berkeley applauding us and admiring Karelia's photographs and Peter's paintings, he would understand how art mattered. Karelia had two groupings, one of images she'd taken of refugees engaged in simple acts of daily life, and another of her *Kalevala* series.

"I have a task to accomplish first, but it shouldn't take long," he said. "Have the Hallgartens gone over yet?"

"I think so."

He tore his eyes away from his drawing with great effort and massaged the fingers of his right hand mechanically. "I wish you luck this afternoon, Joseph." His eyes flicked curiously over the furry coat I wore as my fox costume. "I'm glad you find acting meaningful. I find it puzzling. One person is behaving as if he is a doctor, and another plays the fool. But the fool has memorized his lines just as well as the doctor, so he can't be as much of a fool as he makes himself out to be. And in another play, he has the part of the wise sage, and one is supposed to forget that he was a fool the last time. I don't seem to be able to do so. It's a limitation on my part."

I was moved to hear him speak so plainly to me. Perhaps if Karelia and I had tried to share with him more things that mattered to us, if we had worked harder to explain them in terms he could comprehend, we would all have had more connection and pleasure in each other's company.

"What are you drawing?" I asked.

"Light consists of waves," he said. "These waves travel from the source until they are deflected, reflected, or absorbed. When they come into contact with the retina of the eye—or with film—they cause chemical reactions that lead to the observation or the recording of an image. Do you follow me?"

I said that I did.

"Most light waves leave no lasting record, because they are either absorbed into dark surfaces and translated into heat or diffused and scattered. The light that is absorbed is lost, but it seems to me that that which reflects and diffracts must still carry some knowledge of what it touched. What would be of greatest use to the human race would be a camera that could somehow gather lost images from the light, painstakingly piecing together a precise moment from the past and fixing it."

I stared at him. I wondered if he truly believed he could design such a camera, or if the attempts merely preoccupied him so that he wouldn't have to think of all he'd lost.

He traced the scars along the back of his hand. I feared my refusal to stand for him had finally broken him.

"Two o'clock," I said, and went out.

*   *   *

One hundred and fifty new wooden chairs stretched out before us on the gleaming floor of the Hillside Club's long main hall. Massive columns of unpainted freshly cut cedar, their odor permeating the air, supported the structure. At one end was the stage, at the other a gallery space where Peter's paintings and Karelia's photographs hung. With its airy ceiling and double-height windows, the interior had the feel of a church more than a clubhouse. It was intimidating to think of performing on a real stage, even if it lacked a curtain: we had had only one dress rehearsal in the space.

Backstage, Ina complained of a stomachache. Peter repeated his lines under his breath. Thomasine kept reading her script, though she said she couldn't see the words anymore. Karelia looked tired. I brought her a glass of water and insisted she drink it. She didn't take enough care of herself, and it angered me.

By ten minutes before two o'clock, only a dozen people had arrived, and I began to despair. Why would the wealthy of Berkeley come to see us, when they could very well go to the beach, or for that matter see plays at any number of professional theaters in Oakland. Our idea seemed ridiculous now.

By a quarter after two, however, the crowd had grown to nearly 100, and though many were ignoring the exhibition to chat with each other, it seemed at least the event would not be an utter failure. The audience members moved unhurriedly through the rows, taking their seats. Some of them I recognized as regular attendees from our Sunday performances, but many of them were Hillside Club members, I presumed. When I saw how well-dressed they were, how elegantly they greeted each other, how self-possessed they all seemed, I quailed. Something Peter had muttered the other day—"We are their performing monkeys"—registered for the first time.

Nicholas wore a dark blue robe trimmed with gold braid, and his long black hair spilled around his shoulders. He took Thomasine's script out of her hands and gestured for silence. "No need to be nervous. Remember, this is an insignificant play by an insignificant playwright, which most of our audience won't notice or follow no matter how well we play. No one has paid an entrance fee. If they enjoy themselves, chatting with their friends, then they will feel well-disposed to us. If you forget a line, try to remember the story—you should all have some idea of it by now—" (we laughed uncertainly, unsure whether he was making a joke or teasing us) "—and say something appropriate to the scene. When it's over, everything you've said will have vanished. As Shakespeare wrote, 'These our actors, as I foretold you, were all spirits and are melted into air, into thin air.'"

"Oh, *that's* comforting," Thomasine said sharply.

The seat we'd saved in the front row for my father remained empty. He might have slipped in at the back, hidden from view behind a taller man—though that seemed unlikely. I wondered what task he'd been attempting to finish.

Mr. Hallgarten stepped up on the stage, called for quiet, and introduced us as a band of artists whom he'd had the pleasure of hosting, and who had made it their habit to perform scenes from Finland's great epic poem, the *Kalevala*, each weekend to keep up spirits after the great disaster. "You have the advantage now of seeing them for the first time without risk of sitting in the dirt," he said, and the crowd laughed.

Then Nicholas thanked the Hallgartens profusely for their generosity and kindness, and the play began. Aino's brother Youkahainen sat down at the table with his mother and two sisters and spoke the opening lines that I now knew so well. Nicholas's voice was a bit too dramatic at first, but he sounded more natural as his speech went on:

Feasting with my friends and fellows
came upon my ears the story
that there lived a sweeter singer
on the plains of Kalevala,
better skilled than Youkahainen
better than the one that taught me.
I will travel southward swiftly
to the dwellings of Wainola
there as bard to vie in battle
with the famous Wainamoinen.

Even with our flimsy set and hastily sewn costumes, we somehow managed to pull it off. The audience seemed to hold its breath as Aino lamented that she had ever been born. She said she would rather drown than live to be nothing but an old man's solace.

Three long rows of scalloped pasteboard painted blue served as waves. As Karelia lay down behind the second row and concealed herself from the audience, I stepped forward to witness the drowning. In my terror, I couldn't see individual audience members, only a single entity of indeterminate mass and color, with a gap in the front row where my father ought to have been. I feared laughter at my tail, a bushy thing Ina had contrived from brown and red threads of yarn, its tip black. But the audience remained quiet at Karelia's disappearance—I couldn't see her either, because the third row of waves concealed her from me—and it occurred to me they were waiting to find out if I would rescue her. The audience had no idea what would happen next. I felt a tremendous sense of power.

I cleared my throat to announce my intention to inform the family of her death, and as I spoke, shaky at first, I adopted the sly tone I had developed for the character, but this time adding a note of detachment, as if the affairs of humans were trivial, as if it would never have occurred to me to risk getting wet to save one, as if I had hit upon the idea of bringing news of Aino's death only to try to amuse myself at their distress. I sauntered in a circle to indicate travel while Aino's family carried out their little table and chairs. They sat down at supper, chattering happily. With obviously false sorrow, I delivered the news and relished their horror and weeping.

Thomasine, as Aino's sister, begged me to let her steal away with him. I warned her of the hardships of forest living—sleeping on frost-riddled earth, hungrily eying chickens behind fences, always calculating the risk of farmers catching you, always alert for the approach of horses' hooves. I made my case so ardently that when it was time for me to capitulate, I hesitated, and Thomasine's eyes widened a bit in fear that I might go off-script and refuse her request—a moment I savored. And then I said she had convinced me, and that she must climb on my back so that we could flee swiftly. I could sense the audience's delight in it—I staggered a little, but she was light. In rehearsal, I had loved this moment, to bear her weight, to encircle her legs with my arms and have her arms around my neck, to smell her scent. I had imagined that the experience would be even more intense during the performance, as if it were actually happening, as if I actually were the fox carrying her away with me forever. But the moment seemed to be over.

Once backstage, she pulled my head toward her and kissed my cheek. I pressed my lips to hers. She laughed silently, then ran to Nicholas and lifted her hands—he did so, too, and for the briefest of moments their palms met and their fingers interlaced in a clasp that I suppose they believed to be merely congratulatory, an appropriate and formal gesture for a director and young actress, teacher and pupil. Jealousy flared through me.

Now he mouthed what must have been praise in my direction.

Onstage, Wainamoinen cast his fishing line in the water in search of Aino.

Karelia, still lying concealed, hooked Wainamoinen's line to a large wooden fish and lifted it above the waves. We had worried that this might come off as comical, but the audience seemed absorbed in the seriousness of the moment, or else they were only trying to figure out why a fish was talking. After upbraiding the old wizard, the fish disappeared beneath the waves. Wainamoinen cast his line several times more in vain before giving up and lamenting his folly.

Karelia stood, the actors joined her and Peter onstage to take bows, and I moved forward with them. The applause surged when Nicholas joined us. He bowed modestly. I scanned the audience, but my father was nowhere to be seen.

*   *   *

Thomasine and I rode in the back of her father's car, holding the waves steady between us as they rose from the floor of the front to rest on the top of the seat behind us. The wooden fish lay on our feet. We waved to those we passed, giddy with fatigue. Beneath the waves' scallops, Thomasine took my hand, and I let her, though I was still angry with her. Mrs. Hallgarten seemed pleased with her husband, and he seemed in a good mood.

"It's a shame your father didn't make it today, Joseph," Mr. Hallgarten said. "You gave a fine performance. But it's just as well. He might have considered Wainamoinen a less than flattering portrait."

"A portrait of what?" Thomasine asked.

"Of himself," Mr. Hallgarten said. "It's the story of an old man who wants a young beautiful woman to keep house for him, and she'd rather die than do that. I thought it was a bit pointed of Karelia to choose this tale, though who can blame her."

It was a relief to me that Mr. Hallgarten hadn't interpreted the play as being about himself. But I wondered again where my father was. I worried that rough folk from the tin can camp had come by, hoping to rifle a deserted encampment, and he had surprised them and fought, and now he lay injured somewhere nearby or in the hospital.

Because we had arrived before everyone else, the Hallgartens told me to join them in the house. We would have sandwiches in half an hour, Mrs. Hallgarten said, but first she wanted to lie down.

As soon as her parents were out of sight, Thomasine pulled me up to her room. When she closed the door, I put my arms to her waist and pressed her against the armoire, its smooth wood cool against the backs of my hands. I still had on my fox coat, and it seemed to give me a new boldness that excited us both. I'd been foolish to suspect she was attracted to Nicholas, I thought. She stroked my fur and fumbled with the clasp that bound her cloak. The cloth slithered to the floor. She motioned for me to undo the laces of her dress. With shaking hands, I did so, peeling her shoulders free and helping her yank the dress down so she could step out of it. She backed into my arms and pulled them around her ribs. I felt the heat of her skin through her underclothes.

A sharp noise came from Mr. Hallgarten's study on the other side of the wall. We froze. Her parents' voices still drifted up from downstairs.

Thomasine shrugged, but I had an immediate suspicion, and fear drained into me. I slid free and went out into the hall, ignoring her protest at the opening of the door.

My father stood in the study, facing the window. He hadn't noticed me yet. He held three large, thick folders, which he slapped down one by one onto a pile of folders nearly as high as his hip, using such force that a less meticulous man would have toppled the whole stack. The study had been transformed. All of the heaps that had mixed and swum into each other had been sorted into a dozen orderly stacks, folders with folders, loose papers with loose papers, opened mail with opened mail.

Even on the top of Mr. Hallgarten's desk, the pens and stationery lay at right angles to the blotter. A tennis racket leaned against the back wall.

My father's mouth was twisted, as if he took no pleasure in the order he had created.

"Arthur," said Mr. Hallgarten's voice behind me. I hadn't heard him come up the stairs, but the noise must have drawn him, Mrs. Hallgarten by his side. Thomasine, her dress hastily restored, pushed between them.

My father lifted a dark wooden box from the desk. Flat and square, it bore a woodworked knot or flower on the lid. Had it always been there, buried under papers?

"Arthur, you've gone too far." Mr. Hallgarten's voice was quiet and grim. "I told you not to trespass in my house."

"Have you showed these to your wife?" my father asked. He lifted the box's lid, took several papers from inside, and thrust them at Mrs. Hallgarten. She automatically put out her hands, but he released them too quickly, as if repelled, and she caught only one, the rest fluttering to her feet.

Mr. Hallgarten snatched the one from her grasp. "Are you mad?" he said, squatting and gathering what were, I realized, envelopes, four or five of them. My father removed another from the box and handed it to Mrs. Hallgarten over her husband's head.

"I see you brought these back from San Francisco and gave them a place of honor, Thomas," my father said. "As you would not give to my photographs."

Mr. Hallgarten straightened, crushing envelopes in his large fist. At the sight of his wife holding a letter, he seemed himself to crumple. I recognized the handwriting as Karelia's, the loops of her f's and p's extending excitedly up or down into the next one or two lines, tracing over the words above or below. The envelopes were addressed to Thomas Hallgarten—not at his old office, but at an apartment on Filbert Street in San Francisco.

"*Maman*, what is it?" Thomasine asked.

"Why did you keep meeting her, when you would not visit me any longer?" my father said. "Why did she write to you this way? What hold do you have on her?"

Mrs. Hallgarten was reading the letter. She had turned so white that I feared she would faint. She shoved it back into the envelope, then handed it to her husband. "Return them all to the box," she said, her voice breaking.

Mr. Hallgarten hesitated.

"Put them back," she ordered. This time her words were steely.

My father lowered the box. Thomasine hung on her mother's arm, craning her neck to see inside. At the bottom lay a 5x7 of Karelia, one I'd never seen before. Soft focus, her face in profile filling the frame, head tilted back, eyes closed in reverie, her pale hair spilling around her face. Although she wasn't smiling, she had an air of happiness and calm.

Mr. Hallgarten placed the twisted envelopes on top of it, shut the lid, and removed the box from my father's hands.

"How could you bring her here?" Mrs. Hallgarten said, fixing cold eyes on her husband as if on something loathsome. "There was no Fulvio, was there? She lied to me, and you lied to me. I tried to *help* her. I brought her to my own doctor."

"Celeste." He seemed undecided between trying to pretend bafflement and apologizing. He straightened his shoulders, ready to bluster. My father watched the Hallgartens, horrified.

By now, Mrs. Hallgarten had begun to shake. "Thomasine, go to your room." She turned to my father and me. "It's time for you to go— all of you, leave our property. Pack your things. I want everyone out by tomorrow morning."

Thomasine didn't move.

"Karelia needs to rest," I said. "We can't move her out in the middle of the night. She's already done too much today. It might not be safe for her."

Mrs. Hallgarten closed her eyes. "Tomorrow by noon. That's the latest."

My father looked at Mr. Hallgarten. He crossed the room and with his left hand—his good hand—slapped him hard across the face.

Mr. Hallgarten tumbled backward and fell against the doorway's edge. Thomasine cried out and knelt at his side.

My father headed out the door and disappeared down the hall. I hurried after.

CHAPTER THIRTEEN

The Vissers had returned to camp. My father sped past them into our tent. I headed down the street so I wouldn't have to talk to them. Not wanting to encounter Nicholas, I cut east through a neighbor's lawn. The smell of a roast wafted through the window, and my stomach rumbled.

The sun would not set for another hour and a half, but the bottom of the canyon already lay in shadow. I hadn't been here this late on my own before. I kept an eye out for bobcats, though Peter had said they were too small and shy to bother humans.

I found my way down to the creek and followed its murmur north. Soon I came upon the flat rock Nicholas had slept on during our first photographic expedition. Stretching out on its lumpy surface, I bathed in a cleansing terror, the sky cooling overhead, the grassy slopes of the canyon's flanks curving above me. I didn't move, not even when voices called from a distance.

Gradually I made out the words: they were calling Nicholas's name and mine. At first I thought it was Karelia and Nicholas who were calling, which confused me—why would he call his own name? Then I recognized the second voice as Peter's.

When they were about fifty feet away, I stood. Their backs were to me. I could lie down again and disappear. But instead I called out, and they ran to me.

"What are you doing?" Karelia said, folding me in her arms.

"What time is it?" I asked.

She gave me a strange look. "You know."

I shook my head. I had lost track of time, or rather, I'd turned against the part of my brain that tracked it.

"It was probably seven thirty when we left the camp to look for you," she said. "Are you all right? What happened? Where's Nicholas?" She told me that after the performance, she'd been about to accompany him back to camp when a reporter from the *Berkeley Gazette* detained her for an interview about her photographs. According to Peter, Thomasine stopped Nicholas along the way and pulled him aside to speak to him.

"That's the last I saw of him," Peter said. "When we got back, we saw you and your father come out of the house, but you disappeared, and he said he didn't know where you went. Karelia worried when neither you nor Nicholas showed up for dinner."

As we walked, Karelia told me she'd knocked on the Hallgartens' door to look for me, and finally Sophie had answered. She said we weren't inside. When Karelia asked to speak to Thomas and Celeste, Sophie said they weren't to be disturbed. Karelia told me, "When I pressed her, she said, 'I'm not even supposed to open the door, but you kept knocking, and Adele was afraid.' I wanted to know what she was afraid of, but she wouldn't say more."

"Where's my father?" I asked Karelia.

"Looking for you. He went out toward Boswell's Ranch."

"Did he say anything to you?"

"We didn't speak. What's going on?"

I told her about finding him in Mr. Hallgarten's study, searching for the Book of Months. Because Peter was with us, I said only that Mr. Hallgarten had been very angry and we'd all been ordered to leave the next morning.

Karelia let out a cry. "Why can your father never let go?"

"Why do the rest of us need to leave?" Peter asked. "We put on a splendid performance, we've done them credit. This is outrageous."

"They said we all need to be out by noon tomorrow." We crested the rim of the canyon. The tents of our encampment dully glowed in the moonlight below.

"I'm going to the house to talk to them," Peter said, and strode ahead.

I told Karelia about my father finding the letters and trying to give them to Mrs. Hallgarten. "They were addressed to Thomas Hallgarten on Filbert Street. I thought his office was on Battery Street."

She stood still. "Did Arthur read them?"

"I think he must have."

She grasped the cloth of her coat and balled it into her fists. "Thomas, you fool," she said under her breath. "Why save them, why bring them here?"

"What did you write?"

She hesitated. "I don't remember. Silly things. How many were there?"

"Five or six. And a photograph of you at the bottom of the box."

She closed her eyes. "And Nicholas—he was there too?"

"No. I haven't seen him since I left the play."

"They must have told him somehow. But wouldn't he come talk to me?" She searched my face, as if I would know. "I have to find him."

"There's one more thing. Father slapped Mr. Hallgarten."

She hid her face in her hands.

If Nicholas had learned about Karelia's letters, then he must have figured out that the child Karelia was carrying was Mr. Hallgarten's. Most likely, he had gone to a saloon.

She gathered her coat more tightly about her. "Look at you, you must be freezing. We'll go down and you can sit by the fire. I might not be back by morning."

"You need to rest," I said. "You can't go looking for him. How would you even find him?"

"I know the places he's likely to be," she said grimly. "And I'll be fine."

She looked so fierce at that moment that I let her propel me down the hillside toward the camp. She hurried toward the street. The bonfire was sinking into embers; I struck it with a stick of kindling, and a rush of sparks shot upward.

*   *   *

My father sat motionless on his cot. I'd been preparing a speech about why I hadn't told him about Karelia, but he didn't ask, and he wouldn't look up. I wanted to apologize, but I was halted by the memory of him in Mr. Hallgarten's study, shouting, the box of letters in his hand, the neatly stacked piles all around him. He had missed the performance to do this. He had wrecked our lives again and again because of his obsession. But I was also angry at myself for betraying him by not telling him that Karelia was pregnant. Then I became enraged that I had spent so many years believing in the greatness of his vision. Even when I began to doubt it, I had never been able to extinguish hope completely.

I thought of telling him that it was through my actions that the Book of Months was lost. If I'd left it in Mr. Hallgarten's study, then it would have been found, and my father could have had something to show— who? The scientists he'd imagined as his audience. But were there any?

Now he met my eyes. The pain and anger in them made me flinch.

"You weren't surprised to learn this," he said flatly.

I said nothing.

"I don't know why neither of you came to me," he said.

"I'm sorry." I could hear the fury in my own voice. What would he have had me do? If he had paid attention to Karelia, if he had loved her the way I loved her, he would have seen what was happening long ago. I kicked off my shoes and climbed into my cot.

I was sick with hunger, but I couldn't bring myself to get up again. After a while, my father extinguished the lamp and lay down. It was a long time before I fell asleep. In my dreams, I ran through a forest, the ground covered with ashes, until morning, when voices outside the tent woke me. The Vissers were complaining to each other. It sounded like they were packing too.

Trying to be as unobtrusive as possible, I went out and took a piece of bread, which I ate as I walked around the camp. I checked Karelia's and Nicholas's tents, but both were empty.

Perhaps Nicholas had gotten into a brawl and been arrested. If Karelia had gone looking for him in saloons, she might have come to harm. This last thought turned me cold. I should never have let her go out looking for Nicholas by herself. At every turn, I had failed to look after her.

Peter came out of his tent and said to me, "Thomas tells me there is a family crisis, though he won't say what it is. I still can't understand why we must leave today. He wouldn't answer any of my questions."

"At least they should help us find new places to live," Ina said.

Peter shook his head. "He asked us to give the family privacy and not to approach any of them—they could not give us any more assistance at this time."

"Maybe they will change their minds," Ina said. "How can they kick us out after all these months? We haven't done anything."

"I told him that whatever Arthur had done, we didn't condone it and had no part in it. But he denied that this had anything to do with his decision. I've never seen him so implacable. What happened last night, Joseph?"

I'd been considering an answer to this question ever since I got out of bed. "If Mr. Hallgarten doesn't want to discuss it, then we'd better keep it a private matter," I said stiffly.

"The man is evicting us, what loyalty do we owe him anymore?"

Ina said. I'd never seen her upset before, and this fact alone almost prompted me to confess.

I asked, "Have you seen Karelia?"

"She hasn't been back," Peter said. "But Nicholas came in the middle of the night. He'd lit his lamp and was rummaging around in his tent. I went in to give him the news, but he was already stuffing his belongings into a sack. He was soused. I asked where Karelia was, and he said he hadn't seen her since after the performance. Was he going to meet her? No. Did he have a message he wanted me to give her? No. He pulled out an envelope and said I could give it back to her. Before I could take it, he passed it over the lamp's flame and lit it on fire. I was terrified the tent would blaze up. But he carried it outside and threw it onto the bonfire embers and watched until it had burned up. Then he was gone."

Now everyone was looking at me. Instead of answering, I went into our tent. I had been worried for so long that something would happen that would lead the Hallgartens to evict us, but now that they actually had, I found that I couldn't believe it was over. It seemed impossible that our camp would break up, that we would no longer be rehearsing scripts together, arguing over how the characters would behave, singing the Bonfire Song, passing around the latest painting to admire, laughing or squabbling or all falling silent and staring into the fire together. I had believed that we would soon be transplanting ourselves to Berkeley or Oakland, that we would build a theater and art studios, that we would carry on together as we had all summer.

My father lay on his cot, his eyes open.

"How much money do we have left?" I asked.

"I failed you." It was as if his throat were still full of smoke and ashes.

"I'm sorry."

"You'll need to start your portrait business again."

"The insurance money hasn't come yet. I have little left. It isn't enough to make a start."

I decided I would go to the Hallgartens and tell them we needed money so we could get a place for Karelia to stay. Then I would have to find her.

"I'm sorry too," I said as I went out, thinking I was apologizing, but I couldn't keep the accusatory tone out of my voice.

The Hallgartens' maid, Delia, answered their door. "Thomasine is confined to her room for the week," she said. "And she and Sophie and Adele have all been told not to have anything to do with the refugees."

"I'm not a refugee," I said. "I'm a friend of the family. I'd like to talk to Mr. Hallgarten."

Delia stopped and, quickly glancing at the house as if it watched her, said in a sharp whisper, "I've been told you may not come in."

"But I didn't do anything," I said, and turned scarlet, remembering undoing the laces of Thomasine's dress, the warm curl of her body under my arms.

Delia shook her head. "I'm closing the door now," she said, and did.

I went around to the side of the house. Thomasine's window was closed. If I called up to her, someone in the family might hear me. I picked up a pebble and threw it, as carefully as I could, and it bounced off the glass. I threw another. At the fourth pebble, the curtains abruptly shut. She didn't look out.

I returned to my cot and lay down, defeated. It baffled me that Nicholas had acquired one of Karelia's love letters to Mr. Hallgarten. Then I remembered Peter saying that Thomasine had come to meet Nicholas as they were walking back after *Aino*.

After my father had struck Mr. Hallgarten, Thomasine must have been angry. She might have snatched up a letter. Perhaps she and her mother helped Mr. Hallgarten to his feet, and then her mother ordered

Thomasine to go to her room, against her protests. She sat at the window, reading Karelia's love letter to her father.

And so when she spotted Nicholas coming up the street, she ran out to meet him. I imagine him walking with the Vissers, costumes slung over his shoulder. She took Nicholas aside and said—what? Her dress would have still been unevenly placed at the collar, her hair in disarray. Did they walk down a lane together, away from the others?

I imagine she told him what had happened with an air of shock, as if she simply needed to confide in someone, as if it had escaped her mind that Nicholas had a stake in what happened next. I imagine she gave the letter to him—she touched his hand as she did so—and he unfolded it and read the words Karelia had written to Mr. Hallgarten earlier that same year, in the winter, before Nicholas had met any of us. I imagine his face turning white.

Then he turned away from Thomasine and walked down the hill and disappeared.

*   *   *

Karelia didn't return to the camp. My father and I packed our things along with Karelia's. As we carried our belongings out to the street, I looked back at the house. Thomasine watched us from behind the balcony's French doors. I waved, but she turned her back.

We took the streetcar into town. We trudged the streets of Oakland with our bags looking for a rooming house, speaking to each other as little as possible. I was so worried about Karelia. I pushed away images of her lying dead in an alley somewhere. I told myself that she might have already found Nicholas and explained the circumstances. Maybe he hadn't wanted Peter to give her a message because he had already met up with her and they had a plan. How could he blame her for what happened before she met him, how could he blame her for not telling him that Mr. Hallgarten was the father? We could find adjoining apartments in downtown Berkeley or Oakland, and we could still raise money for our theater. Surely Mr. Hallgarten would not or could not turn all the members of the Hillside Club against us—some of them would invest.

Or Nicholas could join a stock company in Oakland or teach for a theater school. My father would get a job with a portrait company and eventually open his own studio again. And I would enroll in a theater school and continue my training as an actor. I could imagine it all unfolding, although hazily, as when Karelia would stretch a white scarf over her camera lens to give her shot the air of something taking place only in the mists of the mind.

We visited a dozen boardinghouses that afternoon. None had openings. So many refugees, they said. At last we found a narrow room in the Hotel Duncan in the northwest corner of Oakland, a few minutes on the streetcar from downtown. It had a single swaybacked bed wedged between a wall and a dripping sink, and the wallpaper was the color of diseased teeth, but at least it looked out onto a building opposite with a flower box in the third-floor window, thick with mums. We paid the landlord in cash. We had only enough for a couple of weeks of living expenses.

After months in the camp, it was difficult to sleep in a room with walls. I left the bed to my father and wrapped myself in a blanket on the floor. The hotel had rented out its ground-floor music hall for a party, and the revelers made noise well into the small hours. In the morning, the dockworkers down the hall had a loud argument with each other outside their rooms. My father and I were still barely speaking to each other, however, so in a way, I welcomed the relief the sounds brought to our room's terrible quiet.

Three women who I thought might be ladies of the evening shared a room two doors down. One kept a creased ten of hearts dangling from her belt. Whenever she passed me, she liked to point her finger at me without looking, a deadpan expression on her face.

My father began looking for work, and I took over checking our post office box in Berkeley. On Wednesday, a letter from Karelia arrived for me. She wrote that she still didn't know where Nicholas was. She was staying for a few days with Rose, the woman who rented her darkroom to her. She asked me to bring all her belongings to her that night; she couldn't return to the camp herself, now, not ever.

That evening, she met me on the porch of the house where Rose lived. The wind had blown her hair into a chaos. I set down the bundle I'd made of her belongings: a few changes of clothing, her hairbrush and hairpins. I opened my satchel and held out the two volumes of the *Kalevala*.

"They're yours," I said.

"I might be traveling soon," she said. "I won't be able to haul them around. It's better you keep them."

"Leave them with Rose," I said. I wanted so badly to give her something.

But she shook her head. "I don't know what happens next. Come for a walk with me now. It may be a while before we see each other again."

We left everything on the porch. It was a clean, chilly twilight, a bright moon already up. I remembered Mr. Hallgarten saying that his grandmother had said not to look at the moon, that there was something obscene about it. I had interpreted that to mean that its nakedness offended her, but perhaps what was obscene was the way it rose every night and exposed us.

I told her Peter's story of Nicholas's return in the middle of the night, and my theory about how Nicholas had gotten hold of one of the letters.

She gave a sharp sigh. "I went looking for him. I asked everyone I could think of. I looked at Boswell's Ranch, and I even went down to the Oakland saloons. It was awful—Joseph, what are you doing? Walk normally." She trailed one hand down my back, and I returned to my usual way of walking, though I couldn't recall who I had been imitating. "I have to explain everything to him. I should have told him. I don't know if he'll forgive me. He must be very angry. That doesn't matter. I have to try to make it right, that's all."

"And after that?"

She shook her head. "I won't live with Arthur. We've reached the end of that. You understand that, don't you? For now, I have to find Nicholas. I'll write to you."

"I want to go with you. I want to live with you."

Without thinking, we'd walked all the way into the hills. We looked into the shadows among the trees. I closed my eyes and sensed the expanse of space all around, the bay behind us, and, across the water, the charred city we used to call home.

"For now, look after your father," she said. "We'll write to each other. When I find a stable place of my own, then we'll see."

* * *

After a week and a half, my father had had no success in finding work. It must have been difficult for a man in his sixties, whose right hand would never work as well as it used to, to seem like an appealing hire in a time when the city was flooded with people seeking jobs. But when he said, apologetically, "It may be a good idea if you look for work, too, Joseph," I was at first outraged. I had run errands for neighbors all summer to earn us money. It was his turn. If he hadn't foolishly tried to save his photographs from a dynamited building, he would not be injured and he could look after both of us.

At the same time, I needed a change. I'd lost all interest in the

Kalevala, and I was killing time wandering the city, overwhelmed by the shops, the crowded streets, the clang of streetcars, the smell of dung and filth, the people jostling. So I agreed and went out hunting. I offered to hawk newspapers, sell hats, scoop ice cream, sweep hair in a barber shop, deliver for butchers and grocers, carry messages for the telephone company, run errands for a beauty parlor and a bakery and a lawyer and a tailor. Apparently a lot of other boys and even men were competing with me for these jobs. Some I lost because I'd never driven a wagon, others because I didn't own a bicycle, and several because I had no references. I opened cases for a furniture factory for two days, until the manager dismissed me for not being strong or quick enough. The owner of a fish shop said he'd consider training me to scale fish for him, but the next day he'd changed his mind.

Three weeks into our exile, when we had run through nearly all our money, my father found a job as a part-time repairman in a downtown camera shop. The owner was skeptical until my father fixed a Goerz-Anschütz Folding Camera's faulty shutter in less than a minute.

A few days later, a dry goods store, Robinson & Smith, took me on. The manager, a young man named Reed, had a rolling gait that suggested he had been to sea, and his arms were muscled and tanned. He enjoyed correcting my errors and berating me in the stockroom if I failed to sweep a corner sufficiently. It would only be temporary, I told myself, until Karelia sent for me.

A few days later, when I returned from the store, my father was already home. Our ill feelings had eased, but we still had very little to say to each other. The father who'd taken me on expeditions and overflowed with ideas about time seemed to have been another man, and I was still possessed by waves of anger and regret.

He handed me an envelope. It was from Karelia. I'd written her with our new address, and she'd sent me a brief letter from Carmel to say she was all right and promised to write more later. I'd sent her a long response immediately but had been despairing of a reply. Now I slit it open and sat on the crate to read it.

July 26, 1906

Dear Joseph,

I'm sorry not to have written to you properly until now—I've been traveling so much and am only now able to catch my breath a little. You'll never believe it, but I'm writing to you from inside a tent. It stands on a little knoll. A pine forest stretches downhill to the east, and to the west, about half a mile in the distance, Carmel Bay catches the sunlight like a sapphire. (I've never seen a sapphire, but this is what I imagine one is like. When I finally see one someday, I'll say it gleams like Carmel Bay.) I keep thinking I can hear the surf, but Nicholas reminds me the ocean is too far—it's just the wind in the pines.

This tent sits behind the cabin that the Sterlings, George and Carrie, built for themselves here. George is a poet, and he came here to concentrate, he says, away from the temptations and clatter of the city.

It was no easy task to track Nicholas down. I arrived in Carmel a week ago, but no one had seen him, so I continued to Monterey, showing my photographs of him to anyone I could persuade to listen. A hotel clerk sent me on a fool's errand to Salinas. Finally I gave up. But when I passed through Carmel on my way north again, I found Nicholas had arrived at the Sterlings.

It was a difficult conversation we had. But he says Carmel has a restorative effect, and I'm feeling it too—it helped, I think, that we had this conversation while walking along the whitest sand I've ever seen. I told him everything, how Thomas encouraged my photography, how he and I both felt ourselves to be trapped. The Hallgartens have a distorting effect. There's something at the heart of that family that is—not bad, but like milk gone a little off, or like an animal with a wound hidden in its fur.

Nicholas is still angry with me, but we have decided to at least be friends again and continue to talk.

I think of you every day. Tell me you are all right. I will come and visit you soon. I sold a few of my photographs here, but I'm counting pennies. I think I can earn a little money in town somehow.

I'll write more later.

Are you all right? Is your father very angry with me? I tried to write him a letter, but I don't know what to say. I'll try again soon. I imagine that a different uncle, a different niece, would have managed everything so much better.

Love,
Karelia

* * *

That night a brawl broke out on our floor, and our door shuddered as a body slammed against it. As I left the following morning, I spotted a tooth on the hallway carpet. The three ladies of the evening returned, and Ten of Hearts kicked the tooth down the staircase. Before they disappeared into their room, she pointed her finger back at me, unerring. Her playing card had lost a corner.

In August, I should have gone back to school. But with my father working only part-time, and the insurance money still not having arrived, we needed my seventeen dollars a week. I would like to say that I treated my father with tenderness during this period, that we got along more harmoniously. But I spent as little time in that small room with him as possible. After work, I kept roaming the streets. I would look in at windows as dusk fell and wonder what it would be like to live there, or there—each window seemed a stage set, every act within a gesture of a life more real than ours. I fetched our dinner from the delicatessen each night, and he ate what I put in front of him, but we exchanged no more than a few words.

The only thing my father asked from me was an occasional game of chess. Although we followed the traditional rules, we each played slightly different games. I saw the game as an unfolding story, centered around the bishops' plot to overthrow the king and replace him with a knight and a trio of pawns who began as best friends but fell out over love for a beautiful rook. These dramas guided my decisions, and if my pieces had an opportunity to seize one of my father's, they might do so, but sometimes their private grief or fury caused them to rebel against their duties, or left them too limp or absorbed. Against such a moody set of foes, my father's pieces could easily have won, but he seemed to have his own preoccupations. Sometimes he seemed to be seeking to create symmetrical patterns with his pieces, little realms of order within the board's chaos. In one game, he advanced his entire row of pawns one by one down the field. He was not averse to capturing one of my pieces, should the opportunity present itself without undue strain on his main project. And so our two private games intersected from time to time, mine altering the shape of his patterns, his killing a character of mine at a crucial dramatic moment. When the number of pieces on each side had grown small enough to challenge both of our efforts, we would go back to seeking one another's kings.

I missed the nights around the campfire in Berkeley, the conversations and quarrels, the fizz of ideas, the flirtations whose code I could barely make out. I missed watching Mr. Visser's and the Crowleys' sketches and paintings come into being, the way their trees grew, suffered obliteration, and grew again, the way the hills shifted contours until their maker was satisfied. I wanted to be rehearsing again for some new skit, while Ina sewed costumes and Bee and Sebastian tacked together old bedspreads and cast-off fabric with scrap wood to assemble into the lineaments of another world. I walked through the streets at night, hoping I would run into one of them, but everyone was a stranger. They had no connection to me, and I had no connection to them. I wasn't part of anything. When I went home and lay on the other side of the bed from my father, he felt like a stranger, and I felt like a stranger to myself.

CHAPTER FOURTEEN

Karelia's letters arrived irregularly. The Sterlings hosted Sunday afternoon beach picnics, and George and Jimmy (she had never explained to me who Jimmy was) dove into the water by the cliffs and pried abalones off the rocks. Then everyone took turns pounding the abalones with rocks for an hour to tenderize them. To amuse themselves while pounding, they sang the Abalone Song, which George had originated and to which various guests added lyrics. After two hours of parboiling, they cut the abalones into steaks and broiled them on a bonfire. Of Nicholas, she said little, though his name cropped up in her letters, always mentioned as part of a group that went on an expedition somewhere. I longed to join her there, to meet the poets and artists of Carmel, to add my own verse to the Abalone Song, to wake on the beach with salt-stiffened hair. If I could only get down there, I could be useful to them. I wasn't a child anymore. I could become a part of their community.

In September, my father and I moved to a quiet boarding house in the Adams Point neighborhood. In October, Karelia wrote to say that she and Nicholas had gone to the justice of the peace in Monterey and married. They were renting a one-room cabin in the dunes for six dollars a month. It was not much larger than a tent, but they liked having the sound of the surf so close by—it calmed her when she woke in the night. Nicholas built her a closet in the corner to serve as a darkroom and was earning a little money from carpentry when he could, while spending an hour each morning writing plays. She said she missed me, and that I must visit soon.

But somehow delays arose: she caught a cold, and then I did. Their roof needed repair, and they moved back into the Sterlings' tent while Nicholas worked on it in between days of rain. Or it was not a good time to visit because the Sterlings were having many guests. She never mentioned the prospect of my coming to live with her and Nicholas, and I wondered if she had forgotten it, or if she were being discreet so that, if my father read one of her letters, he would not be alarmed. I hadn't told him I planned to live with her.

At last we arranged that I would visit in early November. I asked my employers for a week off, and they granted it on the condition that I work additional hours in December, when others would be taking their holidays. Our insurance money had finally arrived, but my father was now hoping to save enough to open his own camera repair shop. He had a few private customers of his own, and I was glad to see him with a plan, even one this modest. In any case, I had no interest in returning to school.

It was a simple matter to pack, because I owned few clothes. I hadn't opened the *Kalevala* since we'd left the Hallgartens, but now I took the first volume to read on the train ride down, hearing the words in Karelia's voice as if she were reading it aloud to me.

It was raining when I arrived. I hadn't brought an umbrella, so I arrived at their cabin soaking wet. She met me at the door. Her stomach was enormous, and her hair hung longer, past her shoulders. She smelled of ocean and smoke. She ran her hand along my cheek. "You've grown so tall. And your hands—they're gigantic."

She sent me into their bedroom—one corner of the cabin cordoned off with blankets—to shed my wet clothes and borrow some of Nicholas's. When I came out, she was making us hot chocolate on the potbelly stove. We sat and drank it and were so happy to be in each other's company again that we didn't even need to speak for a while. Later, she told me the doctor had pronounced her in excellent health, though he'd ordered her not to overexert herself; the baby was due in a couple of months.

Nicholas arrived a few hours later, drenched. "You're lucky to have come after I fixed the roof," he said. I was glad to see him. The three of us read from the play he was working on while the rain pounded down around us. He asked after the Crowleys and the Vissers, and I confessed I'd heard nothing about them.

The rain let up by nightfall. I had difficulty falling asleep anyway. I'd believed myself happy the whole day, but I was a stranger here, too.

I had so many questions that I felt I couldn't ask—questions about every motive they'd had, every negotiation that had transpired between them. The two of them were more tender and more wary with each other and with me. Perhaps I was upset because they would have their own child soon, a child who had already displaced me.

It rained nearly all that week. After the first night, I slept in the tent in back of the Sterlings' house, because Karelia said I would be more comfortable having space to myself. Many afternoons, everyone gathered at the Sterlings'—Nicholas, Karelia, I, and others who had come to live near the Sterlings or visit them. I had been expecting it to be like our group in the camps, but although a number of them were artists or writers, they tended to talk politics. They were a leaner crew, more gloomy, and they drank more. Some wore a vial of cyanide around their necks, to remind themselves that everyone must die. In fact, many years later, a number of them would end up taking their own lives.

On Sunday, we ate rabbit that George and his friends had shot, and lumpy mashed potatoes, and a sublime chess pie Karelia had baked, and then everyone except Karelia and Carrie Sterling and I drank themselves into a clamor—a chair was broken by a fall, two wine glasses smashed in an enthusiastic toast, a scuffle left one fellow with a black eye. By evening, they subsided into unconsciousness. Karelia and Carrie seemed unperturbed, or at least resigned, and the three of us spent the rest of the night washing up.

After Carrie had gone to bed, Karelia and I sat on the Sterlings' porch, wrapped in blankets, listening to the breeze through the pines. We were too exhausted to speak or sleep. For a long time, we sat in silence. Then she asked about my father. I told her about his camera repairs, about the way he seemed to have lost himself. "It's my fault."

She shook her head slowly. "No, Joseph, you had nothing to do with his despair—it's a grave he digs himself and forces himself to lie in."

"But I'm the one who lost the Book of Months," I said. "And I never told him."

She looked up in surprise.

I told her about Thomasine showing me the photographs in her father's study, and described how I'd hidden them afterward behind her armoire because I didn't want her or anyone else to see them. I said that when I went to look for them, they were gone, and that I had no idea who'd taken them or why.

She leaned back in her chair. The breeze sighed through the pines in sad mimicry of the ocean's sounds.

"I wish you'd told me," she said. "I could have helped."

"I want to live with you and Nicholas," I said.

"Things can't be the way we imagined they would be," she said. "Nicholas and I, we can't stay on here for long. I'm not even sure if we'll have the baby here. He's been going to Los Angeles to try to find work, something stable, a place to live where we can raise our child."

"Then I could live with you in Los Angeles. I'd get a job, too, and help out. Or you could come up to Oakland. I'm working."

"And how would your father get on without you?"

"He would manage. He would have to."

A shadowy form emerged from the pines at the bottom of the hill, then broke into pieces—it was a gang of raccoons, six of them, and they lumbered in their hunched, thuggish way along the edge of the forest until they disappeared into darkness.

For a long time she was silent. Then she rose and kissed me on the forehead. "You're shivering. Go inside—there's an armchair in the living room where you can curl up. I'm going back to the cabin."

I could see she wanted to be alone, and I let her. I picked my way through the snoring men and took the armchair's cushion into the kitchen, where at least it was quieter, and lay awake a long time on the floor, listening to mice rustle and gnaw in the walls.

When Karelia said goodbye to me on Sunday at the train, neither of us said anything about my coming to live with her. It wasn't the same as our little group of artists at the Hallgartens. But I couldn't go on working at the dry goods store. I had to find some way back into the world.

*   *   *

When I returned, my father gathered up the camera parts he had strewn on the bed, rolled up the cloth they'd lain on, offered me half of his cheese sandwich, and asked me how Karelia was. I gave him a brief account of the trip and said that she and Nicholas seemed to be happy in Carmel. "I'm glad to hear this," he said. A sadness permeated the air while Karelia was the subject of discussion, and soon I said I had to run an errand.

I took the streetcar to downtown Oakland and walked for the sake of being among strangers. I felt entirely lost until I passed Ye Liberty Theater on Broadway, which I'd often walked by on my way to work. Its arched entrance was flanked by columns and by the stone masks of comedy and tragedy. A quirk of light, or of craftsmanship, had given comedy more of a twisted sneer than a broad grin. Patrons had begun to line up at the door. That night, for the first time, I joined them and bought a ticket.

Hundreds of small incandescent globes ringed the proscenium arch. I couldn't wait for the curtain to rise, and at the same time, I wanted it to remain where it was, because as soon as it went up, what lay behind it would be fixed; until then, hundreds of sets, thousands of plays remained possibilities.

To my surprise, few of my fellow theater patrons wore finery. Next to me sat a man in khaki breeches and riding boots, smelling of hay and mud. I felt better about the secondhand clothes I wore.

The curtain rose. A college student lied to both his fiancée and the wealthy aunt who supported him as to how he spent his money. I watched, transfixed, until one of the actors, by a slight slowing of his movements, and a particular tilt of his head, and a certain emphasis given to a phrase, signaled intermission: music piped up, the curtain fell, and the audience, knocked from its dream, broke into applause. Everyone stood or wriggled or blinked or stretched, and after nearly an hour of contentedly sitting elbow to elbow, we ceased to be a collective creature and became individuals again. Some went off to smoke or use the restrooms or take some air on the street, some flirted, and some began to complain about the plot. The man next to me hauled out his sweaty wallet from his back pocket and inspected it as if to make sure it hadn't been stolen or substituted by a pickpocket, then shoved it back, leaving a lingering scent of sweat and cowhide in the air.

When I stood, the curtain rose again. It was too early for the intermission to end, but I thought some announcement was forthcoming. Instead, all at once the set began to move to the left—walls, furniture, backdrop and all—first slowly, then picking up speed. As the first act's furniture moved off, a train station hove into view, only to disappear around the corner to be replaced in turn by a grassy meadow beneath the spreading branches of an oak. Next, the first act's furniture returned. The sets, I saw, were mounted on some sort of large turntable, separated by walls so that only one was visible at a time. The stage revolved twice more before slowing and stopping on the train station. The curtain lowered.

I forgot my sadness. I wanted to see what the characters would do next, when they found themselves in the train station and then in the meadow—I knew something of their future before they did. At the same time, I was aware that the actors knew even more of that future—they knew everything up until the end of the play. I wanted nothing more than to climb on that stage and become one of them, or rather two—the actor and the character, one knowing, the other not knowing.

*   *   *

While running an errand for the shop the next day, I stopped in at the Ye Liberty office and asked if I could work for the theater. The answer was no. I inquired at several other theaters on my lunch hour the next day, and the next. I gave up for a few days. One evening, on my way home from work, I returned to Ye Liberty and asked again. This time, the manager said he had just fired a ticket-taker, and I could have his job if I started immediately. I struggled into the uniform of my predecessor, who'd been fired for deliberately thumb-smearing the lenses of opera glasses he was in charge of renting—the apex of a long tale of dissension not worth telling, the manager said. The sleeves and pant cuffs stopped a good two inches short of where they should have, and the uniform retained a memory of my predecessor's cologne. I was instructed in my duties. I kept my thumbs inside my white gloves.

When I returned home, late, my father was in the boarding-house's common room, playing chess against himself. He occupied the sofa I never sat on, because it had a lumpishness and odor that put me in mind of an over-sized, aging sheepdog. Excitedly, I told him what I'd done. "I'll have to miss the beginnings and endings of plays," I said. "But I can stand in the back during the middles. Each week, they run the same play every night. So I can see how the actors vary their performances."

"Will you be able to carry out your regular duties at the store?" he asked.

"I don't see why not," I said, annoyed that he thought the dry goods job mattered. "If I can't, I'll give it up—the store, that is. Ticket-taking doesn't pay as much, but you're earning enough for us."

"It's true that our situation isn't as dire now," he said, and looked away. I knew he'd been hunting for a place to set up his repair shop. I remembered now that he'd said that the rents were proving to be higher than he'd hoped. The happiness of my night at the theater was curdling in the confines of this boardinghouse. On the wall behind my father hung a portrait of George Washington, a watercolor ineptly painted by one of our fellow residents, and which the boardinghouse's owner had accepted as a gift with an exclamation of delight, though the President looked a bit cross-eyed to me, and chinless. I had an urge to rip it down rather than put up with one more minute of its imbecilic gaze.

As if he'd brought the subject up, I said, "Why do you want to have a camera repair shop?" The question had been on my mind for a while. "You worked with Muybridge once. You were a portrait photographer on Market Street. Your work was written up in the newspapers. You were going to show everyone the true nature of time. Why would you settle for a lifetime of sealing up light leaks in people's Kodaks?"

"Heraclitus said a man cannot step twice into the same river," my father said. "I always thought he meant the river changed. Now I think it's the man who changes. I was younger when I had such great ambition."

"Don't you find repairing cameras tiresome?" What possessed me to speak to him this way? The man who'd painted the Washington portrait had proudly told us he'd lived here twenty years, as if he deserved commendation for it. The defeated spirit of this place had infected my father, I decided. It was worse than the Hotel Duncan, where at least the denizens had been lively.

My father dragged the white rook across the board. "It gives people pleasure when I restore to them their cameras as they once were, or better. It's a small way of reversing time."

"I don't believe that satisfies you. What about the book you were writing? You still have the pages, don't you? Why don't you finish it?"

He gave a half-smile. "Do you believe anyone would want to replicate my project? They would encounter the same stumbling block as I—a person is not a horse or a dog. The subject would grow up and have a different dream of his own. He wouldn't want to stand for the camera each day for all his life, and why should he?"

Now everything about the room vexed me—the scratched chessboard, the blue curtains, the low ceiling. "But your thoughts about time. You could at least write those down. And if the problem is that people aren't tractable enough, then why not make a horse the center of the project, or a dog?"

"If there is any value to my ideas, I'm sure another person will think of them too and carry them out. If Stanford hadn't hired Muybridge, some other person would have soon photographed a horse in motion."

I picked up the black pawn and advanced it two spaces, knocking over the rook. "I think you're sulking because you weren't hailed as a genius right away." This was as direct as I'd ever been. I wanted to make him angry, to rouse the person he'd once been.

He picked up his rook and tucked it into his fist, then stole my pawn with his queen. "If there's someone who wishes I'd been hailed as a genius, it may be you, not me." He bowed his head. "But I'm to blame for putting that hope in your head."

I stood and said I was going up for the night, adding something to the effect that all the thoughts in my head were my own, I hoped.

By the time I reached the little two-room suite we shared on the third floor, I was thoroughly embarrassed. It was wrong of me to rub his nose in his lost glory. I stood in his room, spartan and tidy as always. I wanted to write him a note of apology, but I was and was not sorry. It still seemed he should be capable of doing something more. And I resented his claiming the high ground with his apology. I stood hoping he would come upstairs, but after a while, I went to my own room and climbed into bed. The next morning, we avoided each other's eyes, and for a few days the atmosphere between us was painful.

The next week, I quit the dry goods store and moved to a house full of actors, where I shared the attic with a fellow ticket-taker named Johann. He, too, was an aspiring actor, and we pumped the house's other residents for advice, buying them drinks when we could manage it. Alone in the attic, the two of us argued about the merits of this or that person's performance, keeping our voices down so as not to offend anyone who overheard us. Ye Liberty's innovation was to hire only women as ushers, in the belief that this would provide an added attraction for customers. Johann began seeing one of the ushers, and I started seeing another, though I couldn't help comparing her unfavorably with Thomasine in my mind. Every night I worked, I hoped she would turn up in the theater. She would be delighted to see me, I would hold out opera glasses for her to take, our hands would brush.

I brought my father lunch several days a week. We both pretended to have forgotten my outburst. I would tell him stories about the mishaps and occasional glories of our performances. He seemed to listen with interest, as if living with artists for that brief summer had given him a certain protective regard for those who couldn't help but live in the realm of imagination. In turn, he would tell me about his work in the camera store. He and I got along well enough, though it still made me sad that all his talk was of the details of the cameras he had seen that week, his pleasure in coming up with small improvements for his customers. He had never managed to open his own shop, but seemed content enough now to continue working for others. He said that he was glad not to have to manage employees or balance accounts. We avoided discussing the project, and spoke little about the past, although he would sometimes ask if I'd heard news from Karelia.

To my eyes, the vital part of him had dimmed. But he also seemed calmer. I came to think that Karelia had been right, that the project had been a sort of disease he had to recover from, that what had looked like ambition was actually a torment of the mind. He was better off now, I told myself.

CHAPTER FIFTEEN

I took lessons from one of the actors for two years, and then, in much the same way that I'd earned my job as a ticket-taker, I slipped into a nonspeaking role in Ye Liberty's "The Prisoner of Zenda," debuting as a boy who shined the king's shoes. Other small roles followed, then slightly less small roles.

After I joined a traveling theater repertory company, I was able to visit my father only during the summers, when the company took a rest and I waited tables in San Francisco. On my visits, I told him how much pleasure I found in playing the villain's sidekick one week, the hero's loyal confidante the next; how much I loved adopting the cowboy's saunter as much as the bank teller's sly double takes. I told him about the friends, allies, and rivalries I'd found in the company, the petty feuds and the occasional ousting of a director. I said it was difficult sometimes to find books on the road, to sleep in train seats, to find a barber I could trust. I didn't talk about the slow process by which I'd learned not to lunge for the center of the audience's attention in the middle of a scene, or about my love affairs and their complications, or about the arguments the company had over how to break the Syndicate's stranglehold on theaters across the country.

Once or twice a year, Karelia would visit my father, sometimes with Nicholas and their children, Benjamin and Evelyn, sometimes on her own. They lived in Los Angeles now. Nicholas had a position as assistant director for the Alhambra Theatre Stock Company, and Karelia, though too busy to spend as much time in the darkroom as she would have liked, photographed the actors in his company and posed her children as sea sprites on the southern Californian beaches. When we could, we arranged for our visits to overlap. Over time, the strain between my father and Karelia had mostly faded. We would all walk together in Muir Woods. One Sunday morning, my father told the children that the oldest coastal redwoods were more than a thousand years old, and that they received most of their moisture from the atmosphere.

Nicholas laughed. "They feed on fog. How convenient for their families."

My father began speaking, as if to correct him, then looked down at Benjamin, a lively child, who looked very much like Thomasine. "I suppose that would be one way of describing it," he said.

*   *   *

In April of 1914, during a run in Houston, I received my forwarded mail. It included a package just over a foot and a half long and about a foot wide, but surprisingly heavy. As soon as I picked it up, I knew what was in it. I tore it open to discover another package inside; in Thomasine's spidery handwriting were my name and the words DON'T GET YOUR HOPES UP.

Out slid a black leather-bound album and a letter. I ignored the letter and, covering my mouth and nose with the corner of my elbow to ward off the reek of mold, opened the Book of Months.

There they were, every first Tuesday afternoon of me from September of 1891 to November of 1905, four rows of prints per page, from infancy onward. At some point, water must have soaked the album. Now mold blackened most of the images; pages stuck together. The mold had eaten the printing paper mercilessly and then at some point died and turned to dry powder. Here and there a part of my body remained visible: my foot, my face, my flap-like ears.

The odor pricked my nose. I took the letter over to an open window.

Dear Joseph,

Here it is. I've had it since *Maman* died. All the
local newspapers announced her funeral. I thought
you might show up. Afterward, a woman came up
to me who I didn't recognize at all and said she was
Lilly, and that she had worked for us many years ago.
She wasn't my favorite maid. She would straighten
my room even when I told her not to. She handed
me a package and said it belonged to my father. I asked
why she wasn't giving it to him.

"I found it one afternoon while cleaning your
room," she said. "I saw that one of the carved
wooden birds you kept on top of your armoire was
missing, and I thought it might have fallen down the
back. So I poked with a broom handle and found
something else instead. It was hard work getting it
out." I can picture her poking away with her teeth
biting her lip, the way she always looked when she
was determined to make sure nothing ever got lost
or was dirty. The inscription said it belonged to my
father, and when she opened it, she was dismayed by
what she saw. So she took it to my mother. She didn't
look pleased, either. She told Lilly to take it home,
wrap it in newspaper, throw it in the trash, and never
speak of it to anyone.

Lilly said that she thought it wrong to destroy
something that belonged to her employer. What if he
found out? So she wrapped it up and put it on a shelf.
When she graduated from college, she went and

became some sort of nurse somewhere, I think, and left the photographs in a crate in her aunt's attic in Petaluma. She married, and her aunt died, and at some point she took the crate back, but the roof had leaked, and now the photographs were ruined. But for some reason she didn't throw them away. She felt like she'd stolen something. Only after my mother's death did she feel she could return them, and because she'd found them in my room, I was the one she was giving them to.

I figured you must have hid them, though I really can't think why.

I didn't show it to Papa. What good would it do? It would only bring him misery. When Maman fell ill, he started going to services at the First Church of Christ, Scientist, when he'd never set foot in a church willingly before. I thought it was only because he liked the building, which is a pretty thing, it's true. All of the praying they did on her behalf didn't save her, but he's still with that crowd, and Adele goes there too, the little fanatic.

I haven't written such a long letter in years, and now my hand is cramping. Goodbye.

The postmark indicated she'd mailed it from Denver, no return address. She'd signed the letter "Mrs. Jonathan Thierry." So she'd married. Despite myself, I felt disappointment, or perhaps envy.

I took the photographs to a restorer. Most of them were irreparably marred, he said after examining it. He might be able to rescue a few. I asked him to save as many as he could, to err on the side of optimism. If I could send my father even a partial reclamation of his work, it might revive something of his old vigor, the astonishing blaze of his mind.

I traveled back to Houston to pick them up a week later. He pushed a small box across the counter toward me. "Three dozen prints," he said, tapping the box. "That was the best I could do." I leafed through the images. Most were from the first year of my life.

I put the box in my trunk, uncertain of what I should do, and carried them with me from city to city.

A month later, in Butte, I left the trunk for a few hours in the care of my hotel while I handled some business. When I returned, the clerks handed me someone else's trunk, very similar to my own but not as battered. How apologetic the bellhops were. They scoured the back room. Surely the other man would discover their error before he boarded his train, they said.

I was furious, yet I also felt lighter, relieved of responsibility.

On my way out, I saw a man lugging my trunk into the lobby, looking aggrieved. I could still quickly make my exit, I realized, before anyone noticed. I could buy new clothes and toiletries—actors know not to carry anything too valuable with them. If the hotel sent me messages later asking me to retrieve it, I would tear them up. There would be no question of my having to decide whether or not to hand over to my father the disappointing few remnants of his great project, to see his face light up with excitement only to fall as he paged through the evidence of time's preference for dissolution.

The man approached the clerk, who bent over his desk, writing out a message with great concentration, a finger lifted to forestall any request until the missive was completed. Behind me, the doorman let in a woman in an elegant green coat, bringing with her the sounds of the street on a cold breeze.

"I believe that's my trunk," I called out.

*   *   *

That summer, my father seemed very thin and frail, more prone to repeating himself than before, and soon after my return, he fell ill with a high fever and terrible cough that cracked one of his ribs. He spent a week in the hospital. The doctors diagnosed pneumonia: it had left him weakened, with a persistent cough.

I moved into another room in his boardinghouse so I could look after him. I put off mentioning the Book of Months. He might be comforted that some part of his work survived. But it might break up his peace and remind him of everything he had lost. It was hard for him to get out of bed and move around, and I was preoccupied with making sure that he ate and took short walks down the corridor. By the end of summer, he seemed to be mended, so I went back on the road. In October, however, I received a telegram from his landlady. He was back in the hospital, and I should return as soon as I could.

The doctors said he had lung cancer, and they could do nothing. I didn't understand. It was impossible that my father, a grand force even now, should ever be gone. Surely he had years left, though his health would be compromised.

I resigned from the company and stayed in San Francisco to look after him. He'd lost all of the weight he'd gained over the summer. I moved to a boardinghouse nearby and took up part-time work waiting tables. Each night, I would bring him the most tempting leftovers from the restaurant, bowls of pasta or meatloaf and potatoes. In the mornings, I came over to coax him into eating his oatmeal, a process that took more time and patience than his landlady had.

One afternoon—a Monday, my day off—I was alarmed when he didn't answer the door. I called and called, fearing that he had died. At last his footsteps shuffled toward the door and he unlocked it.

"I was photographing," he said, his voice hoarse.

A white sheet hung from the clothesline that he'd strung across the room. I hadn't asked about the clothesline before, assuming that he used it to hang up wet laundry, or that his photographer friends would visit and clip their latest prints to it for viewing. He pushed the sheet to one side, and I saw he'd been using it as a backdrop; his camera stood on a tripod, the window behind it.

"What have you been photographing?" I asked. Even then, I had an intimation. It was a few minutes after three o'clock.

For answer, he waved toward his dresser, seating himself heavily in his armchair, short of breath.

I opened the top drawer and pulled out an envelope of prints.

In each of them, he stood, gaunt and tall, naked, his palms flat and facing the camera, just as I had stood so many years before. Somehow, he managed to stand in almost exactly the same position each day. I glanced at the floor. He had chalked heel-shaped marks on the wood.

The photographs revealed a man slowly wasting away. In the first photograph, dated August 25, he was already thin. By the middle of September, hollows had formed beneath his eyes. Then there was a gap of several days, his most recent stay in the hospital. When the series resumed again, his flesh seemed to have been whittled away, and his ribs showed. His eyes became more prominent; they seemed to cut through the surface of the photograph.

On the back of each print he had written his weight, his height, and the circumferences of his waist, chest, thighs, biceps, and triceps.

"I hope these might be of use someday," he said.

The images struck me as morbid, terrifying proof that slowly, little by little, my father was being removed from the world. I didn't understand how he could contemplate them with such detachment. I wept, and he watched me, kind but removed. He had understood long before what I was only now taking in.

He had printed them beautifully, every line on his body distinct: the edges of his thin muscles, the protuberances of bone, the creases of his face, the circles beneath his eyes, the silver strands of thinning hair on his head and the matted underbrush of hair on his chest and legs.

As his body decreased, the photographs seemed to become luminous. It wasn't because of the printing technique. An air of defiance became unmistakable, a fierceness of purpose I remembered from my childhood. He had captured his own soul, floating to the surface of his skin, flooding him with an inner light.

"Each of us has a finite number of days," he said, taking them gently and slipping them back in the envelope. "We don't know how many we have left, but every day seems to me narrower than the last yet somehow larger. My error was in thinking that all days were units of equal size because they all contained the same number of minutes. But although each day seems to go by more quickly than the one before, it also seems as if a ceiling is moving upward. I understand the great cathedrals now, the high volumes. Not that I have come to believe in a deity, but I understand the desire to invoke awe." He began coughing, the great racking coughs that came over him from time to time now. He hadn't spoken at such length in a while.

*   *   *

The next morning, I brought the box of restored photographs from the Book of Months and placed it in his lap. "I received these in the mail from Thomasine Hallgarten," I said. "Most of the images were ruined long ago, I think. But I was able to have some of them restored."

My father was slow to lift the lid. Today he seemed to be in more pain than the day before, and it had dulled his eyes. But when he saw the contents of the box, he cried out. Here were my infant limbs, swathed in fat and smooth of skin, the muscles just beginning to swell and stretch. Here were Karelia's hands, holding me up. It seemed impossible now that I bore any connection to this child. If the chain of days hadn't been interrupted, if I'd continued to be photographed each day, who would I have become? Who would my father be now?

He leafed through the prints, studying each one as if he could fill in the portions that had been effaced.

"I wish more had survived," I said. "But I was thinking that we could find a way to display the ones in the best condition. We could exhibit them with a few of your new images and call the series 'Youth and Age.'"

My father looked up at me, but I couldn't read his expression.

"If we wrote up a description of your original project," I continued, "and hung these all together, it might be of interest to people. We could even show them at the Panama-Pacific International Exposition."

"Exposition?" My father's voice was weak and uncertain.

"It's been in all the newspapers. The next world's fair. It's opening early next year in celebration of San Francisco's rebirth. They're building eleven huge palaces to display all the accomplishments and inventions of our age, from agriculture to artworks to machinery. I could apply, and we could see."

My father absentmindedly kneaded his right hand. He seemed to be thinking it over. "What if we exhibit the images and people are mocking or indifferent?"

In earlier years, he would never have asked such a question. Even worse, I thought, the exposition might turn down our application, which could send him into a final spiral of despair. I wondered if I'd made a mistake.

He stood, hobbled over to his dresser, and brought out the photographs he'd been making of himself. He laid several of them out on his bedspread along with some of the restored ones, and we studied the two sets, the old photographs of a new child and the new photographs of an old man.

*   *   *

The Panama-Pacific International Exposition opened on February 20, 1915. The governor had declared the day a legal holiday. By pre-arrangement, everyone in the city was awakened at six thirty in the morning: trolleys clanged, factory whistles shrieked, sirens wailed, signal guns at Fort Mason and the Presidio fired, children beat washing tubs with spoons, and in an unlikely collusion of nature, a shower of hail fell from the sky. After hasty breakfasts, tens of thousands of people flooded the streets, San Franciscans and Californians and tourists from every-where, all marching behind a fifty-piece band to the exposition gates.

Karelia and family had come up from Los Angeles for the occasion and were staying at the home of friends, a large ramshackle house in the Mission District. I'd brought my father over the night before to stay in a hotel on the wharf to make the journey as easy as possible. Speaking was prone to make him cough. I pushed him in a wheelchair now.

As we approached the gate, I was momentarily disoriented, as if the world had tilted vertical, until I realized the wall surrounding the expo-sition grounds was entirely covered with green plants. We entered a vast city of domed palaces and towers arranged around great open courts.

Karelia and Nicholas kept their children close. At eight and five, they were old enough to imagine that they could navigate the crowds on their own when they wished. Nicholas had shaved off his beard and had his hair cut short. He wore a white shirt and a white tie with a gray vest. His stock company had dissolved, like so many around the country, squeezed by competition from vaudeville and the movies. Now he was a booker for a vaudeville house. "I love song and dance as much as the next man," he said, taking a turn pushing Arthur. "But it's not the same. And motion pictures are a dumb show—the actor is leached of his voice, which is everything, don't you think? Do you dream of acting in films?"

"I don't," I said. I couldn't imagine playing for the lens of the movie camera rather than for the audience.

"In the movies, the characters always strike me as trapped," Karelia said. "They perform the same actions the same way every time the film is shown."

My father looked at us as if he wished to add something, but he stopped himself. Perhaps the air was dusty and he had decided to conserve his voice.

"If only Muybridge had listened to you," I said, attempting a jest, "and thrown the Zoogyroscope on the junk heap, we would all have been spared the motion picture, and dramatic theater would still be king."

My father smoothed his beard, thinking. "If I could have," he said, his voice raspy, "I would have told him that." The thought seemed to satisfy him, and he gazed around with renewed interest.

At noon, President Wilson himself pressed a key in the White House. The key sent a signal across the continent to an antenna atop the exposition's tallest building, the Tower of Jewels. In response, the Palace of Machinery's great diesel engines sprang to life with a leviathan hum, and water gushed from the fountains.

First we headed to the Joy Zone, hoping to sand down the edges of Benjamin's and Evelyn's excitement, so they could pay attention to the more educational aspects of the exposition. I rode the Aeroscope with Benjamin. We walked through the recreation of Yellowstone Park, and we watched the locomotives tow ships through the miniature Panama Canal. In the Palace of Transportation, a Ford assembly line put together a car in ten minutes before our eyes.

Before long, we went to the Palace of Liberal Arts, where the photography exhibits shared space with booths dedicated to typography, books, the manufacture of paper, instruments of precision, coins, medicine, chemistry, musical instruments, theatrical equipment, and architecture. Beneath the palace's high central dome stood one of the world's largest refracting telescopes, and in the Underwood exhibit stood a fourteen-ton working replica of a typewriter, on which news stories were typed each day in letters three inches high.

Some of my theater friends had helped me construct a small booth for our display. Along the back wall, we'd mounted twelve photographs of my infant self and twelve of my father, cropped from the waist up. My father had sketched a diagram of the original Tetrascope, and it hung next to a description of both his first project and the latest one. A pedestal displayed the logs of fused glass we'd rescued from the ashes of his studio.

My father stretched his hand out, and I helped him stand so he could better see the exhibit—first the photographs of my infancy, then those of his old age. He leaned so close to the fused glass that his breath fogged the surface.

After he'd looked over everything, he held my gaze to make sure I knew—he was pleased with what I'd done. Yet there was also sadness: he could see in his mind's eye all the images that had been lost.

He returned to his chair. I suggested we stay here for a while, to see what visitors made of it, and to answer any questions. I also worried that it was all too much for my father, and that he could use a rest. Karelia and the family went on to the other exhibits, promising to return in a couple of hours.

Soon my father began to doze. He usually woke when someone came near to look at the images. I wondered if he felt as strange as I did, to have become a scientific specimen on display for the public. Reactions from visitors varied from puzzlement to fascination. One spectator burst out laughing, then turned grave and hurried away. Another jumped back in alarm to find my father close at hand, as if he'd stepped out of the frame.

"Are they the same person?" one woman asked.

"No, the old man is the father," said her husband.

"I remember when my grandfather was dying, his skin got mottled the same way," said another man.

"Whose hands are holding the baby?" said a woman. "They look like a woman's hands."

"No one wants to see a woman's hands age," said her friend.

"Are people understanding?" my father asked me. "Do they understand about time?"

"I think they do," I said.

I didn't know if this was true. If we had been able to display more of the Book of Months, it might have made more sense. If we had photographed every moment in my life and bound it all in a book, then the body's passage through time might have become comprehensible by the end. It would take a lifetime to read. You would begin as a newborn, mouthing the frontispiece in your crib, and you would turn the final pages as an old man or woman, and having spent your whole life watching someone else's life unfold, you would sense the ending draw near as the pages dwindled. You would plan to stop right before the final photograph, but how would you know when that was?

"In my own way, I've followed in your footsteps," I said to my father. His eyelids drooped, but he picked his head up at my voice. "To be an actor is to rebel against time. You have an opportunity to capture the same moment over and over again, first in rehearsal and later in performance. You're always changing it, trying it broad and comic, then subtle and tragic, to see what the effect is, the way a photographer develops a print several times in the darkroom, trying to get the image right."

"In life," he said, "time snatches each moment away before you can properly get hold of it."

Toward the end of the afternoon, he fell asleep.

A man asked if I could help set up a table in his booth for some books that had just arrived from the printer. When I returned, my father's chair was empty.

Panicked, I asked a couple in the corridor if they'd seen him. They hadn't, but someone else said he'd seen an old man walking past the display of motion picture projectors.

I hurried in the direction where he'd pointed. All that dozing must have invigorated him. How much he was in his element here, among the fluoroscopes and computing scales, the photographs of diatoms and pollen taken through a microscope, the dental bridges and electro-therapeutic lamps.

But he might have fallen and injured himself. He was so fragile. I told myself that he could not have gone far. I ran through the exhibits, past the device that could record speech and music on a thin steel wire, past the motion picture projectors of all varieties, past the artificial arms and hands made of willow fiber. I asked a woman outside the booth of translucent color photographs if she'd seen a tall, elderly man in a brown suit, and she motioned me to go around the corner on the left. I found him sitting on a chair outside a booth, breathing hard from the effort of walking, watching men demonstrate a machine that could print gold leaf on book covers using electricity.

I brought his wheelchair to him. When the demonstration was over, I pushed him back toward our booth. "There are so many feats of invention here," he said, looking all around with wonder. He coughed, and I prepared for one of the long coughing spells that increasingly overtook him these days, but this one was brief. I had to bend close to hear him. "How many of these will come to fruition, and how many will fall by the wayside?"

"It's impossible to know," I said. "Maybe that doesn't matter. Maybe all these inventions are like seeds floating through the air. Even though only some end up taking root and growing, it's necessary for all of them to be given their chance." I was going to add that our work might lay the foundation for someone else's project to get hold of time, but he had fallen asleep again. I had failed to convince him. But looking around the exhibition hall, hearing the murmur of the crowds, the clank of the fourteen-ton Underwood in the distance, I was happy that my father's work had a representation among all these creations, the pragmatic and the bizarre alike. Perhaps, in the end, my father was both a genius and a madman—one of a great company.

* * *

He would die by the beginning of summer. His last photographs were the final act of his great longstanding defiance of time, his fist raised to stop its clock hands from moving, his insistence that the river of moments halt so we could study each one and finally come to understand them. He saw his work as a series of facts—this day, this day, this day—the antithesis of storytelling. Ironically, I had made a kind of story from the remnants, and only in this way got it before the public eye.

In the *Kalevala*, Aino drowned herself, and Kullervo drove the hilt of his sword into a field and threw himself on the point. Ilmarinen hammered a new wife out of gold and silver, but when he lay beside her she was as cold as sea ice and still as stone. Wainamoinen and Ilmarinen and Lemminkainen stole the magic Sampo from the Northland, but in the sea battle that followed, it slipped from Louhi's claws and broke into pieces and sank, except for a few pieces of the lid that the combatants shared between them, hoping these fragments would bless their fields.

The ancient Finnish singers knew about loss. They lost children to sickness, they lost wives in childbirth, they lost crops and battles, suffered famine and plague, endured seven centuries of Swedish rule before the Russians moved in. They sang in pairs, seated across from each other, right hands clasped, each with a flagon of beer close by to drink from between songs, accompanied by a harpist if they had one.

What became of Ilmarinen and Lemminkainen is not recorded, but the *Kalevala* does say what happens to Wainamoinen at the end of its last, strangest tale, the story of Mariatta. After the priest rebukes Wainamoinen and baptizes Mariatta's son, the ancient singer recognizes that his power has ebbed. He conjures up a copper boat and sails away across the sea to find a place to rest. As he sails, he sings of a time when his people will miss him and come looking for him, asking him to make another Sampo. He's left behind for them his harp, the one he made from the wood of the sacred birch tree and strung with hair given him by a maiden waiting for her lover—his magic harp, the source of all music and songs for the children of his country.

ACKNOWLEDGMENTS

I'm grateful to the Bancroft Library at the University of California, Berkeley, for its treasure trove of letters and other materials about the 1906 San Francisco earthquake and fire. Richard Schwartz's *Earthquake Exodus, 1906* and the Berkeley Historical Society were invaluable resources about Berkeley in that time. Emily Carr's memoir *The Book of Small* provided inspiration for Karelia's early years in Canada, and Susan Ehrens's A *Poetic Vision: The Photographs of Anne Brigman* informed my sense of Karelia's photography and philosophy. Rebecca Solnit's *River of Shadows: Eadweard Muybridge and the Technological Wild West* helped shape my idea of Muybridge. Laura A. Ackley's *San Francisco's Jewel City: The Panama-Pacific International Exposition of 1915* is a jewel of a book.

Ann Cummins, Lisa Michaels, Cornelia Nixon, Ann Packer, Angela Pneuman, Sarah Stone, and Vendela Vida read multiple drafts of this novel and offered much wisdom and insight over the years, as did Nancy Johnson, who is very much missed. I'm also deeply appreciative for the help and support of Andrea Barrett, Charles Baxter, Sylvia Brownrigg, Harriet Scott Chessman, Thaisa Frank, Judy Juanita, Karen Kevorkian, Margot Livesey, Ed Park, Peg Alford Pursell, Cass Pursell, Liz Rosner, Joan Silber, Steve Willis, Rafael Yglesias, and the Bay Area writing community. I learned so much from my teachers and mentors at the University of Michigan MFA program and in the Stanford Creative Writing Program—Jonis Agee, Charles Baxter, Nicholas Delbanco, John L'Heureux, Lorrie Moore, Eileen Pollack, Tobias Wolff, Gilbert Sorrentino, and Elizabeth Tallent—as well as all my colleagues there. And I'm very grateful for the Hopwood Award, the Farrar Prize in Playwriting, the Roy W. Cowden Memorial Fellowship, the Andrea Beauchamp prize in short fiction, and the Wallace Stegner Fellowship. My heartfelt thanks to my editor, Diane Goettel, to Angela Leroux-Lindsey for her careful copyediting, to Zoe Norvell for her beautiful cover and book design, and to everyone at Black Lawrence Press for believing in this book.

I feel so lucky to have my family and Sarah's family; their loving presence underlies everything. And Sarah, you read more drafts of this book than I can count, and I'm forever grateful for your brilliance, your inspiration, your boundless creativity, your companionship, and your love.

ABOUT THE AUTHOR

Ron Nyren's fiction has appeared in *The Paris Review, The Missouri Review, The North American Review, Glimmer Train Stories,* and *Mississippi Review,* among others, and his stories have been shortlisted for the O. Henry Awards and the Pushcart Prize. He is the coauthor, with his spouse and writing partner Sarah Stone, of *Deepening Fiction: A Practical Guide for Intermediate and Advanced Writers,* and a former editor of *Furious Fictions: The Magazine of Short-Short Stories.* He received his MFA in creative writing from the University of Michigan. A former Stegner Fellow, he is currently a freelance writer about architecture and an instructor in fiction writing for Stanford Continuing Studies. He lives in the San Francisco Bay Area.